Darcy Family Holidays, Volume 1

Darcy Family Holidays, Volume 1

Books 1-3 Compilation

LEENIE BROWN

LEENIE B BOOKS
HALIFAX

Cover design by Leenie B Books. Images sourced from Deposit Photos and Novel Expression.

Darcy Family Holidays, Volume 1 (Books 1-3 Compilation) © 2020 Leenie Brown. All Rights Reserved, except where otherwise noted. All books in this compilation have been previously published. Please see each title for its original copyright date and ISBNs.

ISBN (print) 978-1-989410-52-3; (ebooks) 978-1-989410-50-9(mobi), 978-1-989410-51-6(epub)

Contents

Two Days Before Christmas

Chapter 1   3

Chapter 2   21

Chapter 3   37

Chapter 4   49

Chapter 5   59

Chapter 6   75

Chapter 7   85

Chapter 8   97

Chapter 9   107

Chapter 10   121

Chapter 11   135

Chapter 12   149

One Winter's Eve

Chapter 1   161

Chapter 2   171

Chapter 3   183

Chapter 4   197

Chapter 5   209

Chapter 6   219

Chapter 7   231

Chapter 8   245

Chapter 9   259

Chapter 10   273

Chapter 11   285

Chapter 12   297

Chapter 13   307

Chapter 14   321

A Scandal in Springtime

Chapter 1   337

Chapter 2   347

Chapter 3   357

Chapter 4   369

Chapter 5   379

Chapter 6   393

Chapter 7   405

Chapter 8   417

Chapter 9   429

Chapter 10 441

Chapter 11 451

Chapter 12 463

Chapter 13 477

Chapter 14 493

Chapter 15 509

Before You Go 525
Other Pens, Mansfield Park Excerpt 526
Other Leenie B Books 539
About the Author 541
Connect with Leenie 543

Two Days Before Christmas

How does a lady mend her brother's broken heart?

Chapter 1

Georgiana Darcy peered out her bedroom window to see who had come to call and was causing the flurry of activity in the halls. Her eyes grew wide as she saw her brother step down from his travelling coach and give some directives to a footman — likely about his trunk or possibly requesting tea. Those were the things he most often thought of first when arriving home from a trip. Her brows furrowed, and her lips pinched into a displeased pucker. Her brother was not supposed to be here in town. He was supposed to be in Hertfordshire with Mr. Bingley, learning how to be something other than unpleasant.

Honestly! It was her heart that had been broken by that cad Wickham, not his! Hers was mending, but his? She shook her head. If only she could do something to prove to him that, though she had been hurt — and grievously so –, her heart was no longer affected. In fact, she had recently begun to think that it had never actually been touched at all. She had not been in love with Wickham. She was nearly convinced of that fact. She had been in love with the idea of being loved, adored, and cherished by a handsome man. That she had not been and feared she might never be was what still caused a pinching pain in her heart. Her companion, Mrs. Annesley, assured her it was a foolish notion to judge every gentleman by the actions of one, but it seemed prudent to Georgiana to be cautious, just in case. She had been too trusting. No one could tell her otherwise. However, just because she needed to learn a lesson in prudence, did not mean her brother needed to continue to suffer. He had done precisely as he should. Her pain was not his doing. The fact that he still tormented himself with guilt was what made it nearly impossible for her to lay her own, well-deserved, shame aside.

She had spoken in confidence about such things to Mr. Bingley before he and her brother had departed for Netherfield, Mr. Bingley's new estate. He had promised he would do his best to see her brother engaged in activities that would bring him distraction if not pleasure. She had been so hopeful that Mr. Bingley had been successful, for Fitzwilliam's letters had been light in tone, sharing stories of the various people he had met and wishing he was free of the attentions of one particular person, Caroline Bingley. Added to that, yesterday, Mr. Bingley had called to inform her that her brother had done the most unusual thing by dancing with a Miss Elizabeth — the same Miss Elizabeth that had featured in more than one of Fitzwilliam's missives.

Why he was home when things had seemed so promising, she was uncertain. She grabbed a wrap for her shoulders and slipped her feet into her slippers.

"Your brother has returned," Mrs. Annesley said as Georgiana met her in the corridor.

"I saw his carriage," Georgiana replied. "It is very unexpected."

"It is," Mrs. Annesley agreed. "Do you wish for me to attend you?"

Georgiana shook her head.

Mrs. Annesley glanced down the stairs. "You will tell me how he is, will you not?" There was a note of worry in her whispered question.

As far as Georgiana was concerned, hiring Mrs. Annesley to be her companion was the best gift Fitzwilliam had ever given her. Mrs. Annesley's heart was far softer than her angular features and austere manner of dress suggested. She was also aware of far more than the spectacles that perched on her nose while she read and stitched might indicate.

"Of course, I will," Georgiana assured her.

A twinkle shone in the lady's eye. "Then be quick."

Georgiana giggled as she descended the stairs. Mrs. Annesley was quiet and reserved as was proper for one in her position, but she was also curious and lively when she and Georgiana were alone. Reaching the bottom of the stairs, Georgiana stopped and waited patiently as her brother removed his outerwear and apologized to Mr. Wright, his butler, for the unexpected change in plans.

Seeing her, he greeted her first with a smile and then open arms, which she ran into without a second's pause.

"I have missed you," he murmured against her hair before releasing her.

"You did not return on my account, did you?" Georgiana wrapped her arm around his.

"May I not wish to see my sister?"

His avoidance of her question was not a good sign. Such a tactic always meant he did not wish to discuss his reasons for something.

"You may wish to see her, but you should not do so at the expense of breaking your word to a friend." She felt his arm flinch. "Mr. Bingley called on me yesterday. He seemed eager to return to Hertfordshire." Again, his arm flinched.

"He may return anytime he wishes."

Her brows drew together. Her brother's tone was so flat, so uncaring — so very unlike him. "I assume Miss Bingley and the Hursts accompanied you back to town?"

"They did."

She lifted a brow and gave him an assessing look. "You know Mr. Bingley will never persuade Caroline away from town so close to the season. It was a struggle to get her to go with him at Michaelmas."

He shrugged? The only response she was going to receive to such a comment was a shrug?

"He will be disappointed," Georgiana said softly.

"That cannot be helped."

Georgiana's heart sank at Darcy's words. Mr. Bingley had been so eager to return to Netherfield and a particular lady. In fact, he had mentioned taking his mother's fede ring with him when he returned. Not returning would do more than disappoint Mr. Bingley; it would likely break his heart and the heart of the lady he had left behind.

"Now, as delighted as I am to see you," her brother continued, "I am desirous of a long soak in a hot tub of water." He gave her a tight smile. "To wash away the chatter of Miss Bingley."

He had not remembered to ask her if she was well. That was also odd. For the last several months, he had asked her that question at least three times a day and always upon returning from a time away. She released his arm but only to allow her hand to slide down and grasp his. "Fitzwilliam?" She waited until he looked up at her instead of at their joined hands before continuing. "Are you well?"

His eyes left hers and looked down the hall toward his room as he nodded. "I will be," he said as he lifted her hand and kissed her fingers. "I will be."

Georgiana pulled her lip between her teeth as she watched him walk down the hall to his room. His shoulders were not as square as they normally were, and he ran his hand through his hair which was something he only did when thoroughly overwhelmed by a situation. He was not well. Something was most certainly wrong.

Georgiana gasped as a reason for her brother's melancholy came to mind. Unwilling to entertain the troubling thought for hours before she spoke to her brother again, she hurried down the hall and knocked firmly on his door. Then she waited. There was some shuffling in the room, but none that sounded as if a person were approaching the door, so she knocked again. This time she rapt so loudly that she was positive at least one knuckle would bear a bruise from the action.

However, her sore knuckles had produced the desired effect since her brother, minus his coat and cravat, opened his door.

"She has not trapped you, has she?" Georgiana demanded.

Her brother's brows drew together in question. "I beg your pardon?"

"Caroline Bingley. She has not finally succeeded in trapping you into marriage while her brother was gone, has she?" Georgiana's heart raced with trepidation. Caroline Bingley was not the sort of lady she wished to have as a sister, nor did she think her brother would ever be happy married to such a person. Caroline was not horrid, but she was not gentle or lively or particularly witty. She was just not the sort of lady Georgiana knew her brother needed for a wife.

Thankfully, shock suffused her brother's face as he blurted an emphatic no.

"You are not marrying her?" Georgiana asked again just to be certain of his answer.

"No, Georgie, I am not marrying anyone." The light in his eyes faded as he said it.

In spite of her concern for the sadness in his tone and expression, Georgiana smiled at him. "One day you will," she said hopefully.

"Perhaps one day," he replied without so much as a hint of conviction that it was true.

Oh, he was in a deplorable state of mind, and Georgiana was quite certain she knew why.

"Was there anything else?" he asked as he turned to close his door.

Georgiana shook her head. "Not at the moment."

"Then, I shall see you at dinner."

Georgiana stared at his closed door. "Perhaps, nothing," she muttered. "You will marry one day, and you will be happy," she declared to the door, "even if I must see to it myself." Having settled the matter with her brother's closed door, she turned and went in search of Mrs. Annesley. Undoubtedly, her companion would have some advice as to how to help Fitzwilliam.

For a full hour, between songs in the music room, Georgiana and Mrs. Annesley discussed Darcy's mood and the likelihood that he was denying his heart or worse — had been rejected by the woman he loved.

"Miss," Wright said as he stepped into the room. "Mr. Bingley is here to see your brother, but your brother is not available. However, Mr. Bingley is in quite a state, and I would very much dislike sending him away without him having seen someone."

Georgiana stacked her music and rose from her seat. "Thank you, Mr. Wright. Your judgment is always so good." She smiled at the long-time servant. "Mrs. Annesley and I shall receive him in the blue drawing room." She waited until Mr. Wright had left the room before turning eagerly to Mrs. Annesley. "Mr. Bingley might be able to help us understand why Fitzwilliam is so dejected, do you not think?"

Mrs. Annesley exited the music room with Georgiana. "You must remember, that Mr. Bingley was not at Netherfield and that he has already given you his report about your brother's progress when in Hertfordshire. I would not be too hopeful, but I will not say that there is no chance that we might gather some useful information."

"A trace of something to help us is all I wish," Georgiana whispered as they entered the drawing room.

"Mr. Bingley," Georgiana said in greeting. "I do apologize that you must once again be satisfied with seeing only me, but my brother has just returned from the country and is washing away the remnants of his travel." She motioned for him to be seated.

Bingley sat down heavily in a chair, his arms crossed and a scowl on his face. "I know Darcy has returned since my sisters have also returned. What I wish to know is why he has returned."

Georgiana took a seat near him. "I would also like to know that," she said as she smoothed her skirts and folded her hands in her lap.

"Did he not say?" Bingley asked in surprise.

Georgiana shook her head. "He seemed determined to avoid giving me any information at all."

"Huh," Bingley muttered.

"He was very unlike himself," Georgiana added.

"How so?"

"He seemed distant, almost cold."

Bingley rubbed his chin. "My sister declared he was pleased to have arrived in town and that she had never seen him happier."

Georgiana allowed her face to show her disbelief of such a statement.

"I had suspected there was some degree of exaggeration to her words," Bingley admitted. "He is not happy?"

Mrs. Annesley chuckled softly in her corner. "Pardon me," she apologized as she saw them both look at her, "but from what I saw and Miss Georgiana has told me, Mr. Darcy is very far from happy."

"Indeed?"

"Indeed," Georgiana assured him. She smoothed her skirts again and shot a surreptitious glance at Mrs. Annesley. "I was pleased to hear you had called for I am hoping you might be able to help us understand why my brother is so morose."

Bingley settled back into his chair. "I am not certain I can help, but I shall do my best."

Georgiana smiled.

"I shall call for tea," Mrs. Annesley offered. "And some of those little almond cakes you like so much, Mr. Bingley."

Bingley chuckled. "Thank you, Mrs. Annesley. You know how to make a vexed gentleman feel better."

"She is excellent," Georgiana whispered. "There is none better, of this I am certain."

"I would agree," Bingley whispered in return. "Now," he said, raising his voice, "what would you like to know?"

Georgiana tipped her head and arched a brow. "Your sisters are glad to be back in town?"

Bingley blinked. "Yes," he replied as if uncertain why Georgiana was asking such a question.

"Will you be returning to Netherfield?"

Again, he blinked and shook his head. "I cannot say. As you know, I had hoped to return, but my sisters assure me there is no need."

"No need?" Mrs. Annesley repeated as she took her seat once again. "What of the lovely lady you left behind?"

For the second time that day, Georgiana witnessed the light fade from a gentleman's eyes and be replaced with sadness. Fitzwilliam's distress, just like Mr. Bingley's, was, as she suspected, most certainly related to his feelings for a lady.

"My sisters assure me that she holds me in no particular regard."

Georgiana could hear how he tried to keep the pain of such a thing out of his voice. "Do you believe they are correct?" she asked gently.

He shrugged. "I am not good at judging such things."

"Most times," Mrs. Annesley added with a smile. "You are not a good judge of such things most times. It is the same with many men," she explained, "until a man finds a heart that beats in the same rhythm as his own."

He shook his head. "I am uncertain."

"Of course, you are," Mrs. Annesley agreed. "New experiences are always unsettling. I would not place my full trust and future happiness in the hands of another, Mr. Bingley. I would pursue my heart's desires until I had heard from the lips of the lady in question that all hope was vain. We are not all transparent with our affections. We can be as uncertain as any gentleman."

Bingley's brows furrowed. "But what if she smiles at every gentleman and not just me?"

"Then, she has a tender heart," Mrs. Annesley replied. "And it is likely that a tender-hearted lady fears being spurned more than others because she will feel it more grievously."

Georgiana knew there was truth in what her companion was saying. "I know there are those among my friends who would not feel the weight of a refusal as much as I have," she said softly and then shrugged. "Or perhaps they do feel it as much, but, rather than pain and sorrow, it is displayed as anger and viciousness."

"Quite true," Mrs. Annesley muttered.

"You truly believe I should return to Netherfield?"

"Yes!" Georgiana blurted. "That is," she continued, "if you still wish to see Miss Bennet wear that ring as your wife."

Bingley let out a great sigh. "I have no greater desire."

"Then go," Georgiana encouraged. "And invite my brother and me for Christmas."

Bingley's brows furrowed. "I do not think that is a good idea."

"Why?" Georgiana asked as the tea tray arrived. "Your sister will gladly go with you if she can be hostess for my brother."

"It is not that," he said as he took a small bite of an almond cake.

"Then what is it?"

Bingley swallowed his cake. "Your brother has told me

of your ordeal in Ramsgate," he began cautiously. "There is a militia encampment in Meryton."

"I am not swayed by a uniform," Georgiana said lightly. "Nor am I swayed by pretty words any longer," she added more somberly.

"Wickham has enlisted."

Georgiana's mouth dropped open, and her eyes grew wide. "Oh," she said softly. A shiver of cold ran down her spine as she stood and walked to the window. She had hoped that when she heard his name uttered by someone other than herself, her brother, or Mrs. Annesley, she would be able to do so with more composure than she currently felt. His being in Meryton would make going to Hertfordshire more challenging. It was not that she suspected she would be affected by him as she once was, but it was harder to forget the pain of rejection and your foolishness when faced with the source of both. She gasped and turned toward her companions. "Is he why my brother is so miserable?"

Bingley shook his head. "I do not think so. Although..." his left brow rose and his lips pursed as he considered the thought.

Georgiana's steps were quick as she returned from the window. "Although what? What might Mr. Wickham have done that has injured my brother?"

"We met Wickham on our ride one day. Neither of us

expected to see him. I was not as affected by it as your brother was." Bingley paused.

"I know Fitzwilliam despises the scoundrel, as he should, but why would that make Fitzwilliam so miserable and only now, not while you were in Hertfordshire?"

Bingley tipped his head and shrugged. "That is the question, is it not?"

"Yes," interjected Mrs. Annesley, who was sitting forward in her chair, listening eagerly.

"Wickham was not alone," Bingley said

Georgiana took a tentative seat on the edge of her chair as things started to become clear in her mind. "She was with him," she whispered.

"If you mean Miss Elizabeth and her sisters, yes."

"My brother likes her, does he not? She was mentioned in so many of his letters, and you said he danced with her."

"As I told you yesterday, yes. I believe he has lost his heart to Miss Elizabeth."

Georgiana flopped backward in her chair, not caring that it was not how a proper young lady was supposed to sit. "She must have refused him," she said.

Bingley nearly choked on the tea he was drinking. "No, I do not think anything like that has happened, for I am certain my sister would have crowed over such a wonderful event." There was a note of sarcasm in his voice as he said the last part.

Georgiana sat forward again. "Then why would Fitzwilliam say he is never marrying?"

Again, Bingley nearly choked on his tea. "Never marrying? What?"

Georgiana shrugged. "That is what he said. I asked him if he had finally been trapped by your sister –"

Bingley guffawed. "Oh, he must be in a terrible state if you thought to ask him that!"

"He is," Mrs. Annesley assured Bingley.

Georgiana nodded her agreement as she continued. "He assured me that nothing so horrid had happened and told me that he was never marrying. Of course, I replied that he would someday, and he replied with a perhaps. A perhaps! My brother, who has always droned on and on about doing his duty and finding a proper wife, said he would *perhaps* marry! What?" she asked in response to the finger Bingley held up.

"A proper wife is not the same as a lady one wishes to marry," he replied. "Miss Elizabeth is a gentleman's daughter, but her father is of no great standing."

"So?" Georgiana huffed. Her brother could be far too particular at times. She understood following rules and meeting expectations was important but a gentleman's daughter was a gentleman's daughter. It was not as if her brother needed to marry an heiress or a lady whose father held a title. He had said so many times when the subject of marrying his cousin Anne de Bourgh was broached.

"She has an uncle in Meryton and one in town."

"Many people do," Georgiana retorted. "I have an uncle in town — at least, I do when the House of Lords is sitting. And I have several uncles in the country who rarely come to town."

"Yes, but none of your country relations are solicitors and your uncle in town does not live near Cheapside, nor is he a tradesman."

"Oh." That made a bit more sense. A tie to trade was not something that all of her relations would appreciate. "It is her uncle not her father," she argued.

"So I have said," Bingley replied.

"Do you know the name and address of this uncle in town?" Mrs. Annesley asked.

Georgiana turned toward her companion with the same look of shock that Bingley was giving her.

"I thought we might call on her," said Mrs. Annesley. "To be polite and to find out a bit more about Miss Elizabeth."

Georgiana tipped her head. "Do you think it would be beneficial?"

Mrs. Annesley took a sip of her tea. "I do not know, but I would think it would be wise to perhaps caution Miss Elizabeth about some of the members of the militia. Only, of course, if it seems that the aunt is close to her niece." She placed her cup to the side and continued with a sly smile. "And it would not be such a bad idea to have some credible material about the fineness of Miss Elizabeth's relations — provided they are indeed fine people — with which to refute your brother's protests about why he cannot marry a lady he so obviously loves."

Chapter 2

The scheme was settled. Bingley would discover the address of the Gardiners and send it to Georgiana as soon as he was able. Then, she and Mrs. Annesley would pay a visit while out on a shopping excursion. Darcy, of course, was not to know about any of this. It was imperative that they discover the quality of Miss Elizabeth's relations before they attempted any sort of dissuasion of Darcy's beliefs.

Keeping her plans from being discovered by her brother proved to be far easier than Georgiana had expected it to be, for her brother either kept to his room, indulging in sleep, or sequestered himself in his study, pushing books around and consuming far more brandy than was his normal habit. While these actions made for much simpler scheming, it also caused both Mrs. Annesley and Georgiana to worry about Darcy.

He had taken a quiet dinner with them on Thursday, the day of his arrival, but it was not until Saturday afternoon when he once again made an appearance at any sort of table where food and his sister both were.

"I am thinking of returning to Pemberley," he said, taking a seat near the tea table that was laid out in the music room. "I see no need to tolerate the season this year. If we leave soon, we shall likely miss the worst of the cold weather, and the roads will still be passable."

Georgiana lowered her teacup to the table. This would not work! If he was at Pemberley, there would be no way to work on him to return to Netherfield and Miss Elizabeth. "If you do not wish to remain in town, Netherfield would be more convenient," she suggested.

He set his jaw and shook his head. "I shall not be returning to Netherfield."

"Not ever?" She asked in surprise.

"No. Never."

Georgiana recoiled slightly at his harsh tone. "I apologize for my incredulity, Brother. I had thought you a gentleman of your word."

She rose from her chair, leaving her tea and sandwich behind, and crossed to the instrument. She could not enjoy her tea when her brother was threatening to unsettle all her hopes to see him happy. She leafed through her music.

"I shall ask Bingley to join us at Pemberley, where I shall be able to instruct him about estate management from the comfort of my own home."

She turned toward her brother. "You will teach him to manage your estate not his."

"An estate is an estate," her brother argued.

His arms were folded, and he wore that scowl which said his opinion was not going to be swayed. It was unfortunate for him that she was not willing to believe in the immovability of his opinion. His thinking was faulty — moulded and warped by emotions. She knew it was, and because of this, she also knew that with time and persistence, it was not entirely improbable that he would see his error. Had she not also, at one point, been swayed by emotion into believing a falsehood? And though it had taken the crushing blow of the revelation of Mr. Wickham's intentions to help her see her error, she had seen it and was better for it. The same would be true for her brother. She just needed to persist as strongly as she could until he saw how he was wrong.

"He will not come alone," she argued, hoping the dread of being confined to Pemberley with the Hursts and Caroline Bingley for an indefinite period of time would be enough to shake from his mind the foolishness of running as far as he could from Miss Elizabeth.

"Caroline will remain in town for the season. She will not leave."

Georgiana shook her head. "Oh, my dear brother, how mistaken you are! She has no wish to find a husband other than you."

Her brother shrugged. "I will not invite her."

Georgiana sighed. "She will manage to invite herself. You know she will."

"I know nothing of the sort."

"Then you are a blockhead," Georgiana said firmly. She knew that such a comment would draw his anger, but at present, something needed to shake him from his stubborn, morose state of mind.

"Georgiana!"

His tone was harsh and scolding as she knew it would be. She wished to apologize immediately. It was not like her to call her brother names. However, no matter how wrong it was or how red her face burned with shame, she would not retreat from attempting to make him see reason. "What else do you call someone who refuses to see things as they are. You know that Caroline Bingley has long desired to become your wife and mistress of Pemberley. In her three seasons, she has never entertained any gentleman in a fashion that would suggest she was looking for a husband — unless that gentleman was you! She hangs on your every word. She prances and preens to get your attention. She flatters and attempts to make me her sister." She blew out an exasperated breath. "I do not despise her. She is a friend of sorts, but surely, you must see what she is about?" She looked expectantly at her brother, who replied with a shrug. Georgiana rolled her eyes. He was so stubborn at times!

"Very well. Invite Bingley and see if his sisters do not both accompany him." She placed the pieces of music she still held on the piano and marched over to her seat. "I shall not like to live with you once you are married to her. I tolerate Miss Bingley quite well when we are together for a short duration, but I do not wish to be paraded about during my season by her." She blinked at the tears that unexpectedly gathered. Caroline was so very different from Georgiana. Caroline put herself forward. Georgiana did not, nor did she wish to be pushed forward in such a fashion.

"I am not marrying Caroline," Darcy growled.

"Do you truly think that you can survive a full winter at Pemberley without being trapped?" She wiped away a tear that had escaped her fluttering lashes and then took a trembling sip of her tea. "No," she said with a firm shake of her head. "I will not allow it. We will not be leaving town."

"You have very little say in the matter," Darcy retorted.

"If I might," Mrs. Annesley interjected and then waited to be acknowledged. "Miss Darcy's concern is not unfounded. A situation could very easily arise that would call your honour into question if the Bingleys were to travel to Pemberley with you. However, I believe the point to be moot. I understood Mr. Bingley to say he intended to return to Netherfield when last he called. He seemed very determined to do so."

Georgiana wiped away a second tear and looked at her

companion with trepidation. They had agreed that they would not tell Fitzwilliam of Bingley's plans until everything had been arranged.

"Bingley is returning to Netherfield?"

"Yes, sir. I do believe that is his intention." She smiled at her employer. "There is a lovely young lady who awaits him."

Georgiana's eyes grew wide, and she dared to glance at her brother. He was staring open-mouthed at Mrs. Annesley.

"But she is indifferent to him," he finally managed to mutter.

"Has she said as much?" Mrs. Annesley queried.

"No, but Miss Bingley and Mrs. Hurst assure me of its truth, and they were on friendly terms with Miss Bennet."

Georgiana saw her companion's lips twitch just slightly, and she waited eagerly to hear the point Miss Annesley was about to make.

"This would be the same Miss Bingley who insists her brother will marry Miss Darcy?"

"She insists what?" Darcy looked at his sister and then back at her companion.

Georgiana nodded. "Caroline has told me many times how well Mr. Bingley and I suit each other."

"I think," Mrs. Annesley continued before Darcy could form any more words, "that perhaps Miss Bingley does not wish to encourage an attachment between her brother and this Miss Bennet. I am certain that Miss Bennet's dowry and connections are not superior to Miss Darcy's."

"No, not at all," Darcy replied. "Miss Bennet is of little standing."

"That would not benefit Miss Bingley in her quest to rise above her roots, now would it?" Mrs. Annesley poured a cup of tea and placed it before him. "A gentleman does not know the heart of any lady until he has made an inquiry of the lady in question. Until then, it is all hearsay and speculation. Admittedly, listening to such accounts no matter their veracity will save a few from certain heartbreak, but it will just as likely doom many to misery, having given up their heart's desire without so much as a whimper."

Darcy eyed Mrs. Annesley cautiously over the rim of his teacup. The woman had come with impeccable references, and to date, she had proved invaluable to his sister, taking Georgiana under her wing as if she was a mother hen, pushing her out from the safe repose of her room and home when it was needed to advance her recovery, and instructing her in every necessary accomplishment she would require when it came time to make her debut. Surely, she was a lady whose advice was as good for him as it was for his sister, yet, he did not feel particularly ready to admit it. He did not wish to be rational and level-headed, for being rational and level-headed was precisely what had led him to leave Hertfordshire and reduced him to his current miserable existence. He could not remain in town. The temptation to return to Netherfield would be too great. The knowledge that she was so near and yet so unattainable would be agonizing. If there was a distance between them, he might then be able to forget her and her lovely eyes, pleasing figure, and quick wit. He indulged in silence as he drank his tea. Then, when his cup was empty, he placed it on the table and pushed to his feet. "Then, I will go to Pemberley by myself. I will send a request to Matlock House. I am certain Lady Matlock would welcome you to stay with her in my absence."

Georgiana's eyes grew wide and filled with tears, causing him to look away.

"You would leave me? At Christmas?" she whispered.

"Only because you refuse to go to Pemberley with me," he said, moving toward the door. "I will be in my study if you require anything or if you change your mind."

"When do you leave, sir?" Mrs. Annesley asked before he could exit the room.

He would be away at this moment if it were not for those blasted tears in his sister's eyes. His own sorrow somehow deepened at the thought of causing her pain. "Three, four days," he responded uncertainly. "That should give enough time for Mrs. Reynolds to prepare for my arrival." He turned toward his sister. "I will not send any correspondence until tomorrow."

She nodded but did not look up at him. The action was

so reminiscent of how she had been following Ramsgate that he feared he was setting her progress back.

"I cannot remain in town, Georgiana. I just cannot." He gave a nod to Mrs. Annesley and, leaving the music room, headed to his study. He did not, however, reach his destination, before hearing a most unwelcome sound in the foyer. He glanced in the direction of Caroline Bingley's voice, hoping that she had not yet seen him and he might hideaway undetected. From the hand she lifted to wave at him, he knew he was not to be so fortunate.

"Mr. Darcy," she called.

He sighed and turned in her direction.

"I have come to call on your sister. She is such a dear, and I do dote on her," she explained as she removed her gloves and coat. "Louisa and I were uncertain if I would be so fortunate as to see you as well since my brother would not join us. He has been in such a foul mood since our arrival. He stomps about, slamming doors, and replying only in one-word answers. It is absolutely impossible to have a conversation with him about anything."

"He was not pleased with your arrival in town?" Darcy asked.

"Most decidedly not!" said Louisa. "I was thanking the heavens that I did not have to remain under his roof that first night." She shook her head and clucked her tongue. "Such a show of temper!"

Darcy's brows drew together. "A show of temper from

Bingley?" He motioned to the sitting room in invitation to the two ladies. Bingley did not anger easily. He would become disgruntled at times and even cantankerous, but rarely did he become angry to the point of making a display. Darcy wished to rub the small pain that was developing between his eyes. His friend must have been even more attached to Miss Bennet than he had suspected.

"I do not jest," Louisa continued as she moved toward the room he had indicated. "I thought he was going to banish Caroline to our aunt's house."

"He nearly did," Caroline assured Darcy.

How he wished she would walk further away from him than she was. It seemed she always had to be within arm's length of his person — as if being there assured her the possibility of grasping him if he should attempt to disappear, which at this moment he wished he could.

"I should go get Georgiana," he muttered.

Caroline made a small sound of disbelief and favoured him with an amused smile. "Mr. Wright will see to it," she cajoled. "Darcy House only employs the best." She perched herself on a settee near his favourite chair.

He ignored her and walked to the window. "Your brother is truly put out?"

"He is!" cried Louisa. "Did he not seem so to you?"

"I have not seen him," Darcy admitted.

"Count yourself fortunate," Louisa continued. "He shouted about needing to learn estate management and how it could not be managed from town. Then he started in on how he had not taken proper leave of his new acquaintances and moved into something about servants who were depending upon him for their livelihoods. And then, he grabbed his hat and coat and flew out of the house saying he would speak to you and set things right."

"I was indisposed when he arrived," Darcy muttered. He had not thought Bingley would be quite so distraught about his neighbours and servants. Letters could be sent to neighbours, and servants could be kept on. It was not as if Bingley had to be there for them to go about their duties. Both Pemberley and Darcy House still employed staff even when their master was not in residence. It was not the same as employing a worker in a mill or shop who only worked when the place of business was open. "And he would not come with you today?"

"He is rather put out," said Louisa.

Darcy leaned against the window frame. Hopefully, he had not lost a dear friend. That thought was just as jarring as the tears he had witnessed in his sister's eyes a few moments ago. He shook his head. Apparently, he had made a rather large mess of things.

"He was growing far too attached to the area," said Caroline. "We have done him a service in separating him from it. The neighbourhood was not fit for one such as he. If we had remained, he would likely become just as repugnant as the rest."

Darcy tilted his head and studied Caroline. She was looking very pleased with herself. "Not everyone was distasteful. I remember you and Mrs. Hurst found Miss Bennet to be to your liking."

Caroline tittered. "She was the most superior lady in the area, but that does not mean she is to be our equal."

Darcy's brows furrowed. Miss Bennet was a gentleman's daughter, and as such, she was not Caroline's equal but rather outranked her.

"And our brother can surely do better than a penniless country nobody," Caroline added. "No matter how prettily she smiles."

"I suppose you are correct," Darcy muttered uneasily. He had disparaged Miss Bennet and her connections as readily as Caroline when he was convincing himself that removal from Netherfield was necessary, but hearing Caroline speaking now, it struck him how very arrogant it sounded. Again, he considered just what sort of muddle he had created.

"You said just as much, did you not?" Louisa asked.

Darcy nodded. Bingley had the wealth to attract a greater connection, that much was true. However, having spent the last two days in agony, attempting to rid his heart of its desire for a lady who did not even smile at him as Miss Bennet did Bingley, he was beginning to rethink his assessment. He rubbed that pounding place between his eyes. There was no reconciling his heart and his head while here in town. He needed peace and quiet and days of roads between him and Hertfordshire to accomplish such a task.

"I cannot see how a gentleman's daughter is not good enough," said Georgiana, who had just entered the room during the last exchange.

"Georgiana," Darcy cautioned.

She raised a brow and flipped her head. "Why I am only a gentleman's daughter," she said as she took a seat.

"But a wealthy one," said Louisa, "and with relations that are titled."

Georgiana shrugged and fixed her brother with a piercing stare. "Then I suppose I shall have to be content to be sold to the gentleman most in need of my wealth and standing no matter where my heart might lie."

"Georgiana," Darcy scolded. "That is not what was said."

"Was it not?" She fluttered her lashes at him, gave him a small smile, and said, "Then, I do apologize," before turning from him and, to his great annoyance, ignoring him as much as she was able for the remainder of Caroline and Louisa's call.

~*~*~

"Georgiana," Darcy called as his sister passed the door to his study later that day.

Georgiana took four more steps before stopping and abandoning her plan to ignore his summons. There was no need to stir his ire any further; he was likely angry enough with her for her recent behaviour. She had not seen him scowl as much as he had during Caroline and Louisa's call in a very long time.

"You wished to see me?" she asked from the doorway.

"Come in and sit down." He leaned back in his chair and waited for her to comply. "Your behavior today was quite disturbing."

Georgiana bit her lower lip and lowered her gaze to her hands.

"It is completely unacceptable for you to speak as you did — and in front of guests!" He rose and came to stand before her. "It was disrespectful. I expect so much more from you. Where have I erred?"

Georgiana peeked up at him. He was propped against his desk with his arms folded across his chest, looking down at her with such a sad expression that it nearly destroyed her determination to press her point. However, if she truly wished to see that heartbroken look in his eyes removed forever, she must not waiver. Therefore, looking down once again at her hands, which were nervously twisting in her lap, she answered. "Our parents, as well as you yourself, have taught me that a Darcy's word is to be steadfast. I am to consider promises carefully before I make them because a promise should not be broken save for the noblest of reasons."

"This is true," Darcy muttered.

Georgiana lifted her eyes to his. "That is where you have erred. You promised Mr. Bingley that if he leased Netherfield, you would spend the autumn and most of the winter seeing that he had things well-in-hand before Easter, yet you have come home and refuse to return to Netherfield for who knows what reason." She lifted a brow. "I truly do not believe it is to save him from a lady who is beneath him."

"None of that explains your behaviour."

"No, it does not," Georgiana agreed. "But it is my answer to your question. You have not erred with me. I know my behavior was wanting and drastically so. However, it seemed the best way to capture your attention and get you to listen to me." She stood and placed her hands on his folded arms. "You are my brother, and I love you with all my heart and hold you in the highest regard. You have cared well for me. You have even saved me from certain ruin. I wish to repay your kindness if only I knew how."

He pulled his arms out from under her grasp and opened them wide to her in invitation. Gladly, she stepped into his embrace.

"Let me love you," she whispered. "Allow me to care for you and point out your errors when I see them. I am not the foolish girl I once was." She lay her head against his broad chest and listened to him pull in a deep breath and expel it in a whoosh.

"We are all fools at times," he murmured as he squeezed her tight. "If there was a way for you to assist me with my current dilemma, I would gladly seek your help, but I fear there is not."

"You will not keep your promise to Bingley?" she asked quietly.

He sighed. "Your point was valid. I shall consider it."

"Are you still leaving?"

His grip on her tightened. "I do not know. I long to leave, to be far away from..." his voice trailed off and the room was silent for half a minute. "I will consider staying, but I cannot promise beyond that."

"I am sorry," she said.

"You are forgiven," he replied.

She shook her head as he released her. "Not just for my behaviour."

"Then what?" he asked as she moved toward the door.

"That I could not save your heart from breaking." She smiled a sad, knowing smile at him as she said the words that he had repeated to her over and over again after her ordeal with Wickham. He stood quietly, looking at her as if he was uncertain if he should acknowledge that what she had said was true or false. "It is in your eyes, Fitzwilliam. Your heartache is in your eyes," she whispered and took her leave.

Chapter 3

"Are you ready?" Mrs. Annesley poked her head into Georgiana's room.

Georgiana giggled at the unmistakable note of excitement in her companion's voice. "As you can see," she replied, checking her reflection one more time in the mirror. She always wished to look her best, but today, she felt particularly nervous about her appearance. It was not often you presented yourself without an invitation to a person you did not know in hopes of gaining her assistance.

"You are the picture of propriety and elegance," Mrs. Annesley said as she stood in the open doorway to Georgiana's room. "Your green wrap sets off your hair quite nicely, and that hairstyle is very becoming." She waggled her eyebrows and tipped her head toward the stairs.

Georgiana giggled once again. Mrs. Annesley had been surprisingly animated ever since they had laid their plan to see Fitzwilliam happy. Schemes, Mrs. Annesley had assured her charge, were her speciality when she was a girl.

Often, she managed to conduct them without getting into trouble, but not always, which, she said was part of the thrill of it all. Of course, after such a confession, she had to remind Georgiana that schemes were really not the thing for a proper young lady who wished to keep her reputation spotless and her brother from scolding. However, it was allowable this once because the cause was a benevolent one, and apparently, it also helped the permissibility of a scheme to include one's companion instead of undertaking it on one's own. It had been rather entertaining listening to Mrs. Annesley go around in circles about their plan — lauding it one moment and cautioning the next.

"You look very respectable yourself," Georgiana said as she joined her companion in the hall. "The blue of your pelisse is just the perfect shade to declare you serious and austere, while the red trim on your bonnet adds a hint of dashing style that proclaims you are not retiring and should not be overlooked."

Mrs. Annesley chuckled softly. "One should not flatter," she said. "Unless it is to hurry your charge away from her mirror."

The two ladies descended the stairs quickly and slipped out the front door without having to stop and explain their outing. That would be tricky enough to do later when they returned, but to start a mission having to fudge and prevaricate without being outright dishonest would have removed a great deal of the fun of an undertaking such as they were beginning.

"You'll not say a word?" Mrs. Annesley questioned their driver a second time before entering the carriage.

"Not a word, ma'am." He tipped his hat to Georgiana. "I think it's a right fine thing you are attempting if I do say so myself. The master smiles far too little on a sunny day. He doesn't need any clouds of my creation."

"Thank you, Harris," Georgiana said before climbing into the carriage ahead of her companion.

"Are you ready?" Mrs. Annesley said as she settled herself into the carriage.

Georgiana nodded enthusiastically. "Let the games begin."

They travelled to a shop and purchased some perfume and cream as well as a new pair of gloves as a present for Fitzwilliam. Georgiana had noticed the sad state of his gloves yesterday when they had gone to church and had decided a new pair would be just the thing to surprise him with on Christmas morning. Having made their purchases, the two ladies settled in as comfortably as two anxious and excited schemers could for the remainder of their ride to the address on Gracechurch Street that Bingley had given them as they were leaving church yesterday morning.

Mrs. Annesley peeked out the window as the carriage began to slow. "It is a fine looking home," she said as Georgiana joined her at the window. The Gardiner's town-house was not grand nor was it small, but it was well-kept, and the knocker on the front door reflected the light of the midday sun.

"This is a very good sign, is it not?" Georgiana asked.

"Indeed it is," her companion agreed. "They are quite likely very respectable people and, I suspect, of substantial means."

Georgiana's heart raced. "I have never spoken to anyone about *him*," she whispered as she and Mrs. Annesley stood before the door to the Gardiner's home.

"You do not have to say anything if you do not feel it is right," Mrs. Annesley cautioned. "Only share as you feel comfortable."

Georgiana nodded and took a deep fortifying breath as the door opened and Mrs. Annesley requested to speak with Mrs. Gardiner. They waited in a narrow corridor while the housekeeper inquired if her mistress would receive them. There was a scurrying of feet above them and a calling from one child to another followed by a hearty and delighted giggle that caused Georgiana to smile. She could see a maid, sweeping ashes from the hearth in the room next to them, and once the noise from above subsided, Georgiana could hear her humming a tune as she worked. This seemed to be a happy home. That along with the tidiness and smart decor spoke well of the people who lived here.

"This way, ma'am," the housekeeper said, leading them into a cozy family sitting room rather than the more formal one across the corridor from it.

It felt odd to Georgiana to be welcomed by a complete stranger into the heart of where a family spent their time. Even in her friend's homes, she was entertained in the formal sitting room during calling hours.

"Please, be seated," a lady dressed in a modern and stylish blue morning dress and white cap greeted them. "It is such a pleasure to have a full sitting room."

"We appreciate your receiving my companion and myself," Georgiana said as she took a seat and glanced curiously at the other two ladies in the room.

"Miss Darcy, Miss Annesley, may I present my nieces, Miss Jane Bennet and Miss Elizabeth Bennet," Mrs. Gardiner said by way of introduction.

Georgiana's mouth dropped open. "Miss Bennet and Miss Elizabeth?" she repeated, looking from one Bennet sister to the other.

"Yes, that is who we are," said Elizabeth.

Taking note of how Miss Elizabeth's eyes danced with humor and her lips curled ever so slightly upwards, Georgiana gave her head a little shake of amazement. "You are just as he described," she muttered.

"I beg your pardon?" Elizabeth asked.

Georgiana started and, recollecting herself from her shock at seeing the very person about whom she wished to speak to Mrs. Gardiner sitting before her, flushed with embarrassment. "I do apologize, but my brother has written me so much about you."

"Mr. Darcy has told you about me?" Elizabeth asked in surprise.

"Yes, in each of his letters."

Elizabeth's brows furrowed.

"Oh, do not worry, he wrote only lovely things," Georgiana said in an effort to assuage Miss Elizabeth's concern, but instead of having a relaxing effect, her comment seemed to deepen Miss Elizabeth's confusion.

"Mr. Darcy?" Elizabeth's tone was one of complete and utter disbelief.

"Yes," Georgiana replied.

"Huh," was the only reply Elizabeth made as if she was at a loss for how best to respond to such news.

Georgiana looked at her companion, silently begging her to supply some direction in which to proceed.

"We must apologize for intruding on you when you have family visiting," Mrs. Annesley said to Mrs. Gardiner.

"Yes," Georgiana said with a small smile of gratitude. "It is perhaps a bit forward to call without any previous acquaintance, but I assure you we came today with a noble purpose in mind." Her heart began fluttering again as she considered the topic she was about to broach. As always happened when her heart began to flutter as it was, her hands followed suit and began to twist in her lap.

"Have you just arrived in town?" Mrs. Annesley placed a hand on Georgiana's while she asked the question of Miss Bennet.

"We arrived on Saturday," Jane replied.

"And was it a pleasant trip?" Mrs. Annesley asked.

"Yes, thank you."

"Will you be staying in town for long?" Mrs. Annesley gave Georgiana's hand one last pat.

"My nieces will be with us until we travel to Longbourn for Christmas," Mrs. Gardiner said as a loud thud was heard overhead. "I will be grateful for the assistance with the children as we travel," she added with a laugh. "We are expected in Hertfordshire two days before Christmas."

"Three weeks complete then. A very nice length of stay, is it not Miss Darcy?" Mrs. Annesley said with a delighted smile.

"Oh, indeed it is," Georgiana replied.

"We always enjoy our time in town with our aunt and uncle," Jane assured them as tea, and a plate of sweets was set on a small round table near Mrs. Gardiner. "Will you and your brother remain in town for Christmas?"

"Our plans are not yet formed," Georgiana replied. She thanked Mrs. Gardiner for the cup of tea, and then added, "I had hoped to convince him to take me to Netherfield with him so that I might meet you."

"Indeed?" Jane said in surprise. "I had heard he was not planning to return."

Georgiana's lips pursed slightly with displeasure. "Yes, I have heard that as well." She tipped her head. "Did he tell you he was not returning?"

"No," Elizabeth replied, "Miss Bingley informed us that she, Mr. Bingley, Mr. and Mrs. Hurst, and Mr. Darcy would not be returning."

Georgiana smiled. "Well, that does sound like something Miss Bingley would do. She is very good at arranging things to suit her desires. However, I know on at least one count that she is wrong." She gasped. "Oh, dear. This is not good." She turned to Mrs. Annesley. "When did Mr. Bingley say he was leaving town? It was today, was it not?"

"Oh, my, yes. He is likely halfway to Netherfield by now," her companion replied.

"He was returning?"

Mrs. Annesley smiled at Jane. "Yes, my dear, he had a particular reason for returning, but I imagine since you are in town, he will not remain at Netherfield long." She placed her cup of tea on its saucer and balanced it on her knees.

"He was returning to Netherfield for me?"

Mrs. Annesley nodded.

Jane's brows furrowed. "But what of Miss Darcy?"

Mrs. Annesley chuckled. "Did Miss Bingley imply that Mr. Bingley was attached to Miss Darcy?"

Jane nodded.

"He is not," Mrs. Annesley said before taking a sip of her tea.

"Oh."

With that one word, for the second time since Mrs. Annesley and Georgiana's arrival at the Gardiners, a Bennet sister seemed lost for words.

"I am certain Mr. Bingley's lack of attachment to Miss Darcy was not your purpose in calling today," Mrs. Gardiner prompted.

"No." Georgiana placed her cup on the table beside the sofa on which she sat. "Although, your nieces and some information I discovered through Mr. Bingley are the reasons for our call." She drew in a breath. "It was mentioned to me that there was a particular gentleman who had joined the militia who is known very well to my family." She paused to give her heart a moment to calm.

"Mr. Wickham?" Elizabeth asked.

Georgiana nodded and glanced uneasily at her companion.

"You do not have to say anything," Mrs. Annesley whispered.

Georgiana shook her head. "No, I must," she replied to Mrs. Annesley before turning back to Elizabeth. "There are things you should know about him. Things that neither my brother nor Mr. Bingley would ever tell you." She blew out a breath. This was even more difficult than she had imagined it would be. "You must not tell my brother I have said anything. I will tell him eventually." She wished to stand and pace the room or flee it, but she did not. Instead, she twisted her fingers together tightly and continued. "He does not know we have come to call on you," she said to Mrs. Gardiner, "and he will, no doubt, be displeased when he discovers it."

She stopped once again and drew a calming breath. "I apologize, it is difficult to speak of one's foolishness," she said in explanation for why she was dabbing at the tears that had gathered in her eyes. "Mr. Wickham's father was my father's steward, and so I have known Mr. Wickham all my life. He was always kind to me when I was young. He would tease and tell stories, and he would occasionally sneak an extra cake out of the kitchen to share with me. To me, he was a trusted friend. Then, he left to go to school, and I did not see him for many years. His father died, and then so did mine." She crumpled her handkerchief in her hands. Her heart was beginning to slow its pace as she spoke. "I was not aware of the provision my father had left to Mr. Wickham or his refusal of the living at Kympton –"

"His refusal of the living?" Elizabeth interrupted.

"Yes," Georgiana replied. "As I understand it from both my brother and my cousin, Colonel Fitzwilliam — he shares my guardianship with my brother — my brother gave Mr. Wickham a generous sum of money in place of the living. I do not know all the details. My cousin told them all to me this past summer, and I remember some of them. However, at the time when I found them out, I was too distraught to commit them all to memory."

Georgiana looked down at her hands. "You see, until this past summer, I still thought Mr. Wickham a trusted friend. When staying in Ramsgate with my former companion, I happened to meet him again. I had not seen him in years, well before I began thinking of gentlemen as handsome." She could feel her cheeks growing warm. "He was very handsome and as charming as ever. It was a pleasure to stroll on his arm and talk to him of home and his adventures at school. I soon found myself fancying myself in love with him, so in love with him, that I agreed to run to Scotland with him and become his wife. I knew that my brother would never allow me to marry so young, but I was certain that Mr. Wickham was my one true love, and I was his."

Georgiana took a deep breath and lifted her eyes to Elizabeth. "He was not my true love, nor did he care for me beyond my money. My brother arrived unexpectedly, and when the truth of what I had planned was discovered, he vowed that should I elope, not one farthing of my money would be given to my husband. He would see that I was cared for, but my husband would get only me and naught else."

Georgiana could see the horror in Elizabeth's eyes. "It sounds harsh, I agree. I was furious with Fitzwilliam, and, after a time of tears in my room, I descended to the study to tell him that I did not care if he kept every bit of my money. I loved George and would marry him though I was penniless." She shook her head. "I can still hear Mr. Wickham's laugh and words as I pushed the door open and heard him talking to my brother. 'Take her without a pound to her name?' he said, 'I would not take her for less than twenty thousand.' When I gasped, he turned on me with a cold laugh and said 'Surely, you did not think I loved you, did you?' I ran from the room. I am not certain what happened after that." Shaking her head, she continued. "I was so foolish, so duped, and utterly broken-hearted, but I was saved from a life of misery, of that I am certain."

Silence reigned in the room for a full minute before Mrs. Gardiner spoke. "You poor dear," she said. "How horrible."

Georgiana gave her a sad smile. "I have not spoken of this to anyone besides Mrs. Annesley, my brother, and my cousin; however, when Mr. Bingley told me that Mr. Wickham was in Hertfordshire and had made friends with a lady my brother admires, I could not let that lady fall victim to his pretty words."

Chapter 4

Not knowing what to say or how to feel, Elizabeth sipped her tea slowly as she considered what she had heard. The way Miss Darcy had wrung her hands, flushed, and fought tears during her tale made it impossible for Elizabeth to brush the facts away as a fabrication.

She lifted her teacup to her lips and allowed the warm beverage to flow over her tongue and down her throat as she swallowed. It amazed her how Miss Darcy could share such a story. If it had been Elizabeth who had been duped by a cad and come so near to ruin, she would have had to have a very compelling reason to share it. She shook her head slightly before she took another sip of tea. Conversation swirled around her almost as freely as her thoughts twisted and turned in her mind.

There must have been a very compelling reason for Miss Darcy to share such a story with a complete stranger. What had she claimed to be her reason? Elizabeth swallowed the last of her tea. Miss Darcy had said it was because Elizabeth was a lady Mr. Darcy admired and therefore, Miss Darcy did not wish to see come to any harm. Elizabeth rose without a word, placed her cup and saucer on the tea tray, and returned to her seat.

Could it actually be true that Mr. Darcy admired her? Elizabeth's brows furrowed as she attempted to reason away Miss Darcy's claim, but finally, she had to admit that, if Miss Darcy's story about Mr. Wickham was true, then presumably her comment regarding her brother's admiration was true as well.

She considered all that Mr. Wickham had told her. According to Miss Darcy, Wickham had not been injured by anything other than his own actions. The living had been refused. A payment made in its place. And Miss Darcy, the girl that he said was proud and cold was anything but! No wonder Mr. Darcy had looked so angry when he met Wickham and replied so harshly when questioned about the man. Mr. Wickham had attempted to seduce his sister! Oh, how wrong had she been? Had every word of it been a lie? Had she truly been so easily led?

"Mr. Wickham has not been harmed by your brother?" Elizabeth asked when the conversation about something lapsed into silence. She had no idea what topic was being discussed as she had not yet been able to attend to anything more than the troubling thoughts filling her mind.

Georgiana shook her head. "No, he has not. Mr. Wickham has been disappointed by my brother, but he has never been injured by him. Fitzwilliam has always treated him fairly."

Elizabeth nodded and slipped back into her reverie about the conversations she had had with Mr. Wickham. Oh, why had she not questioned his words more? Blind belief was not her normal wont. How eager she had been to hear someone speak ill of Mr. Darcy! And for what reason? To assuage her own wounded pride? To assure herself that she was indeed better than Mr. Darcy had declared? That in so doing, it could be confirmed that his character was wanting, and he was not the sort of man she should long to have notice her?

"I apologize for unsettling you." Georgiana had risen and slipped onto the sofa beside Elizabeth.

"It is startling," Elizabeth replied. "He spoke with such confidence."

"Mr. Wickham is very good at crafting tales. I should know as I was completely fooled by them."

Elizabeth looked at the hand that had taken hers and was squeezing it in a comforting fashion.

"I think," Miss Darcy continued, "that he succeeds because we, ladies such as you and I, are agreeable and friendly with a trusting nature."

Oh, Miss Darcy's words stung! If only she had been agreeable and friendly instead of intent on soothing her pride by hearing anything that would justify her contempt of the man who had injured her.

She shook her head. "No, it is not my goodness that granted Mr. Wickham his success."

She pulled her lower lip between her teeth and looked at the others in the room. She would rather not confess her errors to anyone but Jane, if even her. However, she could not deny the pangs of conscience that smote her as Miss Darcy attempted to reason away Elizabeth's culpability in believing Wickham's tales. Therefore, after expelling one breath and drawing another, she began her confession.

"It was my desire to find fault with Mr. Darcy that caused me to believe Mr. Wickham." Once again, she shook her head at her own foolishness. "Why I did not listen to Jane's cautions, I do not know."

She saw the furrowing of Miss Darcy's brow and the concern in her eyes and squeezed the young lady's hand that still held hers.

"That is not true. I chose not to listen because my pride was injured."

"Not without just cause," Jane interjected. "No lady's pride would be unscathed by such a slighting comment." She looked around Elizabeth to Miss Darcy and then to Mrs. Annesley. "It was at the assembly when the Bingleys had just arrived in the Hertfordshire. We were all eager to meet them, of course. It is not every day a new neighbour takes his place in our small community. The town was welcoming, and Mr. Bingley returned their fervour in kind.

His sisters and your brother, however, were not as enthusiastic to have met our acquaintances."

"Mr. Darcy is not always comfortable in new surroundings," said Mrs. Annesley.

"No, he is not," Georgiana added her agreement. "He had not wished to leave me, although, I assure you, just I did him, that there was no reason he needed to stay with me. He, of course, did not agree."

"I can understand that," said Mrs. Gardiner. "If my child had been through an ordeal such as you had, my dear, I would be in no hurry to be parted from them until I was absolutely certain they were recovered."

Georgiana smiled. "That sounds very much like his protest about leaving. However, he felt obliged, and I insisted he go. Fitzwilliam can be rather surly when he is forced to do what he does not wish, but that does not excuse rudeness, and you said he was rude, did you not?"

Jane nodded.

"Mr. Bingley suggested to him that he should dance with me," Elizabeth said, taking up the story where Jane had left off.

"Oh, dear," Georgiana muttered.

Elizabeth expelled a breath and closed her eyes for a brief moment before continuing. "Mr. Darcy turned, looked toward me and said 'She is tolerable, I suppose, but not handsome enough to tempt me.'" Elizabeth's cheeks felt as if they were on fire. Those words still stung. She had worn her best dress and had her hair styled just as Jane had suggested because it was most becoming. She had hoped to make a good first impression, which was something that was not easily done when one was always compared to such a beautiful older sister. It was not a complete impossibility, however, and Elizabeth had felt she had succeeded that night. She had even been complimented on her looks by many in attendance. Yet, in spite of her efforts, the fascinating and handsome Mr. Darcy had dismissed her as if she were a faded pair of boots, only good for an occasional walk about the country on a muddy day.

Georgiana gasped. "How despicable! And untrue! Oh, he is such a curmudgeon at times!" she cried before she snapped her mouth closed and apologized.

"His words are most certainly untrue," said Mrs. Annesley. "You are a very handsome young woman, and I will be so daring as to say my employer knows it."

Elizabeth shook her head in disbelief. Mr. Darcy had time and time again studied her appearance with a lofty air. Was he not looking to find fault or to prove his words from their first meeting correct?

"I am sorry," Mrs. Annesley said in reply to Elizabeth skeptical look. "I am certain that I am correct. In fact, I will shock you further by suggesting he finds you handsome enough to tempt him into considering marriage."

Elizabeth's eyes grew wide, and a small sound of disbelief escaped her. "That cannot be. I am not good enough for his notice let alone his consideration as a wife!"

Mrs. Annesley's smile in response was very similar — annoyingly so — to the one Aunt Gardiner used when she knew Elizabeth was incorrect in her reasoning.

"Truly, you are mistaken," Elizabeth added. Mr. Darcy had made it clear beyond a shadow of a doubt that she was deficient, had he not?

"I will allow that I might be wrong, but I highly doubt it," Mrs. Annesley replied.

"Oh, she is not wrong," Georgiana added. "Even Mr. Bingley knows that Fitzwilliam admires you."

"It cannot be." Elizabeth shook her head. It could not be true, could it?

"You do not hold my brother in high regard, do you?"

Elizabeth's heart skittered and thumped. How did one answer such a question honestly without causing pain to a girl who so obviously loved her brother?

"Do not worry about offending me," Georgiana added as if reading Elizabeth's mind. "I would not like him much myself if he had said such a thing about me."

Elizabeth saw a curious look that she could not quite decipher pass between Miss Darcy and her companion, which was followed by a small nod of Mrs. Annesley's head.

"Would you be willing to give Fitzwilliam a second

chance?" Georgiana asked. "He is not always as discontented and dour as he likely was when at Netherfield."

Elizabeth shrugged one shoulder. "I suppose I could." How could she say anything else? Miss Darcy was looking at her so hopefully. It would not be so bad a thing to attempt to like Mr. Darcy to keep from offending his sister. There was little harm in being civil after all, was there not?

"Excellent!" Georgiana cried. "I shall tell him that I have met you, and if he does not flee to Pemberley, I will send a note inviting you to tea — all of you, Miss Bennet, Miss Elizabeth, and Mrs. Gardiner. I would be delighted to have such pleasant company for an afternoon." Though her mouth was open as if she were going to continue speaking, she did not do so immediately. Her brows drew together, and her expression became somewhat distraught. Then she shook her head and smiled. "I shall just have to find a way to deal with Miss Bingley if she arrives. All will be well. I hope."

Mrs. Annesley stood. "It has been a delight to meet you, Mrs. Gardiner, and your nieces."

"Yes, indeed it has been a pleasure of the greatest sort," Georgiana agreed.

The sentiment was echoed by Mrs. Gardiner, Jane, and Elizabeth, as was polite. However, Elizabeth's still befuddled mind was not certain if it was either a pleasure or a delight to have met Miss Darcy and her companion as it seemed she was going to be thrown together with a disagreeable, though handsome, man who supposedly and surprisingly admired her. But then, her mind contradicted, it had been an interesting meeting, and she had to admit she was curious to see Mr. Darcy at his home where he might be in a better humor. Added to that was the fact that she rather liked Miss Darcy and would like to see her again. If only her mind would settle on how to think and feel.

"I will send a note even if Fitzwilliam does fly off to Pemberley," Miss Darcy assured them and, with that, Elizabeth's guest, who had borne such unsettling news with her, was gone, leaving Elizabeth to ponder all she knew of Mr. Darcy in as much solitude as a sister and aunt would allow.

Chapter 5

Two days later, Georgiana poked her head around the door to her brother's study.

"Come," he said with a smile.

"I am pleased to see you have not gone to Pemberley," she began.

He shrugged. "I would miss you too much," he admitted. It was true. He had no desire to be parted from her for any length of time, and he knew that sending her to stay with Lady Matlock would not be helpful for Georgiana's state of mind. His aunt was well-intentioned and doting, but she was also fixated on making proper matches and sharing the latest and most scandalous news of the ton. In his opinion, neither would be beneficial to his sister after her recent ordeal — no matter what Georgiana might claim to the contrary.

Therefore, after a frank discussion about Miss Elizabeth Bennet with his cousin, Colonel Richard Fitzwilliam, over a bottle of port and a game of billiards, he had come to realize that staying in town would be the best for all.

Richard had assured him that running from a problem was not the most successful way of overcoming it. Instead, he suggested, Darcy should face and vanquish the problem. This last bit of advice had Darcy considering returning to Netherfield as he had promised.

If he could put Elizabeth from his mind for the next two weeks, then he could surely return knowing that he had merely been infatuated. That was *if* he could put her from his mind. If he could not, well, then a new strategy might need to be employed whereby he could keep his word to Bingley.

"You truly are not going?" Georgiana asked hopefully.

"No, I am remaining here."

"Good," Georgiana replied with a smile, eying a letter with familiar writing on it laying open on her brother's desk. "Is Mr. Bingley returning to town?"

Darcy's brows rose, and his head tipped to the side. "Why would you expect him to return so soon?"

Georgiana smoothed an imaginary wrinkle from her skirt. "Because Miss Bennet is in town," she replied without looking up at him.

Darcy stared at her. "How do you know that?" There was no way she could have read Bingley's letter. It had just arrived, and he had just finished reading it himself.

"I saw her," Georgiana answered, lifting her eyes to him. "Where?"

"At her aunt's house," Georgiana swallowed and waited

for him to reply, hoping that he would not raise his voice too much or worse speak in that low, sad, disappointed tone that always tore at her heart.

"In Cheapside?"

"No, Gracechurch Street," she replied. "The Gardiner's home is very nice," she added. "It's not large, but neither is it small. The furnishings are very tasteful. Everything is well-kept, and the servants seem happy. I suspect Mr. Gardiner is a very well-to-do merchant and no mere shop-keeper." She stopped her rambling as she saw his lips purse and brows furrow.

"Why were you at Miss Bennet's aunt's home?"

"To visit her, of course."

His eyes narrowed. "Why?"

"Mr. Bingley happened to mention that Mr. Wickham was in Hertfordshire, and I did not wish for Miss Bennet or her sisters to be tricked by him as I was." She held her breath. His eyes had grown wide, and his expression did not look pleased.

"You intended to tell a complete stranger about Wickham?"

"Yes."

"Georgiana." Darcy stared at her in disbelief. How could she be so careless with her reputation? He shook his head.

"Fitzwilliam, you know how he hurt me." She scooted forward in her chair so that she could be a tiny bit closer to him. "How could I allow that to happen to another if I had it in my power to prevent it?"

"But a stranger, Georgiana? How did you know she would not bandy your story hither and yon? The Bennets are not heiresses. They have nothing with which to tempt him."

"They are pretty," Georgiana replied. "Even a pretty maid is not beneath his notice, not that he would pursue her for her money, of course." Her cheeks flushed with embarrassment.

Darcy's eyes grew wide. "You know about that?"

"One hears things occasionally," Georgiana replied, lowering her eyes. "It was told to me to assure me that I had lost nothing in not being loved by Mr. Wickham. It helped me understand your disapproval for what it was — not a condemnation of him because he is not a gentleman but because he is a rogue. "

"The connection would not have been good either," Darcy replied, "but you are right, I worried more about your happiness and safety than about his standing." He blew out a breath. "And do you believe Miss Bennet and Mrs. Gardiner will treat what you have told them with care?"

Georgiana nodded. "As will Miss Elizabeth."

Darcy's brows furrowed. "You gave them permission to tell her?"

"No," Georgiana said with a smile, "she is also in town."

In town? Elizabeth was in town? Bingley had not mentioned Elizabeth being in town, only Miss Bennet. Darcy rose from his chair and paced to the window. He was not ready to face his trouble just yet. He had not had ample time to work at forgetting her. Perhaps he should go to Pemberley for a time.

"She is quite lovely," Georgiana said to him as he stood in front of the window, running a hand through his hair. "I can see why you love her."

He spun towards his sister. "I do not love her," he snapped. He did not love Elizabeth, did he? He was only infatuated with her blasted fine eyes and keen mind.

"Do you not?"

"I do not," he answered with little certainty filling his mind. In fact, doubt, great heaping amounts of doubt, was creeping in around the edges of his thinking. Love. Love would explain why rather than thinking of her less with each day he was in town, he had found himself thinking about her more, would it not?

Georgiana stood. "She is a gentleman's daughter, Fitzwilliam. True, she has relations in trade, but so does Bingley, yet you accept him regardless of what any of our relatives say. I do not know the state of your finances, but I cannot believe that, with as careful as you are about everything, Pemberley is in need of funds from a wealthy wife." She crossed to stand next to her brother, who was once again looking out the window. "Fitzwilliam," she said as she wrapped an arm around his waist, "do not sacrifice your heart."

"I am not," he said softly as he placed an arm around her shoulder and drew her close.

"Consider it?" she asked, looking at him with pleading eyes.

He nodded slowly. He would likely be unable to not consider it now that such a thought had been placed in his mind, and his sister knew it. He kissed her forehead. "I will consider it."

"Excellent." She gave him a squeeze and then released her hold on him. "You know she is actually quite beautiful."

"I know," he muttered. She was captivatingly beautiful.

"Then why would you say she was merely tolerable?"

Darcy, who had taken his place at his desk, started and looked up at her. How did she know about that?

"You hurt her, Fitzwilliam."

Darcy blinked, and his stomach dropped. Elizabeth had heard him. No wonder she had done her best to avoid all his attempts to engage her in anything other than an argument.

"You should likely apologize," Georgiana said. "Or, at least, prove to her you know how to be civil."

Darcy gave a sharp nod of his head. Being scolded by one's younger sister was not pleasant.

"Miss Darcy." Mr. Wright stood behind her at the door, "you have callers," he said softly.

"Thank you, Mr. Wright. Would you be so kind as to see that tea is arranged?"

"Certainly."

"Will you join us, Fitzwilliam?"

Darcy shrugged.

"It is not Miss Bingley," she whispered.

Darcy chuckled. "Then who is it?"

A look of pure enjoyment suffused her face. "Miss Elizabeth, her sister, and her aunt."

~*~*~

Darcy stared at the place where his sister had stood before she flounced out of the room. Flounced! He shook his head. Georgiana had actually flounced out of the room. She had not flounced or behaved so carefree for very nearly three-quarters of a year. He smiled as he rose from his chair. It was good to see that part of her personality returning. He straightened his jacket, patted his hair, and checked his neckcloth before exiting his study. He knew that if he was to avoid his sister's displeasure, he would have to make an appearance and at least greet her guests.

He walked the length of the corridor from his study to the drawing room slowly. He could hear the rise and fall of female voices engaged in pleasantries. He paused before he reached the door. Elizabeth was in his home.

Here under this roof where he had imagined her being. He shook his head. His sister's scolding would be better than seeing that vision come to life. How would he rid himself of it once he had witnessed it? He turned and walked halfway back to his study before the pull of curiosity and the shame of cowardice compelled him to retrace his steps to the drawing room. Again, he paused outside the door that stood ajar, but this time, with one last tug at his jacket, he pushed the door open and entered.

He paused and stood like a mute fool just inside the door. Reality was even better than his imaginings. Green was a very becoming colour on her, and she was sitting in the very chair he had imagined she would favor. He wondered for a moment if it had been her choice to sit there or if she had merely taken the chair next to her sister.

"Brother." Georgiana waited for him to turn his attention to her. "I know you have already met Miss Bennet and Miss Elizabeth, but please let me introduce you to their aunt, Mrs. Gardiner. Mrs. Gardiner, this is my brother, Fitzwilliam Darcy."

Darcy turned toward the one lady in the room whom he did not know. He opened his mouth to give her his greeting but upon taking in her appearance, found himself lost for words. She was impeccably dressed. Even Miss Bingley would not be able to find fault with the lady's appearance, but that was not what had struck him about her. He gathered his wits. "Forgive me. It is a pleasure to meet you, but I feel as if I have already met you somewhere. You look very familiar."

Mrs. Gardiner smiled. "I have a twin sister, and we both resemble our mother."

Darcy was unsure why this information might clear his mind. So he waited expectantly for the lady to continue but before she could, his eyes grew wide with recognition as an image of a lady he had seen many times in his childhood flashed through his mind. "Mrs. Pettigrew?"

"Is my mother," Mrs. Gardiner replied.

"You are from Lambton?" Darcy asked with interest as he took a seat.

"Indeed, I am, although, very little of my family remains in Derbyshire. In fact, it is only my cousin, Mr. Cooke, who still remains. Both my sister and I have husbands here in town, and our brother is long since passed — a childhood illness not long after my mother died," she added in explanation.

Darcy slumped from his normal rigid posture. "I remember that year. Illness seemed to be everywhere at once."

Mrs. Gardiner nodded. "It did. Many families were affected. Mine, those of friends, yours." She gave him a meaningful and sympathetic look. "Your mother was a wonderful lady. She frequented my father's shop often and was always so kind. I was telling my nieces about her after your sister's call. Miss Darcy resembles her both in expression and kindness."

"She does," Darcy agreed with a smile for Georgiana. "There are few hearts that are more generous and caring."

"That is a testament to your care for her," Mrs. Gardiner said.

"It was my father," Darcy replied.

"I must disagree," Mrs. Gardiner said with a shake of her head. "Your father may have laid the groundwork, but if I am accounting years properly, when your father died, Miss Darcy was at an age that is a threshold from childhood with several tender years between then and now when she is on the verge of her presentation to society. You, sir, have done well."

Darcy bowed his head in acceptance of the compliment. He was not entirely convinced that he had done much to help his sister become the lady she was. He had paid for school and made certain he was home whenever she had a holiday, and he had now employed two companions to see to her final preparations for her debut — one, Miss Annesley, had been a very good choice, while the other, Mrs. Younge, had been an instrument in bringing Wickham and near ruin to his sister.

Just then, the tea arrived, and Darcy assisted the maid with setting up the table. "Thank you, Nellie," he said as the maid finished arranging the things she was carrying. She curtseyed and slipped from the room without a word.

"I had not thought to see you in town," Mr. Darcy said to Elizabeth when he had returned to his seat.

"And I had thought to see you still in Hertfordshire," she replied, raising one eyebrow. "It was a shock to the whole neighbourhood when everyone from Netherfield left so suddenly."

Though her tone was light and teasing, he could see her displeasure in the flash of her eyes. "It was a sudden decision," he replied. "Perhaps not thought out as well as it should have been," he admitted. "And you? I do not remember hearing you or anyone else speak of a journey to town."

"Must I publish my intentions to travel?" Elizabeth retorted. "One might have plans that are not known to the whole of an area."

"Yet, I am accused of a hasty departure that has caused some acrimony in Hertfordshire."

"Mr. Bingley had said he was to return."

"Which he has," Darcy replied.

"Yes, well, that is not what Miss Bingley's letter said."

Darcy blinked. "Miss Bingley's letter?"

"The one she sent to Jane on the day your party left Netherfield. It made it very clear that her brother was not returning."

Darcy shook his head. "I did not know." Of course, he should have expected that Caroline would have done something like that. That woman could not make a quiet, graceful exit if her life depended upon it.

Elizabeth's head tipped, and her brows drew together

just a touch as she scrutinized his face. "Very well, you are acquitted on that count."

Darcy dipped his head. "You are most generous." A small smile accompanied the statement which seemed to startle Elizabeth. "I do hope you can understand my reluctance to be away from my sister and to be confined to Netherfield with Mr. Bingley's sisters."

The startled expression on Elizabeth's face grew, and he knew that he had most assuredly made a very poor impression on the lady who captivated his every thought. It was quite likely if he were to pursue her and offer his heart, he would have it handed back to him in short order and without ceremony. The thought did not sit well with him. He should count it a blessing for the knowledge of such a thing should make it easier for him to overcome whatever infatuation he had with the woman, but instead, it cut at his heart, causing him to once again wondered if his sister might not be correct. He might indeed be in love with Elizabeth Bennet.

"Miss Bingley would like nothing better than to be the next Mrs. Darcy," Georgiana said. "However, my brother would rather not have her as his wife."

Darcy gave her a disapproving look. These were not things of which she should speak in company.

"There are many that would like to be the next Mrs. Darcy," Mrs. Annesley added. "But, their desires and those of the good gentleman in question do not seem to match.

But that is how it is in the marriage market, is it not? There are the pursued and the pursuers. Things can get jumbled. Feelings can be roused and crushed, or hidden for fear of rejection." She clucked her tongue. "It was not so different when I was young."

"Indeed!" Mrs. Gardiner interjected. "Matchmaking," she said with a shake of her head, "gone wrong is the reason my nieces have come to visit."

Darcy saw both Bennet ladies cheeks grow rosy.

"My husband's sister was not pleased when her second eldest refused an offer she considered adequate for Elizabeth."

"Aunt," Elizabeth cried.

"She has five daughters to see well-married," Mrs. Gardiner continued, ignoring Elizabeth completely. "It is understandable that she would be anxious about accomplishing her task."

"Oh, it is," Mrs. Annesley replied.

"Who?" The question slipped from Darcy's lips. He had not intended to ask, but the shock of Mrs. Gardiner's revelation had him sixes and sevens. Someone had offered for Elizabeth? She could right now be someone else's save for her refusal? Surely, it was not —

"Mr. Collins," Mrs. Gardiner said with a hint of amusement in her tone. "Not exactly the sort of sensible gentleman our Elizabeth would appreciate, but then my husband's sister is more hopeful than sensible at times."

"Mr. Collins?" Darcy repeated in surprise. "They would certainly not suit," he added.

"And why would we not?" Elizabeth demanded. "Am I so deficient as to not be worthy of an offer of marriage?"

Darcy could not contain the shock that such a question brought. His sister was not wrong in that he had hurt the lady beside him most severely. He shook his head. "No, having been admitted to your presence, I would have to say that only an idiot would find you deficient in any way. I meant that the match would be unequal. You are far superior to Mr. Collins."

"Well said, Mr. Darcy," Mrs. Gardiner said. "If only her mother could see that. However, she cannot. At the moment, all she can see is her hopes to have two daughters cared for have been dashed first by Elizabeth's refusal of a good home and then by Mr. Bingley's defection."

Darcy turned his gaze from Elizabeth to Jane, whose head was bowed and a tinge of pink stained her cheeks. Had he been wrong in assessing her feelings for his friend?

"So, Mrs. Bennet has sent them to me in hopes that one might express herself more clearly and the other might, by some miracle of grace, find a man willing to accept her." She held up her hand. "Those are not my words. I find nothing lacking in either of my nieces. A man could not do better than to marry either of them."

"Aunt," Jane pleaded quietly.

"Very well, my dear, I shall leave off." And she did.

The conversation turned to what sorts of activities the Bennets might partake in while in town. Darcy added a few suggestions that he hoped would be appealing to Elizabeth. She had nearly been another's? The way his heart had felt as if it would stop beating to hear such a thing was all the proof he needed that his sister was correct. He loved Elizabeth Bennet. Now, he just needed to decide what he was going to do with such information.

Chapter 6

Darcy paced the length and breadth of the library at Matlock House. It had taken him some time to find his cousin.
He had not been where he was normally wont to be at
this hour of the evening, but Darcy had finally run him
aground.

Richard Fitzwilliam was not the sort of gentleman to be
lounging about home when there were more interesting
entertainments to be found in town. Yet, to Darcy's surprise, home was precisely where Richard was.

"Darcy," Richard greeted as he stepped into the library
and secured the door behind him. "What brings you to
visit and has you looking so..." he tipped his head and
looked his cousin up and down, "unsettled?"

"She is here."

Richard looked around the room. "Who is here?" he
asked.

"Miss Elizabeth," Darcy replied, dropping into a chair
near the hearth. "She and her sister are visiting their aunt."

He scrubbed his face with his hands. "Georgiana told them about Ramsgate."

"Georgiana did what?"

"I was not pleased to hear it either," Darcy assured him. "However, she insisted that she could not allow others to be fooled as she was if she had it in her power to prevent it." He was still surprised that she had shared the story almost as much as he was by her reason for sharing it.

Richard joined Darcy near the fire. "I suppose that is, at least, an admirable reason for doing so."

Darcy nodded his agreement. "I do not think we need to fear Mrs. Gardiner, Miss Bennet, or Miss Elizabeth spreading the tale." As she was leaving Darcy House earlier that day, Mrs. Gardiner had made a point of whispering a promise to protect the information Georgiana had shared.

"Mrs. Gardiner assures me that we all make mistakes when attempting to lead a child into adulthood." He shared a rueful smile with Richard.

"Does she have children that are grown?"

"No," Darcy answered. "I believe the eldest is six. She has been instrumental, however, in Miss Bennet and Miss Elizabeth's lives. As I understand it, they have often visited with their aunt, and she is a sort of confidant for them."

"And you said the eldest Bennet ladies are well-mannered?"

"Yes."

"Then, perhaps she knows of what she speaks."

Darcy shrugged. "Perhaps."

"And is that what has you in a stew?"

"Only partly," Darcy admitted. "I love her."

"I beg your pardon?"

"I love Elizabeth," Darcy clarified, "and I wish to marry her."

Richard laughed. "Last night you wished to avoid any mention of her name."

Darcy rubbed his neck. "I know, but when she called at Darcy House and her aunt said she had refused an offer of marriage...Richard, I thought my heart would stop beating and, though I have tried for the past several hours to rid myself of the feeling of needing her, I cannot. I simply cannot imagine her with anyone else, nor can I imagine my life as even remotely happy without her in it."

"I see."

"Am I being a fool?"

Richard shook his head. "No."

Darcy looked at him, hoping that his cousin would elaborate on his reply.

"What can I tell you that you do not already know?"

"Her family is ridiculous," Darcy said.

"And so is Aunt Catherine."

"Her father's estate is mismanaged."

"That is not Miss Elizabeth's doing," Richard replied

with a smile. "Her father has an estate; that is the relevant point — she is a gentleman's daughter."

"But she has little to bring with her to a marriage."

"Besides herself," Richard countered. "Is Pemberley in need of funds?"

"No, but she will likely bring her younger sisters with her — all three of them, hoping to be thrown into the paths of wealthy gentlemen. Silly younger sisters." Darcy shook his head at the thought.

Richard grimaced. "That could be a problem, but is it great enough to require that you give up Miss Elizabeth to another?"

Darcy scrubbed his face again. "No. I have argued all these points over and over, and the answer is always the same."

Richard cocked a brow. "A fool does not put so much thought into a decision, does he?"

Darcy shook his head. "I suppose not."

"Then marry her. Claim some happiness for yourself."

"Darcy, I had heard you were here," Lord Matlock said as he entered the library through the door that led to his study. "To what do we owe the pleasure of your visit?" He tipped his head and surveyed Darcy from head to toe just as Richard had done.

"He's getting married," Richard replied.

"I am considering marrying," Darcy corrected. "I must convince her that I am worthy of her first."

Lord Matlock leaned against the mantle and looked at his nephew with raised brows. "Have you shown her your bank accounts?"

Darcy chuckled. "She knows I am not poor, but it seems character, rather than wealth, is of greatest importance."

"Then she shall love you."

Darcy shook his head. "I am afraid I made a very poor first impression."

"Ah," Lord Matlock muttered as he nodded his understanding. "Put your foot in it, did you?"

"Indeed, I did," Darcy assured him. "She has an uncle in trade and another who is a country solicitor." He might as well get the disagreeable portion of this interview over with straight away.

"And her father?"

"He has a modest estate in Hertfordshire."

"I see. She is not of great standing, and you are worried that I will not approve."

"Something like that, yes."

Lord Matlock tipped his head from one side to the other and back. "I will not say that everyone will approve, but as far as I am concerned, I trust your judgment. He has thought through every ramification, has he not, son?"

"He has dissected it thoroughly," Richard assured his father. "He has even attempted to change his mind by fleeing her presence."

Lord Matlock chuckled. "That rarely works."

"So it would seem," Darcy agreed.

"You love her, then?"

Darcy nodded. "I do."

"I am glad."

"You truly approve?" Darcy asked in surprise. He had thought there might be some argument about Elizabeth's being of no standing.

"Very much so. I have always wished for you to find someone to love and to love you in return. You need a woman, not a fortune, to wrap your arms around. Now," said Lord Matlock, "I should like to meet this young lady so I will wish you well on your quest to improve her opinion of you, and when you have succeeded, send word. I will deal with Catherine for you."

~*~*~

"You were out late last night," Georgiana said as she took a place at the breakfast table next to her brother.

"I was," he replied, filling his cup once again with tea.

After receiving his uncle's approval to marry where he thought best, Darcy had spent another two hours with his uncle and cousin talking and playing cards. Lord Matlock had waxed eloquent a time or two on felicity in marriage and seeing that an estate had an heir. He seemed most anxious to have a grand niece or nephew whom he could bounce on his knee and tell tales — he had mentioned that more than once as well. The conversation had not all been about marriage or the best way to grovel ones way into the good graces of an offended lady; they had also discussed more mundane topics including the new upholstery Lady Matlock planned to order for their travelling coach once the weather turned warm enough to gad about town in the barouche.

"You were not dressed for a soiree when you left."

Darcy chuckled at his sister's attempt to not ask where he had been while still expressing her wish to know the answer to that very question.

"No, I was not." His plate was empty, so he rested against the back of the chair and cradled his teacup.

Her brows furrowed as she applied herself to cutting her toast into points before topping each with a different jam — raspberry on one, strawberry on the second, apricot on the third, and what Darcy knew to be her favourite, black currant, on the fourth. With that task completed, she filled her teacup and added just a splash of cream.

"I was at Matlock House," Darcy finally said upon hearing her small frustrated huff as she stirred her tea. "Richard was at home, as strange as that may be."

"Indeed? Is he well?" Georgiana asked with a laugh.

"He appeared to be, yes."

"Did you have a good time then?"

"We did. Uncle Henry insisted on playing Casino." Cards of any sort were a favourite pastime for Lord Matlock. However, he was not one to frequent gaming tables for any length of time at soirees or his club since he desired for most of his money to stay in his accounts. A small wager was acceptable to lose, but one must always know his limits. Darcy had heard these words from his uncle many times over the years.

"And did he win?"

Darcy shook his head. "Once or twice. He was far more interested in talking than attending to his cards."

Lord Matlock was not known for being subdued. Richard often said that his father could strike up a conversation with a horse and convince the animal to vote with him on the next bill that entered the house. It was a skill that Richard had inherited, and one that Darcy, at times, wished he possessed.

"Were there any stories of particular interest that might be suitable to relate to me?" she asked as she began eating her toast — strawberry first as was her usual fashion.

Darcy chuckled. "No."

Georgiana's brows rose. "Indeed?" she said with no small amount of curiosity.

"Indeed," Darcy assured her. There was no way he was going to share with his sister about the duties of a husband to his wife, nor was he ready at this moment to admit to her that he was indeed looking for a wife — a very particular wife — Elizabeth.

Georgiana sighed and returned to her toast. "Are you going out today?"

"I have not decided. I might call at Mrs. Verity's. I am

not expected there until next week, but I do enjoy reading to the children." He was considering calling on Elizabeth as well and possibly inviting her to go for a drive or perhaps an evening at the theatre or on a trip to the museum. They were all things that he suspected she would enjoy.

"Mrs. Annesley and I are planning to finish a few projects."

He could tell by the way she was smiling that those projects included a gift for him. "Will you be working on them the whole day?"

"No," she replied before washing down her third toast point with her tea. "Mr. Martin comes for a dance lesson this afternoon, and I have not yet mastered that Bach concerto. "

Darcy placed his empty cup on the table and, leaning back, watched her as she finished her breakfast. She had not looked so happy as she did this morning in a very long time.

"What?" she asked when she noticed his observation. "Do I have jam on my chin?" she whispered.

"No," he replied with a chuckle. "You have a smile on your face and an energy about you that has been absent for some time."

"I assure you, Fitzwilliam. My heart is healing."

"So you have said, and I am beginning to believe."

She smiled at him. "I will be finished soon. Will you

wait for me and escort me to my sitting room before you lock yourself away with your books and whatnot?"

"I would like that," he replied.

Georgiana popped the last bit of black currant covered toast into her mouth and took up her cup. Leaning back in her chair to enjoy the last of her tea, she watched her brother for a full two minutes before he began to squirm under her scrutiny.

"Do I have jam on my cravat?" he whispered.

She shook her head and then, swallowed the last warm drops of tea before returning her cup to its saucer and standing in preparation to leave. "No, just a smile on your face and a relaxed air about you that I feared was lost."

"It would seem," he said as Georgiana wrapped her arm around the arm he offered her, "that my heart has found its hope."

She hugged his arm tightly and rested her smiling face against his shoulder. "I am glad," she whispered. "So very glad."

Chapter 7

"We have just one more place to visit," Aunt Gardiner told Elizabeth as their carriage crawled through the streets of the city.

They had been seeing to errands all morning. Elizabeth had agreed to accompany her aunt while Jane had wished to remain at home with the children. Therefore, Aunt Gardiner and Elizabeth had had ample time to talk about many things. The chief topic of interest for Aunt Gardiner had been the gentleman who had called with his sister on Friday, Monday, and Tuesday.

"The orphan house?" Elizabeth asked.

"Yes, Mrs. Verity's." Aunt Gardiner sorted through her parcels to find the one that Elizabeth knew contained two shirts and three petticoats. "It is not much," she said as she found the correct parcel and placed it on her lap, "but it will be appreciated. Mrs. Verity relies not only on her own funds — substantial though they are — but also on the generosity of her friends to meet every need of her charges."

Mrs. Verity was a wealthy widow, who, having no children of her own, had chosen to use the money left to her by her husband to set up a house for orphans. Her intention was not just to give them a safe place to live, but to educate them in every area of life that might afford them a proper future, free of crime and filled with hope — at least, that is how Aunt Gardiner had described it.

Elizabeth had to admit she was curious to see what an orphan house looked like. There was nothing of that sort in Hertfordshire, and the idea of a lady running her own establishment and aiding the less fortunate intrigued her.

"Mr. Darcy seemed disappointed yesterday when you refused his offer of a drive in the park."

Elizabeth's reply was a tight smile.

Aunt Gardiner sighed. "He is a fine gentleman — handsome and rich — and quite obviously besotted with you. I do not know why you insist on repelling his every advance."

Elizabeth wished she had an answer for that herself — or at least one that did not show her in such a poor light. "I have been such a fool, Aunt. I cannot see him without being reminded of my shame."

"Pride is a dangerous thing, Elizabeth." Her aunt tipped her head and looked at her very seriously. "Apologize."

Elizabeth pulled the corner of her bottom lip between her teeth and winced at that one word.

"Oh, it will smart for a time, to be sure," her aunt continued, "but then, it will be done."

Elizabeth knew it was true. The proper thing to do was to gather her courage and admit her folly. "He will hate me," she admitted in a whisper.

Her aunt's brows rose. "And you wish for him to *not hate* you?"

"Yes," Elizabeth could feel her face turning red. "I believe I have wanted him to not hate me ever since the assembly at Michaelmas. I had hoped when I saw him enter and when his friend paid attention to Jane that he might consider me." She looked down at her hands. "But he did not." It was the first time she had admitted how much Mr. Darcy's slighting comment had humiliated her. She had managed until this moment to wrap that pain in indignation and anger.

"Oh, my Lizzy!" Her aunt reached across the carriage and grasped Elizabeth's hands. "Then let him love you now. He is a good man. Do you not believe that?"

Elizabeth nodded. "He does seem to be a good and kind brother."

"He cares very well for his sister," Mrs. Gardener agreed. "I know many who would not treat a daughter or sister with such care after making such a scandalous plan as to elope with a ne'er-do-well. Why, there is one young lady who found herself in Mrs. Verity's care after being caught with a beau of whom her father did not approve. Miss

Darcy was not ruined as this girl was, but still, to be cast out in such a way." She shook her head. "And you know as well as I that she is one of the fortunate ones to have found a good place to live until she could find a position where she could earn her keep."

Elizabeth nodded. Everything that she had seen or heard about Mr. Darcy since she had arrived in town spoke of his goodness. "I am being foolish, I know."

Her aunt patted her hand. "Learning to love is a fearful prospect."

"Love?" the word jumped from Elizabeth's lips. She did not love Mr. Darcy. She admired him; she found him attractive; she even found his company to be pleasant; but she did not love him.

Her aunt smiled as the carriage drew to a stop. "Yes, my dear, that is the opposite of hate."

Elizabeth's mouth dropped open and then snapped closed. "Just because I do not want him to hate me does not mean I love him. It means...it means..." she stammered indignantly.

"You value his good opinion," her aunt completed. "And when not having it can threaten to rend your very soul, then it is time to consider just how deeply you admire the gentleman. Do not be stubborn about this, Elizabeth, or you may lose something that cannot be replaced."

Elizabeth pressed her lips together and followed her

aunt out of the carriage and up the steps to Mrs. Verity's door.

"Mrs. Gardiner!" A lady with dark hair, streaked with thin ribbons of grey, greeted Elizabeth's aunt as she and Elizabeth entered a spacious study. The walls were lined with book-filled shelves. There was a grouping of chairs near a hearth, and another pair tucked in a window alcove. At one side, a large desk stood before two more chairs. It was to these chairs that Mrs. Verity directed her visitors.

"I have some shirts and petticoats," Mrs. Gardiner said as she placed the parcel she carried between two neat stacks of papers on the desk. "This is my niece, Miss Elizabeth Bennet. Elizabeth, this is Mrs. Verity, the capable headmistress of this fine establishment."

"Oh, be seated," Mrs. Verity waved away Mrs. Gardiner's compliments and chuckled. "Your aunt is always attempting to swell my head even more than it is already swollen."

"I speak only the truth," Mrs. Gardiner retorted with a grin.

"Well, then, I shall leave that to Miss Elizabeth to decide," Mrs. Verity arranged herself in the chair behind the desk and picked up a paper. "This is the young lady who is seeking a position," she said, handing the paper to Mrs. Gardiner. "And this is the lad in need of an apprenticeship." She handed a second sheet of paper to Elizabeth's aunt.

"We instruct all our residence in every useful skill," she explained to Elizabeth. "Both boys and girls are taught to read, write, and do their sums. The boys practice various skills such as placing and removing things from a table without being a distraction, tying cravats, planting, caring for animals, working with their hands, and when an aptitude in one or another of these skills is noted, we attempt to find them a place where they can earn both a bit of money and experience. Master Riley shows an inclination to be very good with figures. He is not meant to work with his hands. He must work with his mind."

"My husband thinks he would do well with Mr. Crenshaw," said Mrs. Gardiner.

"He may lodge here if there is no place for him there," Mrs. Verity turned her attention to Mrs. Gardiner who assured her that all the necessary arrangements would be in place before Riley began any work.

"The girls, such as Miss Clara, are taught cooking, cleaning, tending to and instructing young ones, as well as stitching and the like," Mrs. Verity continued her explanation to Elizabeth. "Clara has a love for fashion and can ply a needle and thread with such skill."

"Mr. Gardiner will surely know of a mantua-maker in need of an assistant," Mrs. Gardiner assured Mrs. Verity. "I see that Miss Clara is also skilled at making bonnets," Mrs. Gardiner said as she continued looking over the sheet of paper she held. "Would she be inclined to work with a milliner?"

"She would indeed. Again, lodging is available here if required, but if a place can be found for her as well as Riley that provides living arrangements, then I can take in two new children."

Mrs. Gardiner nodded her head. "We will see what we can do."

"You always do," Mrs. Verity said with a smile. "Now, your niece has not been here before. Would you care for a tour, Miss Bennet?"

Elizabeth looked hopefully at her aunt.

Mrs. Gardiner laughed. "I dare say I shall not hear the end of her disappointment if we do not have a tour. Elizabeth is an industrious sort of young lady who might need a charity in which to be involved after she is married.

"And is marriage in the near future?" Mrs. Verity asked as she led them from the room.

"No," Elizabeth answered as her aunt replied "possibly."

Mrs. Verity laughed. "The hopeful aunt, but I can see why she is hopeful. You are a lovely young woman."

Elizabeth blushed and thanked Mrs. Verity for her compliment.

"Is there a particular gentleman?" The headmistress of the orphan house asked Mrs. Gardiner.

"I cannot say," Mrs. Gardiner replied while allowing her

eyebrows to flick in a manner that told Mrs. Verity that there was indeed a particular gentleman.

Elizabeth shook her head. "Aunt," she pleaded.

"Very well," said Mrs. Verity, "we shall pursue that topic no further. This room on your left is where the children take all their meals. After they reach a certain age, they are required to take their turns in serving — not just because they may someday be employed in a fine home, but because there is value in learning to serve others."

The room was furnished just as a dining room in a wealthy estate might be furnished.

"It is beautiful," Elizabeth murmured.

"I give them the best," Mrs. Verity said. "They must learn to work in such places as this, so they must be familiar with both sides of the room so to speak. Those who eat and those who wait." She led them down the hall and up a set of back stairs. "The children are required to use these stairs at all times unless descending for lessons. I will show you the classroom last." She led them through the halls, showing them this room and that and introducing each child she met to the ladies.

Elizabeth smiled and curtseyed in response to each polite greeting she received. It was evident that Mrs. Verity and her staff had taught the children very well, and from their clear complexions and bright eyes, they were all well-fed and happy.

After touring the upper levels, Mrs. Verity took them

down to the storehouses and kitchen before returning to the floor on which they had begun their tour.

"There were two drawing rooms and a library when I first purchased the house," Mrs. Verity explained as she stood outside a closed door. "We have kept one drawing room for receiving guests, and the other two rooms have been converted into schoolrooms. This is the room for receiving guests," she said as she pushed the door open.

The room was empty save for a young woman sitting near the window stitching.

Elizabeth stopped and stared at the woman. She looked very much like the maid who had delivered the tea to the drawing room at Darcy House. "Does she work here?" she whispered to Mrs. Verity.

"No," Mrs. Verity paused. "Not all of our children are orphans. Some, such as Nellie's son, are foundlings."

"Nellie?" Elizabeth whispered. It was Mr. Darcy's maid.

Mrs. Verity nodded. "She keeps her son here so that she can continue to work. A maid cannot care for a child and fulfill her duties."

"She has no husband?"

"No, she has never had a husband," Mrs. Verity said softly. "Maids can fall prey to the gentlemen of a house."

Elizabeth's stomach felt as if it had dropped to her toes. "And that is what happened to Nellie?"

"Yes."

The one word answer made Elizabeth blink at sudden

tears. How could she even consider a man who would take advantage of one of his maids in such a way?

"How sad," she muttered, both because it was a dismal realization about the man she admired and because it was sad that a maid should be treated so.

"Indeed, it is. However, Nellie's employer allows her to visit regularly and be involved in her son's life. That is much more than most foundlings are ever given. Her son will be along to see her soon." She looked at the pocket watch which hung with several other baubles and keys on a chain around her waist. "Ten more minutes and reading time will be over, and Robert will be free to visit with his mother."

Elizabeth followed Mrs. Verity to the next door.

"As I mentioned before, the remaining rooms were made over into classrooms — one for the older children and one for the younger ones. The two rooms are connected by a door, and from time to time, the younger and older children learn together. She cracked the door open slowly, and whispered, "such as now. It is good for all ages to hear literature read aloud even if they cannot decipher the words themselves." She held a finger to her lips and did not open the door any further.

"...And I have felt
A presence that disturbs me with the joy
Of elevated thoughts; a sense sublime
Of something far more deeply interfused,*

Whose dwelling is the light of setting suns,
And the round ocean and the living air,
And the blue sky, and in the mind of man:
A motion and a spirit, that impels
All thinking things, all objects of all thought,
And rolls through all things...."[1]

The rich, familiar baritone of the reader wafted into the hall, wrapping itself around Elizabeth's heart with a deep sadness that ran exactly opposite of the sentiments of the poet. She fought to maintain control of her emotions.

Mrs. Verity motioned her forward and pushed the door open just a bit further.

Elizabeth peered into the room, a dozen children of various ages sat attentively listening. Some sat on the floor, others in chairs, and one small boy with blonde curls snuggled into Mr. Darcy's shoulder. Elizabeth looked from that young boy to Mrs. Verity.

"That is Nellie's son, Robert," she whispered.

Her words snatched the air from Elizabeth's lungs. The room felt warm and her legs unstable. "I need a bit of air," she said, and quickly fled the sight of the man, whom she loved, holding his maid's son.

---

1. *from Lines Composed a Few Miles above Tintern Abbey, On Revisiting the Banks of the Wye during a Tour. July 13, 1798, by William Wordsworth*

Chapter 8

Elizabeth hurried through the hall and out the front door of the house. She stood on the step and pulled in several deep breaths of crisp December air. The image of Mr. Darcy with that child nestled in his lap pulled at her heart in two very different directions. Part of her could not help but be charmed by the prospect of a man as tall and handsome as Mr. Darcy snuggling a wee one, but when she thought of how that child had come into this world, her stomach roiled. She had long abhorred the practice of some men to take mistresses or satisfy their desires without the commitment of marriage.

"Pardon me, miss."

A boy, who looked to be about eleven, stood next to her with a broom in his hand.

"Forgive me," Elizabeth said, stepping to the side so that he could continue his work.

"That part of the step is clean if you wish to sit down." The boy kept peeking at her as he worked.

"Thank you. I find sitting would be most welcome."

"Wait, miss," the boy said before Elizabeth could do more than step down a step and prepare to take a seat. "The step is as clean as I can get it, but I should hate to see you soil your dress." He shrugged out of his coat and lay it on the step with the interior facing upward. "Yellow was my mother's favorite color," he said as he returned to his broom.

Elizabeth pulled her shawl more tightly around her shoulders. It would have been far smarter to have stopped during her flight to gather her pelisse. "You remember your mother?" she asked the boy.

He nodded. "I was six when she died. Papa passed the year before."

"I am sorry," Elizabeth murmured. She could not imagine losing both her parents now, let alone at such a tender age.

The boy shrugged. "Rachel, she's my sister, and I were fortunate, I guess. My papa left mother enough money to care for us, and when she got sick, she brought us here. I have wanted for very little."

Save for the love of a parent, Elizabeth thought. "You have lived here for some time then?"

He nodded. "Nearly six years." He gave the corner in which he stood one last good sweep. "There," he declared in a satisfied tone.

The door behind Elizabeth opened.

"Is our guest well, Riley," Mr. Smith, the butler, asked as he stepped out.

"Are you well, miss?"

"You have seen to my comfort very well," Elizabeth assured him. "I shall not inconvenience you much longer. I only wished for a bit of air."

"You will continue to see to Miss Elizabeth?" Receiving a promise from Riley, Mr. Smith handed Elizabeth's pelisse to the lad and then closed the door.

"How thoughtful," Elizabeth said, accepting her coat with a smile. "And, now you may have your jacket back as well. I would hate to be the cause of you catching a chill." She rose and put on her coat. Then, she folded her shawl and placed it on the step. "You may sit with me if it will not get you in trouble," she said as Riley appeared to be taking up a position near the door to watch her.

The boy considered it for a moment and then, just as Elizabeth thought he might refuse, he joined her.

"You are not with the others listening to the reading," she said as Riley made himself comfortable. It might be easier to avoid her thoughts if she were to begin a conversation with someone.

"No, miss. I have my duties to see to, and I am not going to be here much longer, so I must learn here instead of in the classroom." He smiled at her. "I will not lie and say I would not rather be listening to Mr. Darcy read than sweeping a step."

"You enjoy reading?" she asked.

"Very much." His head bobbed up and down vigorously to emphasize his point. "Almost as much as I like adding numbers." A grin split his face. "The others think I am a bit daft for liking sums so much."

"Oh," Elizabeth said as recognition dawned on her. "You are Master Riley."

"Yes, miss."

"My aunt and Mrs. Verity were speaking of you. I believe my uncle is finding you a place with Mr. Crenshaw."

"I am anxious to begin."

"Mr. Crenshaw is a very pleasant man, and his wife makes the best plum pudding."

"He is kind?"

"Very," Elizabeth assured the lad beside her. He might look eager to begin his life, but she could imagine there was at least a small amount, if not a large portion, of trepidation hidden behind his confident smile. Leaving what one knew was never an easy task. Trusting another to care for them and be a good, kind, and giving soul was equally as challenging. Her lips curled up slightly. That was how she felt standing on the precipice of change. She would have to place her trust in another or remain an old maid, listening to her mother's moaning about how unfortunate it was to have a daughter who had never married.

The boy glanced at the door behind him. "I hope he is

as good as Mr. Darcy," he said wistfully. "Mr. Darcy is the best gentleman I have ever met," he added. "Do you know him?"

Elizabeth nodded. Her plan to avoid thinking about that gentleman seemed to be crumbling about her and was about to be swept away completely by the young man next to her.

"I had only been here for a year when I met him. I had met many gentlemen and ladies. They come to see Mrs. Verity and to look at us, you know," he said in explanation. "Sometimes they take one of us to their homes to work. But Mr. Darcy was the first gentleman I had seen bring a maid to us."

Elizabeth propped her elbows on her knees and rested her head on her hands with her face turned toward Riley. "Nellie?" she asked.

The boy's face lit up at the name. "Nellie," he said as he nodded his head. "She let me borrow her handkerchief to dry my tears and never told anyone."

"That is very kind."

"Oh, she is," Riley agreed. "She never once teased me for missing my mother, and she took care of my sister so well. Rachel was only two then and in the nursery, where Nellie worked until she couldn't."

"She couldn't?" Elizabeth repeated in confusion.

The boy next to her nodded his head solemnly. "I

should not tell tales, but she was with child when Mr. Darcy brought her to us."

Elizabeth's stomach once again began to feel uneasy.

"She had never been in the city before."

"She did not work for Mr. Darcy?"

"No, she worked for him, but not here. At his estate." The boys face grew dark. "Some friend of Mr. Darcy had promised to marry Nellie, but he did not. He ran away as soon as he knew she was with child."

Elizabeth's eyes grew wide. "A friend of Mr. Darcy's is Robert's father?"

The boy shook his head. "He is no longer a friend of Mr. Darcy. Mr. Darcy would not tolerate such a rogue."

Elizabeth's lips curled up at the adamant disgust in the boy's tone.

"Nellie was fearful, of course, that she would get turned out from her position, but Mr. Darcy would not hear of it. He brought her here until Robert was born, then, when she was well, she was able to return to work but not at his estate. She was to stay in town so that she could visit Robert. Sometimes she comes on her own, and sometimes Mr. Darcy brings her."

Elizabeth sat silently next to the boy for several minutes. Although her stomach no longer twisted, her heart ached. How wrong she had been once again about Mr. Darcy!

"Robert was sitting in Mr. Darcy's lap while he was reading, " she said when the silence began to feel uncomfortable.

Riley nodded. "He always does."

Again, the pair lapsed into silence.

"Mr. Darcy is a good man," Elizabeth allowed that portion of her thoughts to be uttered. Good, however, seemed to be too small a word to describe a man who would see to the welfare of his maid and her child as Mr. Darcy was doing. Nor was it an adequate word to describe a brother who cared so well for a sister who had nearly been ruined.

She blinked. Those blonde curls! A chill crept up her back and spread down her arms. Nellie's hair was brown, but there was someone who claimed to be a former friend of Mr. Darcy who had blonde hair that curled around his ears and at the nape of his neck. Oh! She had once again been made to think poorly of Mr. Darcy because of Mr. Wickham! She blew out a breath.

"Are you well, miss?"

Elizabeth nodded and then shrugged. "Master Riley, what would you do if you had misjudged a person most severely and had both spoken and thought poorly of this person?"

"Is this person a friend?"

Again, Elizabeth nodded.

The young boys face screwed up as he thought. "Mrs. Verity would say to apologize."

Elizabeth expelled one more breath and rose from the

step. "Then, I must apologize," she said with forced determination. Biting her lip, she looked toward the door to the house beyond which lay the person to whom she needed to address her apology. "A good man would forgive me, right?" she asked her new young friend.

Riley smiled and nodded. "If he is as good as Mr. Darcy he will."

"I pray you are right," Elizabeth replied as she gathered her shawl from the step. "Thank you, Master Riley. I have every belief that you shall one day be as good as Mr. Darcy." The boy stood a little straighter at her words and nodded his head in acceptance of the compliment before moving to open the door for her.

Elizabeth stepped into the foyer and handed her pelisse to Riley who stood behind her, waiting to take it from her.

"Did you get enough air?" Mrs. Verity asked as she approached Elizabeth. "I meant to see if you were well, but Mr. Smith assured me that Riley was seeing to your needs."

"He did a very good job," Elizabeth replied with a smile for both Mrs. Verity and Riley. "He was most helpful."

"Your aunt and I were about to have tea in my study," Mrs. Verity said. "Would you care to join us?"

Before Elizabeth could answer, the drawing room door opened, and Mr. Darcy stepped into the hall.

"Miss Elizabeth," he greeted. "Mrs. Verity said you were here."

"And as you can see, I am. I was speaking with Master Riley outside." Elizabeth was glad she could blame the redness of her cheeks on the cool air so that her embarrassment could be hidden for a few moments.

"Master Riley is a good lad." Mr. Darcy smiled at the boy who was scooting past them toward the back stairs. Immediately, the boy stopped his progress and with a bow, thanked Mr. Darcy for his kind words.

Elizabeth watched him continue on his way. "He adores you," she whispered.

"They all adore Mr. Darcy," Mrs. Verity added. "He is a favourite. Now, shall I pour for two or four?"

Elizabeth drew a breath. "Might I be allowed to speak with Mr. Darcy?"

Mrs. Verity's brows rose, and she shared a knowing look with Mrs. Gardiner. "Is Nellie still in the drawing room with Robert?" she asked Darcy.

"She is."

"Then I do not see why you cannot speak with Mr. Darcy in the drawing room, and when you are through, there might still be a cup of tea for you in my study." She winked and patted Elizabeth's arm.

Chapter 9

Darcy held the door to the drawing room open while Elizabeth entered. "I did not realize that your aunt and uncle were the Mr. and Mrs. Gardiner who help Mrs. Verity with finding positions for some of her charges."

"I did not know it either until yesterday when my aunt proposed my coming with her on her errands today." She took a seat in one of the two chairs tucked into the corner of the room nearest the door and furthest from where Nellie sat playing with her son. "I was intrigued by her description of this establishment and readily accepted."

"Your sister did not join you?" Darcy asked as he made himself comfortable next to her.

"No, Jane had promised the Gardiner children that she would play with them today, and breaking a promise is not something one should do, especially where children are concerned."

"I could not agree more."

Elizabeth drew a breath and expelled it slowly in an attempt to quell the flutters in her stomach. "I wish to apologize," she began. There seemed no better way to get the ordeal over with than to simply begin without a long prelude or drawn out exchange of pleasantries.

Darcy's brows drew together. "For what?"

"I have thought and spoken very poorly of you. I judged your character incorrectly." She dropped her gaze to her hands. It was so difficult to look at the startled and slightly sad look on his face. She would be hurt if she had been abused as she had abused him. "I truly hope that you will not hate me," she murmured.

"I do not see how I could," he replied.

She lifted her eyes and gave him a sad smile. "I believed what Mr. Wickham told me about you. I thought you were arrogant and rude and deserved to be spurned, and so I spoke harshly about you to my friends and relations." Her gaze dropped once more to her hands. "It was wrong, but that is not the worst."

"It is not?"

She shook her head and searched for her handkerchief in her pocket. She was quite certain that she would not complete this part of her confession without needing it. "Your sister made it clear to me that I had been deceived in my opinion of you, and I have seen by your behaviour in the times when we have met here in town that you are not arrogant and rude. You are reserved and perhaps a bit aloof at times, but not improperly proud as I had accused you of being."

She shook her head. Oh, what would he think of her when she told him what she had believed about the child who was squealing in delight over something his mother had said.

"When Mrs. Verity was giving us a tour today, I was surprised to see your maid in this room. Mrs. Verity explained that Robert was one of the children in her care and the result of a gentleman at Nellie's place of employment using her badly. I knew she worked for you." Elizabeth's voice faded as her heart pinched and threatened to break at what she must confess.

"You thought I was Robert's father?"

Elizabeth nodded and then covered her face with her hands.

"You think so little of me?"

Elizabeth could hear the pain in his voice, and the tears that threatened began to fall. She had no voice or words, so she simply shrugged and shook her head. She did not think of him poorly, not now. His good opinion, for which she had longed since their first meeting, was something she knew she had lost forever. How could it not be lost after thinking something so dreadful?

"I see," he said as he rose from his chair. "Thank you for informing me before I made a complete fool of myself."

"Please," Elizabeth choked out. "Please, forgive me. I was so wrong, so very wrong."

"I shall consider it," he replied softly. "Nellie, Harris will see that you are returned to Darcy House."

"Please," Elizabeth begged.

"I will consider it," he replied again. "I need to think," he added and then quit the room, leaving behind a softly sobbing Elizabeth.

She had thought he was Robert's father? She had considered him the sort of man who would use a maid employed in his own service in such a fashion? Did she know nothing about him? Had his insult and the tales of that blasted scoundrel blinded her to seeing anything of value in him?

He took his hat and gloves from the table near the door and, placing his hat on his head, stepped out onto the front step. He looked up the street and then down. Deciding that going up the street was perhaps the best place to find a hackney to drive him to who knows where — anywhere that she wasn't — he descended the steps and after a quick word with his driver, turned right and began walking.

He had not gotten very far before...

"Mr. Darcy! Mr. Darcy!"

He turned to find Riley running after him with a walking stick in his hand.

"You forgot this, Mr. Darcy," Riley said as he finally reached where Darcy was.

"Thank you, Master Riley," Darcy said, taking his walking stick from the lad.

"Mr. Darcy?" The boy called as Darcy turned to continue walking.

"Yes."

"A good man forgives, does he not?"

Darcy's brows furrowed. "Of course."

Riley nodded as a sad look crept across his face. "That is what I thought."

Darcy watched the boy walk back toward Mrs. Verity's. His shoulders were slumped, his hands were stuffed in his pockets, and he kicked at nearly every pebble which lay on the walkway. That was not how Riley normally carried himself. "Master Riley," Darcy called.

The boy stopped and turned toward him. "Yes, sir."

Sir? Darcy blinked. Riley used his name, not sir, whenever they spoke. "Are you well?"

The boy's chin lifted. "I am."

Darcy shook his head. "No, I do not believe you are." He took the few steps necessary to reach where the lad stood. "I have offended you in some way. I can see it on your face and hear it in your words. What is it?"

Riley lifted his chin once again and gave Darcy a very imperious look for one so young. "A good man forgives, sir." He gave a sharp nod of his head. "If you will excuse me, I have duties which need my attention."

Darcy stood staring after the child. Being scolded by

a younger sister was nothing compared to being called to correct behaviour by an orphan who at one time worshipped the ground on which you walked but now hung his head in disappointment at your actions or lack thereof.

He trotted up next to Riley. "I just needed time to think," he explained to the child, "to sort through the thoughts in my mind."

"She was scared," Riley blinked back tears. "I told her good men forgive."

"Miss Elizabeth was scared?" Darcy asked. Now that he thought about it, she had seemed rather nervous when she had greeted him. Her eyes had not met his nearly as much as they normally did.

"Yes."

"Of what?"

"She was afraid that you would not forgive her," Riley replied. "Oh, she did not say it was you, but I could tell."

Darcy felt as if Riley had hit him in the gut.

"She thinks you are a good man," the boy said, adding a second blow.

"She thought I was Robert's father." Darcy was unsure why he felt a need to explain this to a child.

"But you are not, and she knows that now."

When stated like that by a lad of eleven, it sounded rather obvious.

"You did not know she had thunk any of those things."

"Thought," Darcy corrected. "I did not know she had

thought any of those things." He shook his head and slowly expelled a breath as he looked over Riley's head to Mrs. Verity's. "She did not have to tell me, did she?"

"No, but, when she asked what she should do, I told her what Mrs. Verity always says when we do something that is not right."

Darcy's lips curled into a rye half smile. "Apologize?"

Riley nodded.

"It was good advice, and it is advice I should follow." He blew out a great breath. "You are a good lad, Master Riley."

"Thank you, Mr. Darcy." The boy ducked his head, and his ears turned red. "I want to be good like my papa and like you."

Ouch. If Riley's words before had felt like a punch, this new revelation was more like a piercing of a sword directly to Darcy's heart.

"Master Riley, I have no doubt that you shall be among the best of men." He placed an arm around the boy's shoulders. "Is she still in the drawing room?"

Riley nodded. "She was when I left. Nellie was caring for her."

"Then she is in good hands, is she not?" Darcy asked.

"She is," Riley agreed.

"I'm going to tell you a secret, that my father told me," Darcy began as they approached the front of the house. "Good men make mistakes, and when they do, they make amends as best they can." He smiled down at the boy's upturned intent expression. "And making amends becomes even more important if the person you harmed is very dear to you."

A smile split Riley's face. "You love Miss Elizabeth?"

Darcy nodded. "But, that is also a secret. I have not told her, and I do not know that my affections will be returned, especially now." He looked toward the window of the drawing room. "When I first met her, I said something that was not nice, Master Riley. I was in a foul mood, and I allowed it to get the better of my tongue. I have not yet properly apologized for that either. I know," he said in response to Riley's horrified look, "I have been remiss. My sister has already reminded me to apologize, and yet, I have not." He removed his arm from around the boy's shoulders. "Wish me well."

"Mr. Darcy," Riley called to him. "She is a good lady," he said when Darcy turned back to him.

"She is," Darcy agreed.

"Good ladies will forgive, but," the boy's brows furrowed, "not always right away."

Darcy chuckled. "You are far wiser than you know." He gave the boy a small bow and continued on his way up the steps and into the house to offer both his forgiveness and his own apology.

Darcy placed his hat and gloves back on the table just inside the front door and leaned his walking stick in the corner. Then, after straightening the sleeves of his jacket and aligning the buttons on his waistcoat, he sucked in a deep breath, expelled it, and with a slightly trembling hand, opened the door to the drawing room.

Elizabeth still sat where he had left her, but Nellie knelt beside her, rubbing her arm from elbow to shoulder and back as she whispered to her. Robert had climbed up onto the arm of the chair and was patting Elizabeth's back. Darcy closed the door quietly, dug his handkerchief out of his pocket, and approached her.

Nellie looked up at him, displeasure clearly written on her face.

"I have considered it," Darcy began. "I would be a fool to not forgive you." He knelt before Elizabeth. "I only hope you can find it in your heart to forgive me." He placed his handkerchief on her lap as she raised her tear stained face to look at him. How he wanted to gather her into his arms and attempt to erase the pain he had caused! But instead of acting on his desires, he turned to Nellie.

"Thank you," he said.

His maid looked at him warily.

"I promise I will not leave this room until all is resolved," he told her.

Nellie nodded and rose from her position. Then, gathering her son, she retreated to the other side of the room, and Darcy returned his attention to the weeping lady before him.

"I am rarely rational where Wickham is concerned," he

began. "However, that does not excuse my reaction. I was startled."

"And hurt," Elizabeth whispered.

"Yes," he admitted. "I would never use anyone as Wickham does."

Elizabeth nodded as she dried tears from her cheeks. "I know."

Her voice was still soft as if she feared that raising it would open a new wound or bring on more tears. The thought tore at Darcy's heart. "What can I say to make amends? I fear I have erred far more gravely than you. I insulted you at the assembly — a patent lie." He shrugged and smiled softly when her eyes grew wide. "You are beautiful," he whispered before continuing.

"I was disagreeable and standoffish while in Hertfordshire instead of friendly and welcoming as I should have been. My behaviour has been deplorable. I would not think highly of me either. Added to that, is the fact that I returned to town, intending to dissuade Bingley from returning to Netherfield. I judged your sister's attachment to my friend to not be as great as his to her." He shook his head. "Who am I to decide such things? Can you ever forgive me for such arrogance and rudeness? Can we, at least, be friends?" He held his breath as he waited for her to respond.

"You thought Jane indifferent?"

He nodded.

"You would have separated them?" Her tone held a hint of anger.

He expelled the breath he had been holding. It was perhaps too much to expect a ready forgiveness after the sins he had committed. "Yes. I told myself it was so my friend would not be injured."

"It is not because you despised my family?"

He grimaced. "I will admit that I find it difficult to abide some of your family, but that was not the reason."

Her lips twitched for a brief moment. "I find some of them difficult to abide as well," she admitted before her brows drew together in question. "You said you told yourself it was to protect a friend, but that does not mean that Mr. Bingley's welfare was your true reason for separating him from Jane, does it?"

Darcy sat back on his heels. "It was not my sole reason." He swallowed and allowed his eyes to lower from looking at her face to watching her twist his handkerchief in her hands. "You had stolen my heart, but you were not what I thought I should consider for a wife." He heard her soft gasp and lifted his eyes once again to her face. "I was wrong about that as well. I do not believe I have erred as much in the entirety of my life as I have in the past nine months. First, I nearly lose Georgiana, and then, because of my abominable pride and my foul temper, I have likely lost my chance at ever winning your good opinion, let alone your heart."

"You wish for my good opinion?" There was no small amount of incredulity in her voice.

"I do. More than I can ever describe."

Her lips curved into the most beautiful smile of delight he had ever seen.

"I have wished for yours since the assembly," she confessed, ducking her head.

"You have?" It was his turned to be startled.

"I have," she said, meeting his eyes.

"Then, might we begin again?"

She nodded.

"I am forgiven?"

Her lips twitched, and that teasing left eyebrow arched as her lips parted to speak.

"Riley assures me that good ladies forgive," Darcy said quickly before she could say anything.

Elizabeth laughed, the sound filling Darcy's heart with hope that he might one day be able to claim her as his.

"Then, Mr. Darcy, I have no choice but to forgive you."

He grasped her hands. "If you had a choice and did not feel forced, would you forgive me?"

She nodded.

He expelled a satisfied sigh.

"Do you wish to have tea with Mrs. Verity?" he asked as he rose from the floor and extended his hand to assist her from her chair.

Instead of taking his hand as he expected, her hand flew to her face. "I must look a fright," she cried.

"Not to me," he replied. "Never to me."

She pursed her lips and cocked a brow.

"Very well, your eyes and nose are rather red, and your complexion is somewhat wan. However, I assure you that while my eyes might see those temporary imperfections, my heart sees nothing but beauty." He smiled at the way her face reddened at his words. "Be that as it may, I will see if I can persuade Mrs. Verity to allow me to bring you a cup in here."

Chapter 10

Elizabeth peered through the front window of her aunt's sitting room. It had been a week since she and Mr. Darcy had come to an understanding of sorts in the drawing room of the orphan house. Mr. Darcy, with Mr. Bingley at his side, had called at the Gardiners each day, and she had welcomed him most happily. Today was no different. Her heart skipped, and a smile spread across her face of its own accord as she recognized the carriage which was driving up the street. He was nearly here. She tucked her work basket under her chair, making sure the square of cloth she was embroidering with leaves and scrolls was well-hidden before returning to watch out the window for Mr. Darcy.

"I take it our callers are nearly here," Aunt Gardiner commented with a laugh. "To think that the man you criticized so thoroughly in your letters could make you flit about as you are!"

"I am not flitting," Elizabeth retorted. "I am merely hiding a gift."

"You are flitting," Jane assured her sister as she crossed

the room to join her. "And I am certain there is nothing wrong with it."

"Oh, there is nothing wrong with it at all," said Mrs. Gardiner. "In fact, I am quite pleased to have you both flitting about my house in anticipation of your gentlemen's arrival." She also joined them at the window. "I am delighted that you have both found such wonderful young men to love and who love you in return. It will not be long until we hear the banns being read for you both. Of that, I am certain." She placed an arm around each girl's shoulders.

Love. The word had been playing in Elizabeth's mind for two days now — ever since Mr. Darcy had declared his love for her in that drawing room while she used his handkerchief to dry her red eyes and nose. Her aunt had hinted even before that that Elizabeth might be in love with Mr. Darcy, and Elizabeth who could not accept that fact then was equally incapable of denying it now. She woke each morning with anticipation of seeing him in her heart and closed her eyes each night imagining his smile, and the hour or so he spent with her each day was the best part of her day.

"We should likely not be gawking out the window when they arrive," said Aunt Gardiner as the carriage began to draw to a stop before the house. "Come, have a seat."

Jane did as her aunt suggested, but Elizabeth remained at the window until she saw him alight from the carriage.

He stood for a moment in front of the open carriage door, looking toward the house. Seeing her, he smiled and lifted a hand in greeting, which she returned in kind. Then, as he turned to assist his sister from the carriage, she took her seat to wait for him. The wait was not long.

"You are looking well, today." Darcy said as he took his place next to her.

"Do you truly think so?" Elizabeth fidgeted with the seam of her dress.

"Yes, I do. I am correct, am I not, Georgiana?"

Georgiana laughed. "You are rarely incorrect," she said, "which is highly annoying."

He shook his head and held up a finger. "Ah, but when I am wrong, I am grievously wrong." He glanced at Bingley and then gave Elizabeth a sheepish grin.

Elizabeth's cheeks grew rosy. "A trait we seem to share, although I do think I am, in all likelihood, wrong more often but in lesser degrees, punctuated now and again with an error of enormous proportions."

Darcy said nothing but his eyes flickered with amusement.

"See how wise he is to neither contradict or agree with my assessment of myself?" Elizabeth asked Georgiana.

"Another annoying trait," Georgiana assured her.

"Were you successful in finding what you sought this morning?" Elizabeth asked.

"Mrs. Annesley and I have crossed everyone off our list.

Not an item remains that needs to be purchased for our Christmas celebration."

"You will be joining Caroline and me for Christmas at Netherfield, will you not?" Bingley asked.

"Indeed, I would not miss Christmas in Hertfordshire for all the world," Darcy replied.

"I have told Caroline that we are to give a ball on Twelfth Night, which has made her nearly delighted to be returning to Netherfield to display her talents." The amused smile Bingley wore spoke to the truth of his sister's preference to not be returning to Netherfield at all. "Before I left Hertfordshire last, I promised Miss Lydia that I would hold a grand soiree." He clapped his hands. "We must invite your cousin, Darcy. He would add a certain something to our lot!"

"If you mean he will fill your home with copious amounts of tales, and there shall never be a dull moment, then yes, Richard will fill that role admirably."

"I have no doubt the good colonel will keep us entertained, but that is not the particular skill I had in mind." He gave Darcy a pointed look, allowing his eyes to flick to Georgiana for a brief moment.

"I shall be well, even without Richard standing guard." Georgiana crossed her arms and pursed her lips in displeasure.

"I know I would feel much better knowing your cousin

was near, my dear." Mrs. Gardiner interjected. "That scoundrel needs to feel his disgrace."

The subject of Georgiana's travelling to Hertfordshire was one that had been canvassed several times before her brother had agreed that with all the festivities of the season, it was unlikely that Georgiana would have to be in Wickham's company for longer than a brief meeting on the street — if even that.

"I will ask him tonight," Darcy assured Bingley. "I would also feel better knowing he was there." He patted his sister's hand. "And not just for you," he said softly.

The conversation shifted to more mundane topics as tea was served. Then, as Mrs. Gardiner gathered empty teacups and insisted on the gentlemen relieving her plate of the remaining sweets, Elizabeth slipped out of the room and went upstairs to collect her pelisse and refresh herself before leaving for dinner — an engagement that made her stomach flutter and her heart race.

Half an hour later, as she exited Darcy's carriage in front of Matlock House, she was not entirely certain her heart would survive its wild thudding.

Georgiana wrapped an arm around Elizabeth's. "They will love you," she whispered.

"And even if they do not," Darcy said. "I do."

"As do I," Georgiana whispered, "and we shall not leave your side the whole evening."

Elizabeth drew a breath, summoning her courage to face

whatever might lie beyond the threshold to Matlock House.

"Then, let us begin, shall we?" she said with a smile.

Her heart might still be beating faster than was its normal wont in anticipation of tonight's events, but it was simultaneously filled with a most welcome peace, knowing that both Georgiana and her brother would stand with her.

"So this is the lady that has finally captured my nephew?" A distinguished looking gentleman with dark hair, flecked with silver, stood just behind the butler as the Darcys and Elizabeth entered.

"My uncle, Henry Fitzwilliam, Lord Matlock," Darcy introduced as he removed his hat, gloves, and great coat. "Uncle, this is Miss Elizabeth Bennet of Longbourn in Hertfordshire."

As soon as she was free of her outerwear, Elizabeth curtseyed and greeted him with a *my lord*.

"I do apologize. I was far too excited to wait in the drawing room for a proper introduction." He extended his arm to Elizabeth. "Darcy has never brought a female dinner guest with him before who was not his sister," he explained, covering Elizabeth's hand with his free one when she placed hers tentatively on his arm. "There is nothing to fear," he assured her. "We are delighted to meet you."

Elizabeth tried to take in the beauty of the entry hall as

he led her the short distance to a grand staircase, where they left the tiled floor of the entry hall and ascended the steps to the first floor and a very pretty pale blue drawing room. Lord Matlock stepped into the room and cleared his throat, drawing the attention of all who were gathered there.

"May I present, Miss Elizabeth Bennet of Longbourn in Hertfordshire."

It was strange to hear herself presented in such a fashion. She had never before felt quite so dignified as she did standing there, on the arm of an earl, being introduced with her name and place of residence. At home, she was just Miss Elizabeth.

"Miss Bennet," Lord Matlock was continuing, "might I begin by presenting the only lady in the room that outshines you, my countess, Audra Fitzwilliam, Lady Matlock."

Elizabeth dipped a shallow curtsey as anything deeper, though proper, was prevented by her hand still being fastened to Lord Matlock's arm by his hand.

"And this," he said, leading her to stand in front of a very fashionable blonde, "is my daughter, Lady Elinor Fitzwilliam and next to her, my son, Charles Fitzwilliam, Viscount Wyndmere." Lord Matlock leaned closer to Elizabeth and whispered. "He has no viscountess, but we are hopeful." The handsome gentleman before her rolled his hazel eyes at the comment.

"My father is very improper, is he not?" asked the Viscount.

"Indeed, he is," Darcy answered for Elizabeth. Georgiana had taken a seat, but Darcy trailed along behind his uncle and Elizabeth.

"Are you following me?" his uncle asked with a laugh. "I promise I will take good care of her."

"I have no doubt of that," Darcy replied. "But I do not wish for you to seat her on the opposite side of the room from me."

A second gentleman, who shared the same hazel eyes and light brown hair as the viscount, joined them. "Mr. Hughes said our guest had arrived." He bowed to Elizabeth. "Colonel Richard Fitzwilliam at your service."

"Colonel," Elizabeth greeted with another shallow curtsey.

"Well, that is all of us," said Lord Matlock. "Now, I suppose I shall seat you where Darcy can be at your side before he becomes too impatient." He chuckled as he led her to a pair of chairs near Georgiana. "I should not put you in such an uncomfortable position as to endure my teasing, but I cannot tell you how delighted I am to have one of my children so happily attached."

Elizabeth's brows drew together.

"Oh, I know Darcy is not actually my son, but he is very nearly the same." He clapped Darcy on the shoulder and moved to take a seat next to his wife as his son while Colonel Fitzwilliam took a seat next to Darcy.

"My father," he tipped his head toward where Lord Matlock sat, "is not cut from the standard aristocratic cloth as most of his rank are."

Elizabeth glanced at Darcy as she nodded her agreement. She had expected a more reserved greeting from his family. "He seems very pleasant."

"He is unless you are an opponent in the House," Richard assured her. "This assembled lot is the portion of our family that is agreeable — although Mother can be rather exacting at times," he added before continuing. "Our aunt, Lady Catherine de Bourgh is as exacting as Mother but far less cordial. However, my father is the head of the family, and Lady Catherine is too well-bred to cross him." He smiled. "He is perhaps the only person she will not cross."

"Indeed," Darcy muttered as he shifted in his chair. He would rather not speak of his aunt at present. This evening was progressing well, and he did not wish to sour it with thoughts of Lady Catherine. "Bingley would like to have you join us at Netherfield for Christmas if your mother will allow it."

Richard shrugged. "I will petition her, but I cannot guarantee she will be amenable to the idea. Does she realize you will not be in attendance at Matlock House this year?"

Darcy shook his head. "I have not mentioned it yet."

"Ah," Richard said as he nodded.

"Georgiana is going to Hertfordshire with me," Darcy added.

Richard's left brow rose, and his face grew grim. "Is not that scoundrel in Hertfordshire?"

"He is," Elizabeth said softly. "I believe that is why Mr. Bingley wishes to have you join his party."

Richard's features softened, and he winked at her. "Are you certain it is not to foist his sister off on me?" he asked Darcy.

Elizabeth's eyes grew wide.

"She has twenty thousand," Darcy replied with a grin.

Richard paused and rubbed his chin as if thinking, then shook his head. "No, not even for twenty thousand."

"You are both horrid," Georgiana interrupted.

"No," Richard retorted, "Miss Bingley is horrid."

Elizabeth's mouth dropped open slightly. Miss Bingley was not her favorite person, but to hear her spoken of in such a fashion was not pleasant. "I would not say horrid."

"Would you not?" Darcy asked in surprise.

"No," Elizabeth replied.

"Not even after she attempted to separate your sister and her brother?"

Elizabeth's eyes narrowed. "Very well, I will admit she is not my favourite person. However, I do not believe it is best practice to speak ill of another, even if that person is arrogant and disdainful, for you may find that you have done so in error." She cocked a brow at Darcy as her lips curled into a slightly sheepish smile.

He tipped his head, acknowledging he understood of what she spoke. "You are correct, of course."

"But you are not the son of an earl or a wealthy landowner," Richard pursued the topic. "You have no idea how disagreeable it is to be pursued by one such as Caroline Bingley."

Elizabeth tipped her head and studied Richard's face. "Do you mind it so much?" she asked.

"Yes," he retorted.

Elizabeth, who was beginning to feel quite at ease, shrugged. "I will allow it to be true."

"You do not believe me?"

"My belief or disbelief does not prove your words true or false," she replied.

Richard laughed. "I can see why Darcy is enchanted. You argue very well, but do you not believe that being pursued for your name or fortune is unpleasant?"

"I believe, Colonel, that to be pursued for title or wealth is just as disagreeable as being cast aside for lack of either."

"I did not say I am casting Miss Bingley aside due to either of those things."

"No, you did not, but imagine, if you will, being the daughter of a wealthy tradesman. You have a fortune, but your lineage is not what is desirable. Might not those circumstances cause a lady to place herself above others?"

Richard opened his mouth and closed it again, vexation scrawled across his face.

"I may not, at this moment, like Miss Bingley," Elizabeth said, "but I can attempt to understand her. I have been contemplating such things as of late. It seems my judgments of people have at times been wanting."

Richard shook his head. "No, I reject your conclusion."

Elizabeth smiled at him. "Your acceptance or rejection does not make it either true or false."

Richard shook his head and laughed heartily. "Do you read the papers, Miss Elizabeth?"

"Occasionally."

"My father would be thrilled to have a person of your reasoning skills to debate the happenings in the world." He slapped Darcy on the back. "Again, I will repeat, I can see why Darcy is enchanted. You are as astute as you are beautiful, Miss Elizabeth," he said with a bow of his head. "However, I would beg you to feel at least a hint of compassion for me when Miss Bingley begins her barrage."

"Of course, Colonel, as long as you refute her when she disparages either me or my family."

Richard's eyes narrowed. "The way your eyes are sparkling, I fear I am being led into a trap."

Elizabeth pressed her lips together and shrugged.

"Is there a reason why Miss Bingley would disparage

your family?" he asked as he extended his hand to Georgiana to lead her into dinner.

Elizabeth laughed lightly. "Being pursued by Miss Bingley may pale in comparison to being pursued by my mother. She does have five daughters to see well-matched — none with a fortune –, and she does prefer a man in uniform who is a lively conversation partner."

Richard's responding chuckle was deep, rumbling from his belly, and filled with delight. "I thank you for your warning," he said as they began to descend the stairs on their way to the dining room below.

Chapter 11

"Not be here for Christmas?" Lady Matlock repeated what Darcy had just said. "But we are always together for Christmas. It is tradition."

"I have promised my help to a friend." Darcy smiled. "Which is not the only compelling reason to be in Hertfordshire."

"But it is Christmas."

Elizabeth pulled the left corner of her lip between her teeth and looked from the man she wished to have with her in Hertfordshire and his aunt who would clearly be disappointed if he were not here, in town, at Matlock House.

"Georgiana is going with me. I do not wish to be separated from her for this holiday." Darcy reclined in his chair, cradling in his hand the glass that held what remained of his wine. He cast a glance in Richard's direction. "I have asked Richard to accompany me."

"My son? You would take my son from me at Christmas?"

"Not without good reason," Darcy said softly.

"Mr. Wickham is in Hertfordshire," Georgiana interjected.

Lady Matlock, who had been poised to protest Darcy's reason, snapped her mouth closed.

"Is it safe to take Georgie?" Viscount Wyndmere asked.

"With Richard as an escort, I see no need to fear," Darcy answered. "With any luck, just the knowledge that your brother is in Hertfordshire will send Wickham scurrying to some hole to hide." Wickham knew that, while Darcy would not call him out, Richard was not above taking such a risk or, at the at the very least, attempting to find a way within the laws of the land to make Wickham's life miserable.

The viscount allowed Darcy's answer to be true.

"Perhaps you could join Bingley after Christmas," Elizabeth offered.

"No," Georgiana said with a firm shake of her head, "that will not do."

"Are you certain?" Elizabeth asked in surprise. "I would very much dislike being the cause of a less than joyful holiday for your family. I know mine — or at least my mother's side of the family — has always gathered at Longbourn, although it is only my aunt and uncle Gardiner who have to travel to be with us."

"Not your father's family?" Viscount Wyndmere asked.

"They are estranged," Elizabeth answered. She

smoothed the cloth that lay on her lap. "They did not approve of my mother." She could feel her cheeks growing warm. "Her father was a tradesman, as is my uncle Gardiner."

"Ah, so that is how you know it is just as unpleasant to be pursued for your wealth and status as it is to be cast aside for lack of the same," said Richard.

Elizabeth nodded. "My father would never admit it, but I believe he felt the disapproval quite strongly."

"Your father?" Richard asked in surprise. "I thought you were referring to your mother's not being accepted."

Elizabeth smiled. "There is that, too. However, it is my father of whom I was speaking — not that he did not have wealth or standing but that his choice of bride did not." She looked from Richard to Darcy and tears unexpectedly gathered in her eyes. He had fled Hertfordshire because he feared being cast aside as her father had been. She blinked and lowered her eyes to her plate. "There is more on which I based my comments, I suppose. Though I am not penniless, I have no fortune, and I have ties to trade. I know that does not make me a favourable match for many."

"You are a gentleman's daughter," Lord Matlock said. "That is all that matters to me. That and how much my nephew seems to love you."

Elizabeth gave him a grateful smile as her cheeks grew rosy and his wife scolded him softly for having spoken of Darcy's feelings.

"I do love her," Darcy said, drawing the attention of the table. "However, you are speaking as if things have been settled between us. They have not, which is why I would like to spend Christmas in Hertfordshire." He glanced at his aunt. "It is not because I wish to be separated from you. It is just that I..." His voice failed him as he saw the smile that shone in Elizabeth's eyes.

"Then, you may borrow my son," his aunt replied. "Now, if everyone is finished eating, I would suggest we retire to the drawing room. You men can drink your port there. We ladies will not mind. However, you must keep your conversation to acceptable topics." She skewered her husband with a pointed look.

"Yes, my lady," he replied with a chuckle as he rose from his chair. "Darcy, see that your aunt reaches the drawing room unscathed. I should like to escort Miss Elizabeth."

Elizabeth took the earl's hand and allowed herself to be led from the room.

"We will take a turn of the drawing room while the rest are getting the card tables arranged," he said, patting her hand where it lay on his arm. "I would like to meet your father."

"You would?" Elizabeth asked in surprise.

"Yes, I would like to meet both your father and the rest of your family."

They took several silent steps before he asked, "Why do you look so troubled?"

Elizabeth, who had been pondering her mother's exuberant response to meeting an earl and her younger sister's giggling, blew out a breath. "I am not a good match for him."

"I beg your pardon?"

"My lord, along with having no fortune and ties to trade, my family is not what it should be."

He turned her from the card tables and led her back into the hall. "I feel we are not ready to pick up our cards yet," he explained. "Please, continue. I am very much interested in why you feel your family is not what it should be."

"Mr. Darcy is so...so..." she paused, searching for the right word, "dignified. He has been raised to greatness." She shook her head. "I have not."

"That tells me nought of your family," Lord Matlock prodded.

"My father's estate is modest. It produces well, but, I am nearly certain, it could produce better." She sighed. "And my mother." She shook her head. "I love her, but she is not always sensible, and my younger sisters are rather silly because of it." She shook her head again. "He could do far better than me."

"I see," Lord Matlock said as they reached the end of the hall and turned to make the return trip to the drawing room. However, instead of continuing to walk, he stopped and motioned to a couch that stood along the wall under a beautiful painting of an outdoor scene. "It may come as a surprise to you, Miss Elizabeth, but my mother was not the most sensible woman either. She would prattle on for hours about the most inane things and insist on the most absurd strictures at times. I had two sisters. Darcy's mother, Anne, was sweet as could be and not at all like my mother. However, my sister Catherine is the very image of our mother. And my brother?" He grimaced and shook his head. "He was happy to go to sea to be away from both Catherine and our mother. He was sensible to a fault at times and yet unyieldingly foolish at others."

He covered her hand with his. "When my sister discovers Darcy is marrying you." He held up a hand to stop her protest. "I realize you are not yet betrothed, but you will be," he assured her with a squeeze of her hand. "As I was saying, when Catherine realizes that Darcy is not marrying her daughter, she will likely put on a demonstration that would make anything your mother could do pale in comparison. She has said for years that Darcy would marry Anne, and no matter how many times, Darcy's parents or I, myself, refuted it, she would not listen." He smiled. "Did I mention she is not always sensible?"

Elizabeth nodded. Darcy's uncle was a surprisingly easy person with whom to speak. She felt as at ease sitting her with him as she did her own uncle.

"I say all this, Miss Elizabeth, to assure you that your family will not offend me."

"And what of my ties to trade?"

"You are a gentleman's daughter."

"But my uncle and aunt are very dear to me."

"Do you fear not being permitted to see them?"

She shrugged. "I had thought all gentleman, especially those with titles, wanted nothing to do with men of trade."

He squeezed her hand again and smiled. "And what is Bingley? Besides a most amiable man and Darcy's particular friend? He is not yet a gentleman, is he?"

A smile spread across her face as she laughed lightly at her own foolishness.

"In addition to that, my brother did not go to see on a naval ship but on a merchant one. He is in India." He chuckled. "I see I have shocked you. It was quite the scandal." He stood and drew her to her feet. "Miss Elizabeth," he said as they began walking, "I will be delighted if you chose to join your family with mine. Darcy deserves to be loved. That is the only requirement that I will leave with you to consider when you are deciding whether or not to accept his offer when he finally gets around to making it. If you do not love him, then you are not a good match for him. However, if you do love him, then there can be no better match." He patted her hand. "Are we agreed?"

"Yes." Again, Elizabeth pondered that word love as she had in her aunt's sitting room earlier today. "Then, " she said softly as her heart beat a loud and rapid rhythm in her chest, "I am a good match for him."

"I am glad to hear it," Lord Matlock said with another

pat for Elizabeth's hand. "Ah, see, I knew it would happen." He chuckled and nodded toward the drawing room door from which Darcy had just exited. "I knew he would come looking for you," he whispered to Elizabeth. Then, raising his voice as Darcy approached, he said, "I can see my services are no longer needed." He lifted Elizabeth's hand from his arm and held it out to Darcy. "We can play a person or two short. Take a walk. Show her the library."

Darcy looked uncertainly from Elizabeth to his uncle.

Lord Matlock shrugged. "Leave the door open if you must." He smiled at Elizabeth. "I think Miss Elizabeth could use a few more minutes to collect herself after our discussion." He clapped Darcy on the shoulder and took his leave.

"Are you well?" Darcy asked as they walked toward the grand staircase.

"I am."

"The library is just behind the dining room," he explained to Elizabeth as they began descending the stairs. "You do not mind going there do you?" He glanced at her. He did not wish to put her in a place where she was uncomfortable, no matter what his uncle suggested.

"No, I love libraries."

"But we are unaccompanied."

Elizabeth's cheeks coloured, and she carefully watched where she was walking. "We were given permission." She peeked up at him. "Would you rather not go to the library? We can return to the drawing room."

He shook his head. "I would always much rather go to the library than the drawing room," he said with a smile. "The library here is among my favourite rooms."

"Is it? Pray tell, which other rooms are on your list of favourites?" she teased.

"The library at Darcy House, the library at Pemberley, and the library at Netherfield."

She laughed. "Do you enjoy any rooms that are not libraries?"

He shrugged. "My study both at Pemberley and Darcy House are quite comfortable, as are my rooms in both places."

"No drawing rooms?" There was a teasing tone to her voice.

"I do not mind them, but if I had to choose between a drawing room filled with people and a well-stocked library, I would choose the library. I am not well-versed in the art of conversation. It is not something that comes easily to me."

"I do not believe that for a moment," Elizabeth retorted. Her breath caught and whatever she was going to add to her rebuttal was snatched from her mind as she glimpsed the sight which lay beyond the door he was opening. "Oh, how beautiful!"

"You see why it is a favourite then?"

"Indeed, I do!"

Two walls were lined with shelves of books which reached from the floor to the ceiling. One set of shelves was interrupted by a door that Darcy told her led to his uncle's study while the other vast expanse of volumes was broken up by two windows evenly spaced. On the far end of the room and only a short distance from the door to Lord Matlock's study, was a grouping of two chairs and a small sofa with a low table standing before a fireplace. In the midst of the room, were more chairs, a table, a globe, and a few other cabinets and furnishings, all neatly arranged.

"This," Darcy said as he led her toward the fireplace, "is my favourite place to sit. Richard and I have spent a great deal of time in discussions here." He smiled at the memory. "Uncle Henry often joins us and shares his wisdom. Chair or sofa?" He had stopped in front of the sofa and wished to pull her down onto it beside him, but he could not bring himself to be so presumptuous.

"The sofa will be perfect," she replied with a smile. "It is where you wished to sit, is it not?"

"It is," he admitted. "I had hoped you would sit with me."

"And I shall." She took a seat and gave the cushion on her right a pat, inviting him to be seated.

"Before we entered, you said you did not believe I struggle with conversation." He had always felt awkward in drawing rooms — a fact that was painfully obvious to all on many occasions. Therefore, he was curious to hear her explanation of her claim.

"You converse very well, sir, when you are at ease," she said with a smile. "Why, today, at my aunt's house, you did not stumble once, and I would venture a guess that you rarely are without something to say when at Mrs. Verity's. The children would not be so comfortable around you if you were not also comfortable. And this evening, you have carried on a great deal of conversation both in the dining room and the drawing room. Therefore, I suggest that it is not conversation skills which you lack, but rather the ability to feel at ease in unfamiliar places and with unfamiliar people."

He shook his head as a smile spread across his face. She was right, of course. If he looked at it as she was, he had to admit it was a lack of feeling at ease that seemed to tie his tongue. "While I will allow you to be correct, I cannot say you have been completely thorough in your evaluation."

"Have I not?" Her knee brushed against his leg as she turned toward him.

"No," he said, taking her hand. "There are people such as my aunt Catherine who are not strange to me, nor is her house unfamiliar, yet I am as unable to speak in her presence as I was at the assembly in Meryton. I fear I am rather arrogant when I am at Rosings."

"She makes you uneasy?"

He nodded. "She is demanding, and she expects me to marry my cousin." His brows furrowed, and his eyes filled with concern as he mentioned it. "I am not betrothed to her."

"I know. Lord Matlock told me, but," her gaze dropped to the hand that was clasped in his, "I had already heard of your betrothal from both my cousin, Mr. Collins, and Mr. Wickham."

"And yet you have given me leave to call on you without asking me if it was true?"

She looked up at him. "It was not true. I knew that." Her eyes dropped to her hand again. "After hearing your sister's tale when she called and then learning what you did for Nellie and the others at Mrs. Verity's there was absolutely no trace of doubt about your character left in my mind. You are among the best of men. You would not call on one lady while being promised to another."

"I would not place myself there," he said, though his heart thrilled to hear her say it, he still felt woefully inadequate at times, especially when he considered Georgiana's ordeal.

"That is just it," she replied. "The best of men never place themselves in such a category. The scoundrels and rouges attempt it, but never those who truly deserve such a title."

"Thank you," he whispered, unsure of what else to say to such a thing.

"I apologise. I have made you uncomfortable."

He looked at her in surprise. How did she know that?

"You have fallen silent," she whispered.

He chuckled. "I have, have I not? And now, when my heart is so full that it feels as if it will burst from my chest." He lifted her hand and brushed his lips against her knuckles. "I cannot express to you how delighted I am to hear I have won your good opinion. You have long had mine, but it deepens upon each meeting. You are the most handsome lady I have ever met, and not just because of your beauty. Your heart, your integrity, your truthfulness, all that is you cannot now or ever be overshone by another." He lifted her chin to raise her eyes, which had once again lowered to look at her hand, and gazed for a brief moment on her flushed cheeks and her eyes that shone with happiness.

"I love you and would like to speak to your father when I am in Hertfordshire." He cupped her rosy cheek in his hand. "Do I have your permission to ask him for your hand?"

A smile spread across her face as she nodded her consent.

"You would have me?"

Again, she nodded. "If you will have me."

"I should like nothing better," he replied. There was one more thing he wished to know. "Do you love me?"

"Yes," she replied before he could even draw an anxious breath.

"You love me." The words settled in around his heart, wrapping it in a comforting peace he had never before felt.

She nodded. "Very much. So very, very much."

She loved him. The words proclaimed themselves loudly in his mind. She loved him. "May I kiss you?" he asked in a voice that was barely above a whisper.

She saw the longing in his eyes as well as the uncertainty. Such a loving look could not be met with anything less than a willing acquiescence.

Leaning forward, he gently brushed her lips with his. Then, pausing to make certain she was not startled or uneasy, he whispered, "I love you," before claiming her lips in a kiss that both left no doubt in her mind as to the truth of his words and compelled her to respond in kind.

Chapter 12

Georgiana draped her pelisse over the back of a chair and placed her gloves, hat, and reticule on the table beside it. Everything else had been stored away in her travelling case or was tucked under the seat in the carriage just waiting for their departure. Excitement and fear warred within her as she anticipated her trip to Netherfield.

"I am afraid my brother is not home," she said after greeting the people gathered in the drawing room. "However, I do expect him to return at any moment."

"Oh, I am certain we can wait as long as needed," Caroline Bingley said sweetly.

Before stepping into the drawing room, Georgiana had heard Caroline complaining to her brother about having to wait.

"I am sure you are anxious to return to Netherfield," Mrs. Annesley said.

Caroline raised a disapproving brow at the mere servant who deigned to speak and made no reply.

Georgiana bristled at the dismissive action. "I know I

am all anticipation at the prospect of finally seeing Netherfield. I have heard so much about it." Indeed, she had heard plenty about the rooms and gardens from Jane, Elizabeth, and Bingley with a smattering of details thrown in by her brother. Of course, most of the things he mentioned, such as the library, were for Bingley to consider as needing improvement. Once Fitzwilliam had renewed his determination to see his friend well-settled in an estate, he had taken it upon himself to draw up a list of items to which he thought Bingley should see.

Bingley had been eager to listen and learn, of course, while Jane and Elizabeth had preferred to answer Georgiana's questions about the more homely items of furnishing and fabrics.

"You will simply adore it," Caroline cooed.

"Do you?" Georgiana asked pointedly.

"Do I adore Netherfield?" Caroline asked with wide eyes.

"Yes. Do you adore Netherfield? I know that Miss Bennet and Miss Elizabeth both speak highly of it, but until this moment, I have not heard you praise it at all."

Caroline lifted her chin. "You have not been home to callers enough for me to speak to you about such things." The bitterness in her voice was plain to all.

"I do apologize, but I have been out."

A sour look settled on Caroline's face. "Of course." She sighed. "Miss Bennet and Miss Elizabeth have very little with which to compare Netherfield, so they will naturally be more impressed than I am. I have seen Pemberley after all, and Pemberley is an estate without an equal. Be that as it may, Netherfield's gardens are appropriately sized and styled. They are neither grand nor ostentatious. They are appropriate to the grandeur of the house and do not detract from it."

Georgiana smiled and muttered her agreement that simple, dignified gardens were what she preferred.

"The house is impressive. There are none that outshine it in the immediate area. The next largest home is Longbourn." Her lips curled in derision. "And Longbourn is of no great beauty. It has a very small park and," she shook her head and lowered her voice, "it is not well-tended."

"Caroline," Bingley snapped. "Longbourn is a fine estate. It is not so large as Netherfield, but I will not have you disparaging our neighbours."

Caroline's lips pursed and her eyes narrowed. "Our neighbours are much like their estate — of no great beauty and not very well-tended. The youngest Bennets!" She shook her head. "And their mother! I do not know why you would wish to tie yourself to such a family."

"Indeed?" Georgiana's brows rose as she turned amused eyes to Bingley. Bingley had mentioned how his sister was not pleased about returning to Netherfield or his plans to marry Jane — he had already acquired Mr. Bennet's permission and was merely waiting to make his offer and present her with his fede ring. But it was surprising to hear Caroline speak so freely.

"Are they so bad? My brother has not said they are." She knew how Bingley and her brother had described the rest of the Bennet family as well as the cautioning that Elizabeth had given her about her mother and sisters.

"Enthusiastic, a touch unrefined, but pleasant," he responded with a glare for his sister. "And well enough bred to not speak of their neighbours in such a demeaning fashion, but then, you are not a gentleman's daughter, so perhaps that is why your civility is lacking?"

Caroline huffed.

Georgiana's eyes grew wide at Bingley's open and harsh reprimand.

"Civility is not a mark of birth but of character," Mrs. Annesley added, drawing a look of absolute loathing from Caroline.

"My brother should be returning soon," Georgiana repeated. "He had a particular errand to which he needed to attend."

Caroline huffed again. "I cannot see why we must wait while he calls on orphans."

"Because it is nearly Christmas, and he will not be in town to see it done on that day," Georgiana replied. "Ah, here he is." Darcy had stepped into the room with Elizabeth on his arm. Elizabeth was to join Georgiana, Richard, and Darcy in their carriage, while Jane travelled with the Gardiners to assist with the children.

"I am afraid I have one more task that needs my attention," he said. "I will be no longer than five minutes. Has our cousin arrived?"

"No. But he knew you would be busy this morning and likely adjusted his time accordingly." It was not like Richard to be late for an appointment, nor was it like him to arrive early when there were people such as Miss Bingley whom he wished to avoid. Georgiana was curious to see how he would avoid her while at Netherfield.

True to his word, Darcy was only five minutes and had his cousin at his heels. "Richard was in the kitchen," he explained, seeing Georgiana's questioning look. "He was pilfering biscuits and teasing the maids." He shook his head but smiled, letting one and all know that he was not displeased. "It seems the servant's entrance is not guarded well enough."

"Perhaps if your lions roared instead of meowing, they would be more fearsome," Richard quipped as one of those more-friendly-than-fearsome creatures wound its way around his legs.

"They do love you," Georgiana said with a laugh.

"It is because he brings them fish," Darcy assured her. "A few scraps each time he calls."

"I will not have to smell fish all the way to Hertfordshire, will I?" Georgiana asked Richard.

He shook his head and winked at her. "They also appreciate a morsel of cheese now and again."

"If you spoil them too much, they shall not catch the mice as they are supposed to do," Georgiana scolded.

Richard bent and scratched the ear of the tabby that was still weaving around and through his legs. "They know their duty. We have discussed it, have we not, Hattie?"

The cat replied with a meow.

"See?" Richard said with a laugh.

"Are we ready then?" Darcy asked.

"We are," Georgiana rose and allowed Richard to help her with her pelisse. "The blankets and foot warmers are waiting in the carriage as is a tin of biscuits and a few rolls and cheese. Did the children enjoy their gifts even if they were two days early?"

"They did," Darcy replied.

"Gifts? You were giving gifts to orphans?" Caroline Bingley paused at the door to the sitting room.

"No," Darcy said with a shake of his head as he extended a hand to Elizabeth, "We were giving gifts to *children*. It is a tradition that I began about five years ago, and it is one Miss Elizabeth and I intend to continue."

Georgiana was almost certain that Caroline Bingley was about to swoon as she looked from Darcy to Elizabeth and back. "And why would Miss Elizabeth be carrying on this tradition?" she asked in a strained whisper.

"Has your brother not told you?" Darcy made a show

of removing Elizabeth's glove from her left hand as Elizabeth blushed and smiled prettily. "Last week, I asked Miss Elizabeth to be my wife. Two days ago, because I could not wait until we arrived in Hertfordshire to do it, I persuaded her father to accept me, and today, I presented her with my mother's ring." He showed the small gold band inset with diamonds and amethysts to them all.

"I had meant to keep it until Christmas, but Master Riley would not be in Hertfordshire to see it, and he will be gone from Mrs. Verity's after Christmas." His smile was broad as he continued. "I have just informed the household to expect a new mistress in the new year." He allowed Elizabeth to replace her glove. "They are assembling to see us off," he said to her softly.

"Well, we do not need a send-off," said Richard, looking at Bingley and nodding toward the door to indicate they should leave.

Bingley willingly scooted out the door, taking Caroline with him.

"Georgie," Richard called from the doorway.

"In a moment," Georgiana replied.

Richard sighed and leaned against the doorframe to wait.

"I know I said this last week at Matlock House, but I am so delighted," she gave Elizabeth a hug and then turned to her brother and took his hands. "I know I have a parcel tucked away for you in my bag, but this," she reached over and taking Elizabeth's hand, placed it on top of her brother's, "this is my Christmas gift."

Darcy's brows furrowed, and he glanced at Elizabeth, who merely shrugged and shook her head letting him know that she was just as confused as he.

"You saved me from misery when you arrived in Ramsgate, and when I saw you return from Netherfield in such a state of despondency, I vowed I would find a way to save you from misery — a different sort of misery to be sure, but misery just the same." She squeezed the hands that she held wrapped in her own. "I had thought it would be more challenging. I had considered scheming my way to Hertfordshire and pleading your case with Miss Elizabeth." She shook her head. "I did not know if I could succeed in sparing your heart from being broken, but I knew I had to try, in some small way, to repay you for how you have cared for mine." She released her hold on their hands. "I am pleased that it has worked out as it has." She expelled a breath as her brother wrapped her in his embrace.

"Thank you," he whispered and kissed the top of her head. "I could not ask for a better gift."

She placed a gloved hand on his cheek. "No, you could not," she replied with an impertinent grin.

He rolled his eyes and laughed as she left the room. "Are you ready to be greeted by what will soon be your new household staff?" he asked Elizabeth as he brushed a tear from her cheek.

"Your sister...," she said as another tear slid down her cheek.

"She is rather wonderful, is she not?"

Elizabeth nodded.

"Come. We must go," he said, drying her eyes with his handkerchief. "There are celebrations and a new life awaiting us in Hertfordshire." He cupped her face in his hands. "There truly is no better gift she could have given me," he said before bending to kiss her softly.

Elizabeth could not agree more. Darcy's love was the best Christmas gift she could have ever received, and every year, from that one forward, in addition to gifts being exchanged on Christmas morning in the Darcy home, gifts of the heart would be given as well. But these gifts, these special gifts of love, would neither be given nor received on Christmas morning but would always be shared, just as Georgiana's had been — two days before Christmas.

~*~*~

Coming January 2018:
One Winter's Eve, a sequel to *Two Day's Before Christmas*, which will tell the story of how Elizabeth's challenge to Colonel Fitzwilliam to reconsider his opinion of Caroline Bingley plays a part in altering the course of his life

One Winter's Eve

He's an annoyance. She's a puzzle. Together, they make sparks fly.

Chapter 1

Richard Fitzwilliam alternated patting his gloved hands together and swinging his arms as he walked quickly along one of the garden paths near the house at Netherfield. Slivers of light from the windows spilled out onto the walkway, adding to the illumination from the moon which shone down through a clear sky. At present, Richard would have preferred looking up and seeing a blanket of clouds instead of the stars that filled the expanse above him with their wavering silver light. Clouds instead of stars would likely make his trek around the garden a small bit warmer.

"Are you coming in soon," Fitzwilliam Darcy said, coming up beside his cousin. "It is cold out here."

"Is it? I was unaware," Richard said wryly as he smacked his hands together once again. It was no use, they were refusing to warm no matter how he abused them.

"Georgiana is concerned."

Richard sighed. Darcy's concern he could ignore, but that of Darcy's sister, Georgiana, he could not. "Very well,

I will return to the house, but not through the front. I would like to sneak up to my room and warm myself before having to endure any more prattle in the drawing room."

"They have set up the tables for cards," Darcy offered.

Richard shrugged. Cards would, at least, limit the conversation to those with whom he sat instead of the party at large. With any luck, he would be able to claim a spot in a group without Caroline Bingley. "I suppose I can tolerate a game or two."

"Mrs. Nichols mentioned mulled cider."

"Indeed?" Richard's brows rose in interest. Cider — fresh, mulled, mixed with brandy — nearly anyway a person could think of to prepare and serve it was a favourite of Richard Fitzwilliam.

"I thought that might make your returning to the society of the drawing room more palatable," Darcy said with a chuckle.

"Now, if there were a gingerbread or two to accompany it," Richard said with a smile.

Darcy laughed. "I cannot guarantee that as I have not been informed of all the delicacies to be found in the kitchen at Netherfield."

The two men slipped into the house through the servants' door and wound their way up the narrow staircase, hugging the wall as closely as they could to allow room for the servants, who scurried about their duties, making their way up and down the stairs.

"You have made it safely to your room," Darcy said, entering behind his cousin and removing his great coat, which he draped over the chair by the fire.

"You may leave," Richard said as he tossed his own coat and gloves on the end of his bed.

Darcy scowled at him. "Will you appear below?"

"Yes."

Darcy gathered his coat and moved to the door. "If you do not appear in ten minutes, I will be forced to come extract you from your room myself."

"I will be down as soon as my fingers and toes thaw." And his mind was prepared to be in the same room with Caroline without being distracted by her copper-coloured hair, green eyes, and lithe figure. If only he could focus on her faults. But he could not.

"The fire in the drawing room is bigger than the small one you have here."

"There is no need of a large fire in here until I retire for the night," Richard retorted.

"Oh, I agree whole-heartedly. I am only pointing out to you the fact that your extremities would grow toasty much more quickly in front of the fire downstairs, especially with a cup of warm cider around which to wrap your fingers."

"Out," Richard snapped. "I will be down within ten

minutes. Of all the people I thought would understand a man's need for peace, I would have thought it would be you."

Darcy stopped halfway through the door and, stepping back into the room, considered his cousin. "Is it Wickham's presence in the area that has you so on edge?"

Richard shook his head and rolled his eyes. He should have known better than to allow his frustrations to bubble forth in Darcy's presence. "No. It is that blasted Caroline Bingley! She and her infernal twaddle about..." He flopped into a chair. "Everything!"

Incessant chatter about fashion interspersed with gossip was annoying and a favourite of Caroline and her sister Louisa, but they were not any worse than Richard's mother and sister. However, Richard never found it tempting to watch his mother's or his sister's lips as he did Caroline's. He had always found her alluring. If only he could focus on her faults. But he could not. He would not.

"Surely, you can abide a difficult woman for a few days. You have endured far worse on the battlefield, I am certain."

Richard shrugged and remained sullenly silent. The battlefield was a place of terror to be certain, but not nearly so terrifying as facing one's heart and denying it its desire. In battle, one simply destroyed the enemy, but in his present circumstances, the enemy must not be destroyed but rather subdued and locked away. Marriage was not for him. He was not the sort of man who wished to leave a wife and children behind, nor did he wish for them to follow him from camp to camp. He knew that with each campaign on which he was sent, there was every likelihood that he could come back maimed, if he came back at all. Neither a crippled nor a dead soldier was the sort of husband any woman needed or deserved — especially not Caroline Bingley.

"Go," he said to Darcy, who still stood near the door. "I will come down and be civil, as I should be."

"This is not like you," Darcy muttered.

Richard could not agree more. He was feeling very unlike himself. When was the last time marriage had entered his mind? He was certain he could not remember it. It may have been before he crossed the channel to the continent his first time. He shrugged. That was likely when it was.

He worked his feet free of his boots and extended them toward the fire.

And what had caused him to begin thinking of Caroline Bingley in such terms?

He dropped his head back and scrubbed his face.

He blamed Darcy and Elizabeth — Darcy because he was finally marrying, and Elizabeth? Well, she was likely the guiltier of the two. If she had not pointed out to him how to view Caroline as something other than the attractive but annoying sister of Darcy's friend, he would likely be downstairs now with warm feet, taking note of all of Caroline's faults. But Elizabeth had made him consider Caroline differently, and now all his mind saw as he looked at Bingley's sister was a desirable woman with a fortune and a longing to be accepted.

He scrubbed his face again.

He knew what it was like to feel like the unfortunate one. He was a second son with no title, after all, and he was not so handsome and wealthy as his cousin. He had a small inheritance waiting for him, but it was not at all what he had become accustomed to as a child or wished for as a gentleman. It was also not what many ladies sought. Oh, he knew they would have him if he pursued them after they had not been successful with wealthier men. He shook his head. Until a few days ago, these thoughts had not bothered him nearly so much as they presently did.

He blew out a breath and rose from his chair. His feet were no longer cold. He should put on his shoes and his pleasant facade and descend before Darcy returned and either dragged him from the room or a confession of the state of his heart from his lips.

~*~*~

Caroline eyed the man next to the fire as she entered the room.

"Did you find them?" Louisa asked her sister.

Caroline, who had gone in search of a particular pair of gloves about which she had been telling Georgiana, turned her eyes from the colonel and smiled as brilliantly as she could for her sister. "They were in my small bag in my room, just as I suspected. Are they not just the softest leather, Georgiana?" she asked as she placed them on the table where her brother, Hurst, Louisa, and Georgiana were playing. She had bowed out of playing to make the trip to her room to find the gloves — a trip on which she had discovered more than just those gloves. She had also discovered how a particular gentleman viewed her. She stole a glance at the colonel.

Georgiana placed her hand of cards on the table and slipped on one glove. "They are deliciously soft," she said as she bent her fingers and extended them. "And you said you found them at Harding's?"

"Indeed, I did." Caroline was pleased that her selection of an accessory met with Georgiana's approval. Georgiana was one of those ladies born to the knowledge of the fashion and finery of the upper class. Caroline had been born with a love of such things, but her mother had not been the sort to take her on extensive shopping trips. Caroline had, however, listened and observed where she could and, recently, had studied the Belle Assemblée as diligently as she had ever studied a French primer or work of Mozart. Fashion was the visible mark of the well-to-do lady. Other accomplishments, no matter how masterfully learned, would pale and possibly never be noticed if a lady's first appearance in society did not inform others of her status.

Therefore, Georgiana's approbation was confirmation to Caroline that her diligence was not in vain. Soon, she might even be accepted readily in society, a fact that would now surely be harder than she had hoped. Being Mrs. Darcy would have assured her a proper reception, but since that gentleman seemed intent on not having her, she would have to look to her own abilities. Oh, she could pursue him until he was married and perhaps even after, but what point would there be in that? It would only make her look as foolish as she felt after being rejected by him.

She sighed as she took the gloves back from Georgiana. She was stuck here in Hertfordshire where the only gentlemen of worth or interest were either betrothed or, her eyes narrowed as she once again looked at the man standing by the fire and the object of her current thoughts, disagreeable. Twaddle, indeed! The correct knowledge of fashion was anything but twaddle! Insufferable man!

"I will have to visit that shop when I return to town," Georgiana said, drawing Caroline's attention back to the group with whom she was sitting.

"I hope to one day return to town," Caroline said with a pointed look at her brother.

"Hurst can take you any time he likes," Bingley replied with a grin. "In fact, after the new year, I might wish to have you gone." His grin grew, and she shook her head.

Married. He was actually going to marry Miss Bennet — and as quickly as possible. Those blasted Bennets! First,

Darcy and now, her brother. She folded her gloves together and then unfolded them. Perhaps what she needed to do was observe the Bennets and discover their secrets for taking in a rich gentleman and causing him to fall in love with them. Jane was beautiful, but so were others whom her brother had passed over. There must be a look or manner that Miss Bennet possessed which made her desirable. Miss Elizabeth — Caroline's brows furrowed — was not beautiful or charming. There was nothing Caroline could see that would recommend Elizabeth to Darcy, save for her contrary, teasing opinions. Teasing was not something in which Caroline was well-versed. Jane might be the better of the two sisters to attempt to emulate.

"You are rather quiet, Caroline," Bingley said as the round concluded, and he tossed his cards into a pile in the middle of the table.

"I believe I am fatigued from travel," she lied. What tired her was not travel but the state of her life — her desperately unfortunate life — and the thought of remaining unmarried and being passed from brother to sister and back until she became too feeble to be moved.

"You may retire early if you wish," Bingley said with concern. "You are not unwell, are you?"

"No," Caroline assured him with a smile. "However, if Louisa will not miss me..."

"Of course, I shall miss you, but I am fully capable of seeing to our guests in your absence."

"Very well." Caroline rose as Darcy and his cousin approached, their tête-à-tête apparently at a close. "Then I believe I will retire to my room to read."

"You are leaving?" Richard asked. "We have not even had a chance to speak."

Caroline forced her lips into a tight smile. "I am certain you can make do without my twaddle." She fluttered her lashes and added, "*The Lady of the Lake* awaits," before dipping a shallow curtsey and quitting the room.

Chapter 2

A full night's sleep did nothing to aid Caroline in feeling more charitable to a particular gentleman. However, as she dressed, she scolded herself into performing her duties as hostess as flawlessly as she could. She would be civil and polite. Everything would run as it should. Meals and tea would be perfect. She would go over the accounts with Mrs. Nichols and begin her preparations for the Twelfth Night celebration as soon as she was satisfied all was ready for tomorrow.

"Do you wish for this necklace?" Her maid held up a gold chain with a heart-shaped pendant on which was engraved a single rosebud — a precious Christmas rose was what her mother had said it was when she had given it to Caroline. Louisa had a pendant similar to the one that hung from the chain Caroline's maid held. However, instead of bearing a rose, Louisa's was engraved with holly — the crowning glory of the forest.

Caroline smiled and nodded her assent. Her mother might not have been the sort of lady to follow the latest changes in fashion, but she was a lady with exquisite taste. Nothing her mother had ever given to her daughters or created for her home had ever lacked in elegance. Caroline placed a hand on the pendant and held it in place while her maid fastened the clasp.

"Is there anything else you need, miss?"

Caroline studied her reflection in the mirror, tilting her head this way and that as her maid held up a looking glass so that Caroline could see the back of her head as well as the front. Satisfied with her hair, Caroline stood and smoothed her skirts. "You have done well," she said in dismissal of her maid, who scooted out of the room, carrying the items of clothing that would need cleaning.

Caroline took in her full reflection. She was not short, nor was she particularly tall. In her mind, she was just the right height to look good on the arm of any gentleman — even a gentleman of average height. Her figure was slender. Her curves subtle but always displayed to best advantage.

She ran a hand down the front of her gown, smoothing it over her abdomen. There was nothing wrong with her features, not a single thing. She was pretty, she told herself, and definitely not wanting.

"It is only your conversation," she grumbled to her reflection. "Twaddle! Indeed! Perhaps the good colonel has spent too much time with his men and no longer knows how to participate in regular society."

Her eyes narrowed, and she huffed. She really did need to let that comment go and focus on all that needed to be done today. With any luck, she thought as she exited her room, she would be so busy with household affairs that she would not see the colonel except in passing.

"Good morning, Miss Bingley."

Caroline's eyes rolled upward. Of all the people to be first to greet her as she entered the hall, it would have to be him! She should have taken a bit more time with her prayers this morning, but she had lain in bed a few minutes longer than she normally did and had therefore needed to rush through them. This was likely punishment for such neglect. She shook her head and promised herself that tonight she would say an extra prayer before bed. Then, summoning a smile, she greeted the colonel with a cheerful, "good morning."

"Are you on your way to the breakfast room?" he asked, joining her.

Caroline nodded slowly. "Indeed, I am. I like to have a cup of tea as I consider what needs to be done. I doubt there will be any correspondence to which to attend, but there are some lists of things to prepare for tomorrow." She placed her hand on the arm he offered.

"I can imagine it is not an easy task to arrange a Christmas dinner and all with only one day in which to accomplish it."

"Do you think I cannot do it?" she asked sharply as a portion of her checked displeasure bubbled forth.

"No, no. I am certain it can be done. I was just thinking it would be a far easier task if we had not arrived only two days before Christmas."

She felt her cheeks grow warm under his scrutiny. Why was he looking at her with so much curiosity?

"Did you sleep well?" he asked.

"Perfectly," she replied. "And you?"

He shook his head. "Not so well as I would have liked but not so poorly as some nights." He allowed her to enter the breakfast room before him. "The sunshine is a welcome guest this morning. It will make gathering boughs more pleasant."

"Indeed, it will," said Bingley from his place at the table. "And finding a yule log as well."

Richard took a seat next to Bingley after seeing that Caroline had been properly seated. "Has Darcy been here and gone?" he asked.

"I've not seen him this morning," Bingley replied. "Was Mr. Darcy here already?" he asked a footman.

"Yes, sir. About an hour ago."

"And do you know where he is gone?" Bingley asked.

"To the stables, sir. Beyond that, I am uncertain."

Caroline's left brow arched slightly as she lifted her cup. She had a very good idea as to where Darcy had trotted off. Elizabeth was known to take early morning walks. Her lips curled up on one side into a half smile. It was not at all proper for them to be rendezvousing so early and likely alone, but then Elizabeth Bennet was not what Caroline would deem proper. However, she would keep her peace. There was no need to anger Darcy. One must protect ties to well-respected men such as Darcy even if one did not particularly like the gentleman's wife.

Richard watched Caroline from the corner of his eye as he continued his discussion with Bingley about their plans for the morning. She was smiling coyly as if she knew something. There was a smirk that flashed for a moment and then was gone, to be replaced by a small furrow between her brows. He wished he could know what she was thinking.

He took a gulp of his coffee as the room slid into silence, save for the sounds of cutlery on china and cups being returned to saucers. Caroline picked up a pencil and began jotting a few things down in a small notebook. Richard attempted to see what her penmanship looked like. He suspected it would be close and neat with a feminine flourish just as it should be, but unfortunately, he could not see it clearly from where he was sitting. Consequently, his curiosity would have to remain unsatisfied for now. He returned to his coffee to wash down the ham he was eating.

Caroline picked up her cup and cradled it in her hands. That small furrow was back, but this time it was accompanied by a catching of her lower lip between her teeth. Her brows rose, her teeth released her lip, and she drank her tea before returning to the list she was making.

Richard turned his attention away from her and back to his food. He had never spared a moment to notice her subtle behaviours and expressions before this. He had only noticed her decorum in a social setting such as a full drawing room or at a ball. His lips curled into a half grin. He had also noticed her person. It was not an unpleasant task to study her figure. It was just as he preferred for a lady to look.

However, he had never before been granted this close a perusal of her in a setting as intimate as this. She was quite different here from what she was in company. Here she was quiet and thoughtful. There seemed to be no desire to display herself. He sighed. Why he had allowed Elizabeth's words to taunt him into considering Caroline Bingley in a different light? It was maddening and had kept him awake part of the night. Her words upon quitting the drawing room still echoed in his mind — no, it was not so much the words as the bitterness that had accompanied them in her expression. He felt as if he had in some way offended her, but he had no idea as to how that could be. He had walked in the garden and then, when he had returned to the drawing room, he had not spoken to her until she declared she was retiring for the night.

He drained the last of his coffee from his cup and placed

it on the table. Bingley was still eating, but Richard could not remain here to wait for the man and keep his sanity while watching Caroline sip her tea and jot notes.

"I shall be in the billiard's room."

He rose from his seat, gave a small bow to Caroline when she looked up, and took his muddled mind down the hall to where he could argue with himself as he knocked balls around the table.

Caroline blew out a sigh of relief as she lifted her eyes from her list and watched Colonel Fitzwilliam leave the room. It had been trying to keep her eyes from watching him as she wished. Now that he was no longer in the room, she could relax and drink her tea without searching her mind for something — anything — to jot down and appear busy.

"Good morning," Georgiana greeted as she entered the room.

Caroline smiled. "Good morning. Did you sleep well?"

"I did, thank you."

"Do you have plans for today?" Bingley asked as prepared to leave his place.

"I had hoped to call on the Bennets, and it would be delightful to take a tour of the village. I saw so little of the area when we arrived yesterday as the sun sets so early these days."

Bingley paused next to the table. "Have you discussed this with your cousin or your brother?" he asked softly.

She shook her head. "I had hoped to see Richard here."

"You just missed Colonel Fitzwilliam," Caroline said. "He left not two minutes before you arrived. I will be going into the village for a few items, and you could accompany me. However, I was not planning on making any calls today. There is much to be done." She closed her notebook.

"What has not been done already?" Bingley asked. "You have been writing to Mrs. Nichols nearly every day for the last week. I cannot see how there can be an overabundance of things to be completed."

Caroline's left brow rose. "Miss Lydia expects a soiree, and you have promised she will have one. These things do not just plan themselves. I do hope you will not be devoting all your time and means to keeping that child happy."

Georgiana looked from Caroline to Bingley and back.

"She will be my sister, and I have decided I should like to see her entertained and presented with opportunities to find a fitting husband."

"Charles, do be serious. They have assemblies in Meryton, and she has a mother."

Bingley folded his arms and glared at her. It was something he had been doing a good deal since she had returned to London before he had said she could.

"There is a regiment encamped and, while not all of the men are unworthy, there is at least one who is, and I know that he has been paying particular attention to Miss Lydia.

While her mother would not see anything more than his uniform and pretty features, I know better."

Georgiana gasped softly.

"I apologize," Bingley said immediately. "It is not that Mrs. Bennet is without sense."

Caroline snorted.

"She is perhaps lacking some sense," Bingley amended, "but you know the gentleman of whom I speak, and even one who is very sensible could be led astray by his silver tongue."

Georgiana's cheeks grew warm. "Indeed, I do."

"You can travel with Caroline if you choose, but please, make certain your cousin accompanies you. Darcy and I can secure a Yule log and a few boughs without him."

"Why can she not just go with me?" Caroline had no desire to be accompanied by Colonel Fitzwilliam. She was finding things to purchase in the village so that she could be away from Netherfield and him. "I will take a maid and a footman."

"I should not go without him," Georgiana said. "As you are aware, I had my heart broken in the summer."

Caroline nodded. Georgiana had told her that she had been spurned by some gentleman, though she had given very few details.

"Mr. Wickham was the gentleman who duped me."

Caroline's eyes grew wide. Charles had told her that Wickham was not to be trusted because he had treated

Darcy grievously and was a fortune hunter. In fact, she had attempted to warn Elizabeth away from the man. However, she had no idea that he had preyed on Miss Darcy.

"He only wished for my fortune."

Caroline looked at her brother. Was this how he knew to warn her?

Bingley nodded his head as if he could read the question in her eyes.

"I have not seen him since he was sent away by my brother. I do not know how he will react to seeing me, and I think it would be beneficial for Richard to be with me to remind him not to tell tales."

"There are tales to tell?" Caroline asked in surprise.

Georgiana nodded. "I had agreed to elope with him."

"Oh," Caroline exhaled the word as if it had been knocked out of her.

"That is to be told to no one." Bingley's tone was harsh as was the look he gave his sister. "Darcy would be very displeased if it were to be known."

Caroline's hand flew to her chest as she shook her head. "Of course, I would not say a word."

"Thank you," Georgiana said softly.

Had Miss Darcy expected her to gossip about such a thing? She blew out a breath. She knew that Georgiana did not seek her out as a confidant and often seemed less than pleased to see her, but she had never considered that Georgiana thought she would use her ill.

"I would be happy to share my carriage with both you and your cousin if you desire." She could abide Colonel Fitzwilliam for a few hours if it meant Georgiana would learn to trust her and become her friend. She knew they would never be sisters as she had hoped and attempted to scheme into happening, but a friend such as Miss Darcy would be pleasant to have — and not just because of the connection it would bring her. She genuinely liked and admired Georgiana.

"And will you also call at Longbourn?"

She wanted to glare at her brother for asking such a thing. He knew very well that she had no desire to call at Longbourn — ever. However, she would not glare. She would be gracious, no matter how much it pained her to do so. "I believe I could arrange my schedule to include a brief call."

"Very good."

The pleased smile her brother wore as he turned to leave the room was nearly more than she could bear.

"I will not be leaving for half an hour at least," she said to Georgiana as she rose. She picked up her notebook and pencil and acknowledged Georgiana's thanks with a nod of her head. How was she to tolerate a few hours with Colonel Fitzwilliam and a call at Longbourn? She shuddered inwardly. The things she had to endure just to gain a foothold in society! It was nearly enough to drive one to Edinburgh and her aunt's house. Nearly, but not quite.

Chapter 3

"Are you satisfied?" Richard asked as he and Georgiana strolled down the high street in Meryton. "You have seen the village and the interior of nearly every shop." He had not been best pleased to have to escort his cousin around Meryton when she could be safely tucked inside Netherfield, and he could be outside helping Bingley find a Yule log and, most importantly, away from Bingley's sisters.

"I shall be satisfied as soon as we have visited that shop, two doors down from the corner."

Richard drew a calming breath. "We have already visited that shop. I believe it is filled with fripperies."

Georgiana smiled at him. "I know it is dreadful of me to ask you to enter such an establishment twice in one outing, but there is some ribbon that I have been pondering and have decided I would like to purchase."

"It will be a quick trip then?"

"Yes, and you can even stand guard at the door rather than entering if you wish."

He shook his head. "No, I shall stay at your side."

"You are a very good cousin." Georgiana squeezed his arm more tightly.

"Indeed, I am," he muttered. Thankfully, they had not yet come upon the scoundrel from whom he was to shield her, and he hoped that fortune would continue to smile upon them. He had no desire to have to deal with Wickham and Miss Bingley. One troublesome character at a time was enough for any man. How had Darcy managed to endure Netherfield as long as he had when there was a tempting lady at the neighboring estate, a scoundrel in the village, and a scheming huntress residing in the same house with him? It was no wonder Darcy had fled when the opportunity presented itself. It was only Richard's sense of duty to Georgiana that kept him from considering returning to town as a viable option.

Richard nodded and greeted several patrons as he stood next to his cousin, waiting for her to complete her transaction. Finally, after three — or was it four, he had lost count– of the most perfect ribbons had been purchased and wrapped in paper, he found himself stepping once again out of the whitewashed building and onto the street.

"We should find Miss Bingley and Mrs. Hurst," Georgiana suggested.

Richard shook his head. "I will not stroll the streets looking for Miss Bingley and Mrs. Hurst. We could spend hours looking for each other." He chuckled to himself. Meryton was not that large. It would not take hours. He was becoming as cantankerous as Darcy. "I think it best if we return to the carriage and await them there."

"But will they know to not look for us?"

Richard's brows furrowed. Was Miss Bingley or Mrs. Hurst intelligent enough to think of returning to the carriage rather than wandering the streets? Mrs. Hurst was a bit flighty, but Caroline seemed rather shrewd when she applied herself to thinking. "I think it best if we return to the carriage. If they do not join us within a reasonable amount of time, then we can go looking for them."

Reluctantly, Georgiana agreed, but as chance would have it, they had only gotten halfway back to the carriage when they were joined by the very people Georgiana was hoping to find.

"I have completed everything I needed to do," Caroline informed them. "Were you likewise successful, Miss Darcy?"

"Oh, indeed. I have had a pleasant tour and purchased a few things."

"And you, Colonel, did you find everything you wished to find?" asked Louisa.

"The only thing I was looking for was not found, and that is perhaps for the best."

Louisa's brows drew together.

"Mr. Wickham," Caroline whispered.

"Oh, right," Louisa mumbled. "It is very good of you to

wish to see my sister and Miss Darcy protected from a fortune hunter such as he," she whispered.

"He is not only a fortune hunter," Richard whispered in reply, "he is also a rake, a charlatan, and a cad — among other things."

"Then it is indeed a very good thing you did not meet him," Louisa said.

"Yes, but I dare say my good fortune will not last forever. It is likely I shall have to meet with him at some point."

Louisa cast a concerned look at Georgiana. Louisa did not know that Georgiana had nearly eloped with the man, but she did know that Wickham had attempted to ingratiate himself with Georgiana in an attempt to secure her fortune and had treated her very ill. Charles had told her such this morning before they had left to go shopping.

"I had almost hoped to see him," Georgiana said as Richard handed her into the carriage. "Then, that first meeting would be over."

Richard handed Louisa into the carriage and then Caroline. "I think I would like to ride up on the box if you do not require my presence," he said to Georgiana.

"I am reasonably certain I am safe inside the carriage."

He couldn't help his chuckle at her teasing tone and expression. Darcy had told him that she was returning to her former self, and it appeared that Darcy was indeed correct. Richard closed the carriage door and took a seat next to the driver.

They drove past stores, houses, and the church with its graveyard before fields began to open before them. There were houses here and there with their grounds and out-buildings. To Richard, it seemed a rather idyllic area. He was not an expert at discerning such things, but he imag-ined Bingley would do well if he were to remain at Nether-field.

He blew out a breath as he considered what it must be like to have an estate — a home — to call one's own. He would have a small place one day when he retired from the army, should he survive that long. His father had said he would see to it that Richard had at least a small parcel of land to call his own.

"Here we are," the driver said as they turned into a cir-cular drive, leading to a modest-sized manor house. "Long-bourn."

Richard studied the house and gardens. Darcy had said the estate was not properly managed, but Richard could not see it from where he sat. Of course, his eye was not so keen to observe deficiencies in estates as his cousin's was.

~*~*~

"Colonel Fitzwilliam, Miss Darcy, Miss Bingley, and Mrs. Hurst to see the ladies of the house," Richard said to the man who opened the door for them.

"If you would follow me," the man said after they had deposited their outerwear with a footman and maid.

Richard stepped into the sitting room and froze. The

cad he had been hoping to avoid and two other officers sat in one corner of the room with three young ladies — two of whom he assumed from their appearance to be Elizabeth's sisters. He glanced at Georgiana. She seemed to be flustered but not overly so. He greeted Mrs. Bennet and listened to her introductions. Elizabeth and Jane, he knew, then there was Miss Mary, Miss Lucas, Miss Maria –Miss Lucas's younger sister — Lady Lucas, Miss Lydia, and Miss Kitty as well as Captain Denny, Captain Saunders, and the vermin, Wickham.

"Mr. Wickham," he greeted after he had greeted the rest appropriately. "It has been a while since we last saw each other." He held the man's gaze. There was a satisfying uneasiness in Wickham's eyes. The last time they had seen each other Richard had threatened to kill the fool.

"Indeed, it has been some time," Wickham agreed. His gaze shifted from the colonel to Georgiana. "I trust you and your family have been well." There was a slight twitch of his lips when he said it.

Richard wished to yank him from his seat and explain to him exactly how his family — Georgiana, in particular — had been since their last meeting, but he would not. He would muster some civility and refrain from turning the fellow into mincemeat for the Christmas pies.

"We have been quite well, have we not, Cousin?"

Richard could feel Georgiana's hand pressing more firmly on his arm. However, her voice did not waver, her cheeks were rosy, and her smile was convincingly pleasant. He returned her smile. "Indeed, we have been most excellent." He gave a nod of his head, a sort of dismissal and, following Georgiana to a settee, took a seat beside her.

The young lady to his left, Miss Mary, if he remembered correctly, looked at him with a puzzled and somewhat disapproving look on her face. "You did not inquire after his family," she said.

"He has none," Richard replied. Even if Wickham did still have a family, Richard would not have cared to trade pleasantries with the man. He deserved no such kindness in Richard's opinion.

Miss Mary's eyes grew wide, and she returned to reading her book.

That Miss Bennet was rather dull, Richard thought as he turned to greet Elizabeth and Jane. Greetings and pleasantries out of the way, he turned his attention to watching the other end of the room. The younger Miss Lucas and Miss Lydia seemed rather enamoured by Wickham and his friends. That was not good. They were pretty young ladies, and from the sounds of their giggles and exclamations, they were not perhaps the most quick-witted youngsters, making them precisely the sort of young ladies Wickham would prefer to have in his pocket — as well as his bed. Darcy needed to speak to Mr. Bennet. If Darcy did not, he would. No matter how silly a chit might be, she did not deserve to fall victim to Wickham.

~*~*~

For thirty minutes, Caroline listened to Mrs. Bennet prattle on about this neighbour and that — as if Caroline was actually interested in the comings and goings of the neighborhood. With any luck, she would be back in London in January and would find a proper gentleman to take her far away from this hamlet and its annoying matrons.

When she was not attempting to pay attention to Mrs. Bennet and Mrs. Lucas, she was watching the youngest Bennet flirt with the three officers. Kitty tried to follow Lydia's lead, but it was evident that Lydia was the more well-practiced of the two.

How a mother could allow her daughter to behave so was beyond Caroline. A demure smile, a flutter of lashes, a welcoming look accompanied by some light conversation were acceptable means of bringing a gentleman along in his affections. But throwing one's self at him, fawning over his every word, and touching his person every time she found what he said to be delightful was beyond improper. How could Charles wish to see that sort of a young woman presented as his sister!

Yes, it would most certainly be best if she secured a husband before summer. It would likely be impossible to be perceived by society as a worthy match with such connections as Lydia Bennet heaped upon the ties Caroline already had to trade. Her father's birth she could not avoid, but Lydia Bennet she could and would.

So, it was that she entered the carriage in a far fouler mood than she had felt last night standing in the hallway hearing Colonel Fitzwilliam refer to her conversation as twaddle. Her eyes narrowed at that gentleman as he took a seat next to Georgiana. Hopefully, Colonel Fitzwilliam now knew the real meaning of twaddle. If he did not, perhaps he could return for another half hour of torment at Longbourn.

"Are you well?" Richard asked Georgiana.

"You conducted yourself so well," Louisa lauded. "I am not certain I could have been as composed and charming as you were if I had to be in the same room with someone who had treated me so ill." She clucked her tongue and shook her head.

Caroline rolled her eyes. Louisa could be exasperating at times.

"It was not so bad as I imagined it might be, but then, there were friends to talk to, and that made it easier to ignore him."

"Why they even allow his sort into their home, I do not know," Caroline snapped.

Louisa laughed lightly. "He is a fortune hunter. They cannot fear him, for they have no fortune."

"They may not be wealthy," Richard cut in sharply, "but they are pretty and have skirts he would no doubt like to lift."

Caroline's eyes grew wide, and her mouth dropped

open. Gentlemen did not say such things in front of ladies. Did he know nothing of how to behave in fine society?

"Richard," Georgiana scolded.

"It is true," was his only reply as he turned his attention to the scenery outside.

"Then someone should tell them," Louisa whispered. "If he is not looking for a wife but just the benefits that come from a wife, someone should tell their mother."

Caroline snorted. "Mrs. Bennet sees her daughters as prizes to be sought by one and all. I doubt she would be inclined to think of Mr. Wickham or his friends in any other fashion than a possible match. Her eldest daughters have, after all, captured men that one would not think were within their grasp."

Georgiana gasped. "Miss Bennet and Miss Elizabeth are well-worthy of the gentlemen who have claimed them."

"I would agree," Richard muttered.

Caroline's cheeks flushed. She should have remembered that Georgiana considered Jane and Elizabeth to be her friends. "Charles could have done better is all I am saying," she explained. "He could have had a wife with a fortune and a name well-established in the ton, but he has decided against increasing his standing either in wealth or society by marrying a country nobody. Oh, I agree Miss Bennet is pleasant and beautiful, but she brings so little advantage."

"A man who is not reliant on securing a fortune through

marriage can do no better than to find a beautiful lady with a pleasant manner to love and to love him in return."

Caroline blinked at Richard's harsh tone. "And a lady, whose heritage is not thought to be good enough but wishes to marry well, could do much better if all of her siblings made matches that were advantageous."

Richard crossed his arms. "So, it is all about you."

"You would not understand," she retorted. "Your father is an earl. You were born most fortunate."

"Indeed?" His tone was flat and his look hard. "Explain to me how it is so fortunate to have to spend one's life giving orders that you know will lead to the death of many of the men you command. How is it fortunate to sleep exposed to the elements and to know that your limbs and your very life may be taken on the morrow? You have no idea what it means to be the second born of an earl — raised in luxury but required to live without it once you are grown — unless you can find a woman with a fortune to marry."

"Richard," Georgiana said softly as she placed a hand on his arm.

He slipped an arm around her shoulder and drew her close to his side.

Caroline turned her head away. She had never considered what the colonel's life must be like. She was not ignorant. She knew there were dangers in his profession, but his reduction in circumstances had never entered her mind.

"You have no inheritance?" She kept her eyes diverted.

He shrugged. "It is likely as much as you have, perhaps more, since there will be a house and a bit of land."

"And you are free to use that inheritance in any way you choose, are you not?" Feeling her composure and indignation returning, she turned her eyes back to him.

"I am."

"So, there is no brother or uncle to tell you what you may do and when as well as how you might do it?"

Richard blew out a breath. "I will allow that a female has more strictures and is more reliant on marriage than a man, but I will not allow you to say that my position in society is far superior to your own. You will have comforts equal to what you are accustomed or better when you are married. I will not — unless my wife has a fortune. " His lips twisted into a bitter expression. "I am relegated to either a reduction in circumstances or the unpleasant task of being what I despise in man or woman — a fortune hunter."

"You should marry for love," Georgiana said softly. "I should very much dislike seeing you marry without it."

He pulled her tight again and dropped a kiss on the top of her head. "With any luck, I will find that rare woman who both steals my heart and has a fortune."

"For how large a fortune do you wish?"

"Louisa!" Caroline scolded.

"What? I am only asking so that I might be of assistance." She turned her eyes from her sister to the colonel. "How large?" she repeated.

He shrugged.

"Twenty? Thirty?" Louisa prodded.

Again, Richard shrugged. "I suppose nothing less than twenty and ideally far more." He shook his head. "It sounds so crass to quantify a lady with numbers."

"Oh, but you will not decide on fortune alone," Louisa assured him. "There are other accomplishments that will likely help you choose a wife, not to mention her beauty."

Caroline rolled her eyes as her sister asked what Caroline had hoped she would not.

"And what sort of woman do you find beautiful, Colonel?"

"I shall point out all the beautiful ladies I see," he replied with a grin. "Beginning with the three within this carriage."

He was likely just being charming, Caroline told herself. It was what any gentleman would say. It did not mean he thought she was beautiful, did it? Did she hope that he did mean it or that he did not? Caroline's brows drew together. Oh, he was a frustrating man!

Chapter 4

"Yes, just there," Caroline instructed a footman, who was hanging the last of the kissing boughs in the dining room.

The footman secured the bough and then, gathering his things, left the room.

Caroline turned a circle, surveying everything in the room. All was now ready. The puddings and pies had been made. Evergreen boughs and holly were arranged around serving dishes and chargers on the table in here, and the Christmas fire was burning in the drawing room. She sighed contentedly. Not an item of all she remembered her mother doing for Christmas had been forgotten. With everything in place as it should be, she found she did not mind being at Netherfield as much as she thought she would. Things were far more festive looking in this grand home compared to her brother's townhouse.

"It looks very nice."

Caroline's hand flew to her heart as she jumped at the sound of Colonel Fitzwilliam's voice near her ear.

"My apologies," he muttered. "I did not mean to startle you. I was sent to see if there was anything you required."

"I think all is ready," she answered. "You may report back to the rest that we can now take our ease until time to dress for dinner." She crossed to the table and moved a sprig of holly so that the berries could be seen better. "Perfect," she muttered and turned to leave the room.

"You have a critical eye," Richard said from where he leaned on the door frame. "That can be both good and bad."

Caroline lifted her chin. "How so?"

"It allows you to see where improvements need to be made. However, it can also allow you to see only the imperfections and forget to notice anything commendable."

Her brows furrowed, and she shook her head. She was not the sort to only point out flaws. She moved to leave the room. "I give praise where praise is due."

Richard caught her arm, keeping her from exiting the room. "I've been thinking."

"About what?" The grave, nearly stern, expression on his face made her feel as if she were about to be lectured by the headmistress at her school. Thankfully, she had not had to endure too many of those lectures. However, each time she had been summoned to stand before the headmistress, her chest had constricted just as it was doing now. How foolish! She was no longer a schoolgirl, and

Colonel Fitzwilliam was not her headmistress. He was a guest. A fine looking, albeit annoying, guest.

"You would do far better to notice the commendable and stop being so blasted arrogant."

She gasped and tried to tug her arm away from him.

"Your tirade in the carriage about the Bennets," he shook his head. "They will be your relations whether you wish for them to be or not, and if you wish to continue as a friend of Georgiana's, you will need to begin thinking and speaking of her brother's soon-to-be wife with more respect."

Again, Caroline tried to extract her arm from his grasp and leave the room. Other than to instruct her on who was or was not acceptable for Miss Darcy, it was not his place to speak to her about her behaviour. The audacity!

This time, he moved with her into the room and closed the door behind him. Then, when he was leaning against that door, he released her arm. "I have not spoken to your brother about what you said because I do not think he needs to hear your thoughts about Miss Bennet. I am certain he has heard enough of your vitriol. " He blew out a breath. "I have been trying to understand you."

Caroline folded her arms and glared at him. "Have you now?"

He nodded. "Ever since Miss Elizabeth challenged me to reconsider my opinion of you."

Caroline's mouth snapped closed, her retort dying on

her lips. A strange small pain pierced her heart. She had heard him call her conversation twaddle and had argued with him, yet she had not considered that he did not like her at all.

"Finding one's footing in society can be a challenge, especially for someone who has parentage that the elite of society deems undesirable. You said as much today."

Caroline shrugged and lifted her chin. She would not retaliate. Her father was a tradesman, but he was well-respected. He was not disparaging her father. He was stating a fact. Despite her efforts to calm herself, her heart raced and that dreaded feeling of tears forming would not go away.

"To look at you..." He shook his head. "You are beautiful, but to know you?" His eyes swept from her head to her toes and back. "Good heavens, I wish you were as kind as you are beautiful."

That was a step too far, and Caroline could not contain her anger any longer.

"How dare you," she spat. "Who placed you in a position to reprimand me on anything?" She stepped closer to him, her eyes narrowing.

"No one," he replied. "Just me." He left his place of repose against the door and matched her advance with a step of his own. Did she always smell of oranges and spice? The scent fit her.

She lifted a brow. "Why?"

He blew out a breath. "I'll be hanged if I know." He had attempted to keep his thoughts to himself, but for some reason he felt compelled to see her improve, to reach her potential. It was likely that glimpse of her thoughtful, quiet nature at breakfast which had done it.

She shook her head in bewilderment. He was making little sense. How could he not know why he thought it his place to admonish her?

He stepped to the side so that the door was free, but he once again caught her arm as she moved past him. Pulling her close, he whispered, "You are a beautiful, accomplished young woman who does not need to belittle others to make herself look better."

Then, before he could do something foolish like make use of the kissing bough which hung just in front of the door, he released her.

Caroline expelled the breath that had caught in her chest when he had drawn her close and scooted past him and out of the dining room. He had been so close and so tempting even with all his air of hauteur and commanding tone. Those hazel eyes boring down into her own, filled with disapproval one moment and something entirely different the next, were captivating. And there was something she could not describe which seemed to radiate from him and had quelled her anger almost entirely in an instant. She shook herself. He was a frustrating, arrogant, demanding second son of an earl with an appalling lack of civility, she reminded herself. She was not supposed to begin considering him as anything else. She could do better. She would find a man whose profession did not call him away to war. She would be the mistress of an estate as grand as Netherfield if not grander. The season would begin, and she would do her best to secure a proper husband as quickly as possible.

"Oh, I beg your pardon," she mumbled as she entered the drawing room and collided with her sister.

"Are you well?" Louisa asked loudly.

"Yes," Caroline answered quickly as she glanced around the room to see if her sister had drawn everyone's attention. It was bad enough to have been so lost in thought that she had stumbled into another person. There was no need to make everyone aware of it, but Louisa was often lacking in tack.

"You look flushed," Louisa continued. "Are you certain you are well?"

"I am perfectly well. I have just been busy making certain all it ready."

"Perhaps you should go lie down. Just until dinner. I should hate for you to fall ill."

"I am certain I will be well," Caroline insisted with a tight smile. Louisa's continued prattling seemed to have everyone's attention.

"If all is ready, a lie down would not be a horrid thing."

Caroline exhaled her frustration softly. "If you would

allow me to sit and perhaps bring me a cup of tea," she suggested.

"Oh, my, yes! That will be just the thing."

Thankfully, her sister rushed away to fetch Caroline some tea.

"Are you unwell?"

For the second time in less than half an hour, Caroline's hand flew to her heart, and she jumped at the low rumble of Colonel Fitzwilliam's voice so close to her ear. "You must stop startling me," she scolded.

"Must I?" he replied with an impish grin.

"Yes, you must." Her heart did enough fluttering and skipping when he was near her. There was no need to increase its rhythm by creeping up behind her. Did he always walk so softly?

"I make no promises."

As he moved past her, his hand brushed her arm, sending a skittering shiver up it. Frustrating, frustrating man! She was supposed to be furious with him, not wishing to have him near. January and the season could not come fast enough!

"You are not seated," Louisa, who once again stood before Caroline, this time with a cup of tea in her hands, chided. "You are still looking flushed. Perhaps it would be best if you were to lie down."

"I do not wish to lie down." Caroline took the tea from her sister and made her way to a chair with the hopes that in doing so, she could divert her sister's attention from her flushed face.

"Richard reports that we are at our ease. Is that correct, Caroline? Is there nothing left that requires our attention?"

Goodness! She should have retired to her room. Did Charles actually expect Colonel Fitzwilliam to tell him a lie? Or — she took a calming sip of tea — did her brother not expect her to tell the colonel the truth? Did everyone find her offensive? "That is correct unless you remember something that I have forgotten."

"Charles?" Louisa laughed. "He knows little of what it takes to prepare a home for a holiday and visitors."

"I am not without sense," Charles retorted.

Oh, good heavens! Her own siblings were no better than the Bennets at times! "Must we argue? It has been a trying day. Some quiet activity would be nice."

"Are you sure you do not wish to go lie down?" Louisa asked once again.

"No!" Caroline snapped. "I do not wish to go lie down. I wish to sit here and enjoy the roar of the Yule log if you will stop your nattering and find an activity which will allow me to do so. Arguing is not that activity! Everything that needs to be done is done. Please find something to do that will add to the ambiance of what we have created instead of detracting from it."

Caroline closed her eyes and drew and released a slow

breath. Oh, she must look like an utter hag to her guests! She had spoken ill of Miss Elizabeth in the carriage in front of Miss Darcy, then argued her situation in life with Colonel Fitzwilliam, and now, after having been reprimanded for her behavior in the carriage, she was bellowing like a fishwife in the drawing room on the day before Christmas.

"The card tables could be set out," Georgiana suggested.

"An excellent idea," Bingley agreed and proceeded to act on it.

"I could read to you if you do not wish to play. That way you could close your eyes and relax."

Tea sloshed out of Caroline's cup when she jumped. "You must stop startling me."

"I apologize. I swear it was unintentional."

Caroline raised a skeptical brow.

"I swear," Richard replied, placing his hand over his heart.

Caroline shook her head and rolled her eyes. It was difficult to remain properly put-out with such a charming man. "I do not wish to play," she admitted.

"Shall I find us a book then?"

"I do not wish to take you from the game."

"I have no desire to play. In fact, after having spent a great deal of time shopping, followed by a half hour with Mrs. Bennet and Wickham, I think reading would be a very good distraction to smooth the hackles before having to endure one of those things over dinner."

Caroline's eyes narrowed. "Did you not just lecture me about my attitude regarding the Bennets?"

Richard smiled sheepishly. "I did, but that was in reference to treating them with the respect a relation deserves."

"Pray explain yourself further." She took a sip of her tea while skewering him with a challenging look.

"I was not disparaging," he said as he drew a chair closer to hers. "I was merely admitting that there are relations that are at times more challenging to bear than others. For instance, my aunt Catherine is insufferable in her prattling on and on about inane things and her demands for everything to be completed to her specifications because no one else can be trusted to do things properly. I have often allowed myself to express my frustration about her to Darcy, but I would never say the same in front of her daughter, for Anne would be crushed to hear her mother spoken of in such a fashion. You, on the other hand, allowed your frustration to be aired in front of Georgiana, and it was hurtful."

"I see very little difference." Caroline lifted her chin and looked down her nose at him. His quiet reprimand of *it was hurtful* stung more than all his previous admonitions. "If it is wrong to speak ill of relations, then it is wrong to speak ill of relations." Her cheeks grew warm as he studied her face most intently.

"Perhaps you are correct," he said finally. "I will attempt to mend my ways."

She blinked. She was correct? She had not meant to be correct. She had only been attempting to challenge him with the hope of making him admit that her own actions had not been so grievously in error. Oh, he was frustrating! Now, that she had declared her actions as well as his own to be in error, she would also have to mend her ways. "I might need to lie down," she muttered.

Richard chuckled. "Shall I tell Louisa she was correct?"

Caroline glared at him through narrowed eyes. "Just read," she said.

And he did.

Chapter 5

Caroline survived, with great aplomb, the remainder of the afternoon as well as the dinner with the Bennets and Gardiners and even the festivities of Christmas morning. However, by the time the sun was slipping beyond the horizon on Christmas Day, her resolve to remain above reproach in the colonel's eyes was beginning to wane, and she went in search of solitude. Charles, Darcy, and Georgiana had gone to Longbourn. Louisa and Hurst were busy with their pursuits. Louisa was attempting to learn the fingering of a new piece of music which Hurst had given her, while her husband perused a book with a decanter of port at his side.

Caroline stood outside the library door, debating whether she should enter and find a book or retire to her room and review her fashion magazines. There was also her dress for Twelfth Night that needed a few more embellishments, but it did not seem right to take up such an ordinary task on a day like today. A book. She should see if there was a book in the library that would satisfy her need for something out of the ordinary.

The decision made, she entered with the full intention of being the solitary occupant of the room. She would sit near the hearth and read in silence. Her spirit would be restored and when her brother returned from Longbourn with praise for his betrothed — for he had made that official last evening — and quite likely her whole family, she would be able to bear it with only the smallest twinge of jealousy and displeasure. Pulling a copy of *Evelina* from the shelf, she made her way to the hearth and curled into a chair, making herself quite comfortable.

Richard watched her enter, claim her book, and tuck herself away. He had never before seen her remove her shoes and tuck her feet up under her. She had always been the picture of proper posture and carriage. Here, as he witnessed her in such an intimate setting and relaxed pose, he considered her appearance, not as a fashionable lady, but simply as a woman. She was not all that much older than Georgiana, and like Georgiana, she had been left without a mother or father. However, Caroline had been left in the care of a sister and brother, who were only two or three years her elder, not a gentleman many years her senior who could guide her from a place of greater experience. Yet, when he thought of Bingley's house, it was Caroline who came to mind as the person assuring that all was running as it should be. Perhaps her character had not been given the attention it wanted, but her abilities to carry herself through life as a capable mistress of a home were admirable.

He carefully shifted position so that he would not draw her attention. Laying his book aside, he resumed his consideration of his companion. He attempted to recall how he had seen her at her brother's home. There were a few times he had heard her speak crossly to a maid, but for the most part, she was civil and polite with those in positions of service to her. It was a fact that stood in stark contrast to how she spoke of those whom she considered inferiors in society.

He sighed as the reason for the disparity became clear to him. Caroline no doubt felt secure in her position with her maids. She was the mistress. There was no need to prove herself as such. But with her peers or near peers, she lacked confidence, and that was where the truth lay. A smile tipped the right corner of his mouth into a half smile. Caroline, who carried herself with such assurance and shared her opinions and ideas as if they were beyond reproach, lacked boldness within herself.

He turned his attention back to his discarded book, but his mind did not wish to give up its consideration of Caroline Bingley. Instead, it wanted to taunt him with a reminder of how pretty she was and how gracefully she moved. He indulged the thoughts for a moment, pausing to remember how her green eyes had registered her surprise at his words about her as they parted ways in the dining room. She had faltered in her steps, and there had been a brief moment of something...he tapped his finger on his book...something in her eyes when he had declared her accomplished and not needing to belittle others to make herself look better. What was it? Had she been startled? He shook his head. No, her eyes had not grown wide. Was it curiosity that shone in them? Again, he shook his head. Her brows had not drawn together. In fact, her expression had relaxed. Wistful! That is what it was. It had been longing, but a longing for what? For acceptance?

He shifted again. This time, however, the chair squeaked, drawing her attention. "Forgive me," he said, keeping his tone soft to match the peaceful atmosphere of the room. "I did not mean to startle you, nor did I wish to take you from your repose. Please, stay as you were," he added as she began to straighten herself. "You look at ease. It is rather charming."

Her cheeks flushed. "Are you certain? It is not at all how a lady should sit."

"It is precisely how she should sit in her own home when she is enjoying a book in solitude." He grinned. "Even if her solitude is encroached upon by an interloper. I'll not tell," he added with a wink.

His words and tone were so warm that Caroline couldn't help but smile as she returned to her comfortable position and turned her eyes back to her book. However, her eyes would not stay on the page. They kept wandering to the gentleman across the room. He was not so tall, handsome, or rich as his cousin, but there was something about him that was rather compelling. She sighed. If only he were an acceptable choice, but he was not. She wanted what Evelina would achieve. A husband with an estate who was good and kind, gentle and attentive, and behaved as was fitting his rank. Oh, a title such as Lord Orville possessed would make a gentleman even more desirous as a husband, to be sure. However, one of her lot in life must not attempt to reach so high. It was only heroines of novels such as *Evelina* who could hope to rise above their circumstances to such a degree. Still, Caroline thought as she glanced once more at Colonel Fitzwilliam, a lady could hope and dream.

For three-quarters of an hour, Caroline applied herself with diligence to her book while casting an occasional look in the colonel's direction. He was not flipping pages very quickly. His reading yesterday was well done, so it could not be because he found the task difficult. Perhaps it was just not a very entertaining book.

However, it was neither Richard's reading ability nor the story he was reading which kept Richard from progressing through his book. *Robinson Crusoe* had been entertaining enough to hold Richard's attention the two previous times he had read it, but this time it was a trifle difficult to occupy his mind with thoughts of seeking shelter and food on a deserted island when there was a pretty lady whom he was attempting to decipher sitting so near him. Finally, he snapped his book close and rose to leave just as Caroline was beginning to yawn.

"Your sister would suggest you go lie down if she saw you," he teased.

Caroline shook her head as she covered yet another yawn. "I do not need to lie down," she replied with a smile. "However, I do think I would like to lie down."

Richard chuckled and crossed to where she was sitting. "Allow me to see you to your room in safety."

Caroline slipped her feet into her slippers and placed her hand in the one he offered.

"What were you reading?" he asked as she tucked her book under her arm. He had left his book on the table next to his chair. He would return for it later.

"Evelina."

"I have not read that."

"I read it when we were here at Michaelmas and had read it twice before that — not this particular copy, but another at home."

"In town?"

She nodded. "Before Father died."

"Ah."

"He purchased it for me." She missed her father. He was much like the good Reverend Villars in her novel, and she was his heart, his lady, his princess, or so he had said often enough when she was young. She sighed.

"He was a good man?"

"He was. We wanted for nothing, especially affection." She smiled sheepishly up at Richard. "He was perhaps a bit too indulgent."

That lovely deep chuckle rumbled from the colonel's chest.

"Spoiled you, did he?"

"Yes." Her father had given her everything for which she asked if it were in his power to do so. Charles had continued the practice until recently when she had returned to town without his permission. Since then, her brother had been withholding as much from her as he could — except for his displeasure. That he had heaped on her in great doses.

"And your mother? Did she spoil you as well?"

Caroline shook her head. "Not like Father. Mama was determined that Louisa and I grow up to be fine ladies. She knew that Father intended for us to leave our place in trade and rise to that of the landowner, and she believed him absolutely capable of accomplishing that task. Therefore, she educated us accordingly. Things were not her way of bestowing treasures upon us. Knowledge was."

"Your education is good then?"

"It is. Both Louisa and I attended school and were

instructed by masters in all the accomplishments a lady requires."

They had reached the hall on which her rooms were located.

"Then why do you feel inadequate?"

"I beg your pardon?" Did he find her inadequate? She certainly did not think of herself in such terms.

"I believe I know," he replied.

"Do you?" She was not all certain she wished to hear his opinion on her adequacy or lack thereof, but from his confident tone of voice, she knew she would hear it whether she wished it or not.

He nodded and drawing to a stop a few feet from her door, turned to look at her. "I have been considering you for days. You are pretty. You move with grace. You can organize a household and set it to running properly whether you are at Netherfield or in town simply conveying your wishes to Mrs. Nichols by post — I know that yesterday's fete was not arranged in one day." He shook his head, and his brows drew together. "I have yet to witness any area in which you are deficient save your parentage and kindness." He placed a finger on her lips to stop her protest. "You do struggle with kindness, but I am beginning to believe it is not because you do not like Mrs. Bennet or Miss Bennet or even Miss Lydia. There is another reason." He should remove his finger from her lips instead of stroking them as he wished, and with great effort, he managed to make his hand comply with reason.

"And what is that?" she demanded. It was rather ungentlemanly and unkind of him to point out her deficiencies in such a fashion. However, she was interested to hear his theory. She had never encountered anyone who had attempted to unravel her character. Most gentlemen, as well as ladies, only looked at her status and appearance. Therefore, it was rather intriguing to think that the colonel had considered her beyond those things.

He shrugged. "It occurred to me as I was attempting to read and not watch you, that you do not like you."

She gave him befuddled look. "I like myself just fine." Wallflowers that lined the ballrooms, avoiding the notice of one and all did not like themselves. She was no wall-flower.

He shook his head. "No, you do not."

She crossed her arms. "Yes, I do."

He smiled and pulling her arms apart, took the hand that did not hold a book and placed it on his arm. "No, you do not," he replied as they traversed the last few steps to her door. "But do not fear, I shall help you."

"I do not need help in liking myself," she protested. "I think very highly of myself."

He chuckled, but this time she did not enjoy the sound of it.

"It definitely appears to everyone that you do think very well of yourself; however, it is a disguise."

"It is not."

"It is," he said as she turned to open her door, "for a lady who truly thinks well of herself is kind, and we have already established that you struggle with kindness."

She huffed. "You have established. I have done nothing of the sort."

"You have with your actions. Must I remind you of them?"

"No."

"Very well. Do have a good rest." He caught her hand and lifted it to his lips.

She shook her head as she watched him leave. They were having such a pleasant time in the library. Why did he have to ruin that with talking? She entered her room and pushed her door closed rather loudly. She liked herself just fine! She tossed her book on the table next to the bed and slipped off her shoes before flopping onto the mattress and staring up at the canopy above her. Resting would be impossible with his words about kindness and thinking well of one's self chasing each other around her mind. She draped an arm over her tear-filled eyes. Why must he be so disagreeable? And why, oh, why must her heart care so much about what he thought?

Chapter 6

"You have been spending a great deal of time with Caroline." Darcy took a relaxed position in front of the fire in Richard's room two days after Christmas. The two of them had retired there before eventually finding their way to their respective beds and seeking sleep.

Richard tossed aside his jacket and began unfastening his waistcoat. "You have been busy elsewhere as you should be, and Georgiana has happily followed along with you. It is good to see her making friends and returning to her former self." He stopped in his progress of shrugging out of his waistcoat. "You have not mentioned Wickham. I assume he has not been in attendance at Longbourn?"

"We have not seen him."

"Good." Richard's waistcoat joined his jacket in a pile on his bed. "Have you spoken to Mr. Bennet about him?"

Darcy nodded. "I have. Today. Georgiana insisted on accompanying me to the interview."

"She did?" Richard asked from inside his shirt as he pulled it over his head.

"She did, and I believe her presence made the meeting far more successful than it would have been." Darcy's lips tipped up into a half smile.

"How so?"

"Mr. Bennet is not immune to tears."

"Georgie cried?"

Darcy shook his head. "No, but she did dab her eyes a number of times, and it was enough to unsettle the gentleman."

"She was well after?" Richard, wearing only his breeches and socks took a seat across from his cousin. Georgiana's need to tell people about her ordeal did not sit well with him, and he hated to see her hurt or even upset.

"She was."

"Good." Richard pulled his nightshirt over his head. He would keep his breeches and sock on until he climbed into bed. There was no need to get unduly chilled.

"Now, about Miss Bingley."

Richard's brows furrowed. "What about her?"

"It is unlike you to spend any amount of time with her. In fact, you usually attempt to avoid her at all costs."

"There have been few others around."

Darcy's brow rose. Skepticism suffused his face.

Richard shrugged. "I needed something with which to occupy my time. So, I have been attempting to understand her."

Skepticism changed to amusement as Darcy shook his head.

"It is not my fault that your betrothed put the notion in my mind." He folded his arms and leaned back in his chair. "I think I have figured her out — Miss Bingley that is."

"You have?"

Richard nodded. "I have. She wants improvement in a few areas, so I have set myself to the task."

"And this is that with which you have decided to occupy yourself? Improving Caroline Bingley?"

Richard chuckled. "Whether she wishes it or not."

"We will go riding tomorrow," Darcy said decisively. "You should not torment our host's sister even if that sister is Caroline."

"I am not tormenting her," Richard scoffed. "I am acknowledging her proficiencies much to her bemusement." And he was enjoying it. Caroline's look of confusion when he complimented her hair this morning was delightful. But the combs she wore did, in fact, match the colour of her eyes. He was not concocting frivolous flattery. He was not the sort to do that. He was only pointing out her worth so that she could see it. At least, that is what he hoped he was doing. "She is not so bad actually."

"Are you smitten with her?"

"No," Richard said, turning his eyes away from his cousin and toward the fire. "I am not ready to marry." If he were, he might allow his appreciation of her figure and his enjoyment in causing her to become flustered to sway his heart in her direction. However, as it was, he was in no position to be smitten with anyone.

"But if you were ready to marry?"

Richard shrugged. "She has a fortune. Not so large as I might like, but not insignificant. And she is tolerable when she is not cross." And if he were honest, which he would not be with his cousin just yet, at least, not about this, Caroline was rather more than tolerable when she was cross at him. He liked the way she crossed her arm and narrowed her eyes as she glared at him. She also tended to step much closer to him than was entirely proper when she was put out. Even without such an admission, Darcy's mouth had dropped open. "She is pretty."

"So, you like her?"

"I do not dislike her, and you may thank your lovely Miss Elizabeth for that."

Darcy shook his head. "You do not dislike Caroline Bingley?"

"That is what I said."

"Why?"

Richard shrugged. "I'll be hanged if I know." He rose, and Darcy followed suit. "We'll ride before breakfast?"

Darcy nodded. "I prefer it."

"As do I." Richard opened the door for his cousin. "Until the morning," he said as Darcy exited. Then, he leaned against the door frame watching his cousin shake his head and imagined him muttering as he made his way to his room.

"Ah, Miss Bingley," Richard said as he turned his head to see who was walking so lightly on the carpet behind him. "Have a pleasant night." He pushed from the wall and gave her a nod before turning to close his door. He had his door nearly shut before a thought occurred to him.

"Miss Bingley," he said as he pulled his door open once again.

"Yes."

"I... you..." he stammered. She had pulled those two combs out of her hair, and it was spilling down her back in soft amber waves. "Your hair," he said, finally managing to put two words together.

She blushed. "I did not expect to encounter anyone." She gathered her tempting tresses in her hand and began twisting them.

"No, no. I did not mean to say it was improper." Somehow, he had left the open door of his room behind and was now standing near enough to her that he could touch those flowing locks if she were not winding them up. "It is beautiful," he whispered. "Magnificent." He stopped her hands and pulled them away from their work so that her hair would once again tumble down her back.

"Did you want something?" She made no move to pull her hands free from his hold.

Richard's brows drew together. There had been a reason

he had called to her; now what was it? He had just been thinking about Darcy and — ah, that was it! "Do you ride?"

Caroline nodded.

"I am going riding with my cousin tomorrow morning, but if you wished, perhaps you could accompany me for a second ride later in the day when the sun has had a chance to warm things a bit."

"Alone?" Her eyes were wide with surprise.

His brows drew together once again. "Blast. I had not considered that you are a lady."

"Indeed?" she said, snatching her hands away from him.

"It is not that I do not know you are a lady." He allowed himself to take a sweeping, appreciative look at her very lady-like figure. He knew very well that she was a lady. "I had forgotten that you would wish for a chaperone." He tipped his head. "Does Louisa ride?"

Caroline laughed lightly, if a bit uneasily. "Louisa despises the activity. The horses smell too horse-like for her."

Richard chuckled. "They do tend to smell like animals. Then, perhaps Georgiana will join us." His brows knit together for the third time. "You do not despise riding, do you?"

"No. I enjoy it very much, so if Miss Darcy wishes to accompany us, I would be happy to join you for a ride."

"Very good. Until tomorrow then." He should return

to his room now. He should turn himself about and leave her. He should not continue staring at her. He should turn away. However, no matter how many things he told himself what he should do, his feet did not seem to wish to do as he knew they should. Instead, they kept him rooted like a fool to that spot in the hall while he watched her dress sway from left to right to left again as she walked down the hall to her room. Finally, as the click of her door closing rang through the hall, he blew out a breath and forced his feet to carry him to his room and not hers. Perhaps it was time to resign his commission.

~*~*~

Richard tried to avoid allowing Darcy to see him yawning the next morning as they began their ride.

"Tired?"

Drat. He had not turned his head away from his all-too-perceptive cousin in time. "A trifle." That is if a trifle was the same as being ready to dismount his horse and use the nearest rock as a pillow. "I assume you will be going to Longbourn again today?" Changing the subject should keep Darcy from questioning him about being exhausted.

Darcy assured him that he was and then asked, "Did you not sleep well?"

Richard blew out a breath. His cousin was not only perceptive, he was also far too persistent. "No, I slept very ill, if you must know. Now, might we ride. If I wished for tea and a chat, I would not be out here on the back of an animal which is as desirous of exercise as I am."

"You are more than a trifle tired," Darcy said with a grin. "There are only two times when Richard Fitzwilliam tends to become excessively irascible — one, when he is in company with those whom he does not enjoy and two, when he is bone-weary."

"I assure you there are more than two times when I become cantankerous." Richard glowered at Darcy.

"Those trees." Darcy nodded toward a stand of trees to his left and down a small hill. "If you reach them first, I will say no more about your lack of sleep. However, if I reach them ahead of you, you will tell me what kept you from your repose."

Before Richard could mount a protest of the terms, Darcy was off.

"Of all the rotten things." Richard roared into the wind as he urged his horse to run faster and faster. Darcy had always used this very technique to weasel information out of him. His cousin never attempted anything so devious with anyone else but Richard, which was likely due to it being the only way Darcy could force anything out of Richard.

"Does your lady love know how vexing you can be?" Richard growled as he circled the four trees before coming to a stop beside Darcy.

"She likely does. I have not acquitted myself very well

on several occasions." Darcy nudged his horse to walk. "Now, tell me, Colonel. What has been robbing you of sleep?"

"I did not agree to your terms."

"You did not disagree."

"You did not give me a chance!"

"I know." Darcy's grin grew. "At least, you will not have a headache tomorrow from too much drink as I always do when you wish to extract information from me."

Richard rode in silence for a full two minutes before deciding that it was best just to lay out the whole sorry business before his cousin and endure whatever teasing might come. "I am considering selling my commission and applying to my father for the land he has promised me."

"Have you had your fill of military life or is it more than that?"

Richard rolled his eyes both at the question and the way his cousin was tipping his head and studying him. That look always said that Darcy already knew the answer. "I do not wish to ask a wife to either follow the drum or wait for whatever remains of me to be returned to her, nor do I wish to leave fatherless children if there should be any such blessings to come our way."

Richard cast a wary sidelong glance at Darcy, expecting his cousin to have some comment, but Darcy did not. Instead, Darcy just rode on, looking forward with an occasional glance in Richard's direction.

Richard blew out a breath. "It was likely three or four o'clock this morning when I came to the realization that following a lady around and studying her finer qualities to assure her of her worth was not a good way to keep one's heart from becoming attached to that lady."

A lifted brow? That was all the response he was going to get? He sighed. Very well, he would continue as Darcy expected him to do. "In battle, it is good to scout out the enemy, study their tactics, and make notes of their strengths and weaknesses. It is not the same with ladies."

Darcy nodded silently.

He pulled his horse to a stop and turned toward his cousin. "You remember when Elizabeth challenged me to see Caroline in a different light?"

"I do."

"I have always found Caroline's looks appealing. I will not deny I have been attracted to her features and found it challenging to keep my distance from her. However, focusing on her sharp tongue and unkind ways allowed me to keep my baser desires in check. Elizabeth's challenge removed my safeguard." He looked past his cousin. "When I arrived at Netherfield, I knew my best option was to avoid Caroline as much as possible, but not because I could not tolerate her." He shook his head and chuckled. "I did try to avoid her, but staying out in the garden for the duration of my stay is not feasible, nor is skulking about the house."

"No, it is not."

"So instead of hiding, I decided to help her improve, so that when she returned to town for the season, she would be ready to find a husband. If she was married to another, then there would be no danger to me. A diversionary tactic to ensure the enemy's success in attacking someone else instead of one's self, as it were."

"Not your best strategy?"

Richard shook his head. "If I continue on my path, she will improve, and some gentleman will be happy to have her for a wife."

"And you no longer wish for any other gentleman to have her?"

He nodded. That is exactly what he wished, but...

"I am only a second son. I do not have what she seeks." Richard blew out a great breath. "I shall retain my commission."

"No," Darcy replied, "you will not."

Richard's brow drew together. "It is for the best."

Darcy chuckled. "Just as my fleeing Netherfield was for the best?" Darcy reached over and clapped him on the shoulder. "You are the second son of an earl. That will hold some weight, and even if your fortune and estate are not large, you are not penniless. Added to that, you are a good man." He shook his head. "I do not see what you see in her, but if Caroline Bingley is the lady who will bring you love and joy, then I will help you win her. Just tell me what you need, and it will be done."

"Thank you, but I would not wish to be accepted for anything less than love." He smiled sheepishly at Darcy. "I sound like a sentimental fool, do I not?"

"You do," Darcy replied with a grin, "but it happens to us all when our hearts decide on a particular lady." Darcy nudged his horse, and the pair began their journey back toward Netherfield. "I promise not to tell anyone that you are besotted. I will leave it up to you to make a cake out of yourself and reveal it to all."

"Your support is so greatly appreciated," Richard replied sardonically as Darcy laughed and assured him that making a spectacle of one's self was also part of losing one's heart and securing one's happiness.

Chapter 7

Caroline stilled her hand and removed it from fiddling with the hem of her sleeve. Fidgeting was a sign of one who lacked self-assurance. It would not do for the colonel to see her fidgeting like an anxious schoolgirl. And since when, she scolded herself, did she fidget or grow anxious while waiting for a gentleman to arrive to claim her for anything? Never. She had never suffered from flutters of nerves before. Oh, she was not unfamiliar with the feeling of wishing to present herself to best advantage, but she had always carried a list of the other person's imperfections in her mind to use as a sort of salve. However, she very much doubted that the colonel would give two figs whether she found his attire to be fashionable or not. His manners were not so refined as most men who had called on her, so again, she doubted very much if pointing out such flaws would cause the colonel to do anything more than laugh or lecture. He did not seem to be afraid to do either in her presence.

She blew out a slow calming breath when she heard him

whistling as he approached the sitting room. It had been most trying to see him at breakfast in his riding clothes and not imagine him as he had been last night in the hall in such a state of undress as he had been. Her heart fluttered once again at the memory, and her cheeks heated just as he entered the room.

"Georgiana is getting her gloves," he said in greeting. He held a hand out to her to assist her from her seat. "You do not wish to join us do you, Mrs. Hurst?" He winked at Caroline as he asked it, causing her to smile.

"Oh, heavens, no! I have no idea why Caroline enjoys sitting up on those great smelly beasts." Her nose wrinkled in disgust at the thought. "However, if you decide to take a drive. I will gladly join you. In a carriage, behind a horse, is a far better means of travel."

"Perhaps Monday we could take a drive?" Richard offered.

Caroline drew a breath. "And call at Longbourn."

"Longbourn?" The word flew out of Louisa's mouth, laced with incredulity.

"It is our place to be welcoming to our new sister and neighbourly to her family." Caroline's cheeks, which had been warm a moment ago, felt as if they might ignite from the heat that flooded them.

"That is a fine idea."

A ripple of pleasure spread through Caroline at Richard's pleased tone.

"Well," Louisa said with a shake of her head, "I suppose it is the right thing to do, but I cannot say that I wish to do it."

Caroline was not certain she wished to do it either, but when she had decided on doing so this morning, the normal dread of seeing Darcy swooning at Elizabeth's feet had not accompanied it. The idea of having to listen to Mrs. Bennet and Miss Lydia caused some discomfort of spirit. However, she was made of stern enough material to weather the foolishness of a couple of ladies. Had she not often done so at many soirees and balls? The ton was not lacking in foolish matrons and their pert daughters.

"You will accompany me?" Caroline asked her sister.

Louisa sighed. "I will if you feel I must."

"I think it best."

"You know Charles has invited them for dinner twice next week — twice!" Louisa said it as if it were the most ridiculous thing in the world.

"Yes, Mrs. Nichols and I are both aware of that fact."

Richard covered her hand, which lay on his arm, with his free one. "Shall we wait for Georgiana by the door?"

"Please," Caroline muttered and allowed him, after a parting word to Louisa, to lead her out of the room.

He bent his head near her ear. "I am proud of you."

"Thank you," she whispered in response, blinking against the tears that gathered. The last person to have ever said those words to her was her father. He had taken her hand as he sat in his chair before the fire and, after kissing it, had said, "*Remember, Princess, that I am proud of you. You have become a fine young lady.*" He had patted her hand and lifted his cheek for her kiss. Then, with a whispered *I love you* had sent her off to bed for the last time.

"You should wear blue more often," Richard added, drawing Caroline back from her reverie.

"You like it?"

He nodded. "You are beautiful," he whispered as Georgiana joined them.

~*~*~

Caroline, Georgiana, and Richard stopped at the top of the hill. Richard circled his horse around to look behind them. "The sun will begin to sink soon. Shall we go back?"

"A little further," Georgiana replied.

He chuckled. "Your nose is red. Are you certain you will not get too chilled if we do not return now?"

"No, I am well."

"And you Miss Bingley? Are you well and wishing to continue on?"

"I would wish for nothing more than to continue on for a short distance. However, I am looking forward to some warm cider and a gingerbread upon our return." It had not escaped her notice how much Colonel Fitzwilliam enjoyed those treats.

"Well, with such delicacies awaiting us, perhaps we

should return now. I would not wish for the cider to get cold waiting for me to drink it."

"You may have one of my gingerbreads if we continue," Georgiana said.

Richard laughed. "You stand as my witness, Miss Bingley, Georgie owes me one of her gingerbreads." He clucked to his mount and turned him toward the far side of the hill. "To the meadow below, and then we will turn around."

"To the trees at the far end of the meadow?" Caroline asked. "I have not ridden in ages. I am quite enjoying it."

"Then, we will not turn about until we have reached the trees." He drew his horse a bit closer to hers. "You ride very well."

Caroline inclined her head in acceptance of his compliment. "As do you and Miss Darcy." She turned her head away from the gentleman she wished to watch ride and toward his cousin. "I want to thank you for giving up your trip to Longbourn so that I might ride."

"I am happy to be of service. While I might miss seeing Miss Elizabeth and Miss Bennet, I am delighted to be riding. I have not had much opportunity to do so in town, and even when I do manage to get my brother to take me riding in the park, it is not the same as being in the country with its wide expanses and lack of people."

"It is rather peaceful, is it not?" Caroline asked. "I often prefer town to country, but in this instance, I do believe you have the right of it, and the country is far superior."

"I'd prefer the throngs of people in Hyde Park on a pleasant spring day over those three." Richard tipped his head toward three riders who were approaching. "Do you wish to go back?" he asked Georgiana.

"I will be well. They may ride past without stopping."

"You are far braver than I," Caroline said softly.

"I doubt that very much," Georgiana said. "I would wager there is enough pluck in your spirit to not be intimidated by a scoundrel."

"I would agree," Richard added. "Wickham, Denny, Saunders." He greeted the three riders with a tip of his hat.

"Good day, Colonel," Wickham said before the others could open their mouths. "Lovely day for a ride. Sunniest I've seen in weeks."

"Yesterday was bright," Richard replied.

"Not so bright as today," Wickham challenged.

Richard allowed the comment to pass without rebuttal. With any luck, allowing the cad to think he had won such a foolish argument would hasten him on his way.

"Your companions are far superior to mine," Wickham said with a smile for Caroline and Georgiana.

"I would agree with that," Richard replied. "No offense, gentlemen," he added with a nod of his head in Saunders's and Denny's direction.

"None taken," Saunders assured him.

"You did not go to Longbourn with your brother today?" Wickham asked Georgiana.

"As you can see," she replied.

"You know, Miss Elizabeth was in my pocket for a time, but it seems Darcy's money has done its work again."

"It was not his money," Richard growled. "It was his character."

Wickham's eyes narrowed, and his features turned hard as Richard expected they would. There was no one here, save Caroline, for Wickham to flatter.

"It seems there are whispers about my character circulating amongst the good people of Meryton. You would not know how they might have started?" Wickham glanced from Richard to Georgiana. "I've been turned away from many of my friends' homes." His eyes turned back to Richard. "Such as Longbourn. Apparently, I am a fortune hunter and a lothario."

Richard did not reply but simply smiled. Denny and Saunders retreated from Wickham's side a few steps.

"You do realize, Colonel, that there are stories I could share."

"And you realize what I will do to you if you do."

Wickham's friends retreated further at Richard's growled response.

"There are laws, Colonel," Wickham taunted. "And the damage would already be done regardless of what you did after."

"Have you considered the regulars?" Richard struggled to keep his voice flat and his anger in control.

Wickham laughed. "I am not fond of the militia. Why would I wish to join the regulars? Besides that, I do not have the funds to purchase a commission at a rank that would be acceptable." He sighed. "I would prefer to do as you will do and marry a woman with a fortune. However, your family is making it difficult to reach that goal."

"The Bennets have no fortune."

"No, but they are pretty and almost as willing as your cousin to provide — shall we say — companionship of a private nature."

Georgiana gasped. "I never did such a thing!"

"Did you not?" Wickham replied. "I remember you being very fond of my caresses."

"Enough," Richard roared. "You will not spread such a tale if you wish to retain your life."

"See, boys, I told you he would threaten me. Be certain to tell that to the magistrate if anything should happen to me."

Richard moved closer to Wickham and laughed, a deep, foreboding sound. "You think I cannot dispose of the lot of you and within the laws of the land? Boney is still roaming, and his cannons need fodder." His gaze shifted from Wickham to Wickham's retreating friends. "I would suggest you find better company to keep. This one is loyal to none but the crown he wishes to pilfer from your pocket."

Wickham's horse sidestepped, drawing him closer to Georgiana and then alongside her. "You were one of the best," he said with a taunting smile. "At least, that is how I will tell it."

"You will tell nothing of the sort," Richard growled, drawing up beside Wickham.

"Then put an end to these rumors that have shut me out from good society," Wickham returned.

"I cannot refute the truth," Richard replied. "You are a fortune hunter and lothario, among other things. I will not add to the tales, but that is all I can do."

Wickham shrugged. "If there is no society in which to mix and mingle, I shall be forced to spend my time at the tavern, listening to sad tales and telling a few of my own." He tipped his hat and wished them a good day. "Boys," he called to Denny and Saunders as he sat on his horse just behind Georgiana and Caroline, "race you to the ridge." He tipped his hat once more to Richard and then taking it off his head, used it to give a quick but firm whack to the rump of Georgiana's horse as he kicked his horse into a gallop.

Richard grabbed for the halter of Georgiana's horse, but it was too late, the horse had bolted and Georgiana, caught off guard, lost her seat. In a moment, Richard was on the ground next to her. He wanted to race after Wickham and drag him from his horse and across the length of the meadow, but he could not. Not when Georgiana lay on the ground injured. "Where are you hurt?"

"Everywhere," Georgiana said as she attempted to sit up.

"Is there any place that hurts more than others?" Caroline asked, taking hold of Georgiana's arm and helping her to sit. "Your arms, your legs, your head?"

"Ooh," Georgiana moaned. "My hip is very tender, and my ankle is throbbing more than the rest of me, but I do not think anything is broken."

"Did you hit your head?" Richard asked.

"No."

"Good," Richard wrapped her in his arms and pulled her to his chest. "Can you forgive me?"

"For what?" Georgiana asked.

"I was supposed to keep you from harm," he replied. One simple task, that is all he had, and yet he has failed.

"Of course, I forgive you, but I do not think there is anything to forgive. You did not know he would startle my horse."

Richard drew a shuddering breath. "I should not have allowed him to be so near you."

"I am well."

"You are injured."

"Bruised and sore but otherwise unharmed."

"It is enough," he said. "It is more than I can bear to see you suffer."

"We should see her back to the house." Caroline, who still knelt beside Georgiana, placed a hand on his shoulder. "A warm bath and a good meal followed by sleep will help her heal far faster than sitting here on the cold ground." She smiled at him as his eyes met hers. "You could not have stopped her fall."

"I should not have allowed him to be so near."

Caroline tipped her head and studied his face. Her eyes narrowed for a moment, and then, the left side of her mouth tipped upwards as if she found him somewhat amusing. That thought did not sit well with Richard. There was nothing about which to smile at present.

Caroline rose from the ground. "Come along, Colonel. We shall see Miss Darcy delivered to her room, send a groom or two out to find her horse, and then tuck you into a chair near the fire with a cup of cider and some ginger-bread. And then, you may tell me exactly how you are supposed to be able to know every move a scoundrel like Mr. Wickham will make."

She raised a demanding, questioning brow when he opened his mouth to reply. Startled by the expression and the almost harsh glare that accompanied it, he closed his mouth again.

"Miss Darcy needs to be returned to the house. Are you always so slow to follow orders, Colonel? It is a wonder you are a colonel at all with such a lackadaisical attitude." A small teasing smile replaced Caroline's stern look of a moment ago.

Georgiana giggled. "It would be nice to get off the cold

ground." She placed a hand on Richard's cheek. "I am well, and you are still among my favorite cousins. You care very well for me."

Richard smiled at her. "I love you."

"I know, and I love you."

He kissed her forehead. "I dread what your brother will say."

"All will be well," Georgiana assured him as he, first, helped her to her feet and then, onto his horse.

He was not so confident about that as Georgiana was, but he said nothing as he made sure she was seated securely before turning to assist Caroline.

"You do care for her very well," Caroline said as the stood together next to her horse.

"You give orders very well," he replied with a grin.

"My brother's home would not run so well as it does if I were not good at giving direction," she said as she made herself comfortable on her horse. "Miss Darcy is fortunate to have you," she added.

"Thank you," he said softly. "And you are a credit to your brother. He is fortunate to have you."

"He is, is he not?" Caroline replied with a laugh. He was looking at her much as he had last night in the hallway, and it was once again making her feel very uneasy in a peculiarly strange sort of way.

"Extremely."

"Miss Darcy," Caroline whispered.

Richard shook himself. "Right. To the house!"

Chapter 8

As they approached Netherfield, Richard guided his horse toward the side of the house.

"Where are you going?" Caroline asked.

"The servants' entrance," Richard replied.

"No, you are not." Caroline nudged her horse to catch up to his.

"Yes, I am. If Darcy has returned, I would rather have Georgiana already attended to before he finds out I allowed her to be injured."

"You did not allow me to be injured," Georgiana said.

Richard huffed. No matter what his cousin or Caroline said, he had allowed Wickham to get too close to Georgiana.

"How will you manage the narrow stairs?" Caroline asked. "Miss Darcy will get bumped and jostled, and the servants will be delayed in their duties. We cannot have footmen carrying water for her bath if we are in their way."

"But Darcy –"

"Is likely still at Longbourn," Caroline interjected before he could finish his protest.

"She is right," Georgiana said. "Neither he nor Mr. Bingley will be returned just yet."

"But Mrs. Hurst –"

"Can be put to work seeing that a bath is drawn, and the surgeon is called." Caroline raised a brow and gave him a challenging look. "The front stairs will be far easier to navigate should Georgiana need an arm upon which to lean."

Richard scowled. She was making sense, which was incredibly annoying. However, it was not she with whom Darcy would be displeased. Had Darcy and Bingley not expressly invited him to Netherfield to keep Georgiana safe? He shook his head.

"If you promise to remain here, I will inquire if Mr. Darcy has returned."

His scowl deepened. He did not appreciate the tone Caroline was using. It was not as if he were a child in the nursery who needed coaxing to behave as instructed. "Very well," he grumbled. "If my cousin has not returned, we will do it your way, but if he has returned, we will take the back stairs, and the servants can stand to the side for five minutes."

"Thank you, Miss Bingley," Georgiana said with a stern look for Richard.

"Yes, thank you, Miss Bingley," Richard added. However, he did not feel very thankful.

"It is not your fault," Georgiana whispered.

"Perhaps." He shook his head. How stupid he had been to allow Wickham to even come close to Georgiana! True, he had not expected the scoundrel to attempt an attack of any sort in his presence, but he should have been more vigilant.

"Mr. Darcy has not yet returned," Caroline said as she came around the house without her horse.

"Very well," Richard muttered as he turned his horse toward the front of the house. He could just imagine Darcy arriving as he lifted Georgiana down from his horse. But Darcy did not appear, and Georgiana was in her room, resting after having been seen by the surgeon, who had been on a call not far from Netherfield, before Darcy and Bingley returned.

"You had a pleasant visit?" he asked as Darcy and Bingley joined him in the billiards room.

"Indeed, we did," said Bingley. "How was your ride?"

Richard placed his cue on the table and, turning, leaned against it. "It was not uneventful."

"How so?" Darcy asked as he settled into a chair and unbuttoned his jacket.

"We met Wickham."

Darcy's brows rose as he waited expectantly for further information.

"He threatens to tell tales if I do not put an end to the *rumors* keeping him out of polite society."

"You mean he will share about Georgiana's near elopement?" Bingley asked.

Richard shrugged. "There is that, but he threatens to go further and declare her ruined — by him."

"He what?" Darcy's features darkened.

"He will ruin her, but that is not all." Richard walked around to the other side of the table and leaned on his hands on the edge as he faced Darcy, wishing that there could be more space between them when he had to admit his utter failure. "Georgiana has been hurt. Not badly, just a sprained ankle and some bruises." Richard looked down at the balls on the table. "I allowed him to be close enough to her horse to startle it. It bolted, and she fell." He blew out a breath. "I am sorry."

"He startled her horse in your presence?" Bingley asked incredulously before Darcy could utter a word.

Richard nodded. "I did not expect him to, but he did."

"She is well?" Darcy asked from where he sat flopped backward in his chair as if someone had pushed him over.

Inwardly, Richard laughed bitterly. Not someone — he had done it. "She is sore, but well. She said you can come see her whenever you wish to prove to yourself that she is indeed well."

"And Wickham?" Darcy asked.

Richard shook his head. "I let him go. I could not leave Georgie."

"Thank you."

Richard's brows drew together, and he lifted his head to look at his cousin. "For what? Allowing your sister to be injured?"

"No, for staying with her when I know you would have rather chased Wickham down and ended his life." Darcy held Richard's gaze. "I will go see her, but then we must discuss what is to be done about Wickham."

Richard nodded. "I have been considering that for some time now."

"He needs to leave England," Bingley said. "Purchase him a commission or passage to India or toss him down a steep cliff onto some jagged rocks — it matters not so long as he is removed from here."

Richard's mouth dropped open. Bingley was not usually the bloodthirsty sort.

"He will want money and ease," Darcy said as he rose from his chair.

"He does not favor the regulars, I mentioned that while we spoke today," Richard added.

"He wants Darcy's life," Bingley muttered. "It is what he has always wanted — an estate and a fortune to squander on all kinds of rapacious living." He shook his head. "He has injured Georgiana twice now and threatens to continue. He cannot be allowed to do so."

"I know," both Darcy and Richard replied.

Bingley had begun to pace the room but now stood beside the billiard table next to Richard. "You should inform Colonel Forester of his actions. I have heard the man is not lenient with his correction. Then when there is a threat of dire consequence to be escaped, perhaps Wickham would be more receptive to alternative options." He rolled one ball after another down the length of the table as he thought. "I do not know what to do beyond that."

"That is a very good beginning," Richard said. "I had considered calling on Colonel Forester."

Darcy stood near the door. "We will go together after I have seen Georgiana."

Bingley and Richard watched Darcy leave the room. Then, when the door had clicked closed, Bingley turned to Richard.

"Jane said that Miss Lydia has been whispering to Miss Kitty about sneaking out to see the blackguard. Neither knows that Jane has heard them. So, if we could rid the area of the man before rather than after he has ruined a foolish young girl, Jane and I would appreciate it."

"Ah," said Richard, "that explains your comments about seeing him dead or gone."

Bingley smiled wryly. "It was a bit unlike me, was it not?"

"Indeed," Richard replied with a chuckle.

"How Darcy can contain his ire is beyond me!" Bingley had moved down the table and was rolling the balls back to the end where they had been moments ago. "If Wickham had behaved as he did with either of my sisters, I do not think I could harness my anger as Darcy does. I struggled enough to not display my emotions to Jane when she confided in me about her sister — and Wickham has not done anything further than flirt with the girl." He blew out a breath. "Or so we hope."

"Darcy is a special breed of gentleman," Richard agreed. "I have wished to end Wickham's existence since Ramsgate, but there are laws."

"Unfortunately," Bingley muttered. "With what can we tempt him? What would cause him to wish to leave England?"

"Money."

Bingley's head tipped to the side. "Cards."

"I beg your pardon?"

"Is he a good player?" Bingley leaned against the table just down from Richard.

"I could not say for certain, but from the debt he accrues, I doubt he is. Why?"

Bingley shrugged. "We could tempt him with a large sum of money that he gets should he win a game, but if he loses, he takes passage to India."

Richard chuckled. "Bloodthirsty might not be your normal wont, but you fall into the role of sharp quite easily. I had figured you to be a more patient sort, able to put up with a good deal of foolishness before taking action." Richard gave him a nod of respect. "It appears I am wrong."

Bingley smiled. "I do tend to weather foolishness better than some." He blew out a breath. "That is likely why Caroline is as she is. Father spoiled her, and I did not have the fortitude to check her."

"Until she attempted to thwart your plans with Miss Bennet. Since then, she says you have been doing nothing but checking her."

"She has told you this?" Bingley turned so that he was leaning sideways on the table and could look at Richard.

"She did."

Bingley's brows furrowed. "She has been rather docile the past few days." His head tipped. "Have I been too harsh?"

Richard chuckled. "No. She overstepped her place. However, I do believe she has had a change of heart — at least, to a point."

"How so?"

"She intends to call on the Bennets." The way Bingley's mouth dropped open slightly while his eyes grew wide made Richard chuckle once again. "Louisa is not pleased with the idea, but Caroline seems determined. I believe, there is a good heart within her."

Bingley nodded. "She has not always been as she is — or was?"

"Hopefully, was." Richard pushed off the table. It was likely dangerous to continue standing here discussing Caroline with her brother. If Richard were not careful,

Bingley would ferret out of him his desire regarding Caroline. And that was not a discussion Richard wished to have just yet with Bingley. Maybe one day, but not now.

"You know she used to be rather sweet when she was a child," Bingley continued as he followed Richard to the door.

"I can imagine she was, but the experiences of life change us all."

"Too true," Bingley admitted as they exited the billiards room. "However, it would be much easier to find her a husband if she would revert to that sweet child."

Richard shook his head. "It is not a reverting which is needed," he said softly.

"It is not?" Bingley placed a hand on Richard's arm, drawing him to a stop.

Silently, Richard cursed himself for saying anything. "No. It is an accepting which is needed. The lady she has become possesses many good qualities. She just does not know it well enough yet."

Bingley's brows furrowed and then a smile crept across his lips. "You took her riding today."

Richard nodded. "She mentioned she liked riding, so we went riding."

"And that is the only reason?"

Richard shrugged.

Bingley laughed. "Very well, I will not inquire further."

For that Richard was immeasurably happy as the very

lady about whom they had been talking was approaching them.

"Charles, Colonel," she greeted. "How is Mr. Darcy?" She looked past her brother to Richard for an answer.

"I am still standing and have no injuries," he quipped. "He has gone to see Georgiana."

"The horse has been returned. She had not gone much beyond the meadow."

"I am glad." Richard shifted uneasily from one foot to another. Having Bingley watching him as he was, was rather uncomfortable. "Have you finished it?" he asked, indicating the book she carried.

"Oh, no, not yet. Actually, I was not reading just now, but was on my way to find a corner where I could not hear my sister so that I might." She glanced at her brother but returned her eyes to Richard. "I was going to the library."

"An excellent place to find some solitude."

"Or near solitude," she replied with a small smile.

"Darcy and I are planning to visit Colonel Forrester to see what can be done about Wickham, so I will not be intruding on your solitude today," Richard said, extending his arm to her so that he could lead her down the hall to the library and away from her grinning brother.

"Will you be able to keep him from telling tales?" she whispered.

Richard blew out a breath. "That is our goal, but I honestly do not know if it is possible."

They had stopped in front of the library door.

"How is it that there is gossip about Mr. Wickham being a fortune hunter?" Caroline asked.

Richard opened the door in front of them. The hall was not the best place to discuss this particular topic. "How much do you know about Georgiana's interactions with Wickham?"

Caroline stepped into the room before answering. "I know that she nearly eloped with him and that he did not wish to marry her but to get her money. She told me this the day before Christmas when I suggested she could go to town without your accompanying her."

Richard shook his head lightly in disbelief. Georgiana certainly was determined to not let her ordeal remain a heavy weight on her life.

"She shared her story with Mr. Bennet because she did not wish to see any of his daughters fall victim to Wickham's pretty tales." Richard motioned to the chairs near the hearth where Caroline had curled up to read the last time they were in this room together. "She knows Wickham is not above ingratiating himself with ladies for reasons that have nothing to do with marriage, so the fact that the Bennets are not heiresses is not enough to keep them safe from ruin. Forgive me, I do know that it is not proper to speak of such things."

Caroline slipped her feet out of her slippers and tucked them under her.

"I should go," Richard said. "Darcy will likely wish to be on our way soon."

"Was he angry with you?"

Richard shook his head. "Not that I could tell." He shrugged. "He thanked me for staying with Georgie instead of chasing down Wickham."

"Did you wish to chase him down?" Caroline asked in surprise.

"With all that is in me, yes." He still wished to find the man and do him harm.

Caroline smiled at him. "I will say it once again. Miss Darcy is very fortunate to have you. You care for her very well. Every lady should be so fortunate as to be cared for as you care for her." She ducked her head, and her cheeks grew becomingly rosy. "You are a good man."

"Thank you," Richard said, lowering himself into the chair next to her. He should leave. He should go to his room and wait for Darcy. He should not remain here.

"Are you not leaving?"

Richard shook his head. "Darcy can find me here." He leaned back in his chair and stretched his legs out in front of him. "I promise to be quiet."

"And do what?"

"Watch you read. You are very charmingly arranged as you are."

Caroline held her book out to him. "Or you could read to me. You are very good at it."

He took the book from her and opened it to where she had it marked. "Shall I begin here?" He pointed to the top of the left page.

"No, the next page."

He cleared his throat and, after giving her a mock look of hauteur, began reading.

LETTER XLIX

VILLARS TO EVELINA. Berry Hill.

DISPLEASURE? my Evelina!-you have but done your duty; you have but shown that humanity without which I should blush to own my child. It is mine, however, to see that your generosity be not repressed by your suffering from indulging it; I remit to you, therefore, not merely a token of my approbation, but an acknowledgment of my desire to participate in your charity. [1]

---

1. *from Evelina by Fanny Burney*

Chapter 9

Richard entered Colonel Forester's drawing room with Darcy at his heels. He was uncertain where this conversation was going to lead, but he was determined that it should end with Georgiana, as well as Lydia Bennet, being free from the danger that Wickham posed to them. He did not expect to see one of those ladies sitting in the Forester's drawing room with her sister Kitty at her side.

"Colonel," Richard greeted. "Mrs. Forester, Miss Lydia, Miss Kitty."

"We are a popular house this evening, are we not?" Colonel Forester said with a chuckle. "My wife has invited a couple of her dearest friends for dinner." He rose from his seat and motioned toward the door. "I assume you are here on some business and not in pursuit of gossip."

Richard smiled. "That would be correct."

"We will be in my office, my dear," he said to his wife, a pretty young lady of not many more years than Georgiana if her looks were a good thing by which to make such an assumption.

Richard hoped that, with Colonel Forester's having so recently married and to such a young lady with friends who were in danger from Wickham, their conference would go well.

"What can I do for you, Colonel?" Forester asked as he walked behind his desk and lifted a decanter of port in an offer to the gentlemen.

Richard nodded his acceptance as he took a seat before Forester's desk. "I have come to speak to you about one of your men."

Forester placed a glass before Darcy and turned to fill one for Richard. "Let me guess. Would it be Lieutenant Wickham?"

"Indeed, it would be."

Forester placed a glass before Richard, then procured one for himself. Settling into his chair, he sighed. "What has he done?"

Richard took a sip of his drink and pondered the rather annoyed tone with which the question was asked. "Has he been difficult?"

"Not in his training or duties, but I would appreciate it if he would refrain from flirting with my wife — although, I must admit he has not singled her out. It is more just his way, I suppose."

The port in Richard's glass swirled as he turned his glass in his hand. "He is more than a flirt," Richard said. "And I would watch him around my wife if I had one with whom he was overly friendly."

Forester's brows rose as his lips pursed and interest shone in his eyes. "Go on."

Richard glanced at Darcy. "No lady, married or unmarried, rich or poor, is safe from his proclivities. He is as free with his charm as he is with his money at a card table, and he manages both very ill. There are several children born on the wrong side of the blanket who bear a resemblance to him."

"Indeed?"

Richard nodded. "Darcy and I have known him for years. He has been given money and wasted it on licentious living, and there is a maid in Darcy's employ who is the mother to one of Wickham's offspring — not that he cares to know or support the child or its mother."

"I had heard tell that Wickham was a former friend, and a close one of Mr. Darcy's family — his father in particular," said Forester.

"That is not a lie," Darcy replied. "However, my father never knew Wickham as I did. He kept his lifestyle well-hidden from my father. So well-hidden that my father left him a legacy and the living that was in his power to bequeath. The legacy was given, but the living was refused by Wickham in favour of a sum of money. He claimed he wished to study the law instead of taking orders, and, to be honest, I was glad for it."

"He wasted the money in short order and decided the law was not for him," Richard continued. "Not long ago, he wished instead to be granted the living which had just fallen vacant. Darcy refused him his request."

"For which he abused me most severely," Darcy added.

Colonel Forester's head bobbed up and down slowly. "So, the tales he has shared about you are not true — except in part?"

"That would be correct," Darcy replied.

Colonel Forester took a sip of his port. "You have not come to share this tale with me though, have you?"

Richard shook his head. "No. There was an incident today in which Wickham was involved."

"Continue," Forester said as he returned to his glass for another swallow of port.

"This past spring, my sister," Darcy said, "fell victim to his charm — she was not ruined — but she was heart-broken when she discovered his intentions were less than honorable. She has thirty thousand pounds that he wished to claim for his own."

"She has shared her story with the father of the future Mrs. Darcy," Richard added.

Colonel Forester's eyes lit with understanding. "Bennet had mentioned that Wickham was a fortune hunter," he said. "It has caused some grief for Wickham."

Richard placed his empty glass on the desk. "Wickham was less than pleased when he saw me earlier today as I was out riding with Miss Darcy and Miss Bingley. He threatened to tell one and all that he had indeed ruined Miss Darcy. I assured him that such a thing would not be met with pleasure." Richard's lips curled up into a menacing smile as he gave the colonel across from him a knowing look.

Colonel Forester merely nodded and muttered his agreement that such an action would require a measured and severe response.

"He wished for me to refute the tales of him being a fortune hunter, but I cannot. They are true. I did give my word that I would not add to any gossip in return for his remaining silent." Richard leaned forward and allowed the anger he felt to be seen on his face. "I did not expect him to attack her in my presence, so I did not worry about him being too near Miss Darcy's horse. However, I was wrong. He hit her horse with his hat, causing it to start, and Miss Darcy to be thrown. Thankfully, her injuries are not grave."

Colonel Forester drained the remaining liquid from his glass and placed it firmly on the desk with a thump.

"He was not alone. Captain's Denny and Saunders were with him. They, however, spoke not a word beyond a greeting to me and had no interaction with Miss Darcy. I do not know if they will give him up or not as I do not know how their friendship lies." Richard leaned back in his chair. "There is one last item that I think you should know because Miss Lydia is your wife's friend. Her sister, Miss Bennet, has heard Miss Lydia talking about sneaking out to see Wickham."

Colonel Forester cursed and shook his head. "What is to be done with him? Such behaviour cannot be tolerated in my ranks."

"Personally, I would like to see him gone from England," Richard replied.

"I can imagine you would." Colonel Forester went to the door of his office and called to a footman. "Have Lieutenant Wickham, Captain Saunders, and Captain Denny sent to see me with all due haste."

"Right away, sir," the man replied and hurried off to do as he was bid.

"Another glass of port while we wait and plan?" Colonel Forester offered.

"It would be welcome," Richard said with a smile. "I always find it helpful to have a glass or two when dealing with troublesome officers."

Colonel Forester chuckled. "You have them, too, do you?"

"Occasionally, yes," Richard replied.

"I could make a spectacle of him." Forester placed Richard's refilled glass in front of him. "But, I think that would draw too much attention to Mr. Darcy's sister, and I assume we do not want there to be questions regarding her relationship to Mr. Wickham."

"I would appreciate it if nothing of what we have shared about her were to leave this office," Darcy replied. "However, she had given permission to allow you to share that he did attempt to gain her money through false admiration if it is necessary to save another from a similar fate or worse."

"She did?" Richard shook his head.

Darcy shrugged. "I attempted to dissuade her, but she is determined to not let another suffer as she did."

"I will protect what I know as if it were orders from Wellington," Forester assured them. "Now, what are our options regarding Lieutenant Wickham?"

~*~*~

A quarter hour later, Captains Denny and Saunders entered their colonel's office. Each removed his hat and tucked it under his arm as he stood at attention between where Darcy and Richard sat and the door.

"There should be three of you," Forester said sternly, rising and moving to stand before them.

"Yes, sir," Captain Denny.

"Where is Lieutenant Wickham?" Forester's face was mere inches from Saunders's.

The captain swallowed. "I do not know, sir. We parted ways after our ride today."

Forester pulled back and folded his arms across his chest as his brows rose. "Explain."

Again, Richard saw Saunders's Adam's apple rise and

fall as he swallowed. He also saw the man's eyes shift toward his friend; however, his frame remained rigid, and his head did not turn. The rumors about Colonel Forester's lack of leniency seemed to be true.

"He injured a young lady, sir," said Captain Denny.

"That is correct," Saunders agreed. "A bit of fun and flirting with the ladies we can abide but not injury."

"You did not return to assist this lady," Forester replied.

"No, sir." This time, Saunders dared to turn his head and look at Colonel Fitzwilliam. "For that, we are most earnestly sorry."

Colonel Fitzwilliam inclined his head in acceptance as Captain Denny muttered his agreement. Both men appeared to be remorseful and not just terrified of whatever punishment might be doled out to them.

"So, you broke ties with Lieutenant Wickham?" Forester questioned.

"Yes, sir," Denny replied.

"And you have not seen him since you returned from your ride, is that correct, Captain Denny?"

"Yes, sir."

"Saunders, did Wickham threaten to ruin a young lady's reputation?"

"Yes, sir."

"And he then startled her horse, causing her to fall?"

"Yes, sir."

"Colonel Fitzwilliam has informed me that neither you

nor Denny took part in any of the maligning or injury of Mr. Darcy's sister. That is to be commended. However, there is the fact that you did not report the incident to me nor did you return to offer aid." Forester returned to his desk. "You will be assigned some extra duties for your neglect, but I will not make an example of you."

"Thank you, sir," both replied.

"Do you have any idea where Wickham might be?"

"No, sir, we do not."

"But you will find him."

"Of course, sir."

"Be about it then," Forester said in dismissal. "But do not let me hear a word of any of what has happened today leave your lips — most especially the part concerning the lie Wickham was promising to share about Miss Darcy."

"Not a word, sir," both assured him.

Saunders opened the door to reveal the sought-after Wickham.

"You are late," Forester growled.

"I have only just learned of your summons," Wickham replied. He cast a wary look at Darcy and Richard.

"Where were you that you could not be found when I sent someone to summons you?" Forester rose from his desk and approached Wickham, who had taken a place standing where Denny and Saunders had stood moments before.

"Assisting a pretty little maid," Wickham replied with a

smile. "Her mistress's cat had climbed a tree and would not come down."

Forester's brows rose. "You expect me to believe you were only fetching her cat?"

Wickham did a poor job of hiding a smirk as he shrugged.

"I am of a mind to make an example of you." Forester's voice was low and menacing, sending a shiver through Richard, who was not unused to such threats. Of course, he was more likely than not to be the one making them, but there was something dangerous in how Forester growled that could be felt by one and all.

Wickham stood a little straighter. "Have these men been sharing tales about me?"

"Indeed, they have, and Denny and Saunders have confirmed them."

"Denny lost his father's watch to me in a game. He would say whatever was necessary to condemn me — much like these gentlemen."

"Enough!" Forester roared. "You will behave as one who is under my command and show respect to both me and my guests."

Richard bit back a grin as Wickham presented himself properly.

"As I have already said, I am of a mind to make an example of you. However, I have no desire to expose an innocent young lady to possible ruin at your hands."

Wickham's lips twitched, but he held his tongue. The action did not go unnoticed by Forester. "Do not even begin to tell me how you have already ruined her." He shook his head. "Darcy, he is yours. I pray you know what you are about."

"As do I," Darcy replied. "This is the last time we will have any dealings," Darcy began his address to Wickham. "I would like you to leave England. I will purchase you passage to the colonies or any other place you wish to travel, and I will give you money enough to survive in your new land for a year, possibly longer if you are frugal. You will send me notice of your arrival in your new location, and I will send you one more small allotment of money. If it were not for my respect both for my father and yours, as well as my concern for my sister's reputation, I would care very little if you were beaten to within an inch or your life." Darcy shook his head. "If you choose not to leave England, then I see no other profession to possibly accept you save for the regulars. I am willing to purchase you a commission commensurate with the pay you now receive. I will add to that, a sum of money to see you on your way."

"Purchasing my silence?"

"Yes."

"It is a very generous offer," Forester interjected. "Had you dealt with my sister as you have Miss Darcy, I would not be so kind. In fact, I do not believe you would have survived our meeting on the field."

"What if I prefer to ply a trade?"

Richard snorted. "You, a tradesman?"

"A tradesman in the colonies is acceptable," Darcy replied.

"There you have it." Colonel Forester interrupted. "A flogging and who knows what other punishment I will levy upon you to ensure your misery, a new life in the colonies, or a position in the regulars. Those are your options."

Wickham glowered at Darcy.

"I have room in my regiment for an officer," Richard offered.

Wickham's eyes widened just slightly as Richard rose and came to stand near him.

"I would flee the country if I were you," Richard said in a soft but firm voice. "There is a greater chance of you retaining your life if you do. I promise you that you have harmed my family for the last time, and I would caution you to not bring any further dishonour to your father's name. Take what Darcy offers and make something of yourself."

"I would listen to Richard," Darcy said. "I will not seek leniency or mercy for you again but will allow my cousin to do as he sees fit."

Wickham stood silently for a moment. Richard could see from the way his jaw was working and how his nostrils flared as he breathed that he was not pleased to choose any of the options laid before him.

"Very well, I will sail."

"Excellent choice," Forester declared. "You will pack your things and be ready to leave at first light on Monday morning. I have just this minute decided to travel to town to purchase a gift for my wife, and you will attend me."

"Where will you go?" Darcy asked.

Wickham shrugged. "I do not like ships so the closest port you will allow."

"Ireland, Newfoundland, Halifax?" Richard tossed out some close options to his cousin.

Darcy grimaced. "Ireland?"

"Too close?" Richard asked.

Darcy shrugged. "Not if he remains there, I suppose."

"Ireland," Wickham said. "If I must be banished at least let it be to a place that is civilized."

Richard chuckled. "The colonies are not uncivilized, and they do present a greater opportunity to obtain land."

"No, please. Let me find my way in Ireland."

"You will remain there?"

"Transportation usually comes with a term of exile," Wickham retorted.

"Ten years," Richard responded. "You must not return for ten years, and then you will have nothing to do with my family when you do return."

Wickham nodded. "Ten years."

"It is settled then," said Darcy rising. "I will instruct my man to make the necessary financial arrangements, and purchase your passage."

"Thank you, gentlemen," Forester said to Darcy and Richard before turning to Wickham. "Wickham, you are free to go prepare to travel, but if I hear a word about Miss Darcy or see you dallying with any ladies between now and when the sun rises Monday morning. I will not hesitate to extract my displeasure on your back. Do I make myself clear?"

"Yes, sir." Wickham saluted and left.

Forester blew out a breath. "Now, to tell my wife of my need to travel. She will not be best pleased but then, it should not be so bad as she will be delighted to have a new bauble."

Chapter 10

Caroline stood at the window in Georgiana's room, looking out into the deepening shadows of the late afternoon light. This time of year was so dark — she pulled her wrap more snugly around her shoulders — and cold.

"You do not have to stay with me," Georgiana said from where she sat in her bed.

"Oh, I wished to stay." Caroline turned from the window and moved back toward the chair she had occupied for the last half hour. The sick room was not precisely her favourite place to be, but then, Miss Darcy was not ill, only injured, and, knowing just how much Colonel Fitzwilliam cared for his cousin compelled Caroline for some unknown reason to see to the girl's care.

"But it is dull," Georgiana protested. "I would much rather be out of bed and doing something — anything, truth be told. However, I fear my brother would be most severely displeased if I were to act on my wishes."

Caroline smiled at the irritation in Georgiana's voice. "And your cousin? Would he be likewise as displeased?" A feeling of satisfaction and comfort spread through Caroline's being as Georgiana's lips turned up in a smile.

"He would be displeased but not so greatly as my brother. Richard growls and stomps, but he does not get that look on his face that crushes my heart like my brother does." She paused and tipped her head. "However, when Richard is disappointed..." She shook her head.

"It tears at your heart as deeply as your brother's look crushes it?" Caroline asked.

"Yes. How do you know that?"

"My father," Caroline replied. "He was much like Charles — very unbothered by much, always ready with a quick smile and a pleasant word. He tolerated a great deal of foolishness from me and Louisa — and Charles — although I do believe Father was more lenient with Louisa and me." She sighed. "But when I had crossed that border from what he could tolerate to what he could not..." She shook her head. "He never raised his voice but would quietly say 'I expected better' or some such small reprimand. Oh, how those word tore at my heart! I did not like to disappoint Mama either, and her look of displeasure made my heart ache — but not as Father's quiet words did."

"Do you miss him?"

Caroline nodded. "Daily."

"Me, too," Georgiana whispered. "I hope I would make my father proud, but I am uncertain after my foolishness with Mr. Wickham."

Caroline rose from her chair and perched tentatively on the edge of Georgiana's bed. She had never had such a heartfelt conversation with Miss Darcy. The idea that this girl might understand a portion of what she felt drew her to her in a way that Georgiana's brother's fortune and estate never could. "I am positive my father would be disappointed in me," she admitted.

"You are?"

Caroline nodded. "You have trusted me with your story about Mr. Wickham, so I feel I can trust you with this." She waited to get an assurance from Georgiana. "I have not told anyone — Louisa would not understand. She never felt Father's displeasure as greatly as I did." She drew a breath. "One thing my father said to me over and over when I would return home from school for a holiday was that no matter how many accomplishments I acquired, there was truly only one that mattered." She looked down at the bed cover and smoothed the wrinkles with her hand. "Kindness." She sighed heavily. "It has been pointed out to me that I have not been as kind as I should be. Oh, I knew I was not being kind, but it is so much easier to not feel like a pebble among jewels when one chooses to point out the failings of another instead of noticing her own. Eventually, a practice becomes a habit and a habit, a way of life, unless someone forces you to look at yourself in a different light — not as wanting but as accomplished."

Georgiana smiled. "Richard?"

Caroline nodded. "He has not ignored my faults but sees my abilities despite those faults."

Georgiana grasped Caroline's hand. "He is the best at doing just that. Do...do...you...like him?" Georgiana asked cautiously.

"I should like to," Caroline replied. "But I fear it. Soldiers do not always return, and he has no estate. But..." She shrugged. She truly did not know how she felt about Colonel Fitzwilliam. He was handsome and kind, and despite his ability to annoy her at times with his directness, she was beginning to value his opinion, as well as the time she spent with him, and counted him as a friend.

"As far as I know," Georgiana began, "he has a small inheritance, and my uncle would like to see him with some land. However, Richard refuses to speak much about the future. I think he knows that with the war being what it is, he might not have a future or need for land — not that he has ever said as much, but it is the impression I get from him. He will speak of his future lightly but never with any degree of conviction."

The room fell silent for several minutes.

If he would resign his commission... Caroline sighed. She highly doubted that a man as duty-bound as Colonel Fitzwilliam appeared to be would ever resign his commission just to marry a woman of no significance, even if that lady had a fortune.

"Do you think they will rid us of Wickham?" she asked Georgiana.

Georgiana nodded. "Richard will see to it."

"Not your brother?"

"My brother will wish to, but then, he will remember how Father cared for Wickham and how Mr. Wickham's father was a good man, and in respect for those men, he will be too forgiving. Richard does not have that same connection. There is no guilt to rest heavily on him like there is my brother."

Caroline's brows furrowed. She had always seen Darcy as more forceful than what Georgiana described, but then, compared to Charles, Darcy was more commanding. However, she could likewise see how Colonel Fitzwilliam, who was used to giving orders and having them followed, would be even more autocratic.

She rose from the bed.

How often since they arrived at Netherfield had she compared Colonel Fitzwilliam to his cousin and found his cousin – Mr. Darcy of Pemberley in Derbyshire — actually wanting? It was startling. She had been certain there was no one who would ever compare to Mr. Darcy, let alone outshine him. Oh, how she wished Colonel Fitzwilliam were an estate owner instead of a colonel. It would be so easy to love him.

She pulled a magazine from the work basket she had brought with her to Miss Darcy's room.

Love. She closed her eyes against the word and the realization that her jumbled feelings were likely love.

Opening her eyes, she affixed a smile to her face and turned toward Georgiana. "I have a magazine that might make things less dull for you."

~*~*~

Richard knocked on Georgiana's door and, upon hearing her bid him enter, opened it. A smile lit his face as he took in the prospect of Caroline sitting propped up on pillows next to Georgiana in Georgiana's bed as they poured over a magazine. Fashion plates! He would never completely understand the desire of some ladies to study them as if they were a battle plan.

"Were you successful?" Georgiana asked.

"Indeed, we were," he said as Darcy joined them. "Wickham will be on his way to Ireland very soon, and we have only to endure his presence in Meryton for one more day. He and Forester travel to London on Monday." He leaned against the bedpost. "How are you feeling?"

"Bored," Georgiana said, "not due to my company but due to being confined to this bed. Miss Bingley has done a valiant job of keeping me entertained as much as one can be when convalescing." She sent a teasing grin to her brother. "There are at least three new gowns I simply must have."

Darcy raised his brows and shook his head. "Must?"

Georgiana nodded. "And by tomorrow, I shall likely

have two more. These magazines are simply full of wonderful creations."

"It will not work," Darcy said dryly.

"What will not work?" Georgiana fluttered her lashes and affected a look of innocence.

"I am not allowing you out of that bed until morning regardless of how many gowns you decide you must have — a number that will be decided by me, I might add." He looked at Caroline and nodded. "Thank you for caring for her."

"It was a pleasure," Caroline replied as she climbed off the bed. It was odd to hear Darcy and his sister being so informal and teasing each other. She had thought Darcy was incapable of teasing or being teased. It was surprising how little she really knew about him, considering the amount of time they had spent in company. Of course, she should have known that Darcy could abide teasing if he were friends with her brother, but she had never actually stopped to consider the gentleman much beyond his looks, connections, and wealth. How very like a fortune hunter that was!

"Do you wish me to leave this one?" Caroline picked up the magazine that had been discarded near the foot of the bed.

"Would you mind?"

"Not at all," Caroline assured Georgiana, placing the magazine next to her.

"They are such a pleasant diversion from looking at the walls or rereading my book."

"Have you read *Evelina?*" Caroline asked. "I am not finished with it yet, but I am not confined to my room and would be happy to let you read it if you wished."

Georgiana smiled and not that familiar smile that she always had for Caroline when Caroline visited. No, this smile was soft, warm, and filled with something for with Caroline longed — friendship.

"I could not take your book from you," Georgiana replied. "I am certain my brother can keep me entertained for an hour or so and then find me a book to read when he is done." She looked at her cousin. "And then Richard might also regale me with some tale. He is very good at reading. It is quite diverting."

"I know," Caroline replied. "He has read to me twice now and done the actors at Drury Lane proud with his oratory skills."

"Yes," Richard agreed readily, "I have missed my true calling — the stage."

Georgiana giggled, which delighted Richard, but it was the amused sparkle in Caroline's eyes that captivated him.

"Shall we leave Darcy to explain how the meeting with Colonel Forester went?" he asked Caroline.

"Are you not staying?"

Richard shook his head. "Darcy is capable of sharing his news without my help, and since I will be required to perform later for the invalid, I should like to find some refreshment now."

"Dinner is in little more than an hour," Darcy said.

"And at that time, I shall dine with my audience of one," Richard replied. "However, I find I am hungry now and will likely perish before dinner if I do not find the source of that wonderful smell which greeted us on our arrival." He took the basket that Caroline was holding. "Will you allow me to accost your cook for a gingerbread while dinner is being prepared?"

"Richard loves gingerbread," Georgiana interjected.

Caroline laughed lightly as she placed her hand on Richard's proffered arm. "I believe there is a maid who might be willing to procure some for you. She might even be willing to bring you cider instead of tea."

"Ah, the perfect hostess," Richard said as they exited the room and began walking toward her room.

"Thank you, even if it is said in jest."

"It might have been said lightly just now, but it is true. You are very good at seeing to the needs of your guests. Your brother's home runs quite well under your command."

"Thank you," she said once again. "Tell me about your meeting." She liked strolling down the corridor on his arm and chatting.

"There is not really very much to tell. Forester sent for Denny, Saunders, and Wickham — the first two appeared readily — we waited for Wickham. Denny and Saunders admitted their part and Wickham's in what occurred. They apologized for not having returned to lend their aid, and they said they had cut ties with Wickham over it. They have been assigned some extra duties as recompense for their actions. Then, Wickham arrived with his normal attitude of insolence. He was brought up short on it, however, and after a discussion of what happened and what he deserved, we came to an arrangement. He will retire from his position in the militia to Ireland where he will abide for no less than ten years before returning. Darcy will pay his passage and give him funds."

Caroline sighed. "It is a pity that Mr. Darcy has to pay the man who has done him so much harm."

"I agree, but there was little else that could be done. If Wickham is in England, he will likely attempt something foolish once again to secure money from Darcy, and, if he were to receive the flogging that he deserves for Georgiana's accident, there would be too much attention drawn to Georgiana. It seemed the best option to send him away." He handed the basket back to her as they had arrived in front of her door.

"It is wise, I suppose. I am just sorry it must be as it is."

Richard nodded. "It is a sorry tale." He shifted from one foot to the other as he stood there with her outside her bedroom. "Are you going to prepare for dinner now?"

She smiled. "How can I when a guest is in need of sustenance?" She placed a hand the doorknob. "If you will wait for ten minutes, I shall do what I must to make myself presentable for dinner. I promise I will not be long."

Richard looked down the hall to where a pair of chairs flanked a narrow table decorated with greenery. "I shall rest there. Take as long as you need."

"Do you not need to get ready for dinner?"

Richard looked down at himself. "I suppose I could use a little freshening, but I am not dining in the dining room, so there is no need to be too formal."

"Then I shall meet you here, in ten minutes?" Caroline said.

"I shall only be five," he replied with a grin.

He was wrong. It took him a full six minutes to attend to his attire and return. She, however, was not wrong, for it did take her the full ten minutes she had said it would. Be that as it may, when Richard considered how long it took his sister and mother to prepare for dinner, he had to be impressed that Caroline could manage a change of gown and whatever else she might have done to look so fetching in just ten minutes.

"I did not change my hair," she explained when he voiced his wonder at her readying herself so quickly. "That would have taken much longer, and this gown is not so difficult as some to fasten and does not require a maid's assistance."

"You did not rush yourself unduly just because of my

desire to eat gingerbread, did you?" he stopped and turned to look at her.

"And if I did?"

Richard's brows furrowed, and he shrugged. "I guess I would feel guilty as well as pleased." He stepped closer to her. "Did you?"

She pulled her bottom lip between her teeth. It was not his desire to eat that had caused her to hurry but her desire to spend time with him. However, she could not tell him that, so she shrugged and gave him a playful smile.

It was too much. That smile, the biting of her lip, the way she ducked her head and peeked up at him — it was just too much, and before he knew what he was about, his one hand was cupping the back of her head as his other was pulling her near. "Thank you," he whispered against her lips before claiming them as he had desired to do ever since he had seen her in the dining room standing nearly under the kissing bough the day before Christmas.

Chapter 11

Caroline knew she should protest the colonel's actions as soon as he put his hands on her person, but that brief moment of lucidness was promptly overcome by his closeness and then... She sighed as his lips touched hers. Gone was any thought of propriety. In its place, desire and contentment warred for pre-eminence. Rational thought was beyond her. Impulse bid her to wind her arms around him, and readily she complied. She had never experienced such deliciousness as she did in those few moments before his lips left hers yearning for his continued touch.

Slowly, as if he were just as overcome and fighting for comprehension of what had occurred as she was, he released her, backing away but only just a step. "Forgive me," he muttered. His chest rose and fell markedly. "I...I..." He drew a hand across his mouth. "I should not have taken such liberties."

Caroline took one step backward. The colonel's eyes did not look convinced of his words. In fact, he looked very much as if he would like to take the same liberties again.

"I am well," she assured him. "I should not have allowed it, but..."

"It was overwhelming," he concluded, and she nodded.

She would likely never be able to erase this moment from her memory though she should flee from his presence and never return for a thousand years. It — he was forever seared into her very being. She shook her head slightly. How could one moment entwine two people in such a way? It was foolish, a momentary feeling, fleeting in its existence, was it not?

Caroline smoothed her skirts to give her hands something to do other than find their way back to him. "We should find you some cider and gingerbread."

"Right," he murmured. "Cider is definitely needed." He motioned for her to begin walking with him down the hall.

Thankfully, it was only five strides before he offered her his arm, and she could touch him again. Foolish wantonness! She had never expected such a thing from herself.

~*~*~

She was still quietly pondering that kiss and her response sometime later after dinner had been consumed and cards played.

"You do not look well," Louisa said as she took a seat near Caroline on the sofa in the drawing room. "You have been flushed all evening." She placed the back of her hand against Caroline's forehead. "You do not feel feverish, but I must insist that you retire early. Rest will provide you a better chance of not catching whatever it is you are catching."

Caroline was not catching anything. She was caught — well and truly caught. However, she did not protest but allowed her sister to persuade her to go to bed, nor did she protest when Louisa insisted on accompanying her.

"I left my book in the library," Caroline said as she and her sister left the drawing room.

"You should not strain your eyes with reading if you are on the verge of becoming sick."

"I will only read if I cannot sleep."

Louisa huffed softly but allowed Caroline to go to the library to retrieve her book.

Robinson Crusoe still lay on the table. She stopped and ran a hand over it, then picked it up and flipped through it to find the ribbon he had used to mark his place. Blue. She smiled. It was a deep, steady colour and seemed fitting for him.

"Is that your book?" Louisa crossed from the door to the chairs.

"No." Caroline snapped the book closed and returned it to the table. "It is the colonel's." Her hand rested on the cover. "I was just seeing if he had progressed any since the last time we were here reading, and he has not."

"The colonel is the son of an earl." There was a suggestive, matchmaking tone to Louisa's voice.

"Yes, he is," Caroline said, "a second son with no estate."

"Surely, he will not be penniless. Great men often provide some sort of inheritance for those who are not their heirs. Not a one of them would wish to have their sons — second, third, or fourth — fall below the status to which they are born."

"Second sons must have a career," Caroline protested, "as do third and fourth sons."

"Unless they marry well," Louisa persisted. "You have a fortune, and the colonel did say he would consider amounts as low as twenty thousand."

Caroline smiled tightly and took up her book. Hearing she was just barely acceptable was not reassuring. "An earl would not wish a tie to trade."

Louisa wrapped an arm around Caroline's. "Lord Matlock has not protested Mr. Darcy marrying Miss Elizabeth," she whispered as they stepped into the hall.

"Miss Elizabeth is a gentleman's daughter, not a tradesman's daughter."

"Still, you are from a respectable family. Your fortune is not small, and your brother will be Darcy's brother soon enough. I should think all of those things would make you more than acceptable."

"Soldiers do not always return," Caroline whispered as they reached the top of the stairs. "I do not wish to be a widow."

"You will not be. Commissions can be sold."

"He may not wish to sell his commission." She dropped her voice even lower, and Louisa leaned close to hear her words. "I could not ask that of him."

Louisa's eyes lit with delight. "You do like him."

Caroline nodded. "Very much." She glanced up and down the hall before sharing the next bit. "He kissed me."

"Oh!" Louisa squealed softly as she squeezed Caroline's arm. "Then he will marry you."

Caroline shook her head. "Plenty of gentlemen kiss ladies and do not marry them."

"Not the colonel," Louisa insisted.

Caroline rolled her eyes. Why had she decided to say anything to her sister? Louisa was no more sensible than Mrs. Bennet at times. "You do not know that."

"He is very honourable."

That was true.

"But he is not always proper," Caroline refuted.

Louisa huffed and shook her head as if Caroline were daft.

"It matters not," Caroline continued.

Why did her sister have to be so hard to dissuade from an idea once it was in her head?

They were not far from her room now. In just a few moments, she would be in her room and left alone to prepare for bed and consider the very gentleman about whom they were speaking.

"You know I have always wished to marry a gentleman with an estate. Colonel Fitzwilliam does not have an estate. He is a second son and a soldier. These are not on my list of qualifications for a suitable husband. You know this, Louisa. Do not press me on this subject again. I shall not be seeking an offer from the colonel." She would not be seeking one, but she would be hard pressed to reject one. She wrapped her arms around her sister in an embrace. "Do not look so disappointed, Louisa. There is still a season's worth of gentleman to consider." Not that any of them would compare to Richard Fitzwilliam and just the thought of entertaining them made her heart pinch and her eyes mist.

"You make a such a lovely pair," Louisa said dejectedly.

"Good night," Caroline replied. There was no point in arguing any further with Louisa. Her sister was rather unyielding at times. Caroline would do better to save her reasoning powers and words for attempting to convince herself that what she had always desired was what she should still seek, and she knew that it would take a great deal of effort to persuade her heart that it could live without Colonel Fitzwilliam.

She bid her sister one more good night before stepping into her room just as the door to another room not far down the hall, which had been partially opened when they had passed, was pulled the rest of the way open, and Richard stepped into the hall.

"Colonel," Louisa said upon seeing him. "You do not look well." She clucked her tongue. "First, Caroline and now you. I will say to you what I said to her. It is best if you get some rest, for it is far easier to avoid catching whatever it is that you are catching if you are well rested."

Richard nodded. "Excellent advice," he muttered.

"Colonel," Louisa called after him. "Your room is not in that direction."

"No, but the brandy is." And after what he had just heard, brandy was precisely what he needed.

~*~*~

"Go away!" Richard yelled at the infernal knocking at his bedroom door.

"I will not," came the reply from the other side of the door before the knocking resumed once again.

Richard groaned, covered his eyes with his hand, and then, unable to tolerate how the throbbing in his head intensified with each repeated bang, he crawled out of bed, padded across the room in his stocking feet, unlatched the door, and hurried back to bed before the intruder could enter.

"I am not rising," he said as the door opened.

"I am not asking you to rise," Darcy said as he entered. "Mrs. Hurst was concerned that you might require the apothecary. She mentioned that you did not look well after leaving Georgiana's room last night and said that you had gone in search of brandy." Darcy lifted the covers off his cousin who was lying face down. "You are still dressed."

"Yes, I am." Richard's reply was muffled by his pillow. "Go away." He sighed as Darcy's weight caused the bed to sag. "Go away," he repeated. "I am well, but I am not rising until...well, ever."

"Ever?" Darcy's voice was incredulous. "Richard Fitzwilliam is going to remain in bed for the rest of his days?"

"No, just until tomorrow or next week. Now, go away."

Darcy chuckled. "Tell me what you heard in the hall."

Richard rolled onto his side and stared at his cousin. How did he know that he had heard anything in the hall?

"Georgiana said you were well when you left her, but that you had acted oddly when exiting her room. You stood at her door for a period of time, then left without turning to say a final good night. That is very unlike you, so we suspect, after hearing what Mrs. Hurst said about your condition, that you heard something."

Richard flopped back onto his face. "Go away."

"No. Unless you prefer for Georgiana to come question you instead of me."

With a huff, Richard resigned himself to the fact that Darcy was not going to leave without some sort of explanation. "I am not good enough." He rolled onto his side.

"I beg your pardon?"

"I heard Miss Bingley telling Mrs. Hurst that my not

having an estate and being both a soldier and a second son disqualified me as a potential husband. She will not be seeking an offer from me." He turned over fully and draped an arm across his eyes. The sunlight was rather bright this morning. "And that after she seemed rather accepting of me when I kissed her."

"Indeed?"

He peeked out from under his arm. "Indeed," he replied flatly. He had been so certain after the way she responded to his kiss that she felt something favourable towards him. He had even dared to hope that she loved him. However, he had been wrong.

"You are not going to accompany us to church?" Darcy asked.

Richard groaned. "No." Was that all the comfort he was going to receive from Darcy? Could the man not stomp about and declare Caroline lacking in judgment or in possession of deficient faculties?

"Very well. I shall leave you then."

Richard pushed up onto his elbows. "No, you will stay."

Darcy, who had not moved a muscle, smiled. "First, you order me to leave, and now, you order me to stay? Mrs. Hurst may be correct. The apothecary should be called."

Richard narrowed his eyes. "You are not usually so teasing. I do not like it. You are supposed to be steady and the source of rational thinking when I am not. Now do your part."

"What would you like me to say?"

"That she is a fool. That she could do no better than me." He flopped back onto his pillow. "Go away, you're making me into a blathering old ninny."

"I am not leaving," Darcy said softly. "I would gladly think her a fool if she were to refuse you. You are a good man and not without some fortune, such that it is."

Richard glanced at Darcy hopefully.

"However," Darcy continued, "you do not know for a certainty that she would refuse you. Have you told her you are willing to resign your commission?"

"Why would I do that?"

"Why do you think the fact that you are a soldier was listed among her reasons for not considering you? Perhaps they are the same as your reasons for wishing to sell your commission before you marry." Darcy drew a breath and released it. "I never thought I would be convincing anyone of Caroline Bingley's worth, but... There are many women who would gladly marry and become a widow with all due haste because they did not marry for love. You know it as well as I. We have seen some very happy widows."

A half smile that matched the one his cousin wore crept across Richard's lips. There were some ladies who seemed to prefer being a Mrs. with no Mr.

"A lady who has married for love does not wish to be parted from her heart. I would venture to guess that Caroline loves you, and that is why she listed it as a disqualification."

Richard sighed. What Darcy said made sense. "It does not change the fact that I am not good enough."

Darcy's brows furrowed. "When you have slept off whatever remains of the brandy you consumed, perhaps you will figure out why that is not true. Commissions can be sold."

Richard scowled. He didn't need to sleep off the brandy to understand what his cousin was saying. "I am still a second son and have no estate."

Darcy sighed. "And you are as stubborn as Aunt Catherine. Your father will see to it that you have land."

Richard shrugged. His heart and head hurt enough without having to admit that his cousin was right, and he was simply being foolish.

"Elizabeth was right," he said as Darcy moved to rise.

"About what?"

"It is just as unpleasant to be cast aside for lack of wealth and standing as it is to be pursued for it."

Darcy smiled sadly at him. "You have not been cast aside until you have asked for her hand and been rejected. Until then, the battle is not over."

Again, Richard shrugged instead of acknowledging the truth of his cousin's words.

"I will tell Georgiana and Mrs. Hurst that you are only suffering from a headache and a day's rest will improve it."

Richard cocked a brow in disbelief.

"Very well, I shall have to tell Georgiana what you heard, but it will go no further."

Richard nodded, flopped back on his bed, and waved a hand in dismissal. "Now, go away, so I can suffer in peace."

"No alcohol," Darcy cautioned. "Tea, coffee, broth, but no alcohol, not even cider. I will leave instructions for such with your man, and Georgiana is whom you will have to face if you do not follow them."

"Go away," Richard grumbled.

Darcy placed a hand on Richard's ankle, drawing his attention. "She is a fool if she refuses you," he said. Then he turned and left Richard to his miserable wallowing.

Chapter 12

The empty place at the table for breakfast, as well as the lack of whistling in the hallway, had made Caroline's heart ache. Now, as she attempted to pay attention to the scripture that was being read, she wished to hear the colonel's voice joined with the rest of the congregation, lifted in prayer. She glanced at her brother on her right and then at her sister on her left. How was it that standing here surrounded not only by the whole of the worshiping portion of Meryton but also her family, she felt so small, so isolated, so set apart and alone?

She clamped her lips closed and stifled a yawn. She had not slept well. How could she have? Her heart was unwilling to listen to logic. It was fixed, most steadily and assuredly, on the gentleman who was currently missing from their party. She could not fault him for being indisposed, but she could long for him not to be. She knelt and rose, repeated and remained silent as was required, but her mind was not focused as it should be on the words being spoken. As they sat for the sermon, she studied the Bennets. Tomorrow, she would call on them, but today, she felt a stirring within her to begin to mend her ways.

A small smile curled her lips as she remembered with fondness the hours spent with Miss Darcy, talking and looking at fashion plates. It reminded her a bit of how it used to be for her and Louisa. But then, that gnawing fear of failing and being rejected had set in, right around the time when that horrid witch, Miss Smith, had pointed out loudly to one and all who were gathered at that dinner how lacking Caroline was. Caroline could still feel the sting of Miss Smith's words about her father not being a gentleman. How she had degraded him! And he being a well-respected man in their community! It was then that Caroline had begun to actively work to hide her ties to trade and had begun to aspire to marry as wealthy and esteemed a gentleman as was possible. A title she knew was beyond her grasp, but the nephew of a man with a title seemed manageable. And now, that man was betrothed to a lady whom Caroline had treated almost as badly as Miss Smith had treated her. Caroline had not been vocal in her criticism of the Bennets in public, but in private, she had not held her tongue.

Caroline jumped when Louisa poked her in the side with her elbow.

"It is time to leave," Louisa hissed. "Are you certain you are well?"

Caroline blinked and nodded. "I was merely woolgathering."

"In church?"

"I know," Caroline whispered, "Mama would scold."

"And with good reason," Louisa agreed.

Caroline rose and checked the fastening on her pelisse and fiddled with her gloves, making certain they were on snugly as she followed Charles out of the church. They would, no doubt, stand around for a few minutes and talk with the Bennets.

She was not wrong. Charles headed directly for Jane. Caroline sighed. That was what she wanted — a gentleman who longed to be with her and loved her as her brother loved Miss Bennet. It mattered not if he were the captain of a merchant ship or a tenant farmer, though she would prefer him to have an estate.

"Miss Bennet, Miss Elizabeth," she said as she joined them. "I would be very pleased if you would do me the honour of dining with us tonight."

"You would be?"

Caroline gave her brother a pointed look. "Yes, I would be. It is not long until your marriage, and I thought it might be pleasant to give Miss Bennet a tour of Netherfield."

Charles's brows drew together. "That would be pleasant."

Caroline smiled and turned to Jane. "Will you come?"

"She most certainly will," Mrs. Bennet replied.

"And you, Miss Elizabeth? Will you also join us?"

"Yes, I would like that."

Though Elizabeth's words were confident, her eyes held a certain amount of skepticism. Caroline could not fault her for that. They had not been on very friendly terms, and Caroline had attempted to separate Elizabeth's sister from Charles. "I am glad." She turned to Charles. "I will await you in the carriage."

"I will not be long," he replied.

"Do not hurry on my account," she said. It was what would be the expected polite thing to be said, but to her, the words did not fall from her lips without meaning. She truly did not wish for him to rush away from Miss Bennet. He was so happy. How had she been willing to take that from him? It was abominable to treat another in such a fashion — especially a brother one loved dearly.

"You are different," Louisa commented as they walked to the carriage.

"Am I?"

"Yes," replied Louisa. "Hurst, do you not think Caroline changed?"

Louisa's husband shrugged. "She seems friendlier if that is what you mean."

"Yes, yes, that is it exactly!" Louisa cried.

"Miss Bennet is to be our sister, and Miss Elizabeth is to be Darcy's wife. It seems only fitting that we should become friends."

"No, no, it is more than that. You have been friendlier, more contemplative, and well, just more as you used to be before Father died," Louisa said. "It is more than just accepting our fate."

Caroline chuckled. It had a lot to do with accepting her fate. In fact, it had everything to do with accepting that she was the daughter of a tradesman who could run a home as well as any gentleman's daughter, that she was a sister who wished to see her brother happy no matter the lineage of the lady he loved, that she had never been able to capture the heart of a wealthy nephew of an earl, and that she loved a man who was not at all the sort she would choose but was precisely the sort she wished to hear say he was proud of her. Of course, she would not say any of that to her sister.

~*~*~

Everyone had returned from church and eaten their meal before Richard dared venture from his room. His head was beginning to clear, and he was tired of the same four walls and vistas from his window. Quietly, he snuck down the servant's stairs and to the library. He sat down and picked up his book, then noting the fact that the last time he had sat in this chair he had been reading to Caroline, he moved himself to a chair as far from the hearth as possible. Satisfied that in this new location he would not see her image if he should glance up from his reading, he opened his book and began to read. He had consumed two chapters and was beginning to think that lighting a lamp would soon be necessary when the door to the library opened and the vision he did not want to see walked into the room.

He snapped his book closed and rose to leave.

"Colonel, you are out of bed." Caroline greeted him with a smile.

"I was about to return to my bed," he answered. He was not really going to return to bed, but it seemed a good prevarication to aid him in his escape.

Her smile faded. "Are you truly unwell? The apothecary can be called."

"Too much brandy is all," he answered honestly. "Time and quiet are all that are needed to be cured."

"Then you stay. I can read elsewhere," she suggested. "Indeed, I should likely read in my room, so that I can easily prepare for my guests when it is time."

"Guests?" he questioned.

"Miss Bennet and Miss Elizabeth. I have invited them for dinner and a tour of the house. It will be Miss Bennet's home soon." She looked hopefully at him.

"You are correct, and it is a fine thing you are doing. I know it is not easy for you to accept them."

"No," Caroline said quickly, "oddly it is not difficult at all."

"It is not?"

Caroline shook her head. "I have been doing a great deal

of thinking lately, and a friend has taught me to look at things differently from the way I did."

"I am glad." He needed to be away from her. "I fear I must be abrupt and take my leave, but my head is throbbing." It wasn't, but it was better to say it was his head and not his heart.

"Oh, certainly. I should not have detained you."

"You did not. Enjoy your reading and your company." He gave her a small bow and left the room quickly before his heart could keep him there longer. Quickly, he made his way toward he servant's stairs and was halfway up them and drawing close to the safety of his room when...

"Sir."

Richard stopped and turned toward the footman who had called to him.

"A letter for you sir," the footman said as he bounded up the stairs two at a time.

Richard took the letter from the man. "Has the rider been paid?"

"He has."

"Very good. Thank you."

The footman descended the stairs as Richard turned the letter he held over in his hands. Why was his father sending him an express? He broke the seal as he walked down the hall.

Son,

It is my grievous business to inform you that your mother's brother, the one after whom you were named, has died. I am in receipt of some documents which will be of interest to you and pertain to your future. Your mother is telling me to say that you are to dispose of your commission as soon as is possible. You will understand her demand in a moment after she has given me the liberty to impart the news I need to share. There, she is gone to examine some gown that your sister has received but is not pleased with. I will make this brief as it is likely I will be called upon soon to witness whatever travesty has occurred.

Your uncle, as you know, inherited your grandfather's estate on his passing with the stipulation that on your uncle's demise, the estate be passed on to your mother's second son. Your grandfather and your uncle both knew that your brother would have no need of such an estate. Therefore, you were selected to be the recipient of the inheritance.

Your mother has indeed reappeared. The tragedy of fashion was remedied by a well-placed flower. Along with resigning your commission, your mother insists you find a wife.

I will close now before your mother can add any more demands to this missive. However, I will add an admonishment. Your mother will most likely attempt to select a wife for you, but I will tell you as I have told Darcy and your brother. It is far more pleasant to wrap your arms around a *lady you love rather than either her pedigree or fortune. Do not just find a wife, my son. Find happiness as I have done with your mother.*

Send me whatever might be necessary to begin the process of disposing of your commission. Your mother will not rest until that is begun.

Give my love to Darcy and Georgiana.

Your Father,

HF, LM

Richard shook his head and read the letter again. An estate. He was now in possession of an estate? He was no longer wanting. He tossed the letter and his book on the bed and turned to run down to the library to share the news with Caroline. She would have no reason to refuse him now. However, he made it no further than the door when he realized that he did not wish to be accepted because of his estate any more than he wished to be rejected for not having one.

His shoulders sagged. How was he to remain here with her for another week and two days without telling her his news? He was certain his heart would not keep it a secret if it saw that sharing the tale could earn him the happiness he wished to claim.

He paced to the window and looked out into the growing darkness of the winter evening. He turned and leaned against the window frame as his eyes wandered the room coming to rest at last on his father's letter. That was it. He would return to London and begin the transfer of his commission. Tomorrow, Wickham would be gone. Georgiana would be safe, and he would no longer be needed. He looked out the window once more. No branches swayed, and the moon would rise full and bright in a clear sky. Yes, he would return to London, and he would go tonight.

Chapter 13

Caroline placed her wine glass on the table. Charles had suggested that they eat first and tour after. Then, if time allowed, they could play cards. Caroline had declared it an excellent plan with Louisa seconding the approval.

And so, they had eaten.

"Are preparations progressing well for the wedding breakfast?" Caroline asked Jane.

"Yes. Very well. Mama and Aunt Gardiner seem to have every detail of the breakfast as well as the wedding itself well in hand," Jane replied. "Aunt Gardiner is going to extend her stay. It was always their plan to return to town tomorrow, but now, Uncle will go without her and the children. However, he will come again in time for the wedding."

"I do hope the weather cooperates," Caroline replied. "It can be so unpredictable, but at this time of year, it seems worse."

They lapsed into silence for a few moments.

"Will you be returning to town after the wedding?" Elizabeth asked Caroline. "I would assume you would not wish to miss the season. I have never had one, but I hear tell that it can be very entertaining if one likes to dance."

Caroline did not miss the impertinent look Elizabeth gave Darcy. It still surprised her how relaxed Darcy was and just how much he could tease and be teased.

"I do enjoy a good soiree with dancing," Caroline said with a smile. "So, yes, I will be leaving with Louisa and Hurst. After all, I am not yet married, so whether I like participating in the season or not, it is my duty. It is just fortunate that I enjoy it and do not find it to be a burden."

"That is good," Elizabeth agreed.

Caroline's brows furrowed slightly at the silent communication that passed between Elizabeth and Darcy and then Darcy and Georgiana following her comments. Where they assessing her ability to find a husband? Or was it something else?

"I think I will find the season to be somewhat overwhelming when I finally get my turn," Georgiana said. "I do not like being scrutinized."

"You will perform magnificently!"

Caroline cringed slightly at the volume her sister used. It had never before bothered her how Louisa spoke in that particular tone and so loudly when in company, but then recently, many things had begun to bother her, much as they had when she was young.

"You do not have any deficits to overcome," Louisa continued. "You are well-connected and have a good fortune. There shall be many wishing to call on you."

"I would imagine that would be overwhelming," Caroline said with a pointed look for her sister. How did she not understand that? "Not everyone enjoys calls as much as you do, Louisa."

"Do they not?" Louisa looked up and down the table. "I suppose the gentlemen do not all enjoy them, but I never heard of a lady not delighting in calls."

"That is likely because a lady is not supposed to admit she does not enjoy them," Elizabeth inserted.

"Precisely so."

Elizabeth's eyes grew wide at Caroline's agreement.

"I dreaded them for a time," Caroline admitted.

"You did? I am certain I do not remember such a thing," said Louisa.

"It was after that dinner with Miss Smith."

"Oh! She was dreadful!" Louisa cried.

"She was," Caroline agreed. "You see, Miss Darcy, although my fortune is not insignificant, I do not have the connections you do, and my fortune does not come from land — a fact Miss Smith enjoyed proclaiming frequently and loudly."

Caroline placed her fork and knife on her plate, took a sip of her wine, and turned to Elizabeth. There was something she needed to do and had been pondering since arriving home from church this morning. It would cost a pretty penny in pride, but it could not and should not be avoided. "I am afraid I have become Miss Smith. I have not spoken well of you or family. I have criticized them as well as your lack of fortune. For these things, I must apologize. It was wrong."

Out of the corner of her eye, Caroline saw Louisa's mouth drop open.

"It has been pointed out to me by a friend that kindness has become somewhat of a weakness for me, and I am trying to improve," she explained quietly.

"It is a good friend who will help one improve," Darcy said.

Caroline smiled at him. "A very good friend, and one I should not like to disappoint." There. She had admitted aloud both her desire to be what Colonel Fitzwilliam kept insisting she was and that doing so was of great importance to her. Extreme importance. It was always best to be the sort of wife your husband wished to have, was it not? And if she could manage it, she would be Mrs. Fitzwilliam. She wanted no other husband — not Darcy, not some gentleman like Darcy with a great estate and goodly fortune, not even a lord would do. Only Colonel Fitzwilliam.

Darcy's smile in reply was knowing, and Caroline dipped her head slightly. Being forthright about such things was more difficult when the desired outcome was so dear to one's heart. She had declared her intention to marry Darcy many times — not to him, of course, but to her sister. Yet, not one of those declarations had ever caused her stomach to twist with fear that it might not come to pass, and she had been aware that she might not be successful in capturing Mr. Darcy. However, her heart had never been affected as it was now.

"Your apology is most readily accepted, is it not, Jane?" Elizabeth said.

"Oh, yes, of course."

"Thank you." Caroline drew a breath and released it. Then, putting away the awkwardness she felt, she lifted her chin, and, after making a sweeping glance up and down the table to ensure that everyone had finished eating, she said, "If we are all ready, we could begin our tour now."

"Shall we begin in the dining room?" Bingley asked with a chuckle as he rose. "One moment," he whispered to Jane before turning to Caroline and drawing her away a little. "I know that what you said to Miss Elizabeth was not easily done, and I am proud of you." He lowered his voice further. "I suspect your friend would be as well if he were not indisposed."

Caroline's cheeks flushed as she mumbled her thanks.

"Let's begin on the upper levels," her brother suggested, "and then return to the drawing room at the end. I shall instruct someone that refreshments, as well as the card tables, are to be laid out. Would that be acceptable?"

"It is your home," Caroline replied. "It shall be done however you wish."

"It is still your home, too."

Caroline shook her head. "Not for very long and that is as it should be." She grasped one of his hands and gave it a squeeze. "However, I will lead this tour."

He laughed. "And you will likely do it far better than I ever could."

"Quite likely," Caroline agreed. Then, returning to their guests, she declared that they would begin with the bedrooms.

~*~*~

The group made their way down the hall, looking into each room for a moment, commenting on the decor, and listening to Louisa give suggestions on how things could be improved.

"I am sorry to say we will not get a look at this room since the colonel is indisposed. However, it looks very much like the others," Caroline explained, "except the dressing room is to the left here instead of to the right. The furnishings are similar in style to those in the other rooms, but the decor is green with some wheat coloured accents. It is really quite lovely."

"Indeed, it is," Louisa chirped.

"Oh!" Caroline said in surprise as the door before her opened, revealing the colonel's man. Her brows furrowed.

"What are you doing?" she asked as her eyes took in his outerwear and came to rest on the bag he carried.

"What the colonel ordered, ma'am," he replied with a nod as he made to move past her.

"Where are you taking his bag?" She could not keep herself from asking.

"To the stables, ma'am, and then London."

Caroline's hand flew to her heart. "I beg your pardon? The colonel is leaving?"

"Yes, ma'am."

"Without taking a proper leave?" Her heart was beating rapidly first from the shock of the news, and now, from the anger she felt at his creeping away.

"He left a note, ma'am. I was to give it to your maid." He placed the bag next to his feet and, digging inside his coat, withdrew a missive. "There you are, ma'am."

"Did he say why he was leaving?" Georgiana came to stand next to Caroline.

The colonel's man shook his head. "I did not ask. I just do as he tells me."

Caroline unfolded the note she had been given and moved away from the rest of the group, although Georgiana followed.

Miss Bingley,

I wish to express my gratitude for the hospitality and friendship you have shown me during my stay. As you know, W will be gone as of tomorrow and will no longer pose a threat to Georgie. Therefore, my services are no longer needed.

Again, thank you for providing such fine accommodations and companionship. You will do well as the mistress of your own estate one day. Would that I had one to offer.

R.F.

Would that I had one to offer? She passed the note to Georgiana. He would not offer for her because he did not have an estate? She shook her head. No. She would not allow it.

"Charles, Louisa, you will have to continue without me," she said as she made her way toward the stairs.

"Where are you going?" Louisa called after her.

"To the stables."

"Whatever for?"

Caroline stopped and turned toward her sister. "To stop the colonel from leaving unless he has a better reason than the sorry one he gave in that note."

"Oh," Louisa shrank back a bit at Caroline's sharp tone. "Take a coat," she called.

"I haven't time," Caroline shouted back. "I may already be too late," she said to herself.

"The door!" she called as she rushed down the stairs. "Get the door!" She rubbed her arms as the chill of the night air raced into the house and up the stairs to greet her. It was not a warm night. She dashed into the drawing room and snatched the small blanket Louisa kept there. Then, wrapping it around her shoulders, she ran from the house and down the path to the stables.

"Colonel Fitzwilliam!" she shouted as she drew near to the stables and saw him pacing and looking toward the back of the house.

"Miss Bingley," he said in surprise, drawing to an abrupt stop at her call.

Caroline ran the last few steps to where he stood. Next to him, a groomsman was readying a horse for travel. "John, if you wish to retain your position, you will cease your work at once," she snapped at the groomsman. "The colonel is not leaving."

"I am."

"No, you are not. At least, not on that horse."

"I can ready that horse myself, you know." Richard crossed his arms and glared at her.

Caroline raised a brow at his response and turned to the groomsman once again. "John, do not let the colonel near any of the horses unless I say you may, or, I promise you, your position will be at an end."

"Yes, miss."

"You think he can stop me?" Richard said incredulously, looking at the lad.

"No, I do not. However, I do know that your honour will

not allow John to be turned away because of your foolishness."

Richard shrugged and huffed. She was right. He would never willingly be the cause of a man's losing his position unless the reason was justified. His need to escape, though compelling, was not a justifiable reason.

"Offer," she demanded.

Richard blinked. "Pardon?"

"Offer yourself to me — just as you are." She stepped closer to him as he shook his head and lowered his eyes to look at something on the ground. "Your note said you wished you had an estate to offer me, but I do not want an estate."

His brows furrowed, and he looked up at her. "You do not? But you told your sister that you wanted a gentleman with an estate and a fortune and that you did not want a soldier."

Oh, her heart sighed. "You heard that?"

"Yes."

"It is what I thought I wanted, but I was wrong." She stepped closer to him again. "As I lay in bed last night attempting to convince myself that it was still what I wanted, I came to the realization that that for which I truly longed was you." She shrugged in response to his questioning, searching look. "I did not fear being poor. We would not be. My fortune is ample, and you are not penniless. I feared being a widow."

Seeing the tears that glistened in her eyes, he wrapped his arms around her and pulled her to his chest as she continued speaking.

"But I would rather have you for only a short time and endure the heart-shattering pain of losing you than to have never had you at all. I love you."

"Oh, Caroline," he whispered. "You cannot love me half as much as I love you."

"Then offer for me. Make me your wife."

He pulled back and looked down at her. "You would take me just as I am, a second son who must earn his keep?"

"Yes. Gladly."

He bent and brush her lips with his. "Marry me?"

"With pleasure, Colonel."

He kissed her again. "Call me Richard, for I shall not be a colonel much longer."

Her eyes narrowed. "What do you mean?"

He kissed her once more, then reached inside his coat and handed her the letter from his father. "It seems I have inherited an estate."

She looked wide-eyed from the letter she held to him and back to the letter. The light from the lanterns was poor, but there was enough of it so that she could make out most of what the letter said. "You were leaving even though you had an estate?"

He shrugged and nodded.

"Why?"

"I did not wish to be accepted just because I had an estate and, I suspect, since my mother's family was not poor, a reasonable fortune. I knew if I stayed, I would not be able to keep this news from you nor would I be able to stop myself from declaring my love for you, and then, I would never know if you chose me for me or for my estate."

Caroline shook her head. Were men always so daft? "Did you expect to keep the news from me forever or had you just decided that you did not wish to marry me?"

Richard's face scrunched up as he thought about that. "I guess I had not thought beyond needing to be away from you."

Caroline raised a brow.

"Because you tempt me so greatly."

Caroline's other brow joined the first.

"I had a significant amount of brandy last night. My brain was not clear when I made my decision. In fact, it is still a bit foggy now."

A smile tipped the right corner of Caroline's mouth. "Whether your brain has been clouded by alcohol or not, I will not be releasing you from our understanding when it does clear, Colonel."

"Richard," he corrected.

She shook her head as her smile spread. "You will

always be my colonel. Now, it is cold, and I would like to go warm myself by the fire."

"But I have a commission of which to dispense," he protested.

"There are writing supplies in the library. A letter can be sent just as your father said. Come along, Colonel, and, John, put that horse away."

"Yes, miss," the lad replied.

"You are not still thinking of leaving me, are you?" Caroline tipped her head and looked over her shoulder at him when he did not move to follow her.

"Never," he replied, closing the distance between them. "You, my dear, will never be rid of me." He pulled her into his embrace.

"That is excellent news," she replied as he bent to claim her lips.

Chapter 14

"Miss Bingley! Colonel Fitzwilliam!" Mrs. Bennet cried as the two entered the drawing room at Longbourn on Monday. "I hear that congratulations might be in order?" Her brows were lifted halfway to the ruffle on her cap, and one could almost feel the excitement radiating from her as she waited in anticipation of their reply.

"Indeed, they are," Bingley supplied as he took a seat near Jane.

Mrs. Bennet clapped her hands in delight and led Caroline and Richard to two seats near her. "A colonel is a fine catch," she said to Caroline. "Why if my Lydia could capture such a man, I would be delighted! And there is no reason that she should not. After all, she is far prettier than Mrs. Forester and twice as lively," she added in a low whisper with a waggle of her brows.

"Would she mind following the drum or would she prefer to wait at home for her husband to return?" Richard asked.

Mrs. Bennet blinked. "I beg your pardon, but she would

not be marrying a man in the regulars." She shook her head. "I do not mean to offend, Colonel Fitzwilliam, but the militia is preferable to a mother. Colonel Forester has a piece of land that will be his one day, you know."

"I did not know, though I suspected," Richard replied. "However, the fact stands that the life of the wife of a military man is not one of ease. There are always dangers. Why just last week there was more talk of unrest in the north, and, according to my father, it will not be long before the government attempts to put severe measures in place for those convicted of frame breaking. I would suspect that men attempting to escape the noose will become more violent and not less, and who do you think will be called upon to help maintain the law. " He crossed his ankles and folded his arms as he made himself comfortable in his chair. "The regulars who are not deployed elsewhere will no doubt be made useful, but I am equally as certain the militia will not be left standing. They will very much be a part of the effort."

Mrs. Bennet's eyes grew wide, and her handkerchief fluttered for a moment. Then it stilled, and she turned toward Lydia. "Oliver Lucas," she said. "Make certain you dance with him at Mr. Bingley's soiree on Twelfth Night. Twice if you can manage it."

"Mama!" Lydia cried. "Not Oliver."

"There is nothing wrong with Mr. Lucas. He will inherit his father's land, and you would be located so near to me."

"Mama," Lydia whined. "He is nearly thirty."

"He is not," Mary replied. "He is a year younger than Charlotte, and six and twenty is not nearly thirty. Besides, it would do you well to have a gentleman of some maturity to curtail your foolishness."

Lydia gasped and huffed as she turned pleading eyes toward her mother.

"It is not often I say this," said Mrs. Bennet, "but Mary is right."

"You cannot mean it!"

"I do," Lydia's mother assured her.

"If only Mr. Wickham had not left." Lydia cast a displeased look at Colonel Fitzwilliam.

"That skirt chaser!" Mrs. Bennet shook her head. "Lady Lucas said that Mrs. Goulding saw him accosting Mrs. Fletcher's maid not two days ago. Good riddance is what I say to him." She turned to Caroline. "Shocking it was to hear such a thing! He seemed a proper sort of fellow, so charming and handsome."

"He does appear to be that," Caroline agreed.

"But I have heard the same about him myself," Louisa added and then lowered her voice as she leaned toward Mrs. Bennet. "I should not say it in such company as we are in at present, but I would not be surprised to find, come summer, he has left a child behind."

Caroline wished to laugh. How had she been so condemning of Mrs. Bennet and her incessant need to gossip when Louisa was just as bad?

"I would not be surprised in the least," Colonel Fitzwilliam agreed. "It is a pleasant day," he added, abruptly changing the subject. "Miss Bingley, Mrs. Hurst and I had a lovely drive before we arrived here. There is a prominence to the west that Miss Bingley said it might be Oakham Mount."

"Oh, indeed," Mrs. Bennet assured him. "It is a beautiful place for a walk in fine weather, not that I have been there in years. When we were first married, Mr. Bennet and I would often walk there." She sighed. "Perhaps I will have more time for such leisurely pursuits this spring since there will be fewer people about for whom to care."

Caroline smiled at the woman's wistful tone. For all that the lady seemed oblivious to her daughters and their behaviour, she was not, it seemed, without affection for them.

"Your brother and I will visit, and we will take the children for a picnic," Mrs. Gardiner suggested. "And if the Bingleys remain at Netherfield, perhaps they will wish to join us."

Mrs. Bennet sighed once more. "I shall not be able to go there without thinking of my Lizzy. She loves that place."

"I do," Elizabeth agreed. "But that is all the more reason to frequent it often, for me."

"And then Mary can write to you all about it." Mrs.

Bennet seemed to be regaining her spirit and leaving her morose behind.

Mary willingly agreed that she would take up such a task and then the conversation turned to fond memories of places Darcy, Bingley, and Richard had frequented when young. Richard, much to Darcy's chagrin, even shared a tale of when he and Darcy had gotten into a scrape while climbing trees and how Darcy had returned home with rips in his breeches after getting caught on some branches.

To Caroline's surprise, the visit was rather pleasant and was soon over. It had not dragged on interminably as she had feared it would, nor had she found Mrs. Bennet completely unbearable — partially, but not completely.

"You did very well," Richard said as he settled onto the bench next to her in the carriage. Louisa had insisted that it was improper for him to sit with Caroline, but Richard refused to be moved on the subject. And now, he was being glared at by Mrs. Hurst.

"As did you, once we got past the bit about marrying a colonel. I happen to think marrying a colonel is a very fine idea." Caroline gave him a disapproving look.

"Miss Lydia would make a deplorable officer's wife, so I did my part to spare the kingdom of such a travesty." He lifted her hand and kissed her gloved knuckles as she rolled her eyes at him. "However, it seems I have perhaps put Mr. Lucas in a difficult position. Do either of you know him? I have not met that many residents in the area, just the ones who have called at Netherfield, and Mr. Lucas was not among them."

"We have met all the Lucases," Caroline assured him. "Sir William was not shy in putting forward everyone of his acquaintance when we arrive in the autumn. Mr. Lucas struck me as a quiet, thoughtful gentleman."

"And he is not an altogether unpleasant gentleman at whom to gaze," Louisa added. "He is not handsome in the classical sense, but he is a fair bit more than tolerable. His smile and teeth are good. He is of a good height, though a trifle on the tall side of what I would prefer." She paused and tipped her head to the side. "If he wore a longer jacket perhaps the disparity between the length of his legs and the rest of him would be less obvious. It is not a very great disparity, but it is a small grievance. And, if he would wear something other than brown! He was in the same muddy brown jacket every time we saw him, was he not, Caroline?"

"I do not remember."

"I know it is true. Someone should suggest blue. He would look charming in blue with a waterfall cravat. Yes, that is how he would look best. Then, even Miss Lydia would not turn up her nose at him. I shall tell Charles to mention it to him."

"Louisa," Caroline chided. "It is not for you to be giving fashion advice to everyone you meet, and listen to you! I thought you were not fond of this area or its residents."

"I am not," Louisa answered. "However, Charles will insist on presenting all the Bennets to society, and I find it would be best if Miss Lydia found her happiness here, near her mother and far away from town."

Richard chuckled. "Miss Lydia would take the town and its gossip rags by storm, would she not?

"Precisely!" Louisa turned to look out the window.

"You did not tell them of your good fortune," Caroline said quietly to Richard.

Richard shrugged. "She already knew. Did she not congratulate us upon entering?"

Caroline smiled. "That is not what I meant."

He shrugged again. "It is not settled yet."

"But it will be."

He nodded. "Are you certain you accepted me and not my estate?" He winked at her.

"Seeing as you were hiding your estate from me, I most certainly did not accept you for your estate."

He chuckled and lifted her fingers to his lips once again.

"Take a turn in the garden with me," he said as the carriage stopped in front of Netherfield.

"A short one, but then, I wish to find a chair in the library and read. Will you join me?"

"Gladly."

So, the two disembarked the carriage and walked a slow circuit of the garden, stopping now and then, when there was a tree or some structure to obscure the view, at least, in part, to punctuate their new-found love with a kiss before retiring to the library.

~*~*~

For the next week, life settled into a similar pattern. Caroline insisted upon calling on Lady Lucas and Mrs. Philips as well as at Longbourn. On each call, Richard sat by her side in the carriage as well as the sitting room. And on each occasion, he told her how well she had done. And if the weather permitted, they would upon their return take a walk in the garden and then tuck themselves away in the library. Bingley would poke his head inside the open door when he returned from Longbourn with some teasing comment for Richard and a smile for his sister.

However, not all was tranquil and serene. There was a ball for which to prepare. Recipes had to be approved, as did decor and music. The cleaning and arranging of the ballroom were of utmost importance.

"You are a marvel," Richard whispered in Caroline's ear as he came up behind her at the door to the ballroom.

Caroline's hand flew to her heart. "Must you insist on startling me?"

"I assure you it was not intentional."

If his eyes had not sparkled with amusement in contradiction to his words, perhaps she would have believed his penitent look. But as it was, she could only shake her head and mutter about his incorrigibility.

"I have seen my mother prepare for a night such as this,"

he said, taking her hand and placing it on his arm. "I can assure you that she is never so calm as you are at this moment, nor are her preparations without several moments of drama and distress. I admit I had thought you would be the same, but I was wrong."

"Why did you expect me to be the same?" Caroline asked as they began to take a turn around the ballroom to inspect everything one last time.

He grimaced. "I will not say this well."

"Just say it."

"Before this trip to Netherfield, I had always considered you just as I did most of the ladies of the ton. Sharp, demanding, arrogant, and the like."

"And is that how you would classify your mother?" she asked in surprise.

"I told you I would not say this well," he retorted. "My mother can be demanding and aloof at times, but she is rarely sharp. However, I just assumed that if one fits the mold of a lady of the ton, then...well..." His brows furrowed. "It is foolish. Of course, similarities in some areas do not mean likenesses in all."

"Did brandy have anything to do with this logic?"

He chuckled. "It may have."

"Did you receive word from your father today regarding your commission? I saw the express rider when we were arranging these plants." They stood near a group of plants which were placed near a window overlooking the front of the house.

"It is in progress, though I am not a free man yet." He sighed. "I will have to return to town in two days. My presence is required for some paperwork, and my unit will be expecting me until someone else has taken my place."

"I will be in town in two week's time, after the wedding."

"And just a month before ours," he said with a grin. "However, I will be returning to you before the wedding. My cousin is not getting married without his family present. My father said as much in his letter."

Caroline smiled. She had learned so much about how different the Fitzwilliam family was from what she expected of a titled family. She was not certain why she thought they would all be standoffish and cold. Perhaps it was because she had met several ladies at school whose family were that way. Her logic was, she realized, just as faulty as Richard's had been about the ladies of the ton. "Did he say anything about your plans to marry?"

"He is delighted and cannot wait to meet the Miss Bingley whom I have described to him." His smile was sheepish. "I have not always spoken highly of you, I am afraid, so I have had to do a great deal of explaining in my letters."

"I have not been worthy of praise," Caroline admitted. She had thought she was. She was accomplished, attractive, rich, and knew how to navigate the ton. All those things had been, in her mind, worthy of praise, but now?

Now, she knew differently. It was as Mrs. Annesley had said when they were last gathered in the drawing room at Darcy House the day that Caroline's hopes of securing the husband she thought she desired had been crushed and the adventure to realizing that the husband she knew she desired and who desired her had begun. Civility and kindness were not the marks of birth but of character. Her character had been sadly wanting for some time and might have still been wanting had it not been for a particular, persistent, annoying, demanding colonel. The same colonel whose current silence was a telling agreement. "However, I am now, and I shall strive to always be."

"And I shall strive to be worthy of you," he replied.

She shook her head. "No, my dear colonel, you have nothing for which to strive because you have always been worthy of me, and as long as you continue to love me as you do now and will remind me of what is truly praiseworthy should I drift away from my path, you will continue to be worthy of me."

"Even if the house on the estate is ghastly and in need of great quantities of money to repair?"

"Even if we must live in a cottage while it is being repaired," she replied. "As long as I have you, I have everything I will ever need." Her lips turned up and impertinence lit her eyes. "Of course, a new dress at least twice a year would also be good."

"All that I have is yours," he replied with a laugh. "I

just hope it includes a dress or two." He pulled her into an alcove and into his embrace as the musicians began some tuning.

"I truly only wish for you."

"And I you." He kissed her upturned nose. "I am so grateful that I took up Elizabeth's challenge and began to decipher who you really are."

"We shall have to name a daughter for her," Caroline said with a laugh. Then she shook her head. "I cannot say that I ever thought I would say anything complimentary about Elizabeth Bennet; however, instead of owing her my misery at having lost Pemberley, I must thank her for the blessing of my colonel."

Richard dipped his head and captured her lips. "Are you ready to greet your guests, Miss Bingley?"

She nodded and, affixing her glittery, sparkling mask, allowed him to lead her to the entrance hall where her brother, Jane, Darcy, and Elizabeth waited.

Tonight, they would not just celebrate Twelfth Night but also their coming marriages. Music would be played, guests would dance, food would be eaten, and all the gossips of Meryton would talk in hushed tones and loud whispers for some time to come about the splendour of the masque ball held at Netherfield. But for one lady, the splendor of the ball and her success in hosting it would pale in comparison to the radiance of making her debut as the lady she longed to be with the colonel whom she loved at her side on this one winter's eve.

A Scandal in Springtime

Springtime

A tale of insults, apologies, and kisses

Chapter 1

Kitty Bennet paused at the case containing the lace and brooches. There was a piece of lace intricately woven with leaves and flowers swirling along the edge and filling in the body which she would dearly like to purchase so that she could add it to her scarf. Just on the shelf above the lace was a brooch comprised of many tiny pearls which would be perfect for holding the scarf in place.

Perhaps next week when Uncle gave her the allowance her father had sent to him, she would have enough to purchase those two items so that she could wear them to church on Easter Sunday.

"Catherine."

Kitty jumped, her cheeks warming with embarrassment. "Forgive me, Uncle. I was distracted." Thankfully, even though her uncle had used her full name, he did not look put out. "That brooch is just so pretty," she added as she hurried to catch up to him.

"I am certain it is," he replied. "Although I am certain your aunt would know better, my dear."

"Do you think we can bring Aunt with us next time?"

The establishment through which they were walking was a new store that her uncle had said was nearly ready to open. And it appeared he was right, for the cases and shelves were filled with goods, the windows were being washed, and the floor looked as if it had already been polished.

Her uncle chuckled. "I am quite certain your aunt will demand it."

Kitty was not yet completely comfortable with her aunt and uncle – at least, not in the way her older sisters had always been. Jane and Elizabeth were always so at ease whenever the Gardiners visited Longbourn, but that was likely because they had spent so many visits with the Gardiners in town. However, now that her older sisters were married, that was about to change.

She and Mary were to take turns visiting their relations, for their mother hoped that in sending them to London, her remaining unattached daughters might happen upon some nice young gentlemen who would marry them and relieve Mrs. Bennet of two more worries. There was no more significant worry for a mother than to see her daughters well-cared-for. That is what Mama had always said.

Kitty put all thoughts of scarves and brooches, as well as handsome young gentlemen, away as she stood behind her uncle while he knocked at the door to the store's office before opening it when someone inside called *come in*.

"Mr. Gardiner, it is good to see you. With what can I help you?"

"Not a thing, Mr. Durward," her uncle replied. "My wife insisted that we deliver a basket of muffins to you as a gift of goodwill for the success of your store."

He looked at Kitty. "The basket," he whispered.

"I do apologize." Her cheeks burned once again with embarrassment, and she spared a quick glance for Mr. Durward. "I was distracted." How could she not be? The gentleman standing in front of the desk, the one who was not Mr. Durward, was far too attractive not to be distracting.

Her uncle chuckled. "This store seems to have that effect on you."

He took the basket from her and placed it on the desk. "There is one case containing brooches that my niece found of great interest. I think you will have a sale on your first day even if no one else enters the store."

"I am happy to hear it," Mr. Durward said with a friendly smile for Kitty. "Please be seated," he offered.

"I am afraid we are not able to stay today," Mr. Gardiner replied. "There are a few other errands which need our attention. However, Kitty and I wanted to see the basket delivered first." His brow furrowed. "I seem to have forgotten that you have not yet met my niece. This pretty young lady is Miss Catherine Bennet, and she is our houseguest for a few weeks this spring. Kitty, this is Mr. Durward and one of his partners, Mr. Waller."

Kitty dipped a curtsey. "It is lovely to meet you and to see your store. It is very well done up."

"Thank you," Mr. Durward replied, and Kitty found herself compelled once again to remove her eyes from Mr. Waller — handsome, tall Mr. Waller with his golden hair and piercing blue eyes.

"Have you settled into the apartment above?" Mr. Gardiner asked.

Mr. Waller lived here? Kitty's heart sank a trifle at the thought. She probably should not like him if he lived above a store. Mama might not approve.

"I have, and I have even employed a maid and a cook. It is a luxury I have not allowed myself until now. However, I think, even with the extra expense, I shall still be able to save the money I need to secure my future."

That seemed a funny thing for a gentleman to say, and Kitty wondered what it meant. However, she knew better than to ask. It was not right to be nosey, and while in town, Kitty intended to behave properly.

Here, she was not Lydia's sister. Indeed, she was no one's sister when she was alone with her aunt and uncle even if she still had to be Elizabeth's sister when she was attending one function or another with the Darcy's. However, it was not so bad to say that Mrs. Darcy was her sister for Mrs. Darcy was married. But Miss Kitty Bennet was not.

She was still thinking about how delightful it was to not be anyone's sister and have all the beaux to herself when her uncle said her full name – *Catherine* – once again.

"Forgive me," she muttered. She needed to work on not looking like such a distracted fool – especially when in the presence of a very handsome gentleman like Mr. Waller. At least, she had not been caught admiring him.

"It was a pleasure to meet you, Mr. Durward, Mr. Waller," Kitty said in parting before preceding her uncle out of the office as he motioned for her to do.

"You are excessively distracted today," her uncle said as he wrapped her arm around his.

He was likely holding her hand on his arm to keep her from peering into any more of the cases. It was a far more enjoyable way to have one's attention focused than scolding or teasing ever was. She liked how her uncle patted her hand as if he enjoyed having her at his side.

"I get lost in my thoughts sometimes," she admitted.

"And are these happy thoughts?"

She nodded. "Sometimes they are about real life and other times they are about... well... a great number of things that are not real at all."

"Stories?"

She looked at her uncle. He seemed the sort of gentleman who would not make fun of a lady for being less intelligent than Elizabeth, but she was not entirely sure he would not tease her for dreaming up stories in her head. However, she nodded anyway. Lying was not proper, and in town, she was attempting to be proper.

"Would you like for me to stop at my warehouse and pick up a notebook for you in which to write these stories?"

"You would do that?" How shocking!

He nodded.

"You do not think it foolish of me to think up stories?"

He shook his head and held the door open for her. "Not at all. I quite enjoy reading."

So did Papa, but Kitty could not imagine him not saying writing stories was foolish. Stories did not seem to her to be scholarly enough to garner her father's approval. "They are very fanciful."

She waited for her uncle to change his mind about her thinking up stories, but he paid her no mind.

"We will be going to my warehouse," he told the driver before helping her into the carriage. "You do want the notebook, do you not?"

Kitty snapped her mouth closed and smiled while nodding. He was not going to change his mind. No wonder Elizabeth and Jane liked visiting Aunt and Uncle Gardiner so much!

"Uncle," she said as he took his seat, "I know it is not polite to inquire after things which are not my business, but I was wondering if it were possible for you to explain to me what Mr. Waller meant about saving to secure his future."

"Ah." Her uncle gave her a knowing look. "I am afraid that young man is well on his way to being married. He has only to earn enough money to please the young lady's father."

"Oh." That was disappointing. He was very handsome.

"I am sorry," Uncle Gardiner whispered.

"As am I," Kitty admitted. "His eyes are very blue."

Her uncle chuckled. "They are. However, I am certain you will meet with many handsome gentlemen while you are in town. Did you not dance with several when you attended that ball with Elizabeth?"

"Oh, I danced nearly every set and several of my partners were very handsome." She sighed. "However, none of them had eyes as blue as Mr. Waller's." She looked out the window at the passing buildings. Nor did any of them have hair the colour of spun gold.

"There is more to finding a good match than the colour of a gentleman's eyes," her uncle cautioned.

Kitty sighed. "I know. I must also consider his fortune."

"And his character," her uncle added with a raised brow. "No matter what your mother might tell you, a handsome character is far more important than a handsome fortune or face."

"Of course," she said quickly, her gaze dropping from looking at her uncle to her clasped hands.

"I am not reprimanding," Uncle Gardiner said softly. "At least, I am not reprimanding you. Your mother, however..." He chuckled. "She has raised five lovely daughters and prepared them quite well to oversee a household, but..." He paused. "Thinking deeply was never one of her strengths, and I fear, that in her exuberance to see you married to a husband who can keep you in fine dresses, she may have forgotten to instruct you about the qualities beyond face and fortune which qualify a gentleman as a good choice."

Kitty tipped her head and thought about that for a while. What had her mother taught her about how to choose a proper husband other than to seek one who was handsome and had a good income? Her eyebrows rose. Very little.

"I suppose he should be amiable," she said to her uncle. Mama did like agreeable gentlemen such as Mr. Bingley.

"That is a good quality," her uncle agreed. "Although amiability might be hidden at first."

Kitty nodded. "Like it was with Mr. Darcy."

Her uncle chuckled but did not disagree.

"Is there anything else you think a gentleman should be?" he asked.

She pulled her bottom lip between her teeth and sighed as she studied her gloved fingers. "I am not sure I know," she admitted with a shrug. "I wish for a handsome and amiable husband who has a good income."

The carriage began to slow. They were nearly to the warehouse.

"Those are excellent things for which to wish, but do not forget to find a gentleman who respects you and is kind."

"Oh, yes!" Why had she not thought of that? Of course, she did not want a husband who would make fun of her. Heaven knows she had endured enough of that in her life!

"And he should love you with his whole heart – to the point of death should he be separated from you."

Kitty blinked. She might have expected to hear such a statement from her aunt, but not from her uncle. He was a man. Men did not speak of such things. Did they?

"I see I have startled you," her uncle said. "I did not intend for my words to make you feel uneasy. I was just imagining what I would say to Priscilla if she were old enough to be seeking a husband."

He was thinking of her as his daughter? The idea wrapped around her, warm and comfortable, like a blanket made from the softest wool.

"At the risk of startling you more, that is how I feel about your aunt."

"It is?"

"Absolutely. I would be lost without her."

Oh, that was a very lovely thing! Kitty would most certainly like to marry a gentleman who felt that way about her.

"Then," Kitty said as the carriage door opened, "I suppose I must find a husband who is very much like you."

Chapter 2

It did not take too terribly long for Uncle Gardiner to do the things which needed doing at his warehouse. There had been some papers that needed his signature and a question about some tables and where they were to be placed.

After those matters had been seen to, he had taken out a box of notebooks and allowed Kitty to choose one.

There had been several in that crate which she wished she would have been able to take home. However, this one, this plain notebook with its brown binding and floral cover, had seemed the best choice. The ornate notebooks with their attached pencils were beautiful, but they would garner far more attention and curiosity than this one, and they had also contained fewer pages, which would not do at all as she had so very many thoughts she wished to write down.

She ran her hand over the nondescript front of her notebook with satisfaction as she sat in the carriage while her uncle gave a few last instructions to a man about some delivery. Uncle Gardiner certainly was a very busy man — even on a day when he was not officially working.

It was very different from how her father did things. It was not as if her father never stirred from his study. He did. He rode around the estate a few times a week. However, a lot of his business was conducted from his study. He did not have men pushing carts and crates to and fro. Nor did he have urgent papers, which must be signed today, thrust at him when he walked into his book room.

It was a very different life here in town compared to Longbourn. Everything was busier. There were so many more people here than Kitty was used to seeing. The streets were crowded, and travel was not rapid at all. Not even in a carriage. Or, she thought as she saw a young boy carrying a parcel race past, perhaps it was because they were in a carriage that travel was so slow. Be that as it may, she was positive she did not wish to be walking from place to place here, for there were so many streets she was sure to get lost.

"If you had a pencil, you could begin a story now," her uncle said as they started moving down the street. "I am anxious to read one."

Kitty smiled and blushed. "I am not certain they will be good enough to justify your anticipation." She had never before put her imagining down on paper. She was not even certain she knew how to do it, but she was determined to try.

"What shall the first one be about?" Her uncle looked out the window. "How about that man there? The one walking with the stuttering gait. He seems an interesting character."

Kitty pressed her nose against the glass to look back at the man. "Oh, he is interesting!" she cried. "Look at his coat. It looks as if it could have been a very nice coat at one time."

"But was it his when it was so fine, or did it belong to another?" Mr. Gardiner's eye sparkled with amusement. It was as if he was enjoying this game as much as she was.

"I think it must be a tragic story if it was his." She pursed her lips and furrowed her brow as she thought.

"Or," her uncle said, "it could be a disguise."

Kitty's eyes grew wide, and she could not help smiling from the excitement such a thought sent skittering across her skin. But the man's coat was not a disguise, as delicious as that idea was.

"A curse!" she cried. "He has been cursed by a princess and is doomed to wander the world in rags and with a hole in his boot – that is why he walks as he does – until he has paid his dues for some ill behaviour. Oh! I do wish I had a pencil!"

Mr. Gardiner chuckled. "And I must say my anticipation to read your story is growing by the minute. I should very much like to know what this gentleman did to receive his curse."

"That is a very good question." She had not thought that far into the story.

"His penance must be appropriate to his sin," her uncle added, his own brow furrowed as if he were actually contemplating something as fanciful as a story, which was both an odd and a delightful thing to Kitty.

"If he has stolen something or treated someone unjustly," Kitty said, "then he might have to restore four times the value of the stolen item or must endure life as the servant of an ogre until he can serve such a master with equanimity."

Her uncle nodded his head. "Those are excellent thoughts, but, unfortunately, we will have to continue our story later for I see Mrs. Verity's house from here. Do you have the items your aunt wished us to give to Mrs. Verity?"

Kitty placed her notebook on the bench next to her, tucked her story away in her mind, and picked up the parcel with the yellow ribbon.

~*~*~

"These are exceptional, as always," Mrs. Verity said after opening the package Kitty had given her. "But then, I have come to expect nothing less than exceptional from your aunt."

"She is very good at sewing," Kitty agreed. "I hope one day I can sew as neatly as she does."

"I hear you do very well now," her uncle said. "Your aunt has told me so," he added in response to her startled look. "Your mother has taught you well."

"Oh, it was not Mama who taught me," Kitty replied. "It was Jane."

"Indeed?"

Kitty nodded. "Mama was busy with Lydia."

"My sister has five daughters," Mr. Gardiner explained to Mrs. Verity.

"That is a lot of young ladies to teach." She winked at Kitty. "I should know. We have more than five here, but I am fortunate to have several helpers." She rose. "Would you like to meet my young men and ladies?"

"Oh, very much!"

"These," she said, tapping the papers Mr. Gardiner had given her, "I will look at later over a cup of tea. There are no surprises here, are there?"

"No, those are the particulars about the two apprenticeships that my wife told you about last time she was here. She would have brought them here herself, but..." He followed behind Mrs. Verity. "I had several things that needed doing today, and it is not often I get to spend the day with any of my nieces. It has been most pleasurable. However, I wonder if I might put upon both of you to accommodate me with something."

"Most certainly," Kitty said without hesitation. How could she not oblige him after he had been so generous in giving her a notebook and so understanding about her love of creating stories? He had endeared himself to her in a way that no one else had ever done by showing such interest in things that she liked.

"I have one more delivery to make to a gentleman only a few streets from here, and I was thinking that instead of hurrying Kitty through a tour, it might be better if she were to spend an hour and a half or thereabouts with you while I see to my delivery and return. She is very good with her cousins. I am certain your young ones would get on capitally with her."

Kitty sucked in a breath and waited to be granted permission to stay for so long. Elizabeth had told her about this place, and she was eager to see it.

"We are always happy to have willing volunteers," Mrs. Verity said. "I rarely send away anyone who wishes to help." She nodded to a handsome gentleman who had just entered the corridor.

"Mr. Edwards," Mr. Gardiner greeted. "The new tables have arrived."

"Excellent!" Mr. Edwards replied. "We shall soon be able to feed everyone in one sitting instead of two."

"It will be more efficient," Mr. Gardiner agreed.

Kitty looked from her uncle to the handsome gentleman speaking to him and back. What on earth were they talking about? Why was this gentleman, who was dressed as well as Mr. Darcy ever dressed, talking to her uncle about tables?

"Forgive me, Kitty. I see I have confused you."

Well, he did not need to point out her confusion in front of a stranger – especially a very attractive one who looked rather wealthy!

"You remember my telling you about the charity that has been started at my warehouse?"

Oh! She did remember that. "The one where you feed people?"

"The very one. Mr. Edwards was the gentleman who pressed me into starting it. He has a fondness for doing charitable work." Her uncle smirked. "Due entirely to a young lady who he will soon call his wife."

Kitty's eyes grew wide. "Indeed?" Were all the handsome gentlemen in London who her uncle knew married or nearly so? It was no wonder it took Jane so long to find a husband.

"They became betrothed in my office at the warehouse," her uncle whispered loudly.

"Oh! That was you?" she asked Mr. Edwards. She had heard the story from her aunt.

Mr. Edwards smiled broadly. "It was."

He looked as proud and happy as any person could ever look. It was just how Kitty hoped a gentleman might one day look when saying she was his betrothed. She sighed wistfully. "It is a beautiful story."

"Mr. Edwards," Mr. Gardiner said, "this is my niece, Miss Catherine Bennet. Kitty, this is Mr. Edwards, although I suppose you have already figured that out." He chuckled. "I am dreadful at introducing people before entering into a conversation."

"It is a pleasure to meet you, Miss Bennet," Mr. Edwards said with a shallow bow. "If you will pardon my saying so, you look slightly familiar."

"That is because she is Mrs. Darcy's sister," Mrs. Verity said.

"Yes, yes, that is it! You do bear a resemblance to Mrs. Darcy."

"You know her?"

"I met her right here. In this very spot."

"Your boys are waiting," Mrs. Verity said.

"Excellent." Mr. Edwards clapped his hands together and then rubbed them back and forth. "If you are giving a tour, Mrs. Verity, you will wish to skip that room for today, I am to undress and allow them to help me back into my clothes without any instruction."

Kitty's mouth popped open at his shocking words.

"I do apologize, Miss Bennet. I know that was not very proper of me to say in front of a young lady such as yourself. However, I am not very proper."

Mrs. Verity laughed. "That you are not," she said to his retreating form. "Until Miss Barrett came along, I understand he was quite a rake."

"He was a rake?" Kitty had never seen a rake before. She had heard of them, but there were none in Meryton.

"Very much so," her uncle said with a note of caution in his tone. "Town is much different than the country."

"Apparently so," Kitty agreed. "Lydia will be jealous that I have seen a rake and she has not." She pressed her lips together. That was not the thing to say. "I did not mean that we wished to see one or... or... fall prey to one," she muttered.

"All is well," her uncle said. "Just be aware that a rake looks very much like any other gentleman. However, he behaves far less properly."

"I will keep her safe," Mrs. Verity put an arm around Kitty's shoulders and directed her away from the door and down the hallway. "Not that Mr. Edwards has a thought in his head about young ladies these days save for the one to whom he is betrothed. However, he is still improper at times – shockingly so." She chuckled. "He is also very good with two of my older boys and is training them to be butlers and valets."

She removed her arm from Kitty's shoulder and opened a door. "This is the dining room. The children take turns being both the servers and the served in this room. It is important for them to see both sides of the table."

"It is beautifully furnished," Kitty said, strolling into the room to look at the paintings on the wall. "I should very much like to have a dining room such as this in my home."

"Thank you, Miss Bennet." Mrs. Verity was smiling warmly and looking at the dining table with pride in her eyes. "This was the table my husband purchased during our first year of marriage."

Kitty ran a finger along the curved mahogany edge. "He had very good taste."

"He did."

Kitty's companion now wore a faraway expression as Kitty took her time looking at the various dishes and furnishings of the room while supposing that Mrs. Verity was thinking of her husband. She must have loved him very much to look as she did now with that small smile on her lips and the softness in her eyes.

"The room across the hall is used as a classroom," Mrs. Verity said when they exited the dining room. "Mr. Darcy often reads to the children in that room when he visits."

That was surprising. "Is he a good reader?"

"Oh, very. The children hang on his every word."

To Kitty, it was hard to imagine Mr. Darcy reading to children, let alone, in such a fashion as to entertain them, but then, he was so much different now than he had been when she first met him.

"Do you read well, Miss Bennet?" Mrs. Verity looked at the watch which hung on her chatelaine.

Kitty nodded. "I often read to the tenants' children when I accompany Mama on her visits."

"Well, then, you are just in time. I will introduce you."

Chapter 3

"You read very well."

"Thank you," Kitty said with a smile for the pretty young lady who had joined her and Mrs. Verity in the younger children's room while Kitty was reading.

"If Miss Linton is here," said Mrs. Verity, "then it must be time for tea. Shall we retire to my office or the drawing room?" She gave a nod to the children's teacher, who immediately came to take Kitty's book and to send the children to the tables.

"The drawing room," Miss Linton said.

"Excellent choice," Mrs. Verity agreed. "We shall finish our tour after we have had some tea," she assured Kitty before leading them out the door and down the hall toward the front of the house. "The drawing room is set aside for our guests."

She thanked the butler, who she called Smith, for opening the drawing-room door and then asked him to see that tea was brought in directly.

Kitty followed behind Miss Linton and took a seat next to her by the window.

"Miss Linton, now that there are no children gathered around our feet, allow me to introduce you to Miss Bennet. Her uncle is Mr. Gardiner, and he has allowed me the privilege of keeping her for a short time while he conducts some business."

Mrs. Verity had a very pleasant manner, for she made Kitty feel entirely at ease with just a few words.

"And Miss Bennet, this is Miss Linton, who volunteers here at least twice each week at present, but she will soon marry, and then that will change."

"You are betrothed?" It seemed to Kitty as if everyone she was going to meet today was happily matched. Perhaps she had arrived in London too late in the season.

"I am," Miss Linton answered.

"Mr. Crawford, Miss Linton's betrothed is a particular friend of Mr. Edwards, whom you met earlier."

"Oh." It was all Kitty could think to say as she wondered if this Mr. Crawford was also a rake like his friend.

Miss Linton did not appear to be the sort of lady who would court a rogue. She sat just as she should, and she had not once spoken out of turn or put herself forward.

"Since December, I have been very successful in seeing three ladies, who have come to volunteer here, happily betrothed," Mrs. Verity said with a laugh. "Not that any of it was my doing, of course. I just happened to be fortunate enough to meet them. I am no matchmaker. However, I might begin to think of myself as good luck, especially if we can see Miss Bennet well-matched."

"Oh, that would be lovely," Kitty agreed. "I should like to find a husband. It is why my mother has sent me to town, and why Mr. Darcy is taking me to soirees."

"Miss Bennet is Mrs. Darcy's sister," Mrs. Verity said to Miss Linton. "And, she has three other sisters, is that not correct?"

"Indeed, it is," Kitty said. "Jane is the oldest and has married Mr. Bingley." She paused for a moment as Mrs. Verity instructed the maid in how to set up the tea.

The young girl was likely just learning how to perform the service as an older, more experienced looking maid stood behind her.

Once the tea was successfully arranged, Kitty continued while Mrs. Verity poured.

"Mr. Bingley is Mr. Darcy's particular friend, and I must say, he is likely one of the most amiable gentlemen in all of England. After Jane, is Elizabeth. She is now Mrs. Darcy. And then, there is Mary, me, and Lydia. Mary shall have her turn in town at Christmas. She was ill, and so I was sent in her place."

"I hope it was nothing serious," Miss Linton said.

Kitty shook her head. "Just a mild fever and sore throat. Mary is very good about taking all her medicine, so I am certain she will be well before Mama's first letter arrives."

"That is good, then," Miss Linton took a sip of her tea. "Are you all very close in age? I only have a brother and have always thought it would be lovely to have a sister."

"It is not always lovely," Kitty replied, causing Mrs. Verity to chuckle. "In fact," Kitty continued, "I will likely sound dreadful for admitting it, but it has been rather pleasant to be at Aunt and Uncle Gardiner's without a single sister. I love them dearly, but well, yes, we are all close in age, and it is sometimes trying to be noticed. Or, at least, it is for me. And Mary."

"But not your other sisters?" Miss Linton asked.

"Jane is beautiful. Lizzy possesses a quick wit and is second in beauty to Jane. And Lydia?" Kitty smiled. "Lydia will not be overlooked. It is just not possible."

"Miss Lydia is lively, is she?" Mrs. Verity asked.

"Oh, very!" Kitty's youngest sister was nearly always in a state of animation about something.

She turned to Miss Linton. "I have no brothers," Kitty said. "What is it like to have one?"

"I suppose it depends on the brother," Miss Linton said. "Mine is my guardian."

Kitty sucked in a quick breath. How sad!

"He has my aunt to help him. Not that he would need much help. Trefor is exacting and excessively proper, which suits me quite well most times. However, he can occasionally be a trifle too unwavering. That is where Aunt Gwladys' help becomes invaluable."

"Will you miss them greatly when you marry?" Kitty knew she would miss her mother and sisters. Longbourn had felt odd without either Jane or Elizabeth there. How lonely Mama and Papa would be once they were all married!

Miss Linton drew and released a breath as if taking off a heavy mantle. "I will, and I would feel much better about leaving them both if Trefor were to marry. But he says he is not ready for that."

"That is what they all say until they have met just the right lady," Mrs. Verity inserted.

"He has not met the right lady then," Miss Linton said with a laugh. "Not that my aunt has not done her best to suggest which lady might be right for him." She turned back to Kitty after placing her cup on the table. "Trefor is also a good friend of Mr. Crawford and Mr. Edwards."

"How..." Kitty clamped her lips shut. She should not ask what she wished to know. She was attempting to be proper while in town and being inquisitive about things which were not necessary for her to know was not proper. Mary had told her that many times.

"That is a good question," Miss Linton replied with a smile. "I have always wondered why they became friends, but I suppose it goes back to school days before either Mr. Crawford or Mr. Edwards took up their charming ways."

The need to ask about Mr. Crawford was nearly overwhelming.

"You may ask what you will," Miss Linton said. "I can see that you are curious about something." She leaned a bit closer to Kitty. "I will admit to being improperly inquisitive on occasion – especially when there is something of interest about which I wish to learn. Trefor is forever scolding me about asking him things he thinks are not appropriate. So, please ask me whatever it is you wish to know."

"Are you certain?" Kitty asked. "I am attempting to behave as well as I can, but I must confess it is not easy to quell one's curiosity."

"I am positive." Miss Linton looked expectantly at her, making Kitty feel somewhat better about asking what she was about to ask.

"My uncle said that Mr. Edwards was a rake..." Kitty ran a finger around the rim of her cup. "So, I was thinking, if he is a rake and you have said both he and Mr. Crawford are charming, does that mean Mr. Crawford is — was — also one?"

Miss Linton nodded. "He was, but his unscrupulous ways led him to heartbreak which, in turn, led him to wish to change his ways and that, led him to ask me to help him." She shrugged, and a smug grin settled on her lips. "I did a very good job of teaching him how to be a proper gentleman, and my friend was nearly as successful with Mr. Edwards, although I do not suppose Mr. Edwards will ever be entirely proper."

This was all very fascinating and novel information.

"I had thought that rakes were not capable of changing." Was that not what Mama had declared over and over after Mr. Wickham had been sent away?

Her daughters were to beware of such fellows for they were only ever capable of leading a lady to misery.

Of course, Mama had not been able to answer Mary's question about how to know if a gentleman was merely amiable or was a charmer, so between not knowing that and now knowing what she knew about Mr. Crawford and Mr. Edwards, it seemed, there was still much Kitty needed to learn about such gentlemen.

"I would like to think that no one is incapable of change," Mrs. Verity said. "However, it does seem an impossibility for some. I think, and this is only my supposition, of course, but to me, it seems that both Mr. Crawford and Mr. Edwards were not without a good heart buried under their deviant ways. For, if they were corrupted through and through, I doubt they could have retained Mr. Linton's friendship."

"I am sure you are correct," Miss Linton agreed. "As a rule, my brother is not very tolerant of improper behavior."

"From what I understand," Mrs. Verity continued, "change was not without some degree of pain for either of them." She placed her empty cup on the table. "Which, in my opinion, is as it should be. One must suffer the consequences of one's poor decisions to some extent, depending upon how much the good Lord requires."

She pushed up from her chair. "Shall we complete our tour now, Miss Bennet? And then, when we are finished, we will join Miss Linton again while we await your uncle."

For the next twenty minutes, Kitty followed Mrs. Verity up stairs and down corridors, looking into various rooms and hearing the purpose of each.

When the upper levels had been seen in nearly their entirety, save for the one room where two boys named Arthur and Stephen were receiving instruction from Mr. Edwards, Kitty and Mrs. Verity descended into the basement to view the kitchen.

The aroma of roasting meat mixed with that of the fresh bread on the workbench as Kitty stood listening to Mrs. Verity explain how the girls would begin their lessons in the scullery before moving up to assist the cook. Despite the biscuit Kitty had eaten with her tea, her stomach could not ignore the tantalizing smells around her and protested her lack of indulgence in those tasty morsels by rumbling.

Mrs. Verity smiled. "I think a few treats might be nice to have while we sew." She took a tin from the cupboard and handed it to Kitty. "I need to speak to the cook for a moment. Do you remember the way to the drawing room? If not, you may wait here."

"No, I remember."

"Then, will you think me very rude to send you up to Miss Linton without me?"

"Not at all," Kitty assured her. "I would be delighted to be of service."

Mrs. Verity patted Kitty's forearm, gave her a warm smile, and then, turned back to her cook, who was waiting with a book of receipts in hand, while Kitty made her way out of the kitchen, past the servant's hall and the butler's rooms to the stairs that led up to the ground floor.

She was just about to enter the drawing room when the door opened, and a gentleman stepped out. Perhaps if she had not been so distracted by how tall and broad he was or by his light brown hair that fell in waves, she might have been able to move out of his way before he crashed into her. But, sadly, she had been distracted by the handsome stranger, and so it was that she ended up stumbling and nearly falling. Thankfully, she caught his arm and kept her feet. Unfortunately, the tin of biscuits was lost in the action. Biscuits tumbled across the floor as the tin clattered and skipped before coming to a stop.

"My apologies," his voice was deep and wonderfully smooth. Kitty imagined it was what caramel might sound like if it had a voice – rich and sweet.

He bent and retrieved the biscuit tin which lay at his feet. "I shall gather the large pieces while you retrieve a broom, and I will be sure to tell Mrs. Verity that you were not at fault. You should not be punished for my clumsiness."

Kitty's mouth dropped open. He expected her to get a broom? Did he think she was a maid?

"I am sure I do not know where there is a broom." She lifted her chin and affected her most Lydia-like look of disdain. How dare he think she was a servant! Could he not see that she was dressed in a proper lady's blue day dress?

"You do not know where there is a broom?" He looked at her as if she was the most absurd person he had ever met. "How do you not know?"

"I do not know," she said as she folded her arms, "because I, like you, am a guest here."

His hand froze over the biscuit he was about to pick up. "You are a guest?" It sounded as if he were choking on the words which made Kitty smile as she answered, "yes."

"Ah, Miss Bennet!" Mr. Edwards cried as he came down the stairs followed by two young boys. "How do I look?"

"Fully clothed," she answered before she could stop the words from popping out of her mouth. Her cheeks burned as Mr. Edwards' laughed. "And not any different than you did when you arrived," she added. "I believe your students have done an excellent job." Her insides fluttered and flopped with embarrassment. She had been doing so well at being proper until now.

"And these are the fine young fellows who have recreated such perfection," Mr. Edwards said, motioning to the boys behind him. "This is Stephen on the right, and this is Arthur on the left. Lads, this is Mr. Gardiner's niece, Miss Bennet."

"It is a pleasure to meet you, Miss Bennet," Arthur said.

Stephen nodded his head and muttered his agreement.

"I think he is a bit smitten with you," Mr. Edwards, who had crossed the corridor to where Kitty was, whispered. "Not without reason," he added.

Kitty did not know exactly what to say to such a thing but managed to stammer a thank you.

"Linton," Mr. Edwards said to the gentleman picking up biscuits. "Here to collect your sister?"

"*You* are Miss Linton's brother?" Kitty asked in surprise.

The gentleman rose from his crouched position as he nodded.

"You are not at all like her."

"I think I am," he said.

"She would not ask me to get a broom."

Mr. Edwards chuckled.

"You were carrying a tin, and you're wearing blue."

Kitty's mouth popped open, but she quickly closed it while she scowled at him. "And you are wearing black, does that make you a coachman?"

"I have no horses with me," Trefor argued.

"And I have no broom."

"I do, Miss Bennet," Stephen said.

Kitty smiled at him. "Thank you. That is very thoughtful." She took the broom from the lad and handed it to Mr. Linton. "Your broom," she said, and then with a flip of her head, she stepped past him and into the drawing room.

Chapter 4

Trefor Linton stood looking at the drawing-room door which had closed soundly behind the pretty young woman he had assumed was a maid.

"Do you know how to use that?" Charles Edwards pointed to the broom Trefor held.

"Yes," Trefor snapped. "I am not stupid."

"Shall I verify that with Miss Bennet?"

"I'll thank you to leave off with your teasing." Trefor handed the tin he held to Charles. "You may eat them if you do not mind a bit of dust."

"I am not going to eat biscuits which have been on the floor."

"I can sweep for you, mister," Stephen said.

Trefor shook his head. "Thank you, but I shall see to it."

As much as he wished to let the lad clean up the mess he had made, Trefor was not the sort of gentleman to shirk any responsibility – most especially a task that he doubted Miss Bennet would believe he would or could do. She likely *expected* him to pawn the job off on a servant.

"That was not a very good first impression," he muttered.

"No, sir," Stephen, who stood by holding a dustpan, answered. "She was rather put out with you."

Trefor held his mouth firmly closed to keep from uttering some retort, which would likely be something rather rude, seeing as he was also feeling *rather put out.*

"She was wearing blue." He cast a look at his friend. He was uncertain if he were trying more to convince himself or his friend that his assumption had not been as wrong as it was. The fact did nothing to assuage his feelings of guilt for having insulted a lady. He did not do that. He always spoke to ladies properly.

"Many ladies do wear that colour, and if you had paused to notice, it was made of a very fine muslin." Charles leaned against the wall next to the drawing-room door. "And I must say she wore it well."

Trefor glared at his friend.

"I was only commenting on what was obviously apparent to everyone save you."

"She is rather shorter than taller."

"Your logic is still flawed."

Trefor motioned for Stephen to lend his aid with the dustpan.

"I do not know everyone who is here. She seemed the right size for some of the young ladies who live here."

"She's about as tall as Susan," Arthur inserted. "Susan

is going to have an employer soon," he added to Charles. "Your Miss Barrett said so last week."

Charles grinned broadly. "Then, I would imagine it is a good home to which Susan is going."

"She's awful excited," Arthur said. "She'll have her own money soon and a place to live and all that."

"It is a good thing," Charles assured him.

"We'll miss her, of course," Arthur added.

Charles scruffed the lad's hair and merely smiled. He was at ease no matter where he was. Trefor supposed that was likely due to his friend's lack of care for rules and boundaries. Edwards was like a river that flowed over flat river beds as easily as it slipped over the edge of a waterfall and through the boulders in a rapid. Trefor was more like basin of water, staying within its designated confines and seeing to whatever duty for which it was deemed necessary. And creating a fine mess when tipped over, he thought as he scowled at the broom in his hand. He positively felt tipped over.

"Susan proves my logic was not entirely faulty." Trefor spared a glance at his friend, who merely smiled and shook his head.

"Not much left for the mice," Trefor said with satisfaction after giving the floor a thorough looking over.

"You did a fine job, sir," Stephen assured him. "I didn't know a gentleman in fancy dress could do such a good job and almost not soil his clothing."

Trefor's brows furrowed.

Stephen pointed to Trefor's breeches.

With a sigh, Trefor smacked at the dust on his knees. He was certain that he had never before gotten dust on the knees of his breeches when calling on someone. It was just another way in which he felt completely turned on his head.

"You look presentable enough to be properly introduced to Miss Bennet now," Charles said with a laugh.

"I already know who she is," Trefor protested. "Gardiner's niece. I shall await my sister in the carriage as was planned."

"Mr. Linton," Mrs. Verity greeted. "Are you here so soon to steal away your sister?"

"I am. Our aunt reminded me of an engagement we are to keep tonight."

"And what have we here, boys?" she asked Stephen and Arthur.

"Miss Bennet dropped her tin of biscuits," Arthur said. "And we were helping clean them up."

Mrs. Verity looked to the older gentlemen to confirm the boy's words.

"It was I who caused the destruction of the biscuits," Trefor admitted. "I was not paying close enough attention when I exited the drawing room."

He had been thinking of that blasted soiree which his aunt insisted he attend and which he had no desire to attend. He had been, in fact, in a foul mood, which was why he had not wished to stay in the drawing room with his sister and wait for Mrs. Verity. He had only wished to deliver his message to his sister and be gone.

He had not even particularly wished to see Charles, though he had known his friend was upstairs. Charles would be altogether too happy to be going to this particular soiree, for according to Aunt Gwladys, both of his good friends, Charles and Henry, would be there since Constance and her friend, Charles's betrothed, would also be there.

Trefor was in no hurry to marry, but he had to admit that it was becoming less and less pleasant to be the only single gentleman of his set of friends. And his conniving aunt knew it! He was certain of that fact. It was why she was so eager to have him escort her to this poetry reading tonight.

Poetry! He barely refrained from rolling his eyes at the thought. It was not as if he had anything against poetry. He actually enjoyed reading it. However, having to sit in a room as an unattached gentleman of good fortune and standing while simultaneously listening to poetry and being eyed by hopeful matrons and their charges was the surest way to drive any love of poetry from a gentleman.

"Then you have met my guest?" Mrs. Verity asked.

"Not formally," Trefor admitted.

"I was just about to make the introduction," Charles said, opening the door to the drawing room.

Trefor's eyes narrowed. He wished to retort that he was not returning to the drawing room, but that would be impolite to do in front of Mrs. Verity. He had already offended one lady today. He did not need to make it two.

"I understand we had a little mishap with the biscuits," Mrs. Verity said as she entered the room ahead of Charles and Trefor.

Miss Bennet blushed prettily. "I must apologize for that."

"No, no, it was my fault," Trefor interjected.

"It was most certainly mostly your fault," Miss Bennet replied, her chin lifting, "but it was not entirely your fault. There is no need to be gallant on my behalf, sir. I sometimes get lost in my thoughts," she added to Mrs. Verity. "I will own that it is a dreadful habit."

Her eyes darted quickly toward him and Charles.

"Accidents do occur now and then," Mrs. Verity said. "However, I understand that due to the unfortunate events in the corridor, a formal introduction was never made. Miss Bennet, this is Miss Linton's brother, Mr. Trefor Linton, and Mr. Linton, this is Miss Catherine Bennet. If you are to be here often, Miss Bennet – which I assume you will be since your aunt and your sister both are here regularly — you will likely meet on occasion, and it is much more pleasant when each knows the other."

From the expression Miss Bennet wore, Trefor could tell that pleasant was not the word she would use to describe their knowing one another.

"And if you are to call on me," Constance said, "it is best that you know who my brother is."

"Call on you?"

"Yes, brother dear, I was just inviting Miss Bennet to call on me. I think we shall be good friends. I honestly cannot wait to introduce her to Aunt Gwladys and Evelyn."

"Her uncle is a tradesman. Do you think he will have the opportunity to deliver her to our house?" His brow furrowed when he saw Miss Bennet fold her arms as she had in the hallway. "I am not opposed to having Miss Bennet call. I was merely concerned that it would take him away from his work."

"I make calls with my sister," Miss Bennet replied primly.

"Very good then. As long as it will not inconvenience your uncle." For some reason, Trefor felt well out of his depth in this conversation, which was not a normal thing for him. "I must apologize once again for my assumption earlier." He felt his ears growing hot.

"I shall not wear blue when I call on your sister to save you any confusion."

Her lips pressed together, and she ducked her head as if she was embarrassed about what she had said.

"I shall not make the same mistake twice," he assured

her. "Wear whichever colour you like. Blue is nice." Charles had not been wrong in his assessment of Miss Bennet wearing her dark blue dress well. The colour looked lovely against her creamy complexion, and the fit was exceptionally good for it flattered her curves in a most distracting fashion.

She smiled at him. "It is a favourite colour."

"What is?" He could not for the life of him remember what colour had been mentioned now that she was no longer scowling at him.

"Blue," she said. "You just said blue was a nice colour." She cast a worried glance at Constance.

"Oh, yes, right," he stammered. "I am not usually so scattered."

"Neither are the biscuits," Charles whispered before chuckling.

Trefor rose. "I shall wait for you in the carriage, Connie." He needed to get out of this house before he made an even greater fool of himself. "We have that poetry reading tonight."

"Oh, are you going to that, too?" Miss Bennet asked Constance eagerly. "It will be so nice to know someone there."

"You are going to it?" Trefor asked.

Miss Bennet's head bobbed up and down. "With my sister."

His brows furrowed. How had nieces of the Gardiners

received invitations to such a soiree? His eyes grew wide as he realized Miss Bennet was once again scowling at him.

"Mr. Gardiner is my uncle not my father."

"Yes, yes, I know," Trefor defended.

"Do you think I am a tradesman's daughter?"

She was rather direct in the questions she asked! Was she not aware that a young lady was supposed to demur politely by turning the conversation? That was what they were supposed to do, was it not?

Trefor swallowed and smiled sheepishly. "At the risk of offending you yet again, yes."

Her hazel eyes rolled upward as she huffed in exasperation.

"Your father is a gentleman?" he asked quickly.

Mrs. Verity chuckled. "He is, indeed, as is her sister's husband."

"You know him?"

"Not her father," Mrs. Verity clarified, "but yes, I know Mr. Darcy."

Trefor blinked. "Mr. Darcy?"

"Do you know him?" Miss Bennet asked.

Trefor shook his head. "I have never met him, but I know who he is."

"And does *he* meet with your approval?"

Again, she pressed her lips together as if she were frustrated, and his conscience pricked him because he knew he was the cause of her consternation. He blew out a breath. "Yes. But then, so does Mr. Gardiner." He bowed to her. "Until this evening."

And with that, he made as quick an escape as one could make when one was attempting to walk sedately out of the room.

Chapter 5

"I will be surprised if Miss Bennet does call on me." Constance glanced at her brother before taking another bit of her meal.

"Why is that, dear?" Aunt Gwladys asked. "She sounds like a delightful young lady."

Trefor raised an eyebrow at his sister. He suspected he knew exactly where she was going with this conversation. He was about to be reprimanded yet again for his poor behaviour at Mrs. Verity's. He deserved it, but he did not appreciate it.

"Trefor was rather condescending," Constance replied.

"Our Trefor was condescending? To a lady?"

He could not fault his aunt's look and tone of utter incredulity. He was ordinarily polite to a fault when in the presence of a young lady. His father had taught him to be a gentleman, and he had always striven to be the man his father wished him to be.

"More than once," his sister said.

"I was in a foul mood." It was a pathetic excuse, but it was also the truth.

"And what accounts for your foul mood?" His aunt placed her cutlery on her plate and, taking up her glass of wine, settled back in her chair with an expectant look.

"I do not wish to go to the Allen's tonight," he admitted as he stabbed his last piece of chicken with his fork.

"And why is that, my dear?"

"I would rather be at home," he said around his food. "Where there are no debutantes," he added after he had swallowed.

"Ah," his aunt said, knowingly. "You are still attempting to avoid your duty to marry."

"I am not avoiding it," he protested before taking a large gulp of his wine. These glasses were not big enough to hold the full amount of wine for which this conversation was likely going to make him wish. He did not fancy having a discussion of his shortcomings where Miss Bennet was concerned, nor did he relish the thought of having to yet again be reminded of his need for a wife.

"I fully intend to fulfill my duty to the family after I have seen Connie well-settled." And as soon as he could find a lady who was of interest.

He did not wish to marry just to fulfill a duty. He longed for a lady who would do more than provide him with children and be an excellent hostess. He desired companionship. Someone to whom he could talk even more freely than he could his sister and aunt. A lady who would understand and care for his heart and not just his home.

"Your sister has found her happy future," his aunt replied. "So, now, it is your turn." She held up a hand when Trefor opened his mouth to protest. "There is still plenty of time left in this season. I am not saying you must find a wife before summer. I am only suggesting you consider a few ladies."

Trefor drained what remained in his wine glass. "Connie is not yet married." And not a single lady which he had met so far this season had captured his interest in any particularly marriage-inspiring fashion.

His aunt merely raised her brows and pursed her lips in reply. She clearly did not approve of his reasoning. Not that she needed to approve of it. It was the only explanation he felt compelled to share. A declaration of "no lady has met my requirements" would only lead to a list being drawn up and an analysis of all the ladies which either his aunt or sister knew would begin. That was how his sister did things – scientifically. And his aunt would only happily join in for she was desperate to have grand-nieces and nephews.

"I will join you in the drawing room when it is time to leave." He sighed as he rose and paused a moment to look at Aunt Gwladys, "You truly wish to attend this reading?"

His aunt nodded. "I do. For if you will not look for a bride, then I must do it for you."

"You do not need to find a wife for me."

"I did not say I would find one," she replied with a mischievous smile. "I only said I was going to look for one. You, of course, will have the final decision."

"How gracious of you," he muttered before leaving the room and seeking out a haven of peace and quiet.

Discussions of marriage made him uneasy. He had always said that choosing a wife was a monumental responsibility – not that his good friends, Charles and Henry, had ever agreed with him until recently.

He bounded up the stairs as if fleeing from a monster that hunted him in a calculating fashion. There, of course, was no actual monster chasing him. It was only his fear that he would not choose correctly when selecting the companion of his future life.

However, the problem with imaginary monsters was the very real fact that one could not outrun them or hide from them. Not even sleep was effective against them, for even in dreams they were known to torment their victims. There simply was no escape.

He pushed open the door to his apartment. This sitting room had been a safe harbour for him since both his father and mother had died. Here, he found he could hear his mother's voice the most. His father's memories were tied much more closely with the study. That is where he would retreat to contemplate many decisions regarding the effective running of the estate. But here... He took off his jacket and tossed it on the sofa before sinking into his mother's favourite chair. Here he would seek his mother's guidance.

How many times had he sat here on her knee or peered over the arm of the chair as he stood beside it? Too many to be counted, but each had been indelibly engrained upon his heart. He could not accurately tell anyone what had been said or what events had occurred in all those times, but the feeling he had always had here was one of comfort and deep, abiding love.

What would his mother say if she were to hear that he had been rude to a lady – a very pretty lady with expressive hazel eyes and brown hair only a shade darker than the colour of his bay?

He did not need to ponder that for any length of time, for he knew precisely what she would say. He needed to apologize.

It would not matter to his mother that this particular young lady caused his chest to tighten and his thoughts to become tangled. She would take him by his chin, look into his eyes, and remind him that a gentleman always – without fail – corrected his errors. To ignore them was not honourable. Then, she would smile at him and kiss his forehead before sending him on his way to mend whatever needed fixing.

He expelled a great breath. How he was supposed to correct his error when his mind and mouth seemed at odds was beyond him, but he knew he must try.

So it was that later that evening, Trefor Linton entered the Allen's drawing room and immediately began his search for Miss Bennet.

"Are you looking for someone?" Charles Edward inquired.

"Miss Bennet," Trefor said, sparing a quick look for his friend. "Good evening, Miss Barrett," he greeted his friend's betrothed.

"Is there a reason you are looking for this lady?" Evelyn Barrett asked.

"My aunt wishes for an introduction." And Trefor was happy for the excuse it would give him to present himself as a proper gentleman to Miss Bennet and her relations.

Ah! There she was, wearing another blue dress, though this one was not as dark as the one she had worn earlier. This one looked a lot like the sky on a clear summer's day. He smiled.

"Found her, did you?" Charles whispered. There was a teasing tone to his words which caused Trefor to scowl.

"I did, which means I can be done with my duty as quickly as possible." He turned to find his aunt, as well as his sister and Miss Barrett, speaking to Mrs. Allen. "Or perhaps not," he muttered. "What are you doing?"

Charles had lifted his hand as if waving to someone.

"Acknowledging the presence of Mr. Darcy. He was looking this direction. I did not wish to appear rude." His lips twitched, and his brows rose as he said the word rude.

"I was taken by surprise. I did not expect her to be entering the drawing room while I was exiting."

"Of course," Charles replied with the most obviously feigned serious look Trefor had ever seen.

He rolled his eyes and shook his head. Charles had always been incorrigible, and it did not seem that being on the precipice of marriage had changed that entirely. He still enjoyed being shocking and a general nuisance.

"Mr. Edwards."

Trefor swallowed as he turned to find Mr. Darcy had approached them. Hopefully, if the gentleman had heard about the incident at Mrs. Verity's, he would not censure him too severely for Trefor's behavior towards his wife's sister.

"Mrs. Darcy's sister told me that the tables have arrived. Have you seen them?" Darcy asked.

"Not yet," Charles replied, "but I am certain they are perfection if you have chosen them."

Darcy smiled and chuckled softly. "My wife chose them."

"Then I am certain they are far better than perfect," Charles replied with all the ease of a charmer.

"She would be happy to hear it," Darcy said. "And, you are most likely correct." He glanced at Trefor.

"Allow me to present my friend, Mr. Trefor Linton," Charles said. "Linton, this is Mr. Fitzwilliam Darcy."

"It is a pleasure to meet you." Pleasure was perhaps not

the best word for what Trefor felt as Darcy gave him an appraising look.

"I am equally delighted to meet you." Darcy's lips twitched slightly. "I have heard a good deal about you."

Trefor groaned softly. "I had hoped to apologize for that. I was not in the best frame of mind earlier today."

"He had no desire to be here tonight," Charles inserted, "but his aunt insisted he come."

Blasted Charles! Did he not know when teasing was most unwelcome? That bit did not need to be shared!

"My plans had been changed, which meant I needed to collect my sister from Verity House sooner than expected," Trefor explained. It still sounded as sorry now as it had earlier at supper when he had attempted to explain his offending Miss Bennet to his aunt. Such an admission, Trefor was certain, was not going to gain him any favour in Mr. Darcy's opinion.

However, to Trefor's surprise, Darcy chuckled.

"A foul temper can lead to some grave errors," the man said with a knowing smile. "There are chairs near us. How many are in your party?"

"Counting Edwards and Miss Barrett, we are six."

"I think we can accommodate that many," Darcy assured him.

Gaining his aunt's attention, Trefor made quick work of introducing her, as well as his sister and Mr. Crawford, who had joined them by that time, to Mr. Darcy before following the gentleman across the room and going through the formalities of introductions once again. Then, Trefor was obliged to sit beside his aunt who had claimed the seat nearest Miss Bennet and Miss Darcy.

"Are you reading tonight?" Aunt Gwladys asked Miss Bennet, who smiled and shook her head.

"I have only just arrived in town," she explained. "I am certain I do not know enough people yet to be invited to do such a thing."

"But you would like to?" Trefor asked. It sounded to him as if she was disappointed that she could not read tonight. He, on the other hand, was content to sit and listen.

"I enjoy reading," she replied. "Does that surprise you?" She pressed her lips together as if embarrassed for having been direct, just as she had done this afternoon.

"I suppose it does," he answered. "Although, it is likely not for the reason you assume."

"And what reason might you have then?" his aunt asked.

"Performing in front of strangers would be uncomfortable to me, so it is hard to imagine it would not be for everyone." He shrugged. "It is perhaps not a good answer, but there it is."

Miss Bennet leaned towards his aunt, and by extension him. "I would not be performing for strangers."

"You would not be?" She knew no one in attendance.

Even if she knew the host well enough to be asked, she would still not know each of the twenty or so people who sat on the tufted chairs and patterned sofas in the Allen's drawing room.

"No. I would read to my sister."

"But what of the other people?"

She shrugged. "It matters little if they listen to me read to Elizabeth or not, for I would only wish to please my sister."

His brows rose. "That is a different way of looking at an experience."

"But you do not approve."

"No, no," he said quickly. He had most certainly left her with a very sorry opinion of himself. "I think it is quite a good idea actually."

"Then you would not mind reading to me?" his aunt asked.

"What have you done?" he attempted to keep the growl he felt out of his tone of voice.

"Mrs. Allen asked if you would read. It seems one of the gentlemen who was supposed to read this evening has fallen ill, and she was in as desperate state to find a replacement."

"Aunt."

"I know how willing you are to lend assistance." The innocent smile she gave him was anything but. She was up to something.

"And you promised her I would do it?"

His aunt's eyelashes fluttered in response.

He sighed. "When will I get the piece I am to read? You knew I would not disappoint you, did you not?"

His aunt's hand covered his. "You are such a good boy. Mrs. Allen will be over with it in just a moment." She looked across the room to their hostess and gave a nod.

Miss Bennet's eyes were dancing with amusement.

"Do you know what I am to read? Or when?"

"You are starting us off."

"First? I must read first?"

"Yes, the evening is a selection of excerpts from novels..."

"It is not a poetry reading?"

His aunt shook her head.

"Novels?"

"Yes, dear. Those dreadful things."

He rolled his eyes.

"Do you not approve of novels, Mr. Linton?" Miss Bennet's seemed both shocked and horrified by such a thought.

"I cannot say I read them often, but I am not opposed to them. It is just that I was under the impression that we would be hearing poetry tonight. I rather enjoy poetry."

"Did I not say literary reading?"

His aunt was once again attempting to look innocent.

She needed to work on the expression if she wished to be believable.

"No, you said it was, and I quote, 'a poetry or some such thing reading.'"

"Well, then I was not wrong," she said with a sly smile. "You will read a poem to introduce our topic for the evening." She took a paper from Mrs. Allen and handed it to him.

"When you are ready," Mrs. Allen said. "I am going to welcome everyone, and then you can read that."

"Just read it to me," his aunt whispered.

Trefor nodded and rose from his place.

"He is such a good boy," he heard her say to Miss Bennet.

He looked over the poem that was written in neat close letters. It did not seem a difficult piece to read. Still, his heart beat a rather loud and rapid beat as he listened to Mrs. Allen greet her guests and explain how the evening was to proceed before introducing him.

Trefor took a deep breath and looked at his aunt whose smile reminded him a great deal of his mother's. Reading to her would not be a trial.

"'A Receipt for Writing a Novel' by Mrs. Alcock. *Would you a favourite novel make,*" he looked up from his page and caught the look of delight on Miss Bennet's face. Glancing down again at the paper he held, he paused, attempting to find where he had left off. "Forgive me," he muttered. "Let me begin again."

He would read to the paper and only the paper. For looking in his aunt's direction would mean seeing Miss Bennet and, even with words written for him to simply utter, she seemed able to confuse the communication between his mind and his mouth.

With his eyes firmly focused on the paper he began once more.

"*Would you a favourite novel make,*
Try hard your reader's heart to break
For who is pleased, if not tormented?
(Novels for that were first invented.)"[1]

As were poetry readings and pretty ladies with expressive hazel eyes, he thought before reading on.

---

1. *A Receipt for Writing a Novel*, Mary Alcock.

Chapter 6

"Was is not a lovely evening?" Kitty asked with a sigh as she waited to leave the Allen's home. Those who had been in attendance were milling about the room, stopping to chat with one another, as Mr. Darcy and Mr. Edwards were doing right now, and then, slowly moving toward the door to thank their hostess before taking their leave.

"I thoroughly enjoyed it," Georgiana Darcy answered.

"As did I," Miss Linton agreed. "The way each excerpt from the various novels was highlighted using the bits and pieces of the poem that started us off was brilliant."

"It was a very clever way to present it," Kitty's sister, Elizabeth added. The ladies of their party save for Miss Barrett, who was with Mr. Edwards, and Miss Linton's aunt, who was speaking to another lady, were all standing together.

"Well, I am just glad it is over." Mr. Linton was looking over their heads toward the door.

Why could he not be with Mr. Darcy and Mr. Edwards

instead of standing watch over his sister and Mr. Crawford?

"You did not like it?" Kitty asked.

"I apologize. Who did not like what?" Mr. Linton asked.

Kitty blinked. Had he not heard himself?

"You said you were glad it was over," his sister whispered.

"I said that?" His eyes grew wide.

"You most certainly did," Mr. Crawford assured him as Kitty nodded along with his sister and the rest of her companions.

"That was supposed to be a thought," he admitted sheepishly. "It is not that I did not enjoy the reading. I am just anxious to be home."

To Kitty, it did not appear, from the way he diverted his gaze from his group to the door, that he was being completely honest. She firmly believed he was anxious to be home. However she suspected that his desire to be home was most likely due to his longing to be gone from her presence – she was, after all, a tradesman's niece. She rolled her eyes as she thought the bitter words. It really was too bad Mr. Linton was so pompous in his opinions, for he was rather handsome in his wine-coloured jacket and cream breeches. He had, in her opinion, been the most handsome gentleman in attendance. Well, other than his friend Mr. Edwards, that is.

"Who was the gentleman sitting across the room on the

green chair?" Kitty whispered to her sister. That gentleman had also been quite attractive in his black jacket and red waistcoat. His hair was not much darker than Mr. Linton's, and he was likely shorter and less broad than Mr. Linton, but he seemed more willing to smile than scowl, which was very pleasantly unlike Mr. Linton.

"I am certain I could not tell you," Elizabeth answered. "I am not as familiar with everyone as I would like to be."

Kitty sighed. That was the trouble with having a sister so newly married. Elizabeth was very good at meeting people and remembering names, but she had only been in town for a few months. Therefore, she had not had enough time to meet all the truly interesting people about whom Kitty wondered – such as that handsome gentleman on the green chair.

"Mr. Hayes," Mr. Linton answered.

"Were you listening to me speak to my sister?" Kitty asked with no little amount of agitation. How rude! If one were to listen to whispers, one should not let the source of the whisper know that he had intruded on a private conversation. That was why one whispered in public, after all. What was said in a low tone was not meant to be heard by everyone. Surely, that fact was just as true in London as it was in Meryton.

"I did not mean to listen," he apologized.

At least, he knew he was in the wrong. That was a point in his favour.

"I just happened to hear and knew the answer. Was there a particular reason you wished to know who Mr. Hayes is?"

"Yes."

"And what was that?"

He expected her to tell him that? Kitty thought not! And she was certain her expression said so quite nicely since Mr. Linton's brow furrowed.

"Why do you suppose?" Miss Linton gave her brother a pointed glare.

Mr. Linton shook his head for a moment until realization washed over his features. "He is a bit of a fop," he muttered.

"If you mean he appears pleasant, as well as handsome, then I would have to agree," Kitty said, fixing her gaze on Mr. Linton's lovely blue eyes. They were silvery and strong. It really was a pity he was not more civil.

Mr. Crawford coughed, which was likely to cover a chuckle for he looked rather amused. Of course, Kitty did not see anything amusing about such rudeness, but then, she was not a rake. Perhaps rakes found things more humorous than the regular person.

"However," she continued, "if you are only attempting to disparage him to me, I should like to know why."

"Kitty," Elizabeth cautioned.

She should listen to Elizabeth. She knew she should. This was not a particularly good path down which to traverse, but the challenge had been put forth. Therefore, she stood her ground and ignored Elizabeth. She would be improper for just this moment – only long enough to have her point carried that Mr. Linton was being arrogant.

"I will give you that he's handsome," Mr. Linton replied. "But even he would tell you that. And he would likely do it just before he informed you which tailor he used and where to find the best muslin for your dress."

"What is wrong with my dress?" Kitty retorted.

"Not a thing." Mr. Linton looked to his sister for help. However, when none was forthcoming, he continued on by himself, which, as it turned out, was not the right choice. "It is a fine dress, but Mr. Hayes would likely comment on some small detail such as the fact that it will not survive many washings or that it would look better with a different lace on the sleeves."

Kitty's right hand flew to her left sleeve. "This is my favourite lace! And the fabric used for this dress is not catchpenny!"

"I did not say it was." Mr. Linton ran a finger around his collar. "And I can see why you like that lace, it is very nice."

"Nice? Only nice?" Kitty looked at her sleeve. This lace was so delicate that it spoke to a high degree of craftsmanship to create it, and he called it simply nice?

Mr. Crawford was coughing again, which made Mr. Linton glare at him.

"What would you have me call it?" he retorted sharply.

"Something better than nice," Kitty grumbled.

Mr. Linton blew out a breath as they came close enough to the door to feel the coolness of the night. "I was only imagining the sorts of things that Mr. Hayes might say. I was not saying any of that myself."

Kitty accepted her pelisse from a footman. "You sounded very much like an expert."

"That is because I have heard Hayes say such things before," Mr. Linton said, but Kitty paid no attention to him other than to listen and peek at him from the corner of her eye.

"You will still call on me despite my brother?" Miss Linton looked apologetic as she asked.

"Of course," Kitty assured her. "You cannot control your brother any more than I can stop my sister Mary from scolding and lecturing, and I should very much dislike it if I were not to have friends because of her." She pressed her lips together. "That was not kind. I should not speak so about my sister."

Thankfully, Miss Linton smiled at Kitty before turning to thank their hostess for the wonderful evening.

"I like her," Kitty whispered.

"She does seem very pleasant," Georgiana agreed. "And her brother is handsome."

"And boorish." Kitty grimaced. That was not kind, even if it was true. Why could she not behave properly? She glared at the back of Mr. Linton. It was his fault. She had been doing so well until he knocked that tin out of her hands at Mrs. Verity's.

"I think you might be judging him too harshly," Elizabeth said.

A scowl settled on Kitty's face. She did not need her sister to reprimand her. Just because Mr. Darcy had proven to not be so bad-mannered as he had appeared at first, did not mean that all such rudeness was to be readily forgiven. Mr. Linton had thought she was a maid! And when she was wearing her best blue day dress! The one which had only been completed before she left Longbourn for town. Not even her friends at home had seen it. And he – the handsome, frustrating gentleman who read poetry very well – had thought it was no better than what a maid might wear. She pulled her eyes from him and back to her sister and Miss Darcy as first one and then the other thanked Mrs. Allen for the evening.

"I had a lovely time," Kitty said to Mrs. Allen when it was her turn.

"It was a pleasure to meet you, Miss Bennet," their hostess replied. "I do hope we will cross paths at another soiree."

Kitty thanked her and followed her sister and Mr. Darcy out of the house, down the steps, and to their waiting carriage. As she settled into her seat, she knew what she would be writing in her notebook.

~*~*~

After describing her night to her aunt as she readied herself for bed, Kitty settled into the chair next to the small desk in her room and opened her notebook. She was not yet ready for sleep, but a few moments of writing might put the enjoyment and frustration of the evening out of her mind and prepare her for her repose.

Picking up her pen and thinking back to the man with the ragged coat she and her uncle had seen earlier in the day, she began.

The education of Mr. L-, who was cursed for his behavior and doomed to trudge the earth while wearing his character on his back

She smiled. That was a good title. A bit longish, but quite descriptive.

The hall was dank and dingy. The walls were thick, dotted here and there with windows entirely too small for the vastness of the room. There was an enormous fireplace at one end. Large enough for two servants to stand inside when the fires were not lit, which only happened when their master was away. Try as they might maids and footmen attempted to keep it and the whole of the hall clean with the meager supplies their master provided, but the task was impossible. He was a miserly old goat. His coffers were not lacking for gold, but his heart possessed barely a morsel of sense or compassion.

In the midst of this stony portrait was a man, who

had once been nearly as feelingless and hardened as the master of this great estate. This man, this Mr. L, was a relatively new arrival at the mansion, sent there by the princess of the land, whom Mr. L had failed to recognize with the honour she was due.

Today, as every day, Mr. L stood at the ready to fetch whatever his master required, be it his account books, a glass of wine, a piece of bread, or even a chamber pot

Mr. L's coat dragged along the dusty floor of the great hall as he carried an empty basket, which had been filled with warm rolls, to the sideboard. His coat was a ragged old thing, though once it had been a fine blue greatcoat made of the best material that could be purchased in the land. He could not remove it. The curse under which he had fallen would not allow it, and with each passing day, the wretched old coat seemed to grow longer and more tattered. And with each tear and with each time he stumbled over the hem, Mr. L longed to have his old coat back – not to mention his comfortable bed and warm fire, as well as his own servants.

"You!"

Mr. L jumped at the bark of his master.

"Get me more wine!"

More wine was never a good thing. Mr. L knew that very well. Each glass made his master more and more belligerent. However, not bringing the required wine would not make his master any more friendly either. So, Mr. L *wisely hurried from the room to retrieve the desired beverage.*

Perhaps if he was quick enough, he might return before he noticed the cold of the ground through his worn shoes. The floors of the manor house were dirty and hard and not at all like the fine house in which he had once lived, but, at least, they were warm.

Kitty paused and read over the few lines she had written. Smiling, she picked up her pen again.

"Mr. L," a boy called to him, "my mother needs a log for her fire, and I cannot get it."

The man stopped, eying the young lad. The boy did not look frail or terribly undersized. Indeed, he looked quite capable of fetching a log or two. "I must return with the wine," he said. "My master will not be pleased if I delay."

"But my mother is not well," the boy pleaded.

"I cannot," Mr. L said, but upon turning away, his coat, in response to his refusal, tore at the elbow.

With a sigh, he turned back. "Which log?"

He did not have time for this quest, but he also did not wish for any more holes in his coat. There were far too many already that let in the damp, chilled air of this gloomy place.

"The one beside the great tree in the grove of ancient trees. It will burn longer and warmer than any other, and such heat will surely heal my mother."

"The great tree?" *That was a far distance out of the way.*

"Please, Mr. L. My mother is ill."

The man's jacket hung heavily on him, pulling him down. "Could you go to the winemaker for me while I am gone?"

"I cannot leave my mother," the young lad said.

You must show kindness of the greatest kind. The words whispered through Mr. L's mind reminding him of his duty, of the only way he could ever be free of this torn cloak.

"I will get the log," he assured the boy. "See to your mother."

Again, Kitty paused. Her page was nearly filled. A yawn crept over her. Tilting her head from side to side, she attempted to drive the fatigue away, but as another yawn told her, it was no use. Sleep would not be put off for much longer. It had been a long and busy day, and her bed was calling to her. Her body longed for its repose. Reluctantly, she put her pen away and rose from the small desk.

Taking her lamp with her, she crossed to the bed where she placed the lamp on the bedside table. Then, she took off her robe, slipped her feet out of her slippers, and climbed under the covers, sighing into the mattress for a moment before sitting up once again and putting out her lamp.

In the dark, she wiggled deep into her blankets, wrapping them around her shoulders and scuffing her feet against the sheets to help the bedding warm faster.

Once again, she yawned. She would not have to ponder which dream she would like to have tonight, for tonight, she hoped to see Mr. Linton in his ragged, old coat scurrying across a field and over a hill to the ancient old forest as his punishing quest to learn to be kind began.

Chapter 7

The day after the literary reading dawned with a thin layer of fog obscuring the brightness of the morning, but that did not stop Trefor from requesting that his bay be saddled so that he could ride. The feeling that left was right and up was down which had settled on him yesterday afternoon at Mrs. Verity's house had not shifted. It seemed that neither whisky nor sleep could drive it from him, and no amount of scolding from his sister or his aunt – and there had been a fair amount of that – could purge his mind of its jumbled state. Therefore, he hoped that beginning his day as he would any other day would set him on a path to having his well-ordered mind and life set back to right.

However, even eating the exact breakfast he ate every day, while reading the paper in the same order in which he always read it, did not seem to be having the desired effect. Perplexed and a great deal more than a little annoyed, he went to his study to push around a few account books and deal with some correspondence. There was an estate matter about which his steward had written him that needed addressing, and then, he would have to go through the invitations that he and his sister had received to decide which ones he would willingly attend with his aunt.

He knew that Aunt Gwladys would wish to accept them all until she had succeeded in seeing not only his sister, but also him, happily betrothed. However, there was a limit to his tolerance for his aunt's encouragement which was growing smaller and smaller as the season progressed.

That was how it was each year. The season would start with great anticipation. The soirees were a welcome diversion, but then, come March or April, the diversions would begin to grow dull, and he would start longing to be home where he could make himself useful on his estate. As a consequence, when the season would draw to a close, Trefor would be relieved to be packing up house and travelling home.

He poured himself a glass of whisky. It was not his normal wont to consume such a drink while working on his accounts. He usually reserved this particular drink for when the sun had set and he was entertaining himself with a book or partaking in a discussion with his sister and aunt before retiring for the night.

Today, however, he was making an exception to that regular pattern because his books were balanced, his letter had been written, and the stack of invitations had been whittled to an acceptable amount, and yet, he did not feel as he should. Something was off, and so he was willing to take pleasure in a favourite drink while... he shook his head, chuckled, and did what was most certainly out of the ordinary for him — he waited.

He had left the study door open a crack so that the sound of any callers would reach him. He shook his head again. The partially opened door was only more evidence that all was not as it had always been in his world, for he was not waiting for just any callers to arrive. Miss Bennet was to call on his sister today, and he was determined to once again attempt to prove to her that he could behave appropriately even if she did seem eager to misconstrue every word he uttered.

He was just finishing the last of his whisky when he heard that for which he had been waiting. The front door opened, followed by feminine voices wafting down the corridor to his study. Miss Bennet and her sister, Mrs. Darcy, were here.

Trefor remained seated, counting out a minute and a half before he rose. Then, after depositing his glass on his desk in a slow and deliberate fashion, he made his way to the sitting room.

"Crawford," he greeted his friend who was in the entry-way. "I assume you are here to see my sister."

"Indeed, I am, although a game of billiards would not be unwelcome if she is occupied."

Trefor's brow furrowed. His sister did have callers – callers whom he wished to see, or more precisely one in particular whom he did not want to miss seeing for at least a few minutes.

"I think Connie would like to see you first," he suggested.

Henry's brows rose. "But I can hear she has guests."

"There is no harm in saying *good day* before we play, is there?"

"She is not entertaining gentlemen, so why are you so eager to join her?"

That was a good question but not one which Trefor felt prepared to answer. In fact, he was convinced it was a question which would prove impossible to answer should he wish to attempt it, which he did not.

"I am not eager. It is just that I have walked from my study to here, so it seems pointless for me to retrace those steps only to have to return to the sitting room later."

"That makes little sense," Henry muttered.

Trefor shrugged and nodded for the sitting room door to be opened. His reasoning seemed to make sense to him, which should perhaps concern him considering the higgledy-piggledy state of his mind. He motioned for Henry to enter before him. That way he could take in the arrangement of the ladies in the room without it being obvious to his friend.

"You are joining us?" his aunt asked when she saw him.

"I like tea," he replied.

She lifted a questioning brow.

"It is not as if I do not join you on occasion."

"No," she agreed, "but I do find it curious."

"I have a few invitations for you to consider." He ignored her curiosity and gave her the stack he held.

"And were there others?" she asked as he took a seat nearer to where Miss Bennet sat.

"There were, but I thought we would start with those," he replied.

"I am constantly amazed at how many invitations my husband receives," Mrs. Darcy said. "There is just no way we can attend everything, and to be honest, Mr. Darcy is not overly fond of being away from home night after night."

"I can understand that," Trefor said. "I do not find the soirees unpleasant, but there is comfort in being home and quiet now and again."

"And certain soirees are more agreeable than others," Henry added with a smile. "Though I do find I enjoy attending soirees much more than I enjoy being at home. That is likely due to who will be there." He smiled at Constance, who responded in kind.

"Yes," she agreed, "I have developed a fondness for them myself that I never had before I was betrothed."

Miss Bennet sighed as if what his sister said was the most wonderful thing she had ever heard. A romantic. Miss Bennet must be a romantic. That was not something he had ever been. He was more practical and not so flighty as a romantic person was prone to be.

"I find Mr. Darcy enjoys soirees more now that we are married than he did before we were married." Mrs. Darcy shared a secret smile with her sister.

"Oh, yes!" Miss Bennet said with some feeling. "He was positively miserable at the assembly in Meryton." She turned to Constance. "That is where we first met him. He was a guest at Netherfield. That is the estate next to my fathers which Mr. Bingley – Mr. Darcy's particular friend and now my sister Jane's husband – has taken. It is a beautiful home, and the gardens are so inviting."

It was a bit of a wandering way to say something, but there was such animation to Miss Bennet's features when she spoke that Trefor found he did not mind the nomadic path her speech had taken.

"It is a happy thing for your sister to be settled so close to home," he said, attempting to enter the conversation in a way that would not be offensive.

"I think Mama would agree," Miss Bennet replied. "However, I do not expect it to remain as it is."

"You do not?" Mrs. Darcy sounded surprised.

Miss Bennet placed a hand on her sister's. "Jane loves you, and Mr. Bingley will not wish to be separated from his friend. They will find another place to call home soon after you and Mr. Darcy leave for Pemberley."

"But what of your mother?" Trefor asked, genuinely curious to know.

Miss Bennet laughed lightly. "She will not be without company. There are Mary, Lydia, and me, not to mention Mrs. Philips – that is Mama's sister – and Lady Lucas, who is Mama's particular friend." Her brow furrowed as her lips pursed in a most becoming expression of thought. "There are also several other ladies who come to call and all the tenants on whom to call." She emitted a small sigh. "But once my other sisters and I marry, she will have no one to accompany her on those calls."

"You accompany her?" Trefor asked.

"Oh, yes! It is very enjoyable."

"It is?"

"Yes."

Her brow was beginning to furrow. He needed to say something that would not cause that crease between her eyes to deepen.

"What is it about the visits that you like?"

She blinked her eyes as if he was asking something that should be obvious.

"The people," was her simple answer.

"I promise I am not being obtuse," he began, "but what about the people makes the task so agreeable?" He truly wished to understand her thinking and hoped she understood that.

"Well," she said before expelling a breath as if answering was a bit of a chore, but not a disagreeable one. "I find that calls such as this one and the ones in the tenant's homes fill me with..." Her voice trailed off as her features took on that becoming expression she seemed to favor when thinking.

"Lightness?" Constance suggested.

"Yes! That would be one way to say it. And if there are children who need attention," she shrugged, "I do like to read aloud." She blinked and drew a quick breath. "Perhaps that is why you do not understand it."

"Understand what?" he asked cautiously.

"My liking to visit the tenants. You said you did not like to read aloud last night, so could it not be that my enjoying chatting and reading to children seems foreign to you since you would not like it?" She tipped her head and looked at him expectantly.

"I honestly have not attempted to call on the wives of my tenants or read to their children. My mother always did that, and then Connie did it after Mother died."

"Then it seems you will either need to learn how or find a wife," Miss Bennet said in all seriousness before her eyes grew wide with horror. "Not that I am putting myself forward. We would never suit, but if you cannot visit the tenants, you must find someone who can." She ducked her head. "I was doing so well," she muttered.

He was not certain what she was no longer doing well, but her embarrassment caused him to want to say something that would ease it. Of course, he could not think of a single thing, and, therefore, he was not at all put out when his aunt took up the conversation.

"I have told him that he needs to find a wife, and I welcome your support on the matter, Miss Bennet." She smiled kindly at Miss Bennet. "Finding a wife to suit him has been a bit of a challenge. This is not his first season."

Miss Bennet giggled softly at that.

"I have discriminating tastes," he muttered as he was positive his aunt would expect some form of protest.

"We could make a list of what you are looking for in a wife," Henry said with a smirk.

Trefor shook his head. "That might have worked for you, but I prefer not to create a list of ladies and check them off one by one."

"You did that?" Miss Bennet asked Henry in utter shock.

Henry nodded. "I was attempting to reform my former behavior."

"Of course," Miss Bennet said, "you were a rake or some such thing."

"Kitty," Mrs. Darcy scolded softly.

Miss Bennet sighed and apologized.

"I am not offended. I was not what I should have been, and Miss Linton was gracious enough to help me learn to be a proper gentleman."

"And then I created a list of ladies for him."

Miss Bennet looked like she was going to faint away. "No! You did?"

Constance nodded. "It broke my heart to do it, but I had promised I would."

Miss Bennet's hand covered her heart as she shook her head. "How tragic."

"There are several interesting bits to that tale, which I will tell you when we are not beset on every side by gentlemen," Constance assured her. "Suffice it to say that none of the ladies on that list met with Mr. Crawford's approval, and I was fortunate to gain his favour."

Again, the romantic Miss Bennet sighed wistfully. But then, she sat up a little straighter, her eyes shining with excitement.

"Then, perhaps you could help me."

"With what?" Trefor asked before he could think better of it.

"With behaving as I ought while in town. It is not that I am an improper lady like Mr. Crawford was an improper gentleman. I just have never been to town before, and, well, I would like to make a good impression. After all, I would like to marry someday, and, to be frank, there are not many gentlemen from whom to choose in Hertfordshire – at least, there are none to my liking," she clarified.

"If Miss Linton helped me, perhaps her brother could help you by giving you a gentleman's viewpoint," Mr. Crawford suggested.

Miss Bennet shook her head vigorously. "That would not work."

Trefor was inclined to agree. He had seen what had happened when he had allowed his sister to help Henry.

"I am certain I need a lady's advice," Miss Bennet continued as Trefor recalled the article in the paper with his sister's name attached to it.

"Besides, Mr. Linton is far too provoking," she concluded, bringing Trefor's full attention back to the discussion at hand.

"I am provoking?" he asked incredulously.

"Yes."

"I do not see how."

Her brow furrowed as a scowl settle on her lips. "Must you always argue with me?"

"I do not argue with you. You argue with me," he retorted. Blast! That was not what he should have said. It was not what he would have said to any other lady, other than his sister.

Miss Bennet rolled her eyes and while making a sweeping motion with her hand towards him, said to Constance, "You see what I mean?"

Constance laughed. "Yes, I know very well of what you speak. He provokes me regularly, but he means well – most of the time."

"If you say so," Miss Bennet replied, though she did not sound at all convinced of the fact.

It was probably best that he leave now before he made things worse. "Crawford, if you are still interested in billiard, I would not be averse to a game or two." He rose, and thankfully, Henry joined him. However, before he left the room, there was one thing he needed to do.

He turned to Miss Bennet. "I am pleased that you and your sister were able to call on my sister and aunt today. I think Connie would do well to have friends such as you and Mrs. Darcy." He paused. "And, your dress is very pretty. Lavender suits you very well." He smiled at her look of surprise. "It is not at all maid-like nor is it in anyway pinchpenny. I know it cannot completely atone for my poor behaviour yesterday, but I do hope it is a start."

She blinked at him as if she was uncertain what to say. "Yes," she managed after a moment, "it is a very good start."

A feeling of accomplishment settled on Trefor as he quit the room. He had nearly managed to do what he had planned. Had it not been for that small disagreement, that would have been an excellent meeting with Miss Bennet. As it was, it was the best they had had so far, and that was promising. What exactly it promised he was not certain. He was just glad that this time when he left her, he did not do so feeling as low as an ant carrying an apple.

Chapter 8

Candles set high on candelabras stood at both the near and far ends of the ballroom while a chandelier glowed from above. The musicians were tucked neatly into a corner near the far end of the ballroom as the hopeful dancers formed the first set.

Kitty was happy to not be part of this first set. She would much rather sit along the wall and watch her sister and Mr. Darcy while allowing her heart to slow its pace and become acquainted with her setting. A ball was thrilling to be sure and even knowing few in attendance could not dampen the excitement she felt.

She smiled at the gentleman, who was watching her across the room, before quickly turning her eyes in the opposite direction. She should not have even encouraged him with a smile. She was to wait to be properly introduced to anyone she did not already know before accepting a dance partner. Yet, smiling had seemed the most natural thing in all the world to do, for it was what she would have done at any assembly in Meryton.

"The décor is just what it should be," the voice of a welcome companion pulled her from her observation of the ballroom.

"Indeed, it is, Mrs. Kendrick," Kitty agreed as Mr. Linton and his aunt joined her.

"You should be dancing," Mrs. Kendrick said.

"Oh, I will. I am sure I will not have to sit for more than this first dance," Kitty assured Mrs. Kendrick while purposefully not looking at Mr. Linton.

He was wearing a blue jacket tonight with a grey waistcoat and matching breeches. If a combination of colours could be chosen to make his eyes appear to best advantage, blue and grey was it. And while admiring the way his clothing set off his eyes would be excessively agreeable, Kitty did not need to be further confused by him than she already was.

Yesterday, he had been rude – abominably so, in her opinion. But then, today, he had been nearly charming. She ran her thumb across the edge of her folded fan. If he had been as pleasant yesterday as he had been today, she would not have written him into her story as a cursed gentleman.

What would she write tonight? A curse was not just lifted with one stroke of the pen until several trials had been completed. She knew she would have to torture him in some way in her story. However, his attractive attire and smile were not going to make it easy for her to do. Therefore, ignoring him as much as possible was the best course of action.

"My sister informs me that I am to request the second dance of the evening," Mr. Linton said, interrupting her thoughts.

Of course, he was not going to make ignoring him an easy task.

"I would not wish to inconvenience you," she replied with a tight smile. Being asked to dance just to appease a sister's desire was not precisely flattering.

Mr. Linton face was furrowed with confusion. "It is no inconvenience," he said in a cautious tone with a questioning lilt at the end.

"What Trefor is attempting to say is that his sister reminded him of his desire to dance with you," Mrs. Kendrick said.

"That is not precisely what I was attempting to say," he muttered, the look of confusion still on his face.

"Then, what, pray tell, were you saying?" his aunt asked.

The confused furrow between his eyes deepened as he took a seat next to his aunt. "I am not certain I can say without causing greater offense." Again, his statement ended with a questioning lilt.

"I am certain that Miss Bennet can withhold judgment until you have said all you need to say."

"Of course, I can," Kitty agreed.

"I did not mean to say that she could not."

Mr. Linton was looking positively ill, which was odd.

"My sister told me how she had mentioned to you, Miss Bennet, that I would be willing to ask you to dance – which I am." He blew out a breath. "By the by, you look exquisite tonight. The ribbon winding through your curls is very nice."

His eyes seemed to fixate on her head which caused her to touch her hair without thought to make sure all was well with it. Nothing seemed out of place.

"Then, as I was entering the carriage tonight, Connie reminded me that I was to ask for a dance and suggested that the second dance would be best as we were going to be too late for the first dance and having a partner for one of the beginning dances would set you up well for the evening. If you can get one sheep to enter the pasture, the others will often follow."

"Sheep?"

"Yes, yes, I will be the first to dance with you and then the others will follow."

His eyes had left her hair and were now following the dancers on the floor.

"Do you think I am incapable of acquiring a partner without your help?"

His head snapped back towards her. "Is that what I said?"

"It did sound that way," his aunt answered.

"That is not at all what I meant."

Kitty waited for his explanation while he studied first the room and then her.

"You are beautiful, as any gentleman here can see, and you will not lack for partners. However, according to Crawford and my sister, a desirable young woman becomes more so when she has ample admirers. So, I am just to help guarantee that a lady worthy of admiration receives all that she is due."

Kitty could not help but smile and blush at such words. When he was not stumbling over his words, Mr. Linton was capable of being rather worthy of swooning.

"And that is just like the sheep. If one of them can be persuaded to enter the field and eat the fresh grass and flowers, then the others will follow."

And then, he was back to stumbling. Her brow furrowed. She did not want to be fresh grass.

"Not that anyone needs to be persuaded to dance with you." He shook his head.

"It might be best if you stop trying to explain your odd metaphor," his aunt said. "Trefor is fond of strange saying. You are not a field that needs to be eaten to the ground by sheep. It is that sometimes gentlemen need leading." She smiled at her nephew who scowled in reply.

"I am not in need of leading," he muttered.

What was it that Mama had said a gentleman sometimes wanted? "Encouragement." That was it!

"I beg your pardon?" Mr. Linton said.

"It is not that gentlemen need leading," Kitty explained. "They need encouragement."

"I do like that idea better, but it does seem to be rather the same thing," Mr. Linton said in the same disgruntled tone he had used when protesting his aunt's words about needing to be led.

"The first set is half done," his aunt cautioned.

Mr. Linton took note of the dancers taking their places for the second half of the set. "Will you dance with me for the next set?" he asked Kitty. "I would be pleased if you did."

"Yes," Kitty answered. No one else had approached her yet – likely because Mr. Darcy was dancing. There was something about Mr. Darcy that caused other gentlemen to approach cautiously. Perhaps they had not yet learned that Mr. Darcy was not so dour as he appeared.

"You will?"

"Why are you surprised?" No gentleman had ever questioned an acceptance before.

He shrugged. "I do not know. I suppose I expected you to make me wait until the third or fourth set to prove you did not need my help in securing a partner or some such thing."

Kitty laughed. "I wish I had thought of that. My sister Lydia likely would have. She is the best at scheming." Lydia knew precisely how to draw a gentleman along.

"Are the two of you close?" Mrs. Kendrick inquired.

"We are. Lydia is not quite two years younger than me, and we have always been friends."

"But you seem incapable of scheming." Mr. Linton watched the dancers as he spoke.

Was he questioning her intelligence?

His eyes grew wide as he glanced her direction. Her face must be speaking of her displeasure at being thought stupid.

"I meant that you seem too sincere to be a schemer. It was a compliment." His brows furrowed. "Not that I am criticizing your sister in any fashion either," he added before sighing. "It is a pity that conversation is necessary at these soirees, for I seem to be lacking the skill necessary to acquit myself as a polite gentleman." He shook his head. "I am not generally so offensive."

"He is not," his aunt agreed. "Unless, of course, you are Mr. Edwards or Mr. Crawford and in need of a reprimand. Then, Trefor would be the first to point out the error of your ways."

Kitty could tell from the smile that Mrs. Kendrick wore that she truly loved her nephew, and if a lady like Mrs. Kendrick, whom Kitty had decided she admired shortly after they had met this morning, loved Mr. Linton then he was likely not always as he appeared.

She sighed silently. That was not going to make it any easier to torture him on his quest to get the log from the great tree.

Her eyes swept the room, taking note of various dresses and coats, as well as a few fine-feathered hats.

"Who is that gentleman standing close to the musicians?" Kitty asked. "He has been watching me, and I must admit he is rather handsome if a bit shorter than I would like."

"Mr. Densmore," Trefor replied. "He is upstanding, but his estate could use some work — or so I hear. So if you have a good dowry, securing him would not be too challenging."

Kitty leaned toward Mrs. Kendrick. "Does Mr. Linton always give his opinion of gentlemen so freely to ladies?"

Mrs. Kendrick chuckled. "No. Other than his sister, I believe you are the only lady who has ever been given such advice."

"It is very odd," Kitty whispered. "Not that it is unwelcomed intelligence, mind you."

"Do you have a substantial dowry?" Mrs. Kendrick asked in a whisper.

Kitty shook her head.

"But you are Mr. Darcy's sister now, so that will make some think that you might have a hefty purse," Mrs. Kendrick continued.

Well, that was most certainly unwelcome news. "Do you think Mr. Linton could tell me which ones are fortune hunters so that I do not hope where there is none?"

"Gladly," Mr. Linton whispered. "However, I would

hold up my fan while having such a conversation to keep the interested from attempting to decipher what is being said."

There was so much to remember here in town! Kitty opened her fan and held it up.

"Thank you," she whispered.

"Anything to be of service, Miss Bennet," he replied with a relaxed smile.

Until this point, she had not seen him smile so easily, and what a beautiful smile it was, tipping up higher on the right than on the left while the sincerity of his words shone in his eyes.

"Ah, we have only a few more patterns, and then, it is our turn, Miss Bennet."

"Do you dance as well as you converse?" Kitty teased.

Mr. Linton chuckled. "Usually, yes, but then, usually I am not bumbling my words as I seem to do when I am with you." He glanced down at her feet. "I do hope your toes survive."

Kitty laughed. "That is not very reassuring."

"Indeed, it is not, but it is the truth."

"And Trefor is nothing if not honest," his aunt inserted.

Kitty poked her feet out a little further. "These are new slippers. I have only worn them to one other ball while in town."

Mr. Linton stood and held out his hand to her as the

dancers, who were on the floor, began to exit it. "I shall do my best not to ruin them."

~*~*~

As it happened, Mr. Linton did an excellent job of keeping her slippers safe, for other than two stumbles where he seemed to forget his steps, he had danced very well. Kitty was certain, as she made her way to the retiring room with her sister, that she would not hesitate to accept him as a dance partner again.

"Miss Bennet!"

Kitty stopped on the staircase and turned to see Mr. Linton hurrying after her. "It looks as if he has my fan," she said to Elizabeth. "I will join you in a moment."

"Are you certain?"

"You have been waiting this age for me. Go. I will be well."

Her sister looked relieved and hurried on her way.

"My aunt thought you would not wish to lose this." Mr. Linton said as he bounded down the steps toward her. "And so, I told her I would return it to you." He came to a stop two steps below her.

"That was kind of you," she said as she accepted the fan from him. He looked as if he wanted to say something else. However, when he did not, she began to feel foolish and moved to step to the side and continue down the steps to the lower floor where the retiring room was located. However, making a neat and tidy exit was not to be, for in her haste, Kitty caught her toe on the hem of her dress, and then, Mr. Linton caught her.

"Are you well?" he asked as he held her in his embrace.

"Yes, yes, I am well." Mortified, but well. It was only her pride that hurt.

He brushed a curl away from her face. "Are you certain?"

She nodded, unable to speak while he looked at her so intently. Then, his head lowered towards her before he suddenly straightened and released her abruptly.

"If you are well," he muttered.

"Yes, thank you," she replied, feeling a trifle confused by his sudden cool manner.

"Then, I am glad I could be of service." He bowed and left her standing there, looking after him as he fled up the steps.

She raised a brow and shook her head. Mr. Linton was so odd. She fingered the curl he had brushed aside as frustration welled inside of her. He really should have offered his arm and seen her safely down the last few steps, but instead, he fled! Feeling very much as if she had been abandoned, Kitty hurried down the steps and to the retiring room to find her sister.

Chapter 9

"What has you skulking in the garden?"

Trefor looked up from examining the ground to find his friend Charles Edwards standing next to him. "I did not hear you approach."

"That is obvious. Now, what has you out here? Your sister is concerned which, in turn, means Evelyn is also worried." He leaned against the balustrade next to where Trefor was looking out into the small garden.

"I cannot do this." Trefor turned and motioned to the ballroom. "I think I might retire to the country early."

"You know you cannot do that. There are two weddings you must attend."

Trefor blew out a breath and shook his head. "I can return when needed. Aunt Gwladys can see to Connie and whatever needs doing there. Besides, I should see that her things are made ready to be delivered to Crawford's. And if I stay in town, my aunt will expect me to escort her to every function so she can find me a wife."

"And that is a problem because... you do not wish to find a wife?"

Trefor scrubbed his face with his hands. "No. I will need one eventually."

"But you do not want one?" Charles pressed.

"No. I would very much like to marry – eventually – when I have found a lady who interests me in such a fashion. I do not want a pretty face with feathers for brains." He wanted someone to whom he could talk about anything and everything, but also someone who he would wish to take to bed for pleasure and not just to dutifully sire the required heir.

"Miss Bennet is interesting."

Charles was looking at him with that smug expression like he had at the literary reading and just as he had in the hallway at Mrs. Verity's. It was not a look Trefor felt needed a response.

"And she is pretty," Charles added.

Trefor grunted his reluctant agreement. Miss Bennet was more than just pretty. She was intoxicating.

"And I doubt she has feathers for brains if she is happy at a literary reading," Charles said.

Again, Trefor grunted but added a shrug this time. She likely enjoyed poetry as much as novels and would be willing to read such to him. He would not find it a trial to listen to her for he imagined she would read with great expression just as she spoke with animation.

"She dances well."

"And what does that qualify her for?" Trefor grumbled.

"You would always have an excellent dance partner."

A delightful partner to be precise.

"I do not intend to dance once I am married," Trefor objected.

"You do plan to have children, do you not?"

"Of course."

"And they will need to be introduced to society, will they not?"

"As long as I have boys, I shall not need to escort them."

Charles chuckled. "You can no more guarantee that than you can determine the yield of next year's wheat harvest."

A scowl settled over Trefor's face and mind. It was not that he never expected to dance again after he married. He quite liked a country dance now and again. However, he would not need to do it several times a month for several months of the year while his aunt whispered about this or that lady's qualifications.

He should just take a walk around the room, examine the ladies present, and pick the best of the lot so he could be done with it. Not unlike how he chose his horse – which had proven to be an excellent choice.

Again, he scrubbed his face. He could not make this a business transaction. A wife was not something you put out to pasture if she was not a good fit.

"I just cannot do this any longer," he muttered as he turned and looked out at the garden. "Do you know what I did tonight?" He glanced at Charles, who was still looking rather amused at his friend's plight. What Trefor was about to say would likely send the fellow into peals of laughter that would double him over with their intensity.

"No, I really could not guess." Charles turned to lean one hip on the balustrade so that he could look at Trefor.

A breeze rustled the branches below them.

"I nearly kissed her." Trefor braced himself for the hilarity to come, but to his surprise, Charles was absolutely silent.

"Miss Bennet," Trefor clarified.

Still, Charles said not a word for a full minute.

"At a ball?"

"Yes, yes, that is where we are," Trefor snapped. "We were on the steps leading down to the ground floor."

"Here? Tonight?"

It was as if his friend was slow of understanding. "Yes, when and where else would it have been? I have only known the vexing woman for two days."

That caused his friend's eyebrows to lift. "Vexing?"

There was no use in attempting to gingerly step around the subject, Edwards was not the sort to let a curious bit of news die until he had heard the whole story. He was frightfully inquisitive.

"I cannot put two words together without my tongue

running ahead of my brain – not that the grey matter between my ears is even capable of rational thought when Miss Bennet is present." He shifted. "It is not as if I have not been in the presence of many pretty young debutantes. I have. And on each of those occasions, I have performed remarkably well – charmingly, even. But not with her.

"With her, I offend. I say things I did not know I had said, and I find myself nearly kissing a lady on the steps at a ball. And I cannot even apologize to her for my behavior since I will likely make it worse by saying something that I should not say or that she will not take as I meant it."

Charles chuckled. "You could start with will you marry me and extend this delicious torture forever."

"That will not do." The mere thought made his heart race and not in a pleasant fashion but more like he imagined it would when faced by an adder.

"I do not see why not," Charles retorted. "I would put money on it that even if you hie off to the country, she will follow you. However, I have sworn off bets, so you can keep your money."

Trefor only shook his head and turned his attention to the garden. Marriage had never before sent his heart flying like a skittish horse after hearing a loud clap of thunder. It had always been a topic which he could discuss in the calm, serious tone such an important matter deserved.

He blamed Miss Bennet for that. She was the cause of his world being on end.

"I never thought to hear you say that you kissed a lady at a ball," Charles muttered.

"For good reason," Trefor replied. "And it was almost kissed. *Almost.* I did not kiss her." No matter how much he wished even now that he had.

Good heavens! What was wrong with him?

It was most probably due to the fact that he had spent far too much time with rapscallions like Edwards and Crawford. A bad apple was never improved by placing it with the good ones. He should have known that eventually, the company he kept would cause him some trouble.

His brow furrowed. Reprobate friends and decaying morals aside, he needed to apologize to Miss Bennet for taking such liberties as he had. But how?

"Are you returning to the dancing?" Charles asked.

Trefor shook his head. "I think it best if I do not."

"And how much of this conversation shall I share with Mrs. Kendrick when explaining why it is best if you do not?"

"You are the worst friend," Trefor grumbled.

"No, that would be Crawford. I am not marrying your sister."

Trefor shook his head. "Crawford is not out here threatening to tell my aunt about how Miss Bennet has my head in a muddle."

This was met with a chuckle.

"No, I believe he has arranged to meet your sister in an alcove and was unavailable for this task."

"He has done what?" Trefor growled.

"They are betrothed," Charles cautioned as Trefor moved to enter the building. "Which, of course, will mean that Henry is not *almost* kissing her."

"How long until the two of you wed your ladies so I can be rid of this town?"

"At the end of the season, which I believe was a suggestion that you made to Crawford and Mrs. Barrett decided was a good one for me as well."

"Well, it was a stupid one," Trefor grumbled.

"I would not argue that point."

Of course, his friend would not. The past several weeks were the longest single stretch of time that Edwards had ever comported himself appropriately with a lady. Trefor stopped just inside the ballroom. "You are changed."

"How so?" Charles eyed him warily.

"You do not seek out alcoves and flirt."

"True."

"Will it remain this way?"

Charles nodded his head.

"Because of a lady?" A sinking feeling filled Trefor's being.

"Yes. A very demanding, yet excessively wonderful,

lady, whom I love more than alcoves, stolen kisses, and even life itself."

Had the room grown warmer while he was outside or was it just coming in from the coolness of the night that made Trefor wish to mop his brow?

"Are you well?" Edwards asked him.

Trefor nodded but then shook his head. "I hardly know."

His friend slapped him on the back. "Ah, but you will know, eventually. We all do."

Trefor followed behind his friend who was far too optimistic at times such as right now when Trefor felt that his world was tilted in the wrong direction and would never be righted.

"I see you found him," Aunt Gwladys said when they joined her.

"He has a bit of a headache," Charles said.

"Do you need to go home?" his aunt asked.

Trefor considered it for a moment. He did not actually have a headache, but he was not feeling quite right. "It might be best." Not that retiring early would cure what ailed him.

"I will see if Mrs. Barrett will see Constance home," his aunt replied.

"You do not need to leave," Trefor protested. "I can take a hack."

"Are you certain?"

"Positive." He wanted to be alone. He needed to be alone. He did not need to have an aunt questioning him about his wellbeing, and he knew Aunt Gwladys would.

"Well, then, we will see you tomorrow."

He nodded. Of course, she would expect him to be in bed when she got home, and he would be. Whether or not he would be sleeping or merely staring at the ceiling feeling just as bewildered as he did now remained to be seen.

Quickly, he made his way out of the ballroom and down the stairs. He was just retrieving his hat from the butler when he was struck with a solution to his problem.

"Would you happen to have paper and a pen that I could use to leave a message for someone?"

"Of course, Mr. Linton. If you will follow me."

Just down the hall in a pleasant library, he was shown to a writing desk.

"I will be near the door if you need me to deliver it for you," the butler said before leaving him.

Trefor smoothed the paper and dipped his pen in the ink.

Miss Bennet,

I should likely reserve this apology until next we meet when you call on my sister. However, I find that I am too unsettled to do as I should. You have a unique ability to unsettle me which is why I am writing this apology instead of speaking it. I am certain I would say something to offend but hope that in writing, I will be able to express myself in a better fashion.

My behaviour on the stairs tonight was not as it ought to have been. I should have released you as soon as I knew that you were no longer in danger of falling, but I could not. I do not know why I could not, but I could not. I promise you that I do not, as a practice, embrace young ladies or nearly kiss them as I did you. Again, I must repeat myself. You have a unique ability to unsettle me and cause me to do things I would not normally do.

Please forgive me for my behavior. I promise to respond in a more appropriate fashion whenever we next meet – even if you should once again fall into my arms.

I shall call on you tomorrow to learn my fate. Accept me if you will or send me away if you must.

Yours, etc.

Linton

He waited for the ink to dry, then folded the missive and left the library.

"Will you see that Mr. –" No, he could not give this to Mr. Darcy. There was no need for the gentleman to read it.

"– Miss Bennet receives this? She is accompanied by Mr. and Mrs. Darcy this evening."

"I shall see that it is done straight away."

Feeling as if a small burden had been lifted, Trefor thanked the man and made his way out into the night to find his way home.

Chapter 10

"Good morning, Catherine." Mr. Gardiner looked up from his paper.

"Good morning, uncle," Kitty returned his greeting as she sat down at the table in the Gardiner's dining room to have a cup of tea. Was there a reason he used her full name?

Her uncle put his paper aside. His smile was pleasant. Perhaps he had just decided to use her full name for no particular reason.

"Your aunt informed me that you had an enjoyable evening."

"I did!" Kitty exclaimed. "I danced all but two sets."

It had been a delightful ball. She had never felt so wonderful as she had last evening with gentleman after gentleman asking her for a dance. It did not even bother her that some were likely doing it because they thought she had money. However, she had kept a list of names and would ask Mr. Linton when she saw him next. There were three days before she was promised to attend any soirees, so she had plenty of time to discover whatever she needed to know about each and every one of the gentlemen with whom she had danced.

"And I heard you lost your footing on the stairway."

Kitty blushed. "It was foolish. I caught my toe on my dress, but I did not fall."

"No, a gallant young man was there to catch you." He smiled at her. "Your aunt told me. She did not tell me if he has eyes that are bluer than Mr. Waller's, however."

Kitty laughed. "He does not. Mr. Waller's eyes are dark blue. Mr. Linton's are lighter and more silvery but very striking." In fact, they were the most captivating eyes she had seen last night. She quite liked them. Very much, truth be told.

"I also heard that he almost kissed you."

Kitty swallowed the sip of tea she had taken before turning startled eyes toward her uncle. She had not told her aunt that! In fact, she had not even been certain if Mr. Linton had intended to kiss her. Her uncle was not looking at her but was spooning jam onto his toast.

"And," Uncle Gardiner continued as he spread the jam all the way to the edges of his bread, "I hear he is hoping for your acceptance of something – an offer of marriage was implied."

"You heard what?" Kitty forced the words out. Marriage? Acceptance? Of what was her uncle speaking?

"Just a bit of some fantastic tale in the paper. You know

how it is, no names were given, but the clues are hard to miss."

"Paper?"

Her uncle sighed. "I had feared it was a fabricated concoction." He smiled softly at her. "I told your aunt we would have been told if any gentleman were to make an offer to you. I did not think you would keep anything so momentously happy from us."

"I do not know of what you speak." Panic, like an enormous wave, was swelling within Kitty and threatening to break over her and sweep her away when it withdrew from the shore.

Mr. Gardiner took a bite of his toast before picking up his paper. "Four lines," he said. "There is not much to it, just a little mention on the society page." He took another bite of his toast.

How could he eat when her life was hanging precariously close to a violent ocean eager to devour her? Kitty lifted her cup and with effort managed to swallow a bit of her tea.

"Here." He placed his finger on the page. "*Miss B, the new sister of Mr. F.D. of Derbyshire, has made quite the splash in her first season. It has been said Mr. T.L. of Suffolk is anxiously anticipating her reply to his letter of offer. Will there be happiness in store for Mr. T.L. or will he be left with only his memory of holding her in his arms and a near kiss and naught else?*"

A small amount of relief washed over Kitty. The mention of the kiss was disturbing, but the offer could be easily explained away, could it not? "It is only a rumour of an offer. That is not so bad, is it?"

Her uncle shrugged. "It really depends on how those who read it spin the tail. That bit about holding you in his arms and a near kiss is perhaps the worst of it."

That was what she had also feared. "But holding me in his arms could refer to a dance, could it not? There was no one on the stairs with me when I fell."

Again, her uncle shrugged. "It could very much refer only to a dance." His face grew serious. "Why would anyone expect an offer has been made by Mr. Linton? And what of the near kiss?"

Kitty shook her head. "I do not know. He did not kiss me. We talked during the first set, then danced the second, and then later met on the stairs. Could it be that he bent his head to hear me when we were dancing? Could that be a near kiss?" None had seen him bend his head towards her on the stairs.

Her uncle shrugged. "I could not say."

"He did not kiss me," Kitty reasserted. Not that she had not spent a portion of the night wondering if he had intended to and then considering whether or not she wished he had. "After saving me from falling on the stairs, he disappeared. His sister said he was on the terrace and then later Mr. Edwards said Mr. Linton had gone home with a headache."

"He only danced the one set with you? He danced with no one else?"

Kitty shook her head. "He danced once with his sister and another time with Miss Barrett – Mr. Edward's betrothed. Then, he left."

"Then, you were the only lady, other than those of his intimate circle, with whom he danced?"

"Yes."

"I am not well-versed in the gossip of the ton, but when I was courting your aunt, to attend an assembly and only dance with your sister and her friend and then one other lady was seen as paying special attention to that other lady. Such a thing always brought talk of betrothals."

"Oh, dear." Kitty slumped into her chair. "What does this mean for me?"

Her uncle blew out a breath. "I cannot say for certain. It really does depend upon how the gossips weave the tail. I will speak with Mr. Darcy and see what he says. You did not receive a letter from Mr. Linton, did you?"

Kitty shook her head. She knew that correspondence from a gentleman was not something of which Mama would approve if the gentleman had not received permission from her uncle or Mr. Darcy to send her letters. Much could be misconstrued from accepting such. Why, according to Mama, a lady who corresponded with a gentleman was as good as betrothed to the fellow.

"Oh," she groaned. "Must I marry him?"

Her uncle shook her head. "I do not think that things are so serious as that."

Oh, but if she had to! She took a deliberate sip of her tea. It tasted bland and not at all as welcoming as it should – much like her perfect ball had been turned into part of a terrible dream.

"He is not dreadful," she said. But he was disagreeable, and she knew so little about him. She had not thought to ask about his estate or what desserts he preferred or if he liked hunting and riding. She only knew that he liked to argue with her and did not always stop to think before he spoke.

She took another sip of her flavourless tea. It was at least warm. There was a little comfort in that, as there was also some comfort in knowing that she liked both Mrs. Kendrick and Miss Linton. If she were forced to marry Mr. Linton, she would at least have a sister and an aunt she admired.

Marry Mr. Linton? It was a thought with such finality. She had hoped to meet several gentlemen and be called on and taken for drives and such before two or three of them presented their offers. She would then deliberate and choose the one that grieved her heart the most to think of losing.

"I have only just begun my season," she whispered. "It cannot be over before it has begun."

Her uncle rose from his place, came around the table,

and placed a hand on her shoulder. "We must not fret about things we do not know. Will you still be going to Elizabeth's for calling hours as planned?"

"Do you think I should?"

"Your aunt thought it best. We must know what is being said and how you will be received. However, you are staying with us, and it would be no big thing for Elizabeth to inform callers that you were unable to join her."

Stay here and wait to hear her fate rather than discover it as soon as possible? It was tempting to hide, but then one could not hide from worry and curiosity. "I will go."

And she did go. In fact, she and her aunt were half an hour early to their time, but neither Mr. Darcy nor Elizabeth seemed disturbed by that. In fact, it came as a relief to them, for they had wished to speak to Kitty about the article in the paper and one other thing.

"You were given what?" Kitty could not believe what her sister had just said.

"A letter from Mr. Linton to you. You were dancing at the time, and I put it in my reticule and promptly forgot until I was home. I did not think it was something which needed to be delivered to you before you arrived today."

"What does it say?" Kitty could not imagine what Mr. Linton had to write to her about.

"I did not read it."

"Nor did I," Darcy said. "Although I wished to."

Elizabeth laughed. "He was not pleased that the gentleman had left you a letter and had dispatched a footman to give it to you at a ball."

"Indeed," Darcy agreed flatly. "If a gentleman is going to give a letter to a lady, firstly, there should be a very good reason, and secondly, it should be done privately so that not all in attendance knows it has been done."

"Does everyone know that he left me a letter?" Oh! She should have allowed the horrid beast guarding the logs at the great tree to devour him!

"My husband exaggerates." Elizabeth's smile for Mr. Darcy was teasing. "You did not know about the letter, so therefore, it only stands to reason that not everyone in attendance knows about that letter. In fact, it was delivered in a somewhat discreet fashion. I am certain that not more than three of four ladies near me heard the footman say that Mr. Linton had left a message for Miss Bennet and would I be able to give it to her."

Kitty scowled. "He does the stupidest things!"

Mr. Darcy chuckled. "My guess is that he is not usually so stupid. He may have just gotten off on the wrong foot and has no idea how to regain his footing."

Kitty raised a brow. It was not just that Mr. Linton had made a bad first impression. He had made very few good impressions at all in the two days she had known him.

"This is the letter," Elizabeth took a paper from the table beside her. "Mr. Darcy would like to see it, of course, but the decision is yours."

"And you do not wish to see it?" Aunt Gardiner asked Elizabeth with a laugh.

"She was more curious about it last night than I was," Darcy replied.

"And it has been a trial not to peek at it," Elizabeth agreed.

"Oh, my!" Kitty exclaimed. He had almost kissed her! She had not been mistaken. It was somewhat delightful to inspire a handsome gentleman to wish to kiss her, even if it was entirely unexpected and improper.

"What is it?" Elizabeth asked.

Kitty blushed. "An apology." She glanced at her aunt. "You see I almost fell down the stairs last night after Mr. Linton returned my fan to me."

"You what?" Elizabeth exclaimed.

"Mr. Linton saved her," Aunt Gardiner said. "She told me about it before she went to bed."

"And you did not tell me?"

"She did not wish for you to feel badly about doing as she said and going on to the retiring room without her," Aunt Gardiner said.

"And if this letter had not caused the issues it has..." Kitty pressed her lips together. Her excuses were not lessening the look of displeasure on her sister's face. "I truly did not wish to worry you." She took one more look at her letter and then handed it to her sister. "You may read it."

She knew she had to let them read it, but that did not

make her heart hammer any less as Elizabeth read the missive.

"Oh, my, indeed," Elizabeth said before handing the letter to Mr. Darcy.

Everyone waited silently as each person was given a chance to read the letter. Or more precisely, they waited silently except for the small exclamation each made in turn as they read it. Apparently, Mr. Linton wishing to kiss Kitty was just as shocking to them as it was to her.

Aunt Gardiner was just folding the letter and saying, "Well, it seems our Kitty has an admirer," when the butler entered the room and announced...

"Mr. Linton to see Miss Bennet and Mr. Darcy."

Chapter 11

Trefor shifted from foot to foot as he stood, waiting to be allowed entrance to the Darcy's sitting room.

This morning, he had practised his confession to his aunt, his sister, and Crawford. Edwards had not been home when he called, or Trefor would have given his speech to Charles as well.

However, now that he stood here, knowing that *she* was in the sitting room, no amount of practice could keep his thoughts in a tidy order in his head.

She was frustratingly distracting. He closed his eyes but just as had happened when he had attempted to sleep last night, enchanting hazel eyes, beautiful brown hair, and animated features were all he could see.

"Mr. Linton," the butler's voice broke through Trefor's thoughts, "they will see you now."

"Right. Good. Thank you." He looked at the hat in his hand and then held it out to the butler. "Keep it close. I may be sent packing rather quickly." Hopefully, in one piece.

The man nodded and took the hat.

With a final deep breath, he willed his mind to order itself and walked into the sitting room.

"Good day," he bowed to Mr. Darcy and his wife before giving a bow of his head to the lady sitting next to Miss Bennet. Then...

Then, he looked at *her*. And all hope was indeed lost. Not a rational thought remained in his head. So, he plunged forward hoping that he would not overly offend anyone, but most especially Miss Bennet.

"It seems that in my attempt to correct my poor behaviour I have made a muck of things and find myself yet again – or still – in need of apologizing."

"Please, be seated," Mr. Darcy offered.

"Are you sure you wish that?" Trefor asked. "Miss Bennet's name appeared in the paper because of me."

"Yes, I know. Now, sit."

"Of course, sir." Trefor did as he was instructed. He did not need to anger anyone further than they might already be angered. He blew out a breath and rubbed his hands on the top of his thighs. This room was excessively warm.

"Are you well?" Miss Bennet asked him.

He shook his head. "No, and I have not been since you crashed into me two days ago."

"Me? Crash into you? I believe it was you who did the crashing."

This was not a good start to things. Not at all. "You are correct."

"I am?" She blinked at him in surprise.

"Yes. Unless you would like me to say you are not." His eyes were fixed on Miss Bennet, but to his right, he could hear Mr. Darcy chuckle. That was odd. A gentleman whose relation had been named in a story in the paper should not be chuckling – not that Trefor was about to point that out to the gentleman.

Miss Bennet's brow furrowed. "Do you think I am correct or not?"

"I have very little clue as to what I think," he answered honestly. "But considering how we first met and knowing that I was exiting the drawing room in haste and a foul mood, it is most likely that you are indeed correct." He glanced from her to the lady beside her. He had seen her before. Of course, he could not, at his moment, place where.

"This is my aunt, Mrs. Gardiner. Aunt, this is Mr. Linton."

Ah! That was it.

"We are not complete strangers," Mrs. Gardiner said.

"No, indeed, we have seen each other in passing at Mrs. Verity's," Trefor agreed. "However, I have never officially met you, and if it were not for the present circumstances, I would say it is a pleasure to finally meet. Not that meeting you now is unpleasant – it is the circumstances that are unpleasant." He cast a worried look at Kitty as he once again heard Mr. Darcy chuckle. Perhaps his discomfort and apparent ineptitude was satisfaction enough for Mr. Darcy.

"I did not think that my leaving you a message would end with your name in the paper, Miss Bennet." He slipped a finger behind his cravat and pulled at it to try to loosen it some. The room was only growing warmer.

"However, as my sister and my aunt and even Crawford have reminded me, it was poor form to write to a lady without permission from her guardian and some sort of understanding, which two days ago, I would have known."

"It is rather shocking," Miss Bennet said. "I only received it and read it this morning."

His brow furrowed and he looked from Miss Bennet to Mrs. Darcy and then her husband. "I do not understand. The butler said that he would see it was given to Miss Bennet straight away."

"My sister was dancing, and so it was given to me," Mrs. Darcy replied. "I only remembered it once we were home last night and so did not give it to Kitty until just before you arrived."

"Truly?" He had been certain that someone had been reading over Miss Bennet's shoulder or some such thing and that was how the content of his letter had become known. "Then, how?"

"Did you think I told the paper?"

His head snapped toward Miss Bennet. "No, I thought the letter had been seen by someone when you were reading it or dropped and read before it was returned to you."

"The gentry are not the only ones who can read and gossip," Mrs. Gardiner said.

Of course! Trefor ran a hand through his hair. "Apparently, I overlooked that fact as well when I launched my brilliant plan."

"Such things can happen," Mr. Darcy agreed.

Trefor's brow furrowed. The man was too agreeable. But then, nothing had been as it was supposed to be since meeting Miss Bennet. Therefore, he really should not be so startled by Mr. Darcy's lack of stamping and snorting.

"I do not understand how such things can happen," Miss Bennet said.

"You are unsettling," Trefor replied. "As I said in my letter. I did say that, did I not?"

"Yes, you did," Mr. Darcy replied.

He had read the letter and still was not fuming? Trefor thought he had mentioned nearly kissing Miss Bennet in there somewhere. He was almost positive of it.

"I also do not see how I can be unsettling," Kitty said.

"But you are," Trefor assured her. "I assure you that I am a very proper sort of fellow – normally – before you crashed into me." Her eyebrows rose. "Forgive me. Before you crashed into me. No, no, that is not it. Before I crashed into you. I simply cannot think straight around you."

"That is ridiculous," Miss Bennet scoffed.

"I agree," Trefor assured her, "but it is also true." He blew out a breath. "Where do we go from here?" He turned his eyes back toward Mr. Darcy.

"I would suggest a courtship," Mr. Darcy replied.

"A what?" Miss Bennet exclaimed.

"A courtship," Darcy repeated. "There are those who have read the paper who will expect that Mr. Linton has made some sort of offer for you. Any sort of gossip that might ensue can be more easily turned aside if we present an amicable friendship to one and all, and the wags will find something more interesting to discuss."

"But a courtship?" Miss Bennet pressed. "A courtship precedes a betrothal."

"It can," Mr. Darcy agreed, "but only if the young lady accepts an offer of marriage once one is made. For now, you are only agreeing to discover who Mr. Linton is and if you will suit."

"A courtship?" Miss Bennet repeated.

"Yes," Mr. Darcy answered, "I propose that Mr. Linton call on you regularly as would be expected by those who might be watching. He will dance with you at balls – two sets. He can take you for drives and whatever else he might think to do as a suitor, and then you can decide after a period of time if things should continue or be dissolved. Are you agreeable to that, Mr. Linton?"

"If Miss Bennet is," Trefor replied. "It seems a sensible plan."

"But no other gentlemen will call on me," Miss Bennet protested.

"And Mr. Linton will give up calling on any other ladies," Mr. Darcy countered.

"I have never been to town before." Miss Bennet's voice was soft enough to prick Trefor's heart.

"Other gentlemen can still dance with you at balls," he offered, "and if one of them catches your interest –" Oh! That hurt. "—you have only to say so, and I will step away."

"Are you certain this is the best way?" Miss Bennet asked Mr. Darcy.

"I would agree that it is," Mrs. Gardiner said.

"As would I," Elizabeth added. "Mr. Linton is very generous to be willing to give up so much and then step aside as a gentleman who has been shunned if you decide on another." She glanced at him. "And I think he understands what is being asked of you."

"Indeed, I am grieved that you must be put in this situation," he said. "I assure you that this was not my intent whatsoever."

A pretty, though sad, pout formed on her lips. "You are not dreadful," she said.

"I am flattered," he replied flatly, earning him a small smile.

"At least not when you are not being disagreeable. Do you suppose you could refrain from arguing with me?"

"I do not argue with you. You argue with me."

Her eyebrows rose.

"I shall make an attempt, but I cannot promise," he adjusted. "You are provoking."

"Really, Mr. Linton. I am both unsettling and provoking?"

Her eyes were sparkling. He was not doomed to being the fellow who had stolen the light from her eyes. That was a relief.

"Yes, quite."

"I do not see what about me is either unsettling or provoking."

"Have you no mirror?" The thought was out of his mouth before he could capture it.

"Of course, I have a mirror. I do not see what that has to do with anything."

He cast a nervous glance in Mr. Darcy's direction. The gentleman was looking excessively amused. Yes, the man must be taking great satisfaction in Trefor's unease. With that in mind, Trefor hurled himself into what was likely going to be a humiliating admission to make in front of a lady who only deemed him "not horrid."

"Have you used it?"

"My mirror?" Miss Bennet's brows were lifted high.

"Yes."

"Why would I have a mirror and not use it?"

Trefor shrugged. "I would think that one would use a mirror if she had one, and if you have, then you must be aware of one reason why you are profoundly unsettling."

Her brow furrowed.

"You are beautiful."

"Oh!" Her cheeks grew rosy, and her lips turned up into a pleased smile.

"And what makes her provoking?" Mr. Darcy's voice was laced with amusement.

"Her infernal compulsion to argue with me." Trefor smiled sheepishly. "And, more often than not, be correct."

"Yes," Darcy said with a chuckle, "I believe that runs in the family."

"Being correct does," Mrs. Darcy inserted.

Mrs. Gardiner simply laughed, letting Trefor know that what was said must be true.

"I am correct?" Miss Bennet asked.

"Many times," he answered.

A smile spread across her face. "Thank you. I do not think I have been told that before." She tipped her head. "You are really quite charming when you are agreeable. Yes, I think we shall affect a courtship."

"Are you certain you can tolerate it?" Trefor teased.

"No, but we must try." She batted her lashes as she spoke.

Real or no, Trefor expected he was going to enjoy courting Miss Bennet.

"Then, shall we start with a drive in the park?"

"Today?"

Trefor nodded. "If that is acceptable with Mr. Darcy and your aunt."

"But I do not have my driving bonnet."

He could tell from the worried look on her face that she was not just putting forward an excuse to put him off. "Then, tomorrow. If your aunt would be so kind as to tell me where I can collect you."

"Only," Mrs. Gardiner said, "if you agree to come to dinner when you are through. Lizzy and Mr. Darcy, as well as my children, will be there."

"I would be delighted." Trefor rose. "This ended more agreeably than I expected." He gave a bow of his head to Mr. Darcy. "I thank you for not blackening my eye as I did to the gentleman whose name was linked in the paper to my sister's."

Darcy chuckled. "If your reputation had been what Mr. Edwards' was, I likely would have."

"I thank you just the same." He turned to Miss Bennet. "And thank you for agreeing to allow me to pretend to court you." He paused before turning to leave. "Am I forgiven for my improper behavior and not thinking through my solution of sending you a letter?"

Her lips pursed, but her eyes were dancing. "Oh, your

quest has just begun, Mr. Linton. However, telling me I was both beautiful and correct was a fine start."

"And how long shall my quest be?" He must remember that she was a romantic and, as most romantics were, was likely given to flights of fancy.

"I believe the standard is three tests, which means you have to successfully complete two more." She held up a finger. "But you cannot just repeat what you have done today, nor can I tell you what you must do for part of the trial is the discovery. Otherwise, a transformation is not real. It must come from your soul."

"Well, then, I look forward to continuing the quest tomorrow." He tipped his head. "Would flowers help?"

She laughed lightly. "I cannot tell you, Mr. Linton."

"That is a pity. I have already proven myself rather inept where you are concerned. It could be a lengthy quest."

"Or, you might never complete it." She batted her lashes as she spoke.

"Provoking. Utterly provoking," he muttered before taking his leave.

Chapter 12

Kitty pressed the top of her pen against her lip as she thought.

"You look perplexed," her aunt said.

"I am." She sighed. "Mr. L in my story..." She glanced sheepishly at her aunt. "He is who the story is about."

"Yes, I know."

Kitty's face pulled into a slight grimace. "He is also Mr. Linton." She tried not to feel the sting of guilt that accompanied the confession, but it could not be avoided.

"Does your uncle know this?" Her aunt was making a valiant effort not to smile as she applied herself to her knitting.

Uncle Gardiner had read the beginning of Kitty's story just yesterday. He had been impressed with the cause of the worn jacket and the curse that had been cast on poor Mr. L. It had been quite encouraging to hear his thoughts on her work. He had not teased, nor had he looked as if he was attempting to be kind.

"I do not think he does." At least, she had not told him;

however, her uncle was very clever, so it was possible that he had figured it out.

"Are you worried that you have treated Mr. L far more harshly than he deserves by cursing him as you have?"

Kitty's brow furrowed. "Do you know the story?"

"I am afraid your uncle told me last night. He is quite taken with it."

That was a pleasant thought. Having someone as keen as her uncle enjoying the story not only enough to tell her how much he liked it, but also to share it with her aunt was something of importance and should be given its due consideration and the honour it deserved. So, Kitty allowed the feeling to settle into her chest before she continued to speak.

"It is not that Mr. L does not deserve his punishment. He was very rude, but..." She tapped her lip with her pen again. "Mr. Linton did say I was beautiful and right yesterday."

She glanced at her aunt whose hands were still, her knitting momentarily forgotten, as she waited for Kitty to continue. "It is just that perhaps I did not consider why Mr. L was rude in my story."

She placed her pen on the little groove of the writing desk she was using. "What if he was cursed by accident? What if he is not truly as horrid as I first thought? I must consider these things now that we are to be friends."

She still could not bring herself to admit that they were

courting. Friends was a step far enough. She was not prepared to think beyond that.

"What did you have planned to happen to Mr. L in your story?" Her aunt asked. "Were you going to feed him to a dragon or have him drawn and quartered?"

Kitty shook her head. "I had considered allowing the beast at the great tree to eat him, but then, my story would be over before it began, and the boy's mother would never regain her health."

"And at the end? Would Mr. L still have all his limbs?"

Kitty shrugged. "Most likely."

"I am afraid, then, that I do not see the dilemma."

"You do not?" How could her aunt not see it? How was she supposed to torment a friend – even if it was only imaginarily done? Kitty was certain that Mary would say that it was not right to do so.

"Your Mr. L has a quest to complete, does he not?"

"Yes."

"And can he not face the obstacles set before him and rise heroically above them?"

"I suppose he could."

"Would it not be possible for him to discover how he became to be as rude as he was and then learn to not be so again? Discovering such a thing would be a delightful treat for your uncle to read."

"Do you really think so?"

Her aunt nodded. "He does like an interesting turn of

events now and again." She smiled at Kitty. "He is very imaginative himself."

"I had no idea."

"I am certain very few do since he applies his imagination to his work. Only I get to hear the occasional tale he tells one or another of the children." She picked up her knitting. "I think your dilemma lies in your motivation."

Kitty's brow furrowed.

"Why did you decide to write your story about Mr. L?"

"Oh!" Kitty gasped as understanding dawned. She had been angry with Mr. Linton.

"You may either punish your character, or you can help him improve." Her aunt looked up from her knitting. "The two are not the same."

Kitty had set about writing to have a way to make Mr. L suffer. Her cheeks grew warm. Mary would most certainly not approve of someone being vengeful, even in a story.

"Helping someone improve is a very good thing," her aunt added. "A loving thing even."

"I do not love Mr. Linton."

Her aunt chuckled. "I did not mean to say you did. One can be loving without falling in love with someone."

"That is true," Kitty muttered. She was almost sure it was true. It was most certainly true of sisters and cousins, as well as her friends who were not handsome with silvery blue eyes.

"Who knows, you might just find you can love Mr. Linton."

"No," Kitty said emphatically with a firm shake of her head for emphasis.

"He is not a poor option to consider. Your mother would approve of him, do you not think?"

Would she? Kitty's head tipped. She had not stopped to consider what Mama would think of Mr. Linton other than to conclude after their first meeting that Mama would not like him. Mama did not like anyone who did not treat her daughters as she thought they deserved to be treated. Why just look at how she had not liked Mr. Darcy after the assembly! And he had not mistaken Elizabeth for a servant! He had only said she was not tempting. Not being handsome enough to tempt a gentleman was no small thing but to be thought a maid and so far beneath his notice was something far worse. Kitty was certain of it.

However, if her aunt thought that Mama would approve, there must be a reason. Kitty searched for things that would recommend Mr. Linton to her mother.

"He has an estate, though I do not know how large." Mama had always insisted that her daughters should marry someone who owned land and the more, the better.

"And a house in town," her aunt added. "A gentleman with a house in town and an estate is most likely not poor. Mr. Linton does not seem the sort of man to squander his fortune. He was prompt to apologize for his error. That could not have been easily done. Arriving at a gentleman's house to admit that he had placed a sister's reputation in question had to have been a fearful thing."

It had indeed appeared that Mr. Linton was fearful yesterday when he arrived at Darcy House. And so, it seemed he was honourable underneath all his stumbling and bumbling. Not that Kitty wished to admit it to her aunt just yet. It seemed far too soon to be so approving.

"He is handsome." That she could admit. His features were easily admired by one and all. A lady did not need to know a gentleman at all to comment on his appearance.

"I will not argue that. And he is quite tall and broad."

Yes, Mr. Linton was a fine example of what a desirable gentleman should be when observed from a distance. Which is from where Kitty would like to observe him – from a nice, safe distance. Once a lady drew closer to observe the object of her admiration, that was when things began to feel more intimate. That was when hopes and dreams could be aroused and dashed.

It was not that Kitty did not enjoy drawing closer to handsome men. A casual flirtation was an enjoyable thing and was an excellent way to discover if one wished to deepen the acquaintance. That was what Mama had always said. Of course, she had also said that, while engaging in a flirtation, a lady must be careful to keep her heart from being affected by every handsome face.

However, a courtship, even one which was only

affected, was not a casual flirtation. It was something far more weighty, and so her mother's advice was not so very helpful.

Kitty was not even certain that Mr. Linton was capable of flirting. He was excellent at arguing and being disagreeable, but flirting and teasing? He would need to be able to think before blurting to accomplish that, and so far, in their acquaintance, he had not been able to carry off that particular skill — at least, not for more than a few sentences. Even in telling her she was beautiful, he had blurted. Telling someone to use a mirror to discover why they were unsettling was not precisely charming, although, she had to admit she had still enjoyed hearing that she was beautiful.

"You should change your dress and wash the ink off your fingers," her aunt said when Kitty once again picked up her pen. "Mr. L will be here soon." She winked at Kitty.

"Aunt!"

"I promise not to tease you too much, but I must say that I am excited for you."

"Why? He is only courting me because he must."

Her aunt shook her head. "No, you are only allowing him to court you because he must. I think he is quite willing to court you without any persuasion."

"We argue." Kitty placed her ink and pen in the small compartment for them in the desk and tucked her notebook inside the larger section, snapping it closed and turning her key in the lock.

"And so did Lizzy and Mr. Darcy."

"Aunt!" Kitty cried again.

"I am only hoping you will give him proper consideration."

Kitty stood with her writing desk in hand. "I suppose it would be foolish not to consider him as one would a new friend, would it not?"

"Excessively."

Kitty blew out a breath as she mounted the stairs to her room to prepare to spend time with her new friend. Her new, handsome friend. Friend. She repeated the word to herself. That is what they were and naught else. Friends did not endanger one's heart, for one did not marry a friend, did she?

Such troubling thoughts were still perplexing Kitty when the source of her trouble walked into the sitting room looking very dashing in his black jacket and grey waistcoat.

"I know you could not tell me, but I thought it might be best to bring flowers anyway." Mr. Linton handed her a bundle of six daffodils.

"They are very cheerful," Kitty answered as she took them.

"I will make certain they are placed in your room," her aunt said. "There is nothing so nice as waking to fresh flowers." She took the daffodils from Kitty before adding, "And in your chamber, they will be safe from your cousins. I have had more than one bouquet picked clean of its buds. Maxwell loves to present me with treasures even if those treasures are not new to me."

"Max is three," Kitty said to fill the void when her aunt left the room.

"I am afraid I do not know much about children," Mr. Linton said.

"Then, I suppose you do not know if you like them or not."

"I suppose I do not, but I imagine I would like them." His face scrunched. "Or I hope I will. It is expected of a gentleman to have children so that there is an heir to the estate and all that."

Kitty nodded as she was not certain how else to reply to such a statement.

"And do you like children, Miss Bennet?"

"Yes, very much."

"You will wish to have a large family, I assume."

Friends. She repeated to herself once again. Friends could speak of wishes for families and the like. She had spoken to both Lydia and Maria Lucas about such things. However, neither her sister nor their particular friend made Kitty's stomach flutter as Mr. Linton did, and that, along with the thought of being the mother of his children, which would not be pushed out of her mind, made this conversation much different than any she had ever had before about the topic, for while it was a conversation that two friends might have, it felt far more personal to discuss such a thing with him.

"I would not be opposed to such a thing. I have four sisters, after all."

"Right, right." He tugged at his waistcoat.

"And do you wish for a large family?" Kitty could feel her cheeks growing warm at the question as if it were too impertinent to ask. However, it had seemed only proper to inquire after his opinion until the words had exited her mouth.

"Two is expected, I believe. So, I would wish for at least two. I honestly have not considered it beyond that."

"You have not? Never?" Who did not think of the sort of family he wished to have? She had been thinking about it since she was twelve and understood that, one day, she would be a mother. Did boys just not think of such things or was it just Mr. Linton who did not?

"No, never. Is that wrong?" He looked pained.

"It is not wrong," Kitty assured him, though she secretly suspected it was. "It is just odd. I thought everyone thought about such things. The end result of marriage is to have a family, after all, and if one is seeking a husband or wife, I should think that such thoughts would be natural." Either her face was surely going to burst into flames, or her cheeks were going to melt off. Again, such commentary should have been confined to her mind. But he had surprised her. He was often surprising her and causing her to speak before she could think better of it.

"Perhaps it should be natural," he said in a strained voice.

Good, he was as uncomfortable as she. That did make her feel somewhat better.

"Do you have a maid to accompany you?" he asked. "If we are to reach the park and return in time for dinner, we should be off."

"Oh, yes, Fiona." She turned to the maid in the corner. "Are you ready to go?"

"Yes, ma'am," Fiona replied. "Do you require anything?"

"No, I have all I need."

"Then, if there are no other instructions of which I need to be aware, shall we leave?" Mr. Linton asked.

"I had hoped my aunt would return before we left."

"I can tell Mrs. Tuttle that we are going," Fiona offered.

"Thank you. That will work just as well." Relief washed over Kitty. "I did not wish to leave without my aunt knowing," she said to Mr. Linton.

"Shall we wait to see if she has any instructions?"

"No, I have been told the time we must be back for dinner and other than that, I am to enjoy myself but not so far as to kiss anyone." Oh, goodness! She really must learn to filter her words. "I should not have said that last bit. My uncle was teasing me this morning, you see. The story in the paper and all."

Mr. Linton offered her his arm to escort her to his waiting carriage. "My aunt was not teasing when she said the same thing to me."

A giggle burst out of Kitty without warning.

Mr. Linton chuckled. "It may come as no surprise to you, but I am not proficient at courting a lady. I have taken a lady or two for a drive. I am not unfamiliar with sitting in drawing rooms or dancing or escorting someone to the theater and the like, but I have never courted someone in a formal sense." He helped Kitty into his barouche.

"I have never been courted."

"Have you been to the theatre?" He climbed up and took his place beside her.

"Not yet."

His lips tipped into a smile. "Then, we shall have to correct such an oversight. You strike me as someone who would enjoy a play."

"Oh, I think I would." Very much. Especially if he was sitting as close to her as he was now. He smelled of fresh air and cedar. It was an intoxicating mix.

She tucked her skirts around her legs, carefully taking note that nothing of her person was closer than one hand's span away from Mr. Linton. For if it was, thinking of him as a friend and naught else was going to be excessively difficult. As it was, their private conversation and the closeness of his handsome person had her wishing to think of him as more.

Chapter 13

"Are you certain you wish to come inside with me?" Constance asked her brother as their carriage came to a stop in front of Mrs. Verity's.

"There must be something I could do in there that involves children." Miss Bennet liked children and had found it rather amusing that he had not known what to do with her youngest cousin, Lottie, when the child had climbed onto his lap in the Gardiner's sitting room after their meal two days ago.

"It is a home for children."

He glowered at his sister's amusement at his expense. "I know. That is why I assume there must be something I can learn about them here." He climbed out of the carriage and offered her his hand. "Miss Bennet thinks that one should both know if one likes children and if one wishes for a large family or a small one before he begins a season." He shrugged as he tucked Connie's hand into the crook of his arm.

"That does seem wise."

"It does now that I have thought about it."

"You never considered the size of family for which you wished?"

In his sister's tone, he heard the same utter disbelief he had heard in Miss Bennets' voice when she had asked nearly the same thing two days ago. Again, he felt as if he had missed some important lesson in school. "I have not. I know that two is standard, and the Lord may bless beyond that, of course. I just did not know that one was to set plans for such a thing. If I had known, I would have."

Constance laughed. "I am positive you would have. You are a very good planner. Your estate does very well under your watch."

It did. His income was as secure as it could be with only that which could be spared being invested in ventures which were not so proven as he would like. However, ventures must be made into the new and modern if an estate wished to not only survive to be passed on to a future generation but also if it was to prosper and even expand. And now that he had to consider laying aside funds for more than two children, he needed those ventures to thrive more than ever.

"Mother and Father only had us," he said by way of justifying his lack of planning beyond two children.

"It was not for lack of trying to have more," his sister countered.

Trefor blinked. "I beg your pardon." Had his parents wished for more than two children?

"I know you do not like it when I speak so plainly, but Mother told me that she lost two babies before you were born and one after. They were fortunate to have us." She pulled him back from knocking on the door. "They loved each other very much, and when a couple loves one another as Mother and Father did," her cheeks were rosy, and he cringed to hear her say what he knew she was going to say, "they do not limit themselves to only producing two children." Her eyes held his. "Do not make me say it any more plainly. Please use your excessive intelligence to decipher my meaning, or if you cannot, ask Mr. Edwards. I am certain he can present it to you in a more direct and much less proper fashion."

Trefor shook his head in disbelief and self-admonishment. His little sister had just begun a lesson on the duties and pleasures of marriage with him! "Please, do not say any more. I understand your meaning perfectly."

He lifted his hand to knock on the door but then dropped it. "What is wrong with me?" Things were so far from right in his mind.

"Could you clarify your meaning?" Her eyes sparkled with impertinence.

"I should have been able to decipher what you told me. I should have known that a gentleman who loves his wife will... Well, you know. Or I assume you do since you were just talking about it." He blew out a breath. "It is as if half of my brain has been stolen from me, and I would greatly like to get it back. I am not normally so stupid."

"Not normally, but on occasion."

He rolled his eyes at her teasing.

"You do tend to think in absolutes, and sometimes those absolutes do not bend enough for reality," she said softly.

"I like absolutes," he muttered. They were safe and unchanging.

"Love is not an absolute," his sister added.

"Love?" He lifted the knocker and let it fall.

"Yes, my dear brother. Love. I could no more put what love is supposed to be in a list of qualifications than you can slot it neatly into a column in your account book." She squeezed his arm. "Love is unpredictable. Take Henry, for instance. I did not expect the gentleman whom I would love would be anything like him. I imagined someone more like you or father. Proper, always in control of himself, forever knowing what was happening and why. However," she said as the door was opened, "Henry has what I need, and I have what he needs. We compliment each other. We are alike in some ways and so very different in others."

From the entryway, he nodded in greeting to Mrs. Verity, who was just entering the drawing room.

"Perhaps," his sister whispered when she retook his arm

after having removed her outerwear, "the sort of lady you need is not a prim and proper debutante but rather a spirited, young lady who challenges you to think beyond your neat little picture of how things are."

He did not respond to her suggestion. He could not. At least, he could not do so coherently. He had been pondering such a young lady ever since his foolishness had placed him in a position that required him to court that very young lady.

"I have brought you another volunteer," Connie said as they entered the drawing room where Mrs. Verity was sitting quietly at the window doing absolutely nothing.

"That is good news." She motioned to the settee across from her. "And what skills do you possess, Mr. Linton?"

"He is good at reconciling accounts," Connie offered.

He was. Indeed, unlike most, he enjoyed adding rows of numbers and figuring percents and the like. However, that was not why he was here.

"Actually," he began, "I am less of a volunteer than a pupil."

His heart thumped uncomfortably loudly in his chest as if it were attempting to escape and dash away from the embarrassment that admitting his need of instruction was sure to bring.

Mrs. Verity's eyebrows rose. "How so?" Her head tipped as she studied him intently.

"It has been brought to my attention that I am lacking in

knowledge of children." There. He had said it. Aloud. To someone other than his sister. And it was as discomfiting as he had imagined it would be.

Mrs. Verity chuckled. "Indeed?"

Trefor nodded. "I would very much like to learn what to do with them."

"What to do with them?"

Oh, she was enjoying his uneasiness far too much, and he wished to tell her so. However, he also needed her assistance.

"Yes, things such as about what does one speak to children, and what do they like to do?"

Mrs. Verity's lips pursed as she lowered her dancing eyes to study her hands for a moment before looking up at Trefor with a more composed expression on her face, though her eyes still carried her amusement. "What did you like to do when you were young, Mr. Linton? Did you have a favourite toy? Did you favour a particular book or game? What lessons did you love or loathe?"

That seemed simple enough. Incredibly simple actually. So simple that he should have been able to think of it on his own, but he had not been. "I quite enjoyed doing sums," he answered, "I loved any book my mother read me, I had some blocks that the carpenter who was building a new partition in the stable made for me which I treasured, and riding. I loved to ride. I still do."

"Well, we have no horses, so riding with our children

is out of the realm of possibilities. However, we do have some blocks and several books." She leaned forward. "You will find that our little ones, in particular, are very fond of being read to because they have not yet learned to decipher the words for themselves."

"You teach them to read?"

"We do." She stood. "Come along, Mr. Linton. Let's see if we can get you accustomed to our youngest residents."

"How young?" He was feeling rather anxious as he rose to follow Mrs. Verity.

"We are going to the nursery."

"The nursery?" He had hoped to start with somewhat older children before having to face the littlest ones. The older children could likely carry on a conversation about simple subjects, but Miss Bennet's cousin had known very few words, and even then, those words had sounded more like babble than actual words to him.

"Yes, the nursery, Mr. Linton. Those children are far too young to participate in lessons, but, do not fear, there are blocks." She chuckled.

Why was it that everyone found such glee in his discomfort? He found no pleasure in it at all, and as they ascended the stairs, his discomfort rose with each step.

"It is just here," Mrs. Verity opened the door to a room which was busy with sound.

Trefor peeked inside. There were two infants lying in cradles while four others, who possessed various degrees of mobility, were playing on a rug and at a small table. "I might be too large for this room," he whispered to Mrs. Verity.

"You will fit. It is not a tiny room," she assured him.

No, the room was not tiny, but the occupants were.

"Martha." Mrs. Verity stepped inside the room ahead of Trefor. "This is Mr. Linton, and he would like for you to take a rest while he plays with the children."

Martha's eyes grew wide.

Mrs. Verity whispered something to the woman, and her features softened into a smile.

"I think if he is successful here, in a week or two, we might see how he does reading to the older children or perhaps he can help Frank learn his sums."

"That is an excellent plan," Martha agreed.

Trefor was not certain if he agreed or not as he looked down at a little person who had attached herself to his boot.

"Remember, Mr. Linton," Mrs. Verity said before she left him with Martha. "None of these children have parents."

Trefor swallowed and nodded. "Neither do I. Not any longer."

"See, you have something in common already," Mrs. Verity replied with a smile.

"Who is this little one?" he asked, looking down at a pair of dark, curious eyes which were peering up at him.

"That is Emily. She has just had her first birthday last week," Martha replied. "She seems fond of you."

"She does," he muttered.

"You may play with her. She is very good at playing," Martha encouraged.

"How do I do that?"

Martha chuckled. "Emily, where is your baby?"

"Baby?"

Martha gave him a sad smile as if he were the most unfortunate fellow. "Her doll."

"Oh, right. I did not have dolls. My sister did, but she never let me play with them." He crouched down to be closer to Emily's height. "Where is your baby?" He repeated what the nursemaid had said.

Emily smiled and toddled away to pick up a small doll made of cloth.

"Why did your sister not let you play with her dolls, Mr. Linton," Martha asked.

"I would hide them or send them on dangerous missions to capture foreign lands."

Martha laughed. "Then, I can understand why she would keep her dolls from you."

Trefor smiled at the woman. "I promise not to hide Emily's doll."

"And no dangerous missions?"

"Not a one."

"Baby." Emily shoved her doll at him, and he took it. "Book."

Trefor glanced at Martha. He was unfamiliar with the language infants spoke.

"She wants you to read to the baby."

"To a doll?"

"That is her baby," Martha said with a pointed look. "There is a chair over there in the corner that she favours for stories."

"Book," Emily said once again.

Trefor held his hand out toward her outstretched one, and she wrapped her hand around one of his fingers. "Where are the books?" he asked her.

She babbled something in reply as she led him to the corner. There was a book already lying on the chair. He gave her a boost as she climbed into the oversized rocking chair, which looked as if it was designed specifically for reading to a child, and snuggled into the corner leaving ample room for him. Both arms reached toward him. "Baby."

"Here you are."

As Trefor placed the doll in Emily's arms, the door opened, and he heard whispering. However, he dared not remove his eyes from Emily, who was holding the doll in one arm and attempting to pick up the book with her free hand.

"Allow me," he offered. Picking up the book, he settled

into the chair. Only then did he see that the new arrival to the room was watching him very carefully with inquisitive hazel eyes. "Miss Bennet," he greeted with a nod of his head.

"Book!" Emily demanded.

"Yes, yes. Do forgive me. I promise I had not forgotten." He opened the book to the first story.

"*The story of the Two Cocks[1].*" He glanced at Emily, who was arranging her baby in her lap. "*There once was a Hen who lived in a farm-yard, and she had a large brood of chickens. She took a great deal of care of them, and gathered them under her wing every night, and fed them, and nursed them very well; and they were all very good, except two Cocks, that were always quarrelling with one another.*"

Emily made a clicking noise with her mouth, and, to Trefor's great amusement, was shaking her head with a very serious look on her face.

"They were not good where they?" He said before continuing to read. "*They were hardly out of their shell before they began to peck at each other...*"

Two stories later, Trefor closed the book. Emily was sleeping against his side, and the three other mobile children along with Miss Bennet were at his feet.

"You are very good at reading aloud," Miss Bennet said.

---

1. *Lessons for Children Part IV for Children from Three to Four Years Old.* Mrs. Barbauld (Anna Letitia), 1798.

"So good that my audience has fallen asleep," he whispered in reply.

"Hand me the book."

Trefor placed the book in Miss Bennet's hands.

"Emily's cot is the one in the right corner," Martha said.

"You expect me to move her?" She was so little and looked so comfortable where she was.

"Unless you wish to stay there until she wakes up in an hour or so."

Trefor looked at the youngster beside him. She was adorable, but he was not certain he wished to remain here for an hour.

"Scoop her up being careful to keep her head from flopping. A flopping head will surely wake her." Martha had joined them. "Emily does not take kindly to being woken."

"Nor do I," Trefor said with a smile. Carefully, he slid one hand behind Emily's back and the other under her legs. Then, not daring to breathe, he lifted her to cradle her against his chest and pushed out of the rocker — which was harder to do than expected when one did not have any hands to assist in the motion.

"This cot?" he whispered when he had crossed the room.

Miss Bennet nodded.

"The blanket," he said. "How do I pull it back and not drop Emily?"

To his great relief, Miss Bennet came to his aid and soon Emily and her baby were snuggled beneath her covers.

"You performed admirably," Martha commended.

"You did," Miss Bennet agreed. "Why are you here?"

"To learn about children," he answered. "How am I to know if I like them if I do not spend any time with them? I wish to be better prepared should you ask me about them again at some point."

Miss Bennet, who had taken a spot on the floor again, looked up at him in astonishment. "You are here because of me?"

He shrugged. "Yes." Spotting the blocks, he went to the shelf and retrieved them.

"For me?" Miss Bennet replied when he had returned to the rug and taken a seat next to a little fellow.

"No, these are for this young man." He looked at her. "What is his name?"

"That is Jack."

"Jack, would you like to build a castle?"

"I did not mean are the blocks for me," Miss Bennet said.

"You did not?"

She shook her head, her cheeks flushing. "I cannot believe you are here because of me."

"You pointed out a shortfall, and so it must be attended to." He turned his attention back to Jack who was twice the size of Emily. "Now, young Jack. Can you count to three? For we are going to stack them in rows like this.

One, two, three." He handed a block to Jack. "Just here. One. Say one."

The child repeated what sounded like one, and so Trefor handed him another block. "Just on top. Two. Say two. Ah, very good. Now, three, in just the same fashion."

"Why must they all be three high?" Miss Bennet said as she scooted closer to him.

"This is the wall, and the pediment shall be just behind it." He pulled out a soldier from the basket of blocks. "And our guards will stand so." He placed the soldier atop the blocks. "Two," he corrected Jack who had counted one, three.

He smiled at the young lad. "You know," he said to Kitty. "I think I might like children."

"You did think you would," she reminded him.

"Indeed, I did, and that is likely why I like them. After all, the proper attitude in approaching a matter is of great importance." He was quite pleased with himself. "Do you not think?" He turned to Miss Bennet.

"Yes." She smiled as her head bobbed up and down.

He loved how her face lit with her enjoyment. If there were not a child needing attention, he would have gladly admired her features for longer than a brief moment.

"One remembers how to play quite quickly, do they not?" he said.

"You had forgotten how to play?"

"I assure you I have not had my blocks out to build castles in years."

She giggled.

"But I must admit it is rather enjoyable." Tidy columns and rows, all nice and orderly, were very pleasant to build, even if they were eventually going to be knocked through.

"And you are very good at it." Her words were filled with laughter.

"I always was," he answered, feeling just as light as her laugh.

Chapter 14

"I had expected you to be upstairs," Mr. Gardiner said as he came into the sitting room. "Lottie was asking about Mr. Linton, again." Kitty's uncle chuckled. "When she takes a liking to someone, she is not easily persuaded away from it."

"He is coming to call tomorrow."

"I hope he will spare a minute or two for your cousin."

Kitty put down her pen. "I am certain he will." She remembered how sweet little Emily had looked tucked in beside Mr. Linton earlier today.

"I am happy to see you smiling when we speak of him rather than looking anxious as you have for the past three days."

Kitty shrugged but said nothing in explanation. She was not sure she could explain herself for she had still not sorted out her feelings where Mr. Linton was concerned. They were a puzzling mixture of longing and curiosity — and not just because he was handsome. She felt herself being drawn to him, to discover who he was beneath the face he presented to the world — much like discovering who Mr. L was beneath his tattered coat in her story. Neither Mr. Linton or his fictional counterpart were proving to be dreadful under their cover of initial disagreeableness.

"Do you have more of your story for me to read?"

Pulling her lower lip between her teeth, Kitty looked at her notebook. She was at a good stopping point. Mr. L had just completed his second test.

"I promise not to critique it too harshly." Her uncle gave her a pleading look. "But you had left Mr. L with two more tasks to complete. He had only just defeated the great beast and gotten the log he needed. I am anxious to see what trial befalls him next."

Kitty picked up her notebook. "He has just –"

"No. Do not tell me. Let me read it. Please."

"Is my husband begging for stories?" Aunt Gardiner said as she entered the room.

Kitty laughed. "He is, and I was just about to oblige him."

Mrs. Gardiner sucked in a quick breath as her face lit with excitement. "And may I read it after he does?"

Kitty shook her head as she laughed again. "Do you really wish to read it?" Or were they only being kind?

"More than I can say without looking very foolish," her aunt replied.

"But it is only my scribblings."

"Which makes them all the more precious," her aunt

said. "What makes you look so astonished, my dear? Do you not expect me to love everything you do?"

Kitty once again shook her head slowly. A sheepish look settled on her face. "I am not Lizzy or Jane."

"Do they write stories?"

The smile her aunt wore said that the answer to such a question was already known, but Kitty answered anyway. "Not to my knowledge."

"Then, you might have to explain yourself a bit further."

"I think I know this answer," her uncle said before Kitty could do more than open her mouth and begin to organize her thoughts. "Lizzy is bright, and Jane is so proper and good that it is hard not to think one must be those things to be well-thought of. Is that not right?"

"Yes, yes. That is very true," Kitty said. That was a great deal of the issue. How often had she heard one or the other of her sisters praised for such things? Too many to count!

"And is it too hard to believe that you could be either of those things?" her uncle asked.

"Well, yes, but that is not it entirely." That was indeed another piece which made her feel inadequate. But that was only because —

"Then, what is the rest?" Her uncle held her notebook on his lap, ignoring it as if what she had to say was much more important than the pleasure to be found in reading a much-anticipated portion of a story.

"I am," she looked down at her hands, for the rest was not easy to admit, "silly."

"Perhaps at times," her uncle said, "but then so is everyone."

"Not Jane or Lizzy!"

Her uncle chuckled. "Even Jane and Lizzy." He winked at her before picking up the notebook he held.

Surely not!

"I assure you it is true," he replied in answer to her look of shock. "You know." He shifted his focus to the story he held. "I could read this aloud."

Oh, no! She could not sit here and listen to that!

"Please do," his wife cried. "You are an excellent reader."

"What say you, Kitty? May I?"

She looked between her aunt and uncle. They really were the best of people. They loved her despite her silliness, which they claimed was not so terrible as Papa seemed to declare. And at present, they both wore such eager expressions — much like Lottie did when she was awaiting a story. That, coupled with the fact that they had just been so kind to her in saying she was not silly, made it impossible for her to deny them. "Must I stay to listen?" she asked.

"Not if you do not wish to," her uncle said.

"Then, yes, you may read it aloud. However, I do not think I am equal to listening." She rose from her chair.

"Catherine."

She was beginning to like hearing herself called that by her uncle, for, while it might from time to time be followed by a gentle scold, whatever followed it was always said as if he thought her an equal and not a child.

"Thank you," he said when she turned toward him. "For sharing this with us." He held up the book.

A smile spread from her lips to her heart. "You are most welcome."

She ducked out of the room and closed the door until it almost latched. Then, she leaned against the wall next to the door and listened.

"*Several minutes later, Mr. L rounded a bend in the road, looking behind him to make certain that the beast was truly dead and not following him. To his immense relief, there was only path behind him and naught else.*

He put the log down and sat on it for a full five minutes. His legs burned from running and his breathing was labored. His arm that had been cut was growing cold and sore.

This path back to the village was longer than the way he had come, but it had seemed the best direction to escape from the beast. However..."

Kitty smiled. Her uncle was a very good reader, and it was not so very dreadful to hear her words read by him. She pushed off the wall and moved toward the stairs. It was not right to listen at doors, even if one was listening to her own words. It was not proper, and in town, she was trying to be proper. For the past several days, she had achieved her goal. She had said what was proper, refrained from saying too much that was improper, and behaved as she thought a proper lady should. She had even managed to accomplish being proper at Mrs. Verity's today. And all this had happened despite Mr. Linton being present. Perhaps there was hope for them to be good friends, or maybe even more, if they could continue to meet without arguing.

She slipped into her room and sat quietly on her bed in the light of the lamp she had brought up from downstairs. Today had been a perfect day, and she was reluctant to have it end. However, after five minutes of watching the flame flicker, tiredness began to creep over her, and so, she rose and prepared for bed, taking extra care when deciding which dress she would wear tomorrow for callers.

Before climbing into bed, she placed that dress next to the ball gown she would wear to tomorrow night. Then, with thoughts of dancing and tea mingling in her mind with blocks and children, she slid into her dreams which were filled with a tall, handsome fellow with the most perfect silvery grey eyes.

~*~*~

"You look beautiful." Elizabeth wrapped her arm around Kitty's. "I wish I was half as pretty."

Kitty's brow furrowed.

"You are becoming quite as pretty as Jane," Elizabeth

whispered. "But do not tell her or Lydia I said so." She laughed.

"You truly think I am beautiful? Like Jane?"

"Oh, most certainly," Elizabeth assured her. "I will tell you something else, but you must promise me you will not be too startled."

"I will try to keep my composure," Kitty assured her eagerly. Elizabeth did not tell anyone secrets, save Jane. Well, perhaps she also told Mr. Darcy now, but before she was married, she only ever told her secrets to Jane.

"Mr. Darcy and I are quite impressed by the fine young lady you are becoming. Even in the face of disaster, you have done quite well. I am not certain I could glide into this ballroom with the grace with which you have tonight. There is almost an elegance about you which makes me think you are no longer my little sister, but a wonderful lady I know."

"You are teasing me." There was no way that she fit Elizabeth's description. Her stomach was twisting, her heartbeat was as quick as if she had been dancing already, and her thoughts whispered doubts that she might do or say something which would be her ruin.

"No, I assure you I am not," Elizabeth said. "You are different here compared to at home. I can see why Mr. Linton is so taken with you."

"Please, I am not as you say." Kitty would also like to refute that Mr. Linton was taken with her, but he had declared her beautiful in front of Elizabeth, Mr. Darcy, and Aunt Gardiner. So, there was no way she could honestly deny it. Nor could she truthfully wish to be able to deny it.

"You are." Elizabeth gave her a firm glare.

"Thank you." What else did one say to such a thing when she neither wished to start an argument or provoke Lizzy into scolding her?

"And there is Mr. Linton now." Elizabeth sounded nearly as excited as Mama might about a potential match for Jane. "Remember, you and he are to dance two sets."

Kitty nodded her understanding and sucked in a quick breath when she saw him. He was wearing dark blue. Goodness! He looked handsome in dark blue.

"Miss Bennet," he greeted with a bow, "are you ready to make one and all believe we are happily courting?"

"As long as you do not provoke me." She fluttered her lashes and smiled coyly just as Lydia would do when she was attempting to sway a gentleman to like her. Kitty gasped.

"Are you well?" Mr. Linton asked.

"Perfectly," she hurried to reply as her cheeks grew warm. "I just was thinking. It was nothing." Nothing that was going to make her feel at ease that is.

Why had she fluttered her lashes at Mr. Linton? They were friends. One did not flirt with a friend.

However, her brow furrowed, they were supposed to appear to be more than friends. She smiled. That was it.

She was just playing her part so well that she did not need to think about it. Unless...

No, it was not because she was enamoured with him. Was it?

"Do you still wish to dance?" He was looking utterly befuddled.

"Most assuredly."

She would need to put startling thoughts out of her head. For each time she and Mr. Linton had met where he looked confused had not ended well.

"Truly forgive me for woolgathering." She took his hand. "The room is splendid; is it not?"

"Indeed, Mrs. Belmont is known to host an excellent ball. It is her second this season. The first made the papers."

He was wearing a smirk that begged her to ask if there was some pleasant memory from that ball that caused him to look amused, and so she asked.

"You will likely think me horrid if I tell you," he replied.

Again, his lips lifted in a teasing smirk. It was almost as if he were flirting with her! But gentlemen such as Mr. Linton did not flirt; did they?

"I promise not to think you are horrid," she assured him as she took her place across from him.

"My sister nearly ended up married to Mr. Edwards after that particular ball."

The first notes of *Strawberries and Cream* were played,

and Kitty's curiosity about what Mr. Linton had said was left to fester and grow as she wound her way through the dance, swaying side to side, hopping, turning, crossing, and returning through the line as required.

"You must tell me more," she said at one point when she actually had a moment to speak when they joined hands.

"I will." He parted from her again. It was many steps later before he could reply further. "Perhaps a walk in the garden?"

"Oh, yes," she said before they were once again parted.

Some dances provided more chances to speak. She scowled wishing that this was one of them — no matter how invigoratingly delightful she found the patterns. Indeed, she was to be frustrated by dancing for the rest of the set, as well as two others, before she finally found herself on Mr. Linton's arm and strolling through the small garden.

She glanced back toward the terrace where Lizzy stood with Mr. Darcy. Their presence gave approval to Kitty's wandering the paths with Mr. Linton, while lanterns stood tall along the side of the path, providing ample light. The breeze was cool, but not too cold. However, if they remained outside for too long, she was going to wish she had worn her shawl as her sister had suggested.

"There are a few alcoves on your way to the retiring room," Mr. Linton said.

"Yes, I noticed them. They have lovely red drapes."

"That hide a couple quite nicely, or so I hear," Mr. Linton's steps faltered.

"I suppose they would. They did look as if they would be a pleasant place to find some solitude and quiet."

"Solitude and quiet are not precisely why a couple might seek out such a place."

He was using that tone of voice which seemed to be very natural for him to use. It was the one that sounded a great deal like a tutor, instructing his students on the best way to do something.

"I do know that," she said, looking up at him. "However, I did not think it would be best if I mentioned any other activities." She fluttered her lashes and smiled.

"Right, right. Forgive me." He sighed. "Would you mind not looking at me?"

Kitty's brow furrowed. "I do not see why I cannot look at you. Is there something wrong with how I do it?"

"No, no. There is most certainly nothing wrong with how you look. In fact, it is quite the opposite which is the problem."

"You make very little sense at times," Kitty muttered, a small pout forming on her lips.

"I would have to agree."

"You would?"

"Yes. Now, please mind your steps so that I can speak without becoming any more turned about than I am."

Kitty giggled. "Am I being vexing again, Mr. Linton. I promise I had not meant to be."

"Vexing, unsettling, alluring, tempting." He blew out a breath. "Perhaps we should return to the house before I forget myself entirely."

"You have not told me your story. We cannot go back until I know how your sister nearly became betrothed to Mr. Edwards at a ball which was held here."

"She met with him in one of those alcoves – not by herself, mind you. Miss Barrett was with her, but the gossips do not always care about the details. To make a long story short, the incident found its way to the paper, and I stormed off to demand that Edwards marry her."

"Did she not tell you the story was wrong?" She could not imagine that he would not listen to his sister.

"She did." He paused and chuckled to himself as if thinking. It was a rather disparaging sound. "Perhaps I should have listened to her and not sought out Mr. Edwards, but a reputation is a fragile thing. How could I, as her brother and guardian, allow her reputation to be destroyed. There was only one way to save her from disgrace, or so I thought." Again, he made a small disparaging chuckle sound. "However, I was wrong, and it all ended with Connie happily betrothed to Mr. Crawford, which, before that story in the paper, was what I had hoped to have happen."

"You did?" Kitty was feeling rather confused. "Was not Mr. Crawford a rake like Mr. Edwards?"

"He was until he decided not to be and, against my wishes, sought help in affecting his change from my sister."

Kitty stopped walking. "Wait. You did not wish for your sister to help him, but you then wished for her to marry him?"

Mr. Linton nodded.

"You are perplexing."

"Let me explain," he said. "When I first heard of Connie's willingness to help Crawford, I feared she would lose her heart to him, which she did, and then, once it was lost, of course, my hopes had to be that it would not be broken."

That part was understandable, but... "Yet, you were going to make her marry Mr. Edwards?"

"Her reputation..." he said with a shrug.

Kitty shook her head. "I would have talked to Mr. Crawford and asked him to offer for her."

"As Mr. Darcy did of me?"

Kitty laughed lightly. Mr. Linton was looking at her rather intensely, and she wondered if he realized how unsettling such a look was capable of making him be.

"I suppose it is rather the same, except we are only courting," she leaned closer and lowered her voice, "or pretending to be."

"I'd very much like it if we were not pretending," he said. "Indeed, I wish we were not courting."

Kitty stepped backward. Her heart stung as if it had been slapped. "Well, I can break our arrangement at any time. You only need to tell me that you do not wish to continue. I am sure I shall not care one jot if you do." Except that she would, and the tears in her eyes were surely giving away her lie.

He grasped her hand. "That is not what I meant. It is not that I do not wish to court you. It is that I wish to," his mouth dropped open as a furrow formed between his eyes.

"You wish to what?" Kitty prodded. Such a look of surprise and bewilderment on a gentleman's face was far too tantalizing to a curious lady such as herself.

"Marry you?"

There was nearly as much question in his voice as there was in her mind. It was as if the idea was as utterly new and disquieting to him as it was to her.

"We have known each other only a short time," she managed to say after a moment of staring at him with her mouth agape and a million thoughts, many of them startling, running through her mind.

"You are right," he said quickly. "It makes no sense. I am sure it must just be the lantern light and the music."

She saw his throat move up and down.

"And your enchanting eyes and the flowers in your

hair." Hesitantly, he touched her cheek. "I do not understand it," he whispered.

Such a soft touch both by his fingers and his words was intoxicating. Kitty felt herself slipping from the garden in which she knew she stood to some other place that was filled with stars which shone like precious jewels and with warm breezes that caressed and soothe one's soul. And then, in a moment, she was plopped back in the garden as Mr. Linton, stepped away from her, leaving her feeling bereft.

His chest was rising and falling deliberately. "We should go back." His voice was strained.

"We should?"

"Straight away," he said with a nod.

"Why?" She really did not wish to leave this place, this feeling of something she did not understand but craved.

He stepped closer to her again. "Because if we do not, I will likely kiss you, and then, you will have no choice but to marry me."

"And that is bad?" Her mind should know the answer to this. A compromise was never a good thing, and yet, at this moment, it seemed anything but bad.

"It is." He cupped her cheek in his hand. "I could never force you to do what you do not wish."

"And if I wish it?" Did she? Was that for what she longed? Was the ache in her chest the result of wishing for him to ask her to marry him and him not doing so? Did she love him?

He shook his head, his eyes filling with sadness as his thumb caressed her cheek. "You do not wish it. It is the garden and the lanterns' light."

"That is rather disappointing." Excessively so. "Are you certain it is not your eyes? They are the loveliest mixture of blue and silver."

He smiled. "I am almost certain it should be more than even my eyes or your beauty that precipitates a marriage. Although, you are unsettling so I could be wrong." He shook his head once more and stepped back. "We should wait until we know for certain, do you not think?"

She shrugged but put her hand on his proffered arm. "If it is what you wish and think is best."

"Best, yes. What I wish?" He shook his head. "It is most certainly not what I wish."

It seemed, Kitty thought as they began walking back toward the terrace, that she and Mr. Linton finally agreed on something, for returning to the house was also certainly not what she wished. And that was indeed unsettling — deliciously so.

Chapter 15

"You are in the paper again," Charles Edwards dropped into a chair at the table where Trefor sat in their club.

"Yes, I saw."

"Is that why Darcy is glaring at you?"

Trefor turned toward the far corner of the room. "He is not glaring at me. He is looking nowhere in particular."

Edwards! Always attempting to stir up trouble. It was a good thing his sister was marrying Henry and not Edwards. Miss Barrett and her mother were far better equipped with the sternness and resolve needed to deal with the likes of Edwards.

Charles smirked. "You'd be glaring."

"No, I would not." He leveled a harsh look at his friend. "You should know."

Edwards leaned back in his chair, completely unaffected by either Trefor's look or words. But then, that was how Charles was. It should not surprise him. Trefor finished the last of his cup of tea and rose.

"Where are you going? I just arrived," Charles said.

"To speak to Darcy."

Edward's eyes grew wide. "Indeed?" Rising, he followed along behind Trefor.

"Darcy," Trefor greeted as he reached where the man was sitting.

"Linton." Darcy folded his paper and placed it on the table. "I was wondering how long it would be before you came to see me." He motioned for Trefor to take a seat. "I am meeting a friend here, but I do not expect him to be on time. He rarely is."

"Is that so?" Edwards asked.

"Quite," Darcy replied. "Bingley follows his own schedule. Neither the sun nor a watch is going to dictate his plans." He chuckled. "That is not entirely true. He intends to be on time. It just never seems to happen." Darcy took a sip of his tea. "There is always someone to speak to on his way."

"A friendly sort is he?" Edwards asked.

"Very." Darcy took another sip of his tea. "His wife is my wife's sister. They have not seen each other since we married over two months ago, so we men are letting them get reacquainted without us." His lips tipped into a smile. "Especially since they intend to spend their time together visiting some new shop that is opening today."

"Durward, Waller, and Eldridge," Trefor said with a nod.

"That is the very one."

"I am on my way there as soon as Crawford arrives. He is collecting my sister and aunt before he comes here. Crawford's sister is marrying Durward, and since Crawford is marrying my sister, it is imperative that we show our support, or so my aunt says." Trefor shrugged. "I suppose she is correct."

"It seems logical," Darcy agreed. "My wife's other sister will be there as well."

Trefor nodded as his ears grew warm. "I know. She told me."

Miss Bennet was the reason he was happy to do as his aunt suggested and visit the shop on its opening day. He even intended to spend some money on something in the shop if he could discover something that Miss Bennet would like.

"The gossips will surely have a grand time with that bit of news should they see you with her," Darcy said. "They are already enjoying themselves judging by the account in the paper." His left brow rose. "I did not see any amorous actions from the terrace last night."

"There were none." Trefor was not about to admit to having caressed Kitty's cheek to Mr. Darcy. If the man had not seen it, he did not need to know about it.

"She did seem not quite herself after your walk."

Trefor's brow furrowed. "How so?"

"She was more distracted than normal and did a lot of smiling and sighing." The gentleman's lips pursed as if attempting not to laugh. It seemed that Mr. Darcy took great pleasure in causing Trefor to feel uneasy.

"You do not know the reason for that, do you?" Darcy asked, causing Edwards to chuckle.

"No," Trefor lied. He was nearly certain that he knew the reason.

"Indeed?" There was no little amount of disbelief in Darcy's voice.

Trefor shook his head.

"No idea whatsoever?" Darcy prodded.

Again, Trefor shook his head.

"Out with it, Linton," Edwards said as he gave Trefor's arm a jab. "Not even you can be so clueless as to not know if something said on a garden stroll caused a lady to be distracted. What was it? Did you confess your undying love?"

"No," Trefor snapped.

"Did you propose marriage?" Edwards asked with a laugh that fell silent when Trefor did not reply. "You did not? Did you?"

Trefor shrugged. "No, although the word might have come up in conversation."

"You talked about marrying?" Darcy leaned forward.

Trefor shook his head. "I did not intend to. I had not even thought I wished to marry her until..." He shrugged again. "Until it came out of my mouth. I honestly do not know what is wrong with me. I do not blurt things. I do not almost kiss ladies at balls. My name does not appear in the paper."

Edwards grasped his shoulder, turning Trefor toward him. "Did you almost kiss her again?"

"No."

Edwards grinned. "But you wanted to. I can see it in your eyes."

"You see nothing of the sort," Trefor snapped.

"Convince her to marry you," Darcy said. "There is no other option."

"Do you really think so? The article in the paper did not seem so bad as all that to me. A push towards it perhaps but not something which would require it," Trefor said.

Darcy shook his head. "I am not speaking about the paper. Trust me when I say I know of what I speak." He smiled. "I tried to avoid marrying my wife."

"Do tell," Edwards was once again leaning back in his chair looking for all the world like there was nothing more important than the weather being discussed.

"Suffice it to say, my sister was good enough to push me in the right direction," Darcy said. "Which is what I am now attempting to do for you. If you love her, do not let her go."

Love. That was the thing about which Trefor had been thinking since that moment in the garden. How did one know if one was merely attracted to a lady or in love? He wished to ask someone but to do so felt so foolish. It was something he thought he should know. He had been able to see it in his sister. Why was he not able to see it for himself?

He was still pondering this thought when he entered Durward's store. And he likely would have continued thinking about it, if it had not been for seeing *her* standing at a case next to her aunt, exclaiming about something. As soon as he was able, he moved in her direction. However, by the time he reached where she had been, she had moved.

The store was busy. There were customers at every display case. Many were having parcels wrapped while others were deliberating over a purchase while the shop assistant stood waiting to either wrap up the purchase or put the item back on display.

Crawford's sister was marrying a shrewd businessman from the look of this store and the brisk business being conducted. She would likely never want for anything.

Finally, it was his turn to speak to the man behind the display case. "There was a young lady here who seemed taken by some item in this display just a moment ago."

"If I am thinking of the same lady," the shop assistant said, "she was looking at this lace." He placed a length of lace on top of the case.

Lace. Of course, Trefor thought with chuckle. They had discussed lace once, although discussed was perhaps not the best choice of words. He had offended her over lace. "It is lovely."

"It is large enough to wrap around one's shoulders on a fine spring day. It would most certainly set off the lady's features."

That was true. Miss Bennet would look lovely wearing it.

"She seemed to think that this brooch would be just the thing to keep it in place."

"A young lady with hazel eyes and brown hair who was just here with her aunt?"

"She was with Mrs. Gardiner," the assistant said. "There was something in the back that caught Mrs. Gardiner's ear, and so they left to see to that without completing the purchase."

"I will take them both. If you would wrap them up and tell me the total."

"Immediately, sir. I will not be long."

"I will just wander this direction and return. I promise to not leave without that parcel." Trefor wandered toward the back of the store, looking in one case after another and stopping to admire the tea caddies.

The door to the back was open. Not fully, but halfway. Trefor moved to look through to the hall beyond, hoping to see Miss Bennet. She was there, but the sight made his heart lurch.

Turning away, he went back to the case to wait for his

purchase to be wrapped. Who was that gentleman and why was Miss Bennet holding his hands? And why was her aunt allowing such an intimate gesture?

He placed his money on the counter. "Will you see that Miss Bennet gets this?" They were for her. No matter what he had witnessed. No matter if her heart belonged to another.

"Was there a name to tell her?"

Trefor shook his head. "Just a friend who thinks she has an excellent eye for lace of high quality."

"Very well, sir. I will tell her."

With a nod and a thank you, Trefor parted from the man.

"Where are you going?" his aunt asked when he passed her on his way toward the door.

He closed his eyes at the frustration of being stopped in his escape. "Outside."

"Is something amiss?"

"No." He moved toward the door.

"Trefor," his aunt hurried to follow him.

"Please, Aunt Gwladys," he said. "I am just not in the right frame of mind to enjoy this little adventure." Although, in that brief moment of seeing Miss Bennet standing so close to another gentleman while engaged in what looked like a serious conversation, his world, which had been set on akilter upon his first meeting with Miss Bennet, had righted itself before crumbling at his feet.

"Are you going home?"

"Eventually."

Aunt Gwladys put her hand on his arm. "Are you well?"

"I just need some air." And to be far away from here. "It is a bit stuffy in here."

His aunt's brow furrowed. "How are you getting home?"

"I will walk the street for a few minutes, and then, if possible, I will take a hack if you and Connie are not finished."

"We planned to make one more stop on our way home," his aunt cautioned. "But you could sit in the carriage. We have Henry to escort us."

How he wished he had ridden his horse. A ride through the park would be just the thing. "I think I shall take a hack and then go for a ride when I get home."

"In the park?"

He nodded. "Rotten Row," he said before ducking out of the store. He looked up the street and then down before deciding on a direction.

An hour later, he was feeling no less agitated, despite the pleasure of riding.

Love. He scoffed at the notion. It was a tricky fellow this thing called love. Skirting the room, poking at the occupants, disguising itself as attraction and friendship, hiding itself in a laugh, peeking out of a pair of fine eyes, but never fully revealing himself until he stood ready to rend a heart in two and dispose of the pieces. Why anyone sought such a thing as love was at this moment beyond his understanding. And he had no desire to attempt to understand it. He knew enough. With any luck, his heart would heal and not be utterly destroyed, though he suspected it might be too late for such a wish.

Tomorrow or the next day, the papers would carry his name again in a story. This time he would not be the gent hopeful of acceptance but rather the one who had been spurned. There was no need to continue with the charade of courting when Miss Bennet's affections lay elsewhere.

He stopped and dismounted, choosing to lean against a tree as he watched others driving past in their carriages — happy couples tempting love to show his darkness.

He laughed bitterly and closed his eyes, revisiting the scene in the back of Durward's store and feeling the disappointment which threatened to crush him. It was best to get such melancholy thoughts out of the way before he returned home to his questioning aunt and sister.

"What did you think you were doing?" a familar and angry voice penetrated his troubling thoughts.

His eyes popped open. A carriage was stopped in front of him. It was his own carriage with the canopy lowered, driven by Henry and containing his sister, his aunt, and a much displeased Miss Bennet.

"I was taking a moment to enjoy this tree before continuing my ride."

Miss Bennet glared at him. "Mr. Crawford, if you would

be so kind as to help me out of the carriage. I would rather not yell at Mr. Linton from here."

With a laugh, Crawford, the wretched traitor, immediately offered his assistance.

"How might I be of service?" Trefor eyed her suspiciously as she approached him.

"You can tell me what you thought you were doing." She folded her arms and glared at him.

"I already did."

"Not now." She huffed as if he were being difficult, which he was not – not intentionally at any rate.

"Then, when?"

"You bought me a gift?"

Oh!

"Was it not right? I can see if we can exchange it for something else."

She stamped her foot. "It was perfect!"

His brow furrowed. "Then, I do not understand the issue."

"You cannot just give a lady a gift and leave without allowing her to either accept it or not."

"If you do not want it, I will take it back."

She huffed again. "I do not not want it."

"Then, you are accepting it?"

"Yes." If exasperation had a face, it was Miss Bennet's, although Trefor was not sure why she was exasperated.

She seemed to know what she was talking about which was a great deal more than what he knew.

He shook his head. "I do not understand," he said apologetically.

"You left."

"I did not think you would notice."

Her look of exasperation changed to one of perturbation. "Why would you think that?"

"I saw you."

Her brow furrowed.

"And him," Trefor added. "Whomever he is. You looked rather cozy, holding hands and standing so close."

Her brow remained furrowed.

"In the back hall of the store," he explained. "Some tall, handsome chap."

"Of all the stupid things," she spat. "You, Mr. Linton are provoking and excessively vexing and..." She stamped her foot before moving closer to him. "And stupid. You do not know what you saw, yet you assume that I am the sort of lady who goes around cozying up to every handsome fellow."

"No, no. I did not think that. I just thought your uncle owns the building, and so you might have met this gentleman before and had..." he shrugged, "lost your heart to him, but you could not tell me just yet since you know there was that letter and the pretending to court thing."

He looked down. "I could not stay and see you happy with him."

"Why?" her eyes were wide.

He searched her face for any sign of understanding, but there was none. "Do you truly not know?"

She smiled at him, softly, in the most becoming fashion, and then said, "yes" gently, just as she might to Emily or Jack in the nursery at Mrs. Verity's. Such a response told him that there was understanding behind her look of surprise from just moments ago. He longed to be given the years he knew he likely needed to discover how to read her expressions and understand her way of thinking.

"My heart would not survive it," he explained. "It is barely holding together as it is."

She stepped closer to him, tears gathering in her eyes. "That is how my heart feels."

"It is?" Hope leapt within him as she nodded.

"Do you think," she paused and tipped her head, "do you think we might now know what we did not know last night?"

"Is there any way you can speak plainly?" he begged. He was not capable of deciphering much of anything presently. Hope and joy clung to the edges of his mind, waiting either to be allowed entrance or to be dashed to the ground.

"Do you not remember saying you wished to marry me?"

Oh, that he remembered. He stepped so that he was less than an arm's length away from her.

"And I thought I might wish the same." Her voice was only just louder than a whisper.

"And do you?" He sucked in a breath and waited.

"I am mostly certain I do." She fluttered her lashes and smiled at him. Did she know just how tempting she was when she did such a thing?

"Mostly certain?"

She shrugged. "I suppose you could kiss me, and then, I would have no choice but to be completely certain."

"That is a rather scandalous option," he cautioned. "There would be no changing your mind."

She smiled. "It makes no sense, you know. You are impossibly annoying, and I have only known you for a short time. However," she shook her head. "It is just ridiculous. It is likely too foolish."

He nodded. "You are right. There are those who would say it is. How can I love you when I know so very little about you?"

"Precisely!" she agreed. "I should not love you so soon. It is not how it is done, you know." Her forehead wrinkled. "Except my sister Jane assured me that it is not impossible because she loved Mr. Bingley from the first time she danced with him."

"I have heard that it happens," he agreed as he took her hands, "though I thought it only happened to less logical people than me." She was smiling at him as if he had missed something. But what was it? Oh! Yes. "You love me?"

She nodded. "I do. You are a good man with a noble heart."

"And lovely eyes," he added with a smirk.

"Yes, perfectly lovely eyes." She stepped a fraction of a step closer to him as if she felt the same pull that he did.

"And under all your provoking vexingness," he said, "you are just the sort of lady I need, for you see things as I do not, and you are genuine. There is no artifice in you. And your heart..." He pulled her into his embrace. He knew he should not, but he was powerless to resist the compulsion to hold her. "The care contained in your heart shines through your eyes and displays itself in your actions. Will you, Miss Bennet, allow me the chance to get to know you better and better for the rest of our lives?"

"As husband and wife?" She fluttered her lashes at him again.

"Yes, my provoking love. Will you be my wife?"

"Considering the scandal you are creating by holding me as you are, I think I must." She made no move to extricate herself from his embrace and instead, placed a hand on his cheek. "But I submit to my destiny happily. It is a most willing surrender."

Then, with a whispered *I love you* from one to the other, they sealed their union and their future with a kiss that was as pure as it was passionate, stirring desires and mingling souls as only love of the truest sort, which inspires tales of brave quests to break curses, can do. And there, in the park, on the edge of Rotten Row, on a fine spring day, a gentleman, who was a stranger to scandal, and a lady, who was bent on being proper in town, inspired yet another story for the society pages that would keep the gossips' tongues wagging for some time as they whispered behind fans and smiled over teacups, sharing their version of this delicious scandal in springtime.

Before You Go

If you enjoyed this book, be sure to let others know by leaving a review.

~*~*~

Would you like to read the story that Kitty wrote about Mr. L?

Or, do you want to know when the next Leenie B book will be available?

You can do both when you sign up to my mailing list.

Book News from Leenie Brown
(bit.ly/LeenieBBookNews)

~*~*~

Turn the page to read an excerpt of another one of Leenie's books

Other Pens, Mansfield Park Excerpt

If you would like to discover more about who Trefor Linton and his friends are, you can find them in my Other Pens, Mansfield Park series. Below is the first chapter of book 1, Henry: To Prove Himself Worthy, where we first meet both Charles Edwards and Trefor Linton.

Henry: To Prove Himself Worthy

Chapter 1

Henry Crawford paced the edges of the ballroom, surveying the latest crop of debutantes with a critical, assessing eye. Not just any beauty would do for him this season. The lady he selected to pursue would need more than beauty to capture his admiration. He had had his fill of games, dalliances, and chits who thought too well of themselves. He was looking for a woman of substance who would stand by his side as his wife. Not that he truly felt worthy of such a lady.

His eyes narrowed as he scrutinized a group of ladies standing in a corner to the right of the ballroom door.

There were several in the group who stood head and shoulders above the rest. They would never do for him. He did not possess great height, and a gentleman must not have a partner — even for a dance — who was taller than he.

Of the ladies of acceptable height, there were those who held their chins very much like a particular young lady whom he would like to forget. She was full of airs and invitation, but... He shook his head. Maria Bertram had been more beauty than substance, and what substance she had possessed was, as it turned out, unpleasant. He shuddered in remembrance of that particular lady's sour disposition.

Then there were one or two in the group who were of a proper stature and appeared shy — almost fearful. They were the ones whispering to their chaperones and fidgeting uneasily. They would likely be the ones still standing by the wall when the dancing began — not because they lacked beauty, for they did not. Some were slightly more attractive than others as was the normal scheme of things, but all were elegantly dressed and expertly coiffured, showing themselves to best advantage. However, their reserved manner and lack of sparkle would likely see them overlooked. That might be the best place to begin, with the wallflowers, if he could bring himself to approach anyone at all.

He paused at the door to the terrace, which was not quite closed, and pulled in a gulp of cool air. The room seemed rather warmer than he remembered it being. Perhaps it was the crush of people, or — he swallowed at the strange uneasiness that rose in his throat — perhaps it was the disapproving eyes of the many matrons and male folk guarding their precious treasures that made him wish to pull at his cravat and straighten his jacket and caused him to feel so warm. That was likely it, he had to admit to himself. He had always been welcomed in the past, but tonight he did not feel that former welcome. It was his own doing, however, and he knew it. Had he considered one sweet lady as the precious treasure she was, he would likely not be here scouting for someone with fair eyes and a pleasant smile to fill the void that Fanny Price had left in his heart.

"Have you settled on the next scandal?" Charles Edwards drew up beside Henry and lifting his quizzing glass, looked down his nose as he surveyed the room. "It is an excellent crop with many beauties."

"Aye, it is that," Henry agreed with a half smile.

"Which shall it be?" Edwards cast a quick glance at his friend of many years.

"I do not know. I see their beauty, but..." He turned toward Edwards so that his lips could not be read by anyone.

"I do not think I am ready for this," he admitted in a low whisper. "I should not have allowed you and Linton to talk me into attending."

"Do not be foolish, my man, you are exactly where you must be to assuage a disappointment." Edwards' smile had a wolfish quality to it as it usually did when he was speaking of ladies. "A broken heart does a lady good. It hurries her on to consider matrimony at a faster pace. In reality, their guardians should be thankful for those of us who provide such a service."

Henry chuckled. If there was one thing at which Edwards was good, besides seducing a lady, it was twisting logic into some rational explanation about why his actions were not so reprehensible as most might consider them. The truth was that Edwards was a rogue through and through, but he had enough charm and good looks to make him not only acceptable to many young ladies but also desirable. Likely one of them fancied herself as capable of ensnaring the man's heart and reforming him into all that was proper. Henry wished her well, for the task would not be an easy one.

"The Price chit you liked. She's married now, is she not?" Edwards pressed his point.

For a moment, Henry paused to consider that Edwards might be correct. After Henry's departure last spring, Fanny had not been long in securing an offer from her cousin Edmund. He shook his head. No, his friend was not correct, for Fanny's heart had not been broken, and that was a truth which, as of yet, never ceased to cause his own heart to pinch. She had been kind to him and caring, and perhaps she might have been persuaded to love him, but she had not loved him as he had wished she would.

He knew his foolishness had hurt her, and he imagined her disappointment in him had been great. How could it not have been? Fanny was all that was good. She scowled — very prettily and softly — at all that was less than virtuous. How she must have censured him in her heart, if not in her words! And he deserved it. He knew he did. He had failed her. He had acted rashly, in a fit of misguided passion. He was likely very unfit for any lady of such good taste and character.

Henry's morose contemplations were brought to a halt as a burly gentleman wearing a green jacket attempted to pass between Henry and the doors behind him. "You must dance at least once before you escape." Trefor Linton gave Henry a nudge with his shoulder. "When the horse tosses you on your arse, you have to ride it again."

Henry flashed a grin at his friend. "You are not also going to tell me how breaking the hearts of poor innocents is somehow a service to them, are you?"

"Good heavens, I should say not!" cried Linton. "Has Edwards been spouting his regular rubbish?"

"I will have you know it is not rubbish," Edwards defended. "Why just last year, three young ladies made very eligible matches after I had shown them particular attention. I tell you, I am a good luck charm for the matrimonially-minded miss."

"I dare say at least one of them felt a very pressing need to accept the first offer she was given after receiving your attentions." Linton raised his left brow and looked down his nose imperiously at Edwards.

Edwards shrugged. "I heard no word of scandal."

"That is because you refuse to listen," Linton muttered.

Henry shook his head. How Linton had remained friends with Edwards and him for all these years was a mystery. Linton was level-headed and honorable to a fault. He would never be caught in a dark corner with a chit. Edwards, on the other hand, made it something of a sport to see how many dark corners he could frequent with a different chit in each one. And Henry? Well, he was more inclined to participate with Edwards and tease Linton for his refusal to join them than he was to deny himself such pleasure. He drew a breath. No longer. He hoped.

"So who shall it be?" Edwards prodded again. "Her?" He directed his gaze at a curvaceous blonde to their left. "She would be quite delightful, I imagine."

Linton's long arm reached behind Henry and thwacked Edwards. "Have a care. That's Hodson's sister."

"Indeed?" Edwards did not remove his eyes from the lady. "I had not thought such beauty could be found in his family." He tipped his head as he studied the beauty across the room. "She has definitely defied the Hodson odds and lost her awkwardness. Does Hodson still frequent Gentleman Jackson's?"

Linton nodded. "Daily."

Edwards lowered his glass and gave it a wipe before

putting it in his pocket. "Then who else might there be of interest?"

"Start with Constance," Linton suggested. "No harm will befall you. She will be all that is proper, and perhaps others, seeing that I trust you with her, will stop scowling at us. It is very unnerving. How do you bear such looks of displeasure so frequently, Edwards?"

Edwards laughed. "The pleasure of a few stolen moments is worth the discomfort, my friend. You should try it."

"Not likely," Linton retorted.

"You know Crawford is nearly as skilled as I at finding secluded corners." Edwards once again had his quizzing glass out and was wiping it. "I am surprised you would trust your sister with him."

"It is one dance in my presence, and he knows I would kill him if he were to so much as think of stealing a kiss from Connie." Linton crossed his arms and glowered at Edwards. "I believe Crawford currently has enough sense to heed such a warning, and that is why I will allow him to dance with my sister. You, however, still lack such sense and are to keep your distance."

Edwards shrugged. "Her tongue is too sharp for my liking." He answered Linton's growl at the disparagement with a smile. "I prefer not to be lectured when I am attempting to seduce a lady."

"I should give such ungentlemanly comments the reply

they deserve, but knowing they will likely fall on deaf ears, I shall spare my breath. Come, Crawford," said Linton. "We will leave Edwards to his dissipated ways and go find Connie."

~*~*~

Constance Linton huffed softly as she stood beside her aunt.

"Stand up straight and do not scowl." Gwladys Kendrick's instructions to her niece were accompanied by an appropriately stern look and a slight nudge forward. "No man will ever find you if you attempt to sink into the shadows."

"I would be quite happy not to be found." Constance favoured her aunt with a charming smile.

"Do not be ridiculous, child. There must certainly be at least one gentleman here that will rise to your exacting standards of dullness," a smirk pulled at the corners of Aunt Gwladys's mouth.

"Dull is not the proper word, Aunt."

"Yes, I know. Intelligent, forward thinking, and so on." Aunt Gwladys waved her hand in a small circle, indicating that she knew Constance's description of her ideal gentleman would go on and on for some time if she was allowed to begin such a topic of conversation. "Many intelligent beasts, such as your brother, dance, you know."

Constance linked her arm with the lady who had been her companion and guide for these past six years, filling neatly the void left by the death of Constance's mother. "I know. I just find this whole sifting through the dross process to be quite tedious."

Aunt Gwladys patted Constance's hand. "Ah, but the prize for such effort is well worth it." Her brows furrowed, and her lips pursed for a moment as she caught sight of her nephew. "Why your brother insists on keeping some of his friends, I will never understand."

"Because one does not turn out a stray just because it has a bad eye — or some such thing," replied Constance with a laugh.

"There is more than an eye that is bad with that one," Aunt Gwladys muttered as her nephew and Henry Crawford approached.

"He is not so bad as Mr. Edwards," Constance whispered. "In fact, Mr. Crawford has been making improvements, according to Trefor."

She was not certain why she felt compelled to defend Henry Crawford. She did not hold him in high esteem herself, but there had been an aura of melancholy about him lately that was so unlike him. She had never been one to enjoy seeing the suffering of others even if they did deserve to feel wretched. Of course, she knew that it would likely not keep her from reprimanding him if the opportunity arose. It was a serious inconsistency in her character, and one she wished to remedy. But, should she continue to reprove and learn to bear the sorrow of the transgressor without qualm, or was it better to bite her tongue and pat the offender's arm while saying "there, there, poor dear"?

"Mr. Crawford," Aunt Gwladys gave a nod of her head in greeting while her features spoke of her hesitance in doing so.

"Mrs. Kendrick, Miss Linton." Henry bowed and smiled. "It is a pleasure to see you. You are both looking fetching tonight — quite the brightest jewels at the ball." He took the hand that Aunt Gwladys had offered him and gave it a kiss.

"Your silver tongue will not work with me, young man. I know your sort." Her tone was stern despite the small smile that played at her mouth in response to his flattery. "And your lifted brows and raised chin will not scold me into being civil," she said to Linton while tapping her cheek with her fan, indicating that he should kiss it.

Linton obliged. "Tonight shall be trying enough for Crawford. There is no need of increasing his discomfort," he said softly.

"Consequences are consequences," Aunt Gwladys retorted.

"You are correct, of course, but they are not for you to award or laud," her nephew responded.

Henry pulled at his sleeves and attempted to keep a smile on his lips. How many times had he had to plaster such a look of nonchalance on his face over the last year?

"Linton will not allow me to leave until I have danced," he explained.

"You were leaving just after you arrived?" Constance asked in surprise.

Henry shrugged. "I might have found the card room for a while before making my exit, but yes. I am uncertain I am prepared for the close, and may I say just, examination, I appear to be receiving."

"Surely, you knew it would be thus?" Constance snapped her mouth shut and smiled sheepishly at her brother, who had cleared his throat rather loudly at her comment.

"I expected as much," said Henry. "However, I had hoped some of my infamy had faded."

"There are likely many gentlemen in the card room whose only interest in your past activities is to place a bet on if they are likely to be repeated," said Aunt Gwladys. "The ladies tend to be longer in coming to terms with the idea of accepting a gentleman back into society who has shown disdain for the solemnity of marriage. They fear you will be unfaithful as a husband, you see. However, you are not without your particular charms." Her lips curled into a smile. "Pin money and an estate with ample carriages and servants as well as a townhouse and fine gowns are very alluring to some young ladies."

"Crawford is a changed man, are you not?" Linton turned to Henry. "Henry here has learned the value of a good woman, and that is precisely what he seeks — not some fortune hunter." Linton waved his hand as if brushing away some disgusting bit of dirt.

"I am trying to be," Henry replied as the musicians began to play something recognizable rather than just the few notes of tuning they had been playing for some minutes.

"I have assured Crawford that you would be happy to partner him for the first dance if Aunt Gwladys has not harpooned someone else for you."

Constance's mouth dropped open at the audacity of such a statement. "I can assure you that I would have garnered several names on my card had I wished to do so. I do not need them to be harpooned."

Henry bit back a smile at the way Linton's sister crossed her arms and glared at her brother. He had seen them nearly come to blows before over some careless comment that Linton had made and to which Constance had taken exception. It did not matter that she was half the size of her larger and older brother. While others might find the man intimidating, his sister did not. There was no denying the fiery blood of the Kendrick family ran in the lady's veins. In fact, she seemed to have received all of her own on that account as well as a portion of her more relaxed brother's.

"She would have secured many a partner, had she not

been doing a valiant job of avoiding the majority of them," muttered her aunt.

"Then, am I in luck?" asked Henry with a bright smile for Constance. "Might I have the pleasure of enduring the stares of the masses with such a lovely partner to hold my attention?"

Though she knew him to be a charmer, Constance had to admit, as she accepted his offer and his arm, that Mr. Crawford's words were very pretty and did make a lady feel a particular happiness that crept unbidden to her cheeks.

Other Leenie B Books

You can find all of Leenie's books at this link
bit.ly/LeenieBBooks
where you can explore the collections below

~*~

Other Pens, Mansfield Park

~*~

Touches of Austen Collection

~*~

Other Pens, Pride and Prejudice

~*~

Dash of Darcy and Companions Collection

~*~

Marrying Elizabeth Series

~*~

Willow Hall Romances

~*~

The Choices Series

~*~

Darcy Family Holidays

~*~

Darcy and... An Austen-Inspired Collection

Leenie Brown has always been a girl with an active imagination, which, while growing up, was both an asset, providing many hours of fun as she played out stories, and a liability, when her older sister and aunt would tell her frightening tales. At one time, they had her convinced Dracula lived in the trunk at the end of the bed she slept in when visiting her grandparents!

Although it has been years since she cowered in her bed in her grandparents' basement, she still has an imagination which occasionally runs away with her, and she feeds it now as she did then — by reading!

Her heroes, when growing up, were authors, and the worlds they painted with words were (and still are) her favourite playgrounds! Now, as an adult, she spends much of her time in the Regency world, playing with the characters from her favourite Jane Austen novels and those of her own creation.

When she is not traipsing down a trail in an attempt to keep up with her imagination, Leenie resides in the beautiful province of Nova Scotia with her two sons and her very own Mr. Brown (a wonderful mix of all the best of Darcy, Bingley, and Edmund with a healthy dose of the teasing Mr. Tilney and just a dash of the scolding Mr. Knightley).

Connect with Leenie

E-mail:

LeenieBrownAuthor@gmail.com

Facebook:

www.facebook.com/LeenieBrownAuthor

Blog:

leeniebrown.com

Patreon:

https://www.patreon.com/LeenieBrown

Subscribe to Leenie's Mailing List:

Book News from Leenie Brown

(bit.ly/LeenieBBookNews)